ABOUT THIS BOOK

Welcome to Havenwood Falls, a small town in the majestic mountains of Colorado, where nobody is what you think, where truths pose as lies, and where myths blend with reality. A place where everyone has a story, including the high schoolers. These are only but three...

Somewhere Within by Amy Hale

Zoey Mills has been the target of bullies since childhood, and she expects nothing to change when her family relocates to Havenwood Falls. What she doesn't expect is to discover that she's the next generation of a long line of frost dragons. When Zoey falls for a human boy, elitism and prejudice take on whole new meanings. While she wants to trust her instincts and follow her heart, Zoey discovers that hiding who she really is and playing by the rules would make life a lot simpler. But simple doesn't mean easy.

Awaken the Soul by Michele G. Miller

Breckin Roberts has known Vivienne his entire life, but they aren't friends. They're merely two classmates—her human and him not so much. Until one fateful December afternoon, when Vivienne almost dies. Breckin saves her, but when he interferes with Death, he awakens a connection. A connection one Reaper finds highly appealing and could turn Vivienne into a pawn in the battle of Good versus Evil—a battle about to descend on Havenwood Falls.

Bound by Shadows by Cameo Renae

Eris Blaekthorn can't believe what she and her father learn when two strangers show up and remove a memory spell that had caused them to forget their past—including her older brother, who's in a coma caused by dark magic. Her father agrees to return to Havenwood Falls—a place he'd left to keep Eris safe—where she discovers who she really is. When events spiral and danger rises, Eris turns to Rylan, her brother's best friend, for help in saving her brother's life.

HAVENWOOD FALLS HIGH BOOKS

Written in the Stars by Kallie Ross

Reawakened by Morgan Wylie

The Fall by Kristen Yard

Somewhere Within by Amy Hale

Awaken the Soul by Michele G. Miller

Bound by Shadows by Cameo Renae

Fata Morgana by E.J. Fechenda

Forever Emeline by Katie M. John

Reclamation by AnnaLisa Grant

Avenoir by Daniele Lanzarotta

Avenge the Heart by Michele G. Miller

Curse the Night by R.K. Ryals

Blood & Iron by Amy Hale

Shadows & Spells by Cameo Renae

Falling Deep by J.L. Weil

Saving Infiniti by Rose Garcia

Willful by Liz Ferry

Cast in Moonlight by Ali Winters

Promise the Moon by Kallie Ross

Blurred Lines by Daniele Lanzarotta

Ascending Darkness by J.L. Weil

Finding Infiniti by Rose Garcia

Unicorn's Lament by Megan Linski

Paper Bird by Amy Richie

Predestined by Valia Lind

Rediscovered by Morgan Wylie

Ashes of Fate by Apryl Baker

Stay up to date at www.HavenwoodFalls.com

HAVENWOOD FALLS HIGH
VOLUME TWO

A HAVENWOOD FALLS HIGH COLLECTION

AMY HALE   MICHELE G. MILLER   CAMEO RENAE

SOMEWHERE WITHIN

BY AMY HALE

Havenwood Falls High

Somewhere Within

AMY HALE

~ A Havenwood Falls Young Adult Novella ~

OTHER BOOKS BY AMY HALE

Ulterior Motives

THE SHADOWS TRILOGY
Shadows of Jane
Shadows of Deception
Shadows of Deliverance

Catching Whitney

Letters From Jayson

For all the young people who fight to be normal.

Normal is boing and overrated.
Be unique.
Aim for extraordinary.
Show the world why it's great to be you.

CHAPTER 1

$\mathcal{I}$ glanced at the boxes still waiting to be unpacked as I attempted to relax in my new bedroom. The excitement that generally accompanied a new house was missing. I felt like we moved more than we stayed still. My dad had assured me this would be the last time, and while I thought he believed that to be true, I had my reservations.

My first memories of moving took place at age seven. I don't remember all the details, but I do recall a loud commotion, after which Mom had run out to the backyard to get me. She rushed me into the car, and we left. Just like that. No goodbyes to the neighbors. No "grab a few things for overnight." We just left. Two days later, my dad arrived at our hotel room, two states away, driving a moving truck containing all our belongings. At the time, I was afraid to ask what happened, but it had certainly crossed my mind with every successive move. I'd had an unpleasant sensation down in my gut each time I attempted to mention the subject, so I'd always chickened out.

So there I was, on move . . . what was it? Move eight? Yeah, I thought this was move number eight. One would think I'd be used to starting over, and over, and over. But the truth was that with every packed box, I felt like I'd left a part of me behind. Even if that part wasn't important, it was a segment of my scattered life that no longer felt valid. Those memories now lived in the past.

This latest move had been prompted by a family member. It turned out I had a grandfather here in Havenwood Falls, Colorado. My parents had never talked about him before, so I'd assumed my dad didn't know who his father was. It was the only logical explanation for never hearing about Grandpa Mills. You couldn't talk about someone you didn't know, right?

My parents had received a letter that my grandfather, Lawrence Mills, had become very ill, and was possibly dying. Mom and Dad seemed frustrated by the phone conversations they'd had with him afterward. Ultimately, I held the impression they'd decided it was time to mend fences. Granted, they'd never told me what busted the fences to begin with, but maybe someday I'd learn all the deep, dirty family secrets. All families had a skeleton or two in their closets, so I'd heard. I suspected my family to be no different.

I stood and opened the box closest to my bed. It contained some of my clothes and the most beautiful jewelry box I'd ever seen. It'd been a gift from my parents for my sixteenth birthday. I hadn't actually had that birthday yet, but it was only about a month away. Dad had said that he wanted to give it to me before the move. "Something special for your new room," he'd said. I thought he'd been attempting to bribe me so I wouldn't complain about changing houses and schools yet again. It kinda worked.

I ran my fingers over the smooth metal casing, and I could almost feel it vibrate beneath my fingers. I didn't know how to explain it, but it felt as if the box itself was alive. Every time I touched it, I felt a zing of positive energy pulse through me. No doubt these sensations all took place in my mind, but I allowed myself to indulge the fantasy just the same. As long as I didn't say it out loud, I should be safe. Admitting it to others would have been like saying I'd grown a third leg, but no one could see it.

I placed the gold box on my nightstand and studied the intricate design on the lid, which looked much like a maze, with lines darting out from the center in odd geometric patterns. From the moment I laid eyes on it, I'd tried to figure out if there were some kind of labyrinth hidden in all the chaos, but if so, I had yet to solve it.

Regardless, it was another great addition to what my mother lovingly called my "jewelry hoard." I did have a slight obsession with jewelry, but really, what teenage girl didn't? I wouldn't call it a hoard.

"Zoey, here's another box with your name on it." Dad pushed through my bedroom door and set the box on the bed beside me. "Sheesh, that's heavy. What do you have in there? Anvils?"

I rolled my eyes at him. "Yes, Father. I have an anvil addiction. You've found me out."

He smirked. "So much sass in such a little person."

I reached over and pulled the tape from the top of the box, then glanced inside. "Oh," I said.

Dad simply raised his eyebrows in curiosity.

"It's my jewelry boxes," I said quietly.

His soft laughter followed him to the door, and he sent me a wink. "Enjoy." He walked out of the room and gently closed the door behind him.

I looked into the box again. I had several jewelry boxes, most of them very full. *Okay, maybe I do have a jewelry-hoarding issue. Is there a therapy for that?*

AFTER LUNCH, Dad had some things to take care of at his new job running Simple Treasures Pawn Shop, so that left just Mom and me cleaning and unpacking in the kitchen.

Mom crossed her arms and leaned against the tan Formica counter. "What do you say we run into town for coffee? A latte sounds great, and I noticed a nice-looking shop as we drove through town."

I put away the last plate in the stack I'd unpacked and wiped my hands on my jeans. "Sure. Sounds good."

She smiled at me. "Perfect. As much as I love this new house, I'm eager to get out for a few minutes."

I didn't comment. I knew she wanted to hear me gush about the new place. After all, it was a nice house. A relatively new brick ranch house, it contained three bedrooms and loads of extra space. My bedroom easily overshadowed the dimensions of any other room I'd ever had. I even had my own bathroom. The pale yellow walls and white gauzy curtains gave my room a cheery feel. My white bedroom suite fit perfectly within the space. Much to my mother's delight, there were hardwood floors throughout. All I could think about was how cold those floors would be first thing in the morning. I made myself a mental note to ask for a rug in my bedroom.

The main part of the house had an open floor plan with the living room, kitchen, and dining room all in one large area. The fireplace had to be my favorite feature of the house, aside from my bedroom. The large grate could hold a decent-sized load of wood, and I could imagine the relaxing crackle as the flames warmed my fingers and toes while the smell of the fire saturated my clothes.

I had every reason to love our new home, yet all I could muster for my mother was a less-than-excited smile. As for the town—it was lovely. The gorgeous mountains surrounding the town boxed us in and lent a cozy, protected feel. As it was November, the air felt frigid and crisp, but also clean. Air this fresh was foreign to me, since all our other homes were in larger cities filled with smog and the various odors that accompanied living in a crowded area with several thousand people. One apartment had been so poorly located that a few times I wondered if I'd ever get the stench of garbage out of my nostrils. There was nothing like living a few blocks from a landfill when the wind blew just right. Thankfully, that stay was short-lived.

Havenwood Falls was perfectly sized for exploring. I hadn't had a chance to look everything over yet, but Mom assured me I could easily walk from one end of town to the other. Since I'd always felt pulled to the outdoors, I should have been thrilled, but moving and leaving what little stability we'd had dampened my spirits. The unknown was always scary. I'd never been good with change.

Mom pushed away from the counter. "C'mon, kiddo. Let's get some caffeine."

She wasn't kidding about the size of Havenwood Falls. We'd only been on the road a few minutes when we pulled into a spot in front of a collection of cute little storefronts on the town square. We stepped onto the sidewalk, and I glanced at the surrounding businesses. It seemed to be the typical small-town America kind of place, except for a few eclectic shops, which oddly didn't seem out of place. I spotted Madame Tahini's, whose sign advertised potions, palm readings, and other services. I couldn't say I'd ever been in a store like that. It intrigued me. It was at the end of the block, next to Simple Treasures Pawn Shop, which was owned by my grandfather and now managed by my dad.

Directly in front of our parking space was Coffee Haven. The bell over the door greeted us with the light tinkle of chimes as we entered the shop. The scent of coffee and baked goods hit me immediately. I was suddenly thankful for the distraction and the promise of chocolate. I wasn't as into the whole froufrou drink thing as my mom was. If it had a weird name and complicated list of ingredients, she'd try it. I honestly preferred hot cocoa over coffee. Thankfully, most coffee places offered both. With it being the first week in November, the weather was perfect for a warm drink.

I glanced around the cozy space, and my eyes were instantly drawn to a section near the back of the shop. Shiny silver, copper, and gold hung from various displays, and the overhead lights caused a sparkle from the beads and gems as I moved to the right or left. My quest for hot chocolate was all but forgotten.

"I see that look in your eye," Mom teased.

"What?" I shrugged. "I'm just looking around."

"Well, why don't you go look closer, and I'll order your drink. You want your usual? With peppermint?" She asked.

"Yeah, that'd be great. Thanks." I wasted no time in getting to the jewelry display. Several gorgeous pieces were front and center, and I couldn't help but reach out and touch them. I had an affinity for all jewelry, but these were expertly handcrafted by someone named Serena Alverson, and I found myself wishing I had such a creative gift. Of course, if I did, I'd likely end up with more jewelry than all the stores in town combined, so it was probably fortunate I didn't possess that talent.

I glanced down at the bracelet hanging from my wrist. It was my favorite, and my parents had gifted it to me on my tenth birthday. The green and yellow crystal beads were strung together on a delicate gold chain. Inside the gift box there had been a note indicating that the crystals were fluorite and yellow jasper, providing the dual function of an energy shield and a protective amulet. I wasn't sure I bought into all that, but I loved wearing it just the same.

"Zoey, here's your drink." My mom's voice pulled me from the allure of shiny objects, and she motioned for me to join her at a small table near the large picture window in front. My mother and I were opposites. Her short brown hair barely reached her shoulders, and her eye color matched it perfectly. Naturally petite, she possessed an inner grace and beauty. She preferred more casual clothing, but no matter what she wore, she made it look classy. She oozed charm and confidence. I did not. I was more comfortable reading in my room than I was socializing. Outside of us both having pale complexions and being short, I appeared to be nothing like her—a disappointing realization.

My dad was a tall man, easily over six feet in height with only a slightly darker skin tone and a muscular build. His hair had a thick texture with waves, and while dark, it was nowhere near the raven black of my own hair. His eyes were blue, where mine were gray with hints of blue. His self-assurance inspired me, and I had idolized him for as long as I could remember. He was my hero. I seemed so very different from them both. I often wondered if, upon my eighteenth birthday, they'd tell me I was adopted. It wouldn't have surprised me.

I took a seat opposite my mother and cupped the warm mug in my hands as I sipped it cautiously. Perfect. I looked up at the counter and noticed the young woman behind it smiling at me. Her name tag said Willow. *Such a pretty name!* I gave her a thumbs up to indicate my pleasure, and she winked at me, then turned to wipe down one of the espresso machines.

"So, what did you think of the jewelry? Anything you can't live without?" my mom asked as I took another careful sip of my drink.

"There are a few that are amazing, but I should probably at least get my room unpacked before I start adding more to my collection." I thought back to the various jewelry boxes in my room still waiting for my attention.

She laughed and reached across to pat my arm. Bad timing on her part, or on mine. As she moved, so did I—I scooted my mug to the side, directly in her path. Her fingers hit the cup and tipped it over, spilling the scalding hot contents all over my right hand.

I yelped in pain, and my mom jumped up to help me. Willow appeared at our side quickly, and I vaguely remembered hearing her ask how she could help. My instinct was to blow on the back of my hand, and to my amazement, impossibly cool air passed over my lips and cooled my skin. I watched in shock, and honestly some horror, as ice crystals formed over the burned area.

My mom wrapped her arms around me, shielding my hand and face from the view of those around us. A towel was thrust between our heads by a tight-smiled Willow.

"I've got this. Go take care of her before anyone notices." Willow's voice barely registered above a whisper.

She and my mom exchanged a look that I couldn't understand, then Mom nodded and ushered me out the door.

"It's okay, baby. Let's get you to the hospital to have that looked at." Mom spoke louder than necessary, and I began to think I was losing my mind—or dreaming.

The pain had disappeared, and I had a morbid eagerness to peek under the dish towel to see how bad my injury really was. I glanced back into the shop and saw Willow quickly cleaning up the mess we'd left behind.

It seemed like only seconds before I found myself sitting in the passenger seat as Mom backed out of her parking space.

I peeled the towel back from my hand, expecting to either see the worst, or see that I'd imagined the severe burn, but found nothing but a small mark. What I didn't expect to see . . . I didn't even know what it was. It was white, shimmery, and hard—almost like a shell.

Panic welled up in my chest. I struggled to breathe.

"Mom?" I could hear the fear in my own voice, so I knew she heard it too.

"It's okay, sweetheart. It's gonna be fine." She pulled out her cell phone and hit a button. "Call Tristan," she said loudly.

The phone answered back, "Calling Tristan Mills."

Mom put the phone to her ear and waited only a few seconds, then said, "Tristan, it's happening. Meet us at home as soon as you can."

I heard the muffled voice of my dad say, "On my way," and then the line went dead.

"Mom?" I asked again. "What is this? What's happening?"

She glanced at me and sighed a deep, worried-sounding breath. "It's a long story. Dad and I will explain it all when we get home."

We drove in silence until we reached our new house—not the hospital, by the way. My gut told me something big loomed before me. Something I was totally unprepared for.

CHAPTER 2

*W*e pulled into our driveway just seconds before Dad arrived in his black Toyota RAV4. He ran to the door and unlocked it, then waved us inside as quickly as possible. I worried about the cool air and the weird burn, but I was even more concerned by the way my parents reacted.

Once inside, Mom sat me on the sofa between her and Dad. She gently grasped my wrist and flashed me a reassuring smile. "We need to show your father."

I looked at my hand, then back up at her, and felt the previously unshed tears start to roll down my face.

"It's okay, sweetheart. Let me see," Dad said with a calm assurance he hadn't previously displayed. He pushed up the sleeves of his red sweater and held out his hand.

I removed the towel and gingerly placed my hand in his. He frowned and closed his eyes. "Well, I guess that settles it."

Mom nodded. "Yeah, it does."

I grew annoyed at all the completely unhelpful answers. "Settles *what*? You guys are scaring me!"

Mom grasped my left hand as Dad continued to hold on to my right. He gave my fingers a tight squeeze. "We aren't like other families."

I rolled my eyes at that. "No duh. I've known that for a long time. What does that have to do with this freaky scab on my hand?"

Mom slipped her other arm behind me and around my shoulder. "No, sweetheart, you aren't understanding your dad. Just give him a few minutes to explain."

"We are different because we aren't completely human. We're called shifters. Our specific species is dragon—frost dragon to be exact." Dad's demeanor was as if what he'd just told me wasn't completely bonkers. He acted like he'd just announced he'd taken a new job or something.

"Dragons?" The high pitch of my voice gave away my lack of emotional control.

"Sweetheart," my mom said. "Stay calm."

"Calm?" I screeched. "What the hell? How can we be dragons? We are people! Shifters, or whatever you called it, aren't real!"

Mom frowned at my use of the word hell, but at that point, I wasn't worried about dropping a dollar in the swear jar. Crap, I'd have been happy to dump my entire life savings in there if it would have allowed me to truly express how I felt at that moment.

"Dragons?" I repeated. "Huge, lizardish, winged creatures? That kind of dragon? How is this even possible? You're joking, right? Please say you're joking!"

Dad ran a finger over my weird scab. "This is a scale. It's a method of protection for us. Like armor." He glanced at my mom.

Mom frowned. "I accidentally knocked hot chocolate on her hand. She blew on the burn and . . . well . . ."

"Ah," said my dad, as if that cleared this entire enigma up.

I stood and paced in front of them. "Why do I have a scale?"

Mom spoke again. "Your natural instinct was to blow on your burn, as most would do, but unlike most, your inner dragon kicked into protection mode and blew frigid air out to stop the burn. Then it formed a scale to protect the skin until it's fully healed." She sounded a little in awe by this process.

I held up both hands. "Wait a minute. How come I'm just now learning about this?"

"Well," Dad said as he leaned back on the sofa, "if you possess the gene, it's triggered around your sixteenth birthday. You're only a few weeks away from that. Now that we know for sure you possess that gene, we can prepare you for what to expect next."

"Next?" I gulped. That sounded ominous.

"It's kind of like going through puberty." Mom smiled. "You'll notice minor changes up to your sixteenth birthday, when the gene is fully developed. What those changes will be? We can only guess. Everyone is different."

"Fully developed? What does that mean? Will I become a huge creature or something?" I could feel myself begin to hyperventilate.

"It's not quite like that. It's more—" Dad was interrupted by the doorbell. "Hold that thought." He ran to answer the door.

Mom motioned for me to join her again on the sofa. I sat next to her and stared at the scale on my hand.

Dad re-entered the room moments later. He clutched a letter between his fingers, his face solemn.

"What is it?" Mom asked.

"It's from my father. He'd like us to join him for dinner tonight." Dad didn't look pleased, which confused me. *Isn't Grandpa the reason we moved here to begin with?*

Mom nodded, but also appeared disturbed by the idea.

Dad sighed and looked at me. "I'm sure you'll learn more tonight, but I'll give you the summary. We come from an old line of frost dragons that originated in Iceland. Your Grandpa Mills is the patriarch of our family. Grandma Mills passed away before you were born. Everyone in my family has the shifter gene." He glanced at Mom. "Your mother is human, so there had always been the possibility that the gene would skip you."

I looked at my hand once again. "So I'm half human and half dragon?"

"More or less." Mom gave my shoulders a squeeze.

"I can't believe I'm hearing this. It's crazy," I muttered.

"It gets crazier," replied Dad. "Your great-grandfather settled in Havenwood Falls as one of the original founders of the town. This place came to be because supernatural beings from all over needed a safe place to live."

My eyes widened. "So there are other dragons here?"

"Other frost dragons? Outside of our family, none that I'm aware of, but there are other dragons, as well as witches, werewolves, vampires, fae, ghosts . . ." His voice trailed off when he noticed I was getting the point.

"Ho-ly crap." I couldn't believe what I heard. "All those things in fairy tales and horror stories are real?"

"Yes, but don't believe everything you read. Not all supernatural creatures are bad. In fact, many just want to be left to live in peace. Again, this is why Havenwood Falls is perfect for us." His eyes were full of emotion that bordered on pain, but something else lurked there too. Sadness? Longing? I wasn't sure.

"So why have you never mentioned Grandpa before?" I had to know why they kept all this from me for so long, especially since there was a possibility this secret would be life-changing for me.

"Havenwood Falls is protected by a memory ward. Once you leave, it's only a matter of time before you forget it exists. I think the memories were hidden somewhere in our minds, including your grandpa, but for the most part, we simply forgot." His shoulders were tense, and I sensed his discomfort.

"There's more to this story, isn't there? With Grandpa?"

"Yes," he stated. "But we'll have to continue this discussion later. I have to take care of some things before dinner tonight."

I opened my mouth to protest, but he held up one hand to stop me. "I promise you'll be told all the details. It'll just have to wait a bit longer. You have the bulk of the information you need for now."

I turned to my mom. "We live in a town full of supernatural creatures."

She nodded.

"How do all the regular people in town deal with that?" I could imagine the terror the human townspeople must have felt upon learning something so bizarre.

"Well," Mom sighed. "Most of the humans in town don't know

about the supernatural beings that live here. This is a secret. One you need to be very careful with."

How am I supposed to pretend all is normal when I have this huge secret?

"Wait, what about Willow? From the coffee place?" I remembered how she jumped right in to help. She and my mom working in tandem.

"Willow is fae," Mom stated in a matter-of-fact tone.

"Fae," I repeated. "She looks so human."

"Faerie glamour. It helps them blend in, just as you do as a shifter. No humans will ever know you're a dragon, unless you tell them or they see you in that form."

The memory of that first, frantic move came rushing back. "When we moved, when I was seven. What happened? Why did we act like we were escaping something?"

Mom closed her eyes. "Dragons are territorial." She smiled at my dad a moment before turning back to me. "Understandably, human men are, too. Your father came home and found our neighbor trying to touch me. I was fighting him off, but I wasn't winning. Dad shifted in the backyard, and the other guy peed himself before passing out. We couldn't safely stay there after that." She squeezed my hand. "I'm sorry we've had to move so much. The other moves were job-related, with a touch of restlessness. I think we missed Havenwood Falls and didn't even realize it."

Mom brushed the hair back from my face and kissed my temple. "Now, we'll put a bandage over that scale so no one will see it, then you need to get some rest. You're going to need it for tonight."

Great, more cryptic talk that tells me nothing. "Is something bad happening tonight?" I mustered the bravery to ask.

"Not if I can help it." Dad's face grew stern, and I knew that asking more questions right now would only be met with silence.

~

I SPENT the better part of my afternoon online, looking for anything relating to dragons in Iceland. To my frustration, I didn't find much, and what I did find was based on video games or something similar, so I had no confidence the information could be trusted. I also searched for dragons in general, but there were many various sources, all giving conflicting information. I was frustrated and scared. Mom and Dad seemed perfectly cool with it all, but then, they'd had decades to adjust. Or maybe more. I realized then that I didn't know exactly how old my dad was. We had birthdays, and his age had been mentioned, but he still looked much like he did in my kindergarten days. I had always assumed that good genes were responsible. I obviously wasn't far from the mark, except that there weren't human genes involved.

I searched until my eyes burned, then slammed my laptop closed in frustration. I'd considered talking to Mom about it more, but I had yet to address how I felt about them keeping this from me. I acknowledged the sense of betrayal, even if they did have a good reason. I rested my head on my pillow and tried not to think about anything. It seemed a better option than losing my mind. I closed my eyes and inhaled, trying to relax.

When I opened my eyes, darkness greeted me. My vision adjusted, and my room resembled a jail cell. I rubbed my face, trying to shake off the dream I knew I was having. It didn't work. I rolled off the small bed and walked to the bars.

"Hey! Is anybody there?" I yelled at the top of my voice.

A man walked out of the darkness and sneered at me. "Quiet!"

"Sir, please. Let me out." I tried not to cry.

"We don't let monsters roam free." His caustic tone and expression of disgust terrified me as he stepped closer.

"Me?" I asked. "I'm not a monster. I'm just a girl."

"No. You're the worst kind of monster imaginable." He reached through the bars and started to strangle me.

I fought back with all my might, but couldn't break free of his grasp. A roar ripped from my lips, and in an instant, I was looking down on the man from a great height. Fear filled his eyes, and I roared again, then bent my head down and ate him with one bite.

I woke up drenched in sweat from the nightmare. It turned out I did take a short nap, and I was surprised at just how exhausted I really was. I guess finding out you're part dragon will do that, with the obvious addition of horrific dreams.

Moments later, my mom entered my bedroom with a garment bag.

I rubbed my face and fanned myself, still feeling overheated from the dream. "What's that?"

"Your dress for tonight. It's almost five." Mom walked to the end of my bed and draped it across my blanket.

"I gotta wear a dress?" I frowned. While I didn't mind dresses, I wasn't particularly fond of them, either. Especially in wintry weather. This was Colorado in November—not exactly tropical. I preferred my jeans and baggy hoodies.

Mom gave me a tight smile. "Yes."

"Because?" I asked.

"Because your grandfather is very old-fashioned, and we are trying to ease him back into our lives. He believes dinner should be a formal affair, so to appease him, we are going to follow his rules . . . for now." She seemed just as annoyed by the idea as I did.

I huffed. "Whatever." I rolled off the bed and grabbed the dress. "Can I wear my tennis shoes?"

Mom shook her head, and I fought back a pout. I hated dress shoes. Like really hated them.

"Are you okay? You look a little haggard." She gazed at me with concern.

"I'm fine. I just had a bad dream." I didn't really want to discuss it. I shuffled into my bathroom and hung the dress on the towel rack. After unzipping the garment bag, I slid it down to land in a pile on the floor.

"Hmm." It wasn't the worst thing I'd ever seen. The simple, light pink dress had an elegance about it. It had a round collar, three-quarter sleeves, and a princess seamed bodice. I slipped the dress over my head. I'm a petite person at five feet two inches tall, but this dress fell just below the knee, as I suspected it should have—like it was custom made for me.

I yelled through the doorway, "Mom, I need you to zip me up!"

She stepped inside and took a moment to look at me. "Oh, honey. It's beautiful on you." She smiled, and I could tell by the look in her eyes that this wasn't one of those mom-goggle moments. She meant what she'd said.

I glanced at myself in the mirror. I'd never felt particularly pretty before. My raven black hair landed just below my shoulder blades, and while it wasn't curly, it wasn't perfectly straight, either. My pale skin often stood out, even when I spent time in the sun. It seemed as if I was immune to tanning. I'd learned not to wear eyeliner too. When I did, it framed my blue-gray eyes in a way that made them look ominous. I couldn't count the number of times I'd been asked if I was into gothic stuff. I always replied, "No, I just naturally look like death."

Pink had never been a color I'd considered trying, but if this dress were any indication of all pink clothing, I thought I might reconsider that. I kinda felt pretty, or at least, not quite so much like a freak. Given what I'd just learned about myself earlier in the day, feeling somewhat normal was a good thing. I'd take it.

Mom ran her fingers through my hair, then gathered it on top of my head in a messy bun. "What do you think? Should we put it up?"

I shook my head. "Not if I don't have to."

Her reflection winked at me in the mirror. "No, you absolutely don't have to. We'll just pull the sides back so they aren't in your face."

I nodded and enjoyed that moment with my mom. I couldn't remember the last time she'd styled my hair for me. Probably because I'd always thrown a fit when she'd tried. But tonight, everything felt off. I wasn't going to shun the comfort of my mother's care, in any form. I needed her to be my calming presence, even if I still felt annoyance with her. She was exactly that.

WE DROVE through an area called Havenwood Heights. As we passed several large estates, Dad explained that the homes in this area had been here for several generations. The one we were heading to was among the biggest homes on the street.

As we approached, I took notice of multicolored stones that towered upward, supporting dark shingles. I could make out several chimneys, and I silently wondered why anyone would need that many fireplaces. One corner of the house had a large round room that reminded me of a turret like on the old castles they always showed in horror movies.

Dad stopped the car in front of an impressive set of stone steps. My eyes were immediately drawn to the two large statues that flanked the entryway. Dragons. My hopes that I could temporarily forget about all this shifter business were immediately dashed.

A tall, broad-shouldered man in a suit and tie greeted my father at the bottom of the stairs. They shook hands and exchanged a few words I couldn't hear, then Dad motioned for us to exit the car and follow him. Mom waited for me to shut my door, then she clasped my hand in hers as we followed Dad up the stairs. I could feel the tension pulsing through her muscles. She was uncomfortable, and that made me even more apprehensive.

The man in the suit sat behind the wheel of our car and drove it around the side of the house and out of sight. Dad gave Mom and me a wink and pushed open the large oak doors. We stepped into the grandest entryway I'd ever seen, not that I had a lot to compare it to.

Tall beige walls connected to exquisitely polished oak flooring. An enormous crystal chandelier hung from the vaulted ceiling, projecting colorful sparkles on everything in the room. I struggled to tear my eyes away from its beauty. Dad stepped beside me and cleared his throat, so I moved my gaze from the crystal drops above to the elderly man who seemed to suddenly materialize in front of me.

"Lawrence Mills, I'd like to introduce you to your granddaughter, Zoey." He turned to me. "Zoey, this is your Grandpa Mills."

Grandpa stood about average height. His frame appeared wiry, and he had wild white hair that looked as if it took real effort to tame. His black suit was impeccable, and even his shoes were shined to perfection. He squinted his pale green eyes and leaned in a little closer.

While his vision might have been somewhat impaired, I believed he was a shrewd man that didn't miss anything.

"She's a little wisp of a thing, isn't she." He stated that as a fact, not a question.

Dad placed a hand on my shoulder. "Yes, but she's mighty in spirit."

Grandpa's lips turned up a little at that. "I've no doubt she is. She's a Mills!" Then he glanced at my mother. "Well, half Mills anyway." His voice held a hint of disgust.

Mom squeezed my hand a little tighter, but didn't reply. It signaled to me that I shouldn't worry about the insult. It would all be fine.

Dad put his arm around Mom. "Lawrence, if this is any indication of how the night will go, then I suggest we say our goodbyes now."

"Eh! Don't get your shorts in a wad, boy. Come on in and eat some dinner." He turned to go, taking his first step with a cane that looked every bit as old as he was. Before his second step, he turned his head toward my dad. "And stop calling me Lawrence. You know I hate that. I'm your father."

Dad shrugged. "No, I can't say that I do know what you hate. I don't remember much, thanks to this town's special wards."

I looked up at my mom.

"There's a spell on the town that makes people forget about Havenwood Falls and everyone in it. It becomes more like a vague dream." Mom glanced at Grandpa Mills. "Some people get their memories back in a rush, others in small chunks. Some memories trickle back in slowly. Dad and I are getting them back in little segments."

We followed Grandpa through a set of double doors and into a large, elegantly furnished dining room. The gleaming mahogany table looked as if it could have seated at least ten people. I tried not to openly gawk.

"Well, look who the cat dragged in," said a female voice from the back of the room.

Dad stood still for just a moment, then turned to the woman and smiled. "Jetta? Is that you?"

She gave an over-pronounced bow and then walked toward us. "In the flesh . . . for the moment." She smiled slyly as she seemed to take a moment to appreciate her own joke. Her skin-tight black dress looked as if it were made of leather, and matched her knee-high boots perfectly. Jetta's pixie-cut hair was a radiant silver color, and I thrilled to see her eyes were very similar to mine—a pale gray with blue mixed in. Despite the hair color, she appeared to be in her early twenties, with a vibrant energy about her.

Dad turned to address us then. "Bianca. Zoey. This is my younger sister, Jetta."

Aunt Jetta smiled. "It's wonderful to meet you, Zoey! And I remember Bianca, although I'm sure she doesn't remember me. Not yet, anyway." She gave my dad a small shove on his shoulder. "You stayed away far too long, big brother."

Dad shrugged. "If it hadn't been for Lawre . . . uh, Dad's letter, I wouldn't be here now."

Grandpa grunted out something I didn't understand, then barked an order. "Everyone sit down. I can't think or talk on an empty stomach."

We all took a seat at the table, and a kind-looking older woman entered the dining room with a wheeled tray full of all kinds of meats and vegetables. She made her way around the table, filling plates while no one said a word. The tension was too much for me, and I couldn't resist the urge to say something to break the silence. I looked over at Aunt Jetta and took in her appearance. Several beautiful pieces of jewelry graced her neck, arms, and fingers. She also had quite a few tattoos, and I found that fascinating.

"I like your piercings, Aunt Jetta." I tried to make it sound as cheerful as possible.

Aunt Jetta reached up and ran a finger over the gold hoop in her eyebrow, then the diamond stud in her nose. She had several in her ears too, but they weren't as unusual. "Thanks, kiddo. I'm glad someone in this family appreciates individuality." She shot a frustrated look at Grandpa.

Grandpa snorted. "You look like a damn pin cushion."

Jetta batted her eyelashes at him dramatically. "Aw, I love you too, Daddy."

Grandpa just snorted again and picked at his food.

Well, I guess asking about her tattoos is a bad idea. I'll save that for another time.

Dad spoke up next. "So, Dad, tell me why we're here."

Grandpa looked at him like he'd sprouted a second head. "To eat, you moron."

"No, I mean why did you really summon my family to Havenwood Falls? My memories are still a bit fuzzy, but I do clearly remember you telling Bianca and me you never wanted to see us again."

My eyes grew wide. *Harsh!* Dad started right off with the elephant in the room. He didn't just mention it—he shot it between the eyes.

I noticed Mom fidget a little in her seat. I reached over and took her hand in mine. I felt her relax a little.

Grandpa stared Dad down a moment, then placed his fork beside his plate. One bushy white eyebrow rose as he spoke. "To be frank, I'm getting old. We dragons aren't immortal, and someone needs to carry on the Mills legacy. It's gotta be you."

Aunt Jetta laughed out loud. "Yes, darling brother, it has to be you. Do you want to know why?" She glanced at Grandpa, then back at my dad. "Because the old man here still won't forgive me for wanting to be my own person."

Dad looked at them both. "When are you gonna bury that hatchet? It's been years!"

Grandpa shook his head. "I can't abide defiance and disobedience."

It was Dad's turn to laugh. "But you're forgiving mine?"

The room became so quiet, you could've heard a pin drop.

"No," said Dad. "You aren't. You just wanted me back here so I can be under your thumb. If you still can't accept Bianca as a part of this family, then we have nothing more to talk about." He stood. "Girls, it's time we left."

Grandpa stood as well. "Now, wait a minute. You can't just come in here—"

Dad cut him off. "When you're ready to act like a proper father and grandfather, you know where to find us. Until then, don't bother."

Grandpa roared, and it shook the windows. It wasn't merely a loud yell. It was the kind of supernatural sound that made the very ground quake beneath your feet. I clung to my mom as I watched Grandpa's eyes change from pale to a vivid green with a narrow slit for a pupil.

Aunt Jetta put a hand on Grandpa's shoulder. "Dad, calm down. Keep that up, and you'll have the Court here."

Grandpa closed his eyes, then sat back down in his chair. He took a deep breath. "Does she have it, Tristan?" he asked quietly.

Dad looked at me, then back at Grandpa. "Yes, she has the gene."

"May I talk to her?" He sounded exhausted.

Dad studied Grandpa for a moment, then turned to me. "Your grandpa would like a word with you. Are you comfortable with that? If not, you can say no."

I looked at my grandfather. He seemed to have calmed down now. "Sure, I don't mind." I wasn't quite as brave as I tried to sound, but this man was family, and I knew Dad wouldn't allow him to hurt me.

Aunt Jetta walked to where we stood and put her arm around my mom. "Let's get reacquainted while they chat." Mom looked at me, and I nodded my head.

"I'll be fine, Mom. Go ahead." I pasted on a smile to reassure her.

"Okay, if you're sure." Mom looked at Grandpa. "I don't care how you feel about me, but don't you dare disrespect my daughter." She shot him a fierce and protective glare I'd never seen her give anyone.

Grandpa sent her a silent nod, and Aunt Jetta led her out of the dining room.

Dad put a hand on my shoulder. "I'll be just outside these doors if you need me."

I gave him a thumbs up, and he winked at me, then shut the doors behind him.

There I stood—alone in a huge room with a cranky grandfather I'd just met, who happened to be a dragon. What could possibly go wrong?

I took the seat next to Grandpa and tried to calm my nerves. He was intimidating.

"You probably don't know a lot about our family history yet. Would you like me to fill you in?"

I nodded my head. "That'd be nice. Thank you."

He leaned back and closed his eyes a moment before focusing his gaze back on me. "Settle in, Zoey. It's a long story."

CHAPTER 3

"Family records go back far enough to indicate that Iceland is where we originated. My father, his father, and his father's father were all frost dragon shifters. Obviously, we didn't start out that way. In the beginning, we were fierce, mostly solitary beings—protective of the resources in our lands. Dragon families would grow together, then scatter to make our own homes and families. When humans began to settle in our area, it was a source of constant conflict." Grandpa Mills frowned as he relayed our history. "No matter the intention, it always ended in a bloody battle. Both sides became exhausted and broken, tired of losing members. After one particularly devastating loss for the humans, a sorcerer approached us with a proposition. Due to his magic, he could speak to us much the way we communicate with each other. He said that if we'd allow him to change us into humans on occasion, we could communicate with their king and work on a peace treaty."

I felt my eyes grow wide. "Seriously?"

He nodded. "It's the truth. So, we talked among ourselves, and a few volunteered for the task."

He grew quiet and pensive.

When it seemed he wouldn't continue, I had to ask him, "What happened next?"

His eyes snapped to mine. "The humans betrayed our trust. The sorcerer worked for the king, and our agreeing to the deal was all that it took to change our entire clan into humans. They changed us, then attacked us. As humans, we were as vulnerable as they, or so they believed." His lips turned up into a wicked grin. "But there was a kink in their plan. When threatened, our dragons emerged to protect us. We wiped out the entire kingdom after that."

My jaw dropped. "You killed them all?"

"I didn't. I wasn't around. Our ancestors did." He shrugged. "This is the story that's been passed down for generations. I don't know if it's one hundred percent accurate, but it's close enough."

He sighed. "The humans kept coming, and eventually, we had to learn to hide among them to survive without casualties. When we heard news of a journey to this continent, and the search for sanctuary, our family decided to tag along."

It was a lot to take in. "Is there anything else I should know?" Fear almost kept me from asking.

"I think you know the most important parts. There are trivial things. We tend to be paler than most humans and can't tan no matter how hard we try. The details are unclear to me. Evolution to adapt to our climate or some kind of genetic hokum." He waved his hand around as if it was of no consequence, then tapped his index finger on his bottom lip as he reflected on his next words. "I hear you like jewelry."

I nodded, wondering about the sudden change of topic. "I do."

"You've heard the tales of dragons and treasure?"

I nodded again.

"All legends start from a truth. Our truth is that we have an affinity for beautiful things. Jewelry certainly falls into that category. It's in your blood, so to speak."

I felt a sense of relief at his words. At least I had a reason for my obsession, outside of just being odd.

"Other things you'll likely notice," he said, "you may prefer solitude to large crowds. What do they call that now?" He took a moment to think. "Introverts. Yes, that's it. Dragons are generally solitary creatures, although with frost dragons, we do sometimes exist in small clans, such as our ancestors did. The human side of us craves family and companionship, which is why we now do our best to exist in peace with each other, as well as other creatures." He scowled, as if the thought of coexistence angered him.

"You don't like this arrangement?" I asked.

He turned his gaze to mine, and his eyes felt like they were boring into my soul. I adjusted myself in the chair, trying to shake the discomfort of his stare.

"I tolerate it," he stated. "Humans are the reason we are in this mess, so I have very little use for them. But we do what we must, and I am willing to grant concessions . . . for now."

The way he said "for now" sent a chill down my spine. I amended my earlier thought. At that moment, he wasn't intimidating—he was terrifying.

Grandpa Mills crossed his legs and then pointed to my hand, noticing the bandage. "What happened there?"

"I had an accident. A burn." I glanced down at my hand.

"How is it now?" His words indicated a question, but his expression spoke volumes. He knew what my answer would be.

"It's healing . . . under the scale." I pulled the bandage off and pushed my hand forward to allow him a look.

He nodded. "One of the numerous benefits of being a frost dragon. When needed, we can create frost, ice, and blasts of arctic air at will."

I pondered that for a moment.

"What other uses does it have, besides the obvious?" I asked as I held up my hand.

"Well, you can cool a drink in no time flat." He winked at me, and I was taken aback by the levity of his demeanor. He'd been so grouchy just moments before.

"There was a time when we froze our food, for consumption later. It's not so necessary with modern technology, but when I was young, it was all we had."

"When exactly was that, if you don't mind my asking?" I couldn't help but be intensely curious as to his real age. He looked to be in his eighties, but I felt sure he was much older.

"I'm almost two hundred, give or take a few years." He scratched his chin absentmindedly. "I was in my early twenties when we relocated from the old country. My family joined the original band of travelers searching for sanctuary. In 1854, they discovered what we now know as Havenwood Falls."

My mouth gaped open. "Two hundred? That's insane!" I couldn't decide if that could be classified as awesome or horrifying. "How long do frost dragons live?"

His expression grew sad. "Not long enough. Once we hit twenty, we age about half the rate of humans. I'm nearing the end of my lifespan."

I could feel a bit of sadness creep over me. I didn't know this man at all, and he didn't appear to be a popular member of the family, yet the thought of losing him hit me deeply. It made no sense.

"It's okay, child. When I go, I'll be with your Grandma Christine again. I can't ask for anything better." He patted my hand, and for a moment, I felt a kindness he withheld from the rest of the world.

"How long has she been gone?" I asked with a quiet reverence.

"I lost her in the Massacre of 1876." He paused and his expression grew hard. "I lost of lot of family and friends that day."

"Massacre?" I felt the word stick in my throat.

His eyebrows drew together, almost meeting in the middle. "You'll learn about it at school." He stood abruptly and gripped his cane so tightly, I thought I heard it crack.

"I will?" I wasn't quite sure what that meant.

"What are you, a parrot? Yes, you'll get the public version. The real events of that day are only known to a few of the humans that live here. It's not something we discuss openly." He began to hobble toward the door.

I sat motionless, trying to grasp all the information I'd gleaned so far.

He turned and glared at me, his intimidating side returning full force. "Well, girl, are you gonna sit there all night? Let's get your parents back in here so we can eat before the meal is completely ruined."

I returned to the seat I'd occupied before everyone left. My appetite had abandoned me.

~

TWO WEEKS HAD PASSED since I'd learned the truth about my family. I'd had a lot of time to think about my true identity. I'd once believed there was nothing special about me. The last two schools I had attended had hammered that point home. A month ago, I existed as just a below-average teen girl, approaching her sweet sixteen and wishing she could be someone else. Anyone else.

Don't get me wrong. I loved my parents, and I really had nothing to complain about, but I didn't like me. Despite all the "you must love yourself first" stuff my parents had fed me every time I'd been snubbed or my heart had been broken, I knew the truth. I was a weirdo, and I always had been. But the joke was on me. Weird didn't begin to cover it. What was sad was that I now lived in a town full of weirdos, and I still didn't feel like I fit in.

My mom used to call me unique and say that's why I didn't click with people easily. She said, and I quote, "Average people don't understand you, so they lose out on an amazing friendship. Only people that are very special will bond with someone as amazing as you."

The previous times she'd said that, I'd think "Yeah. I wish." But knowing what I knew now, a lot of things made sense. I was beginning to understand the logic behind our love for this part of the United States. We were evolved for a snowy climate—one of many reasons Havenwood Falls was a perfect home for us. The closer my birthday loomed, the more I found the cold comforting. While my schoolmates wore heavy coats, I fought the urge to wear T-shirts.

There was also my tendency to be introverted. I'd generally rather read than attend parties. That part, coupled with my unusual looks, had caused me a butt-load of grief growing up.

The day after I learned the truth, Dad took Mom and me to meet the Court of the Sun and the Moon. As a supernatural being, I had to be registered, per the Court's law. I also had to get a tattoo. Sounds cool for a soon-to-be sixteen-year-old, but the bummer part was nobody could see it. Magic tattoos, secret councils, and a town full of all the scary things the human world was told didn't exist. Once I adjusted to the idea, I realized it was kinda cool. Too bad I had to keep this secret hidden. I felt like the one thing that made me interesting, I couldn't tell anyone. The existence of non-human beings had to be kept secret. This rule kept us safe. It was the reason Havenwood Falls existed.

I pondered all of this new information and exhaled a deep sigh as I watched the scenery fly by the passenger-side window of my dad's car. It was the end of November, and I'd been incident-free since the coffee shop accident, so I naively wished that'd be all there was to it. To be honest, the idea of becoming a full-blown dragon terrified me, especially since I didn't know how the transformation process worked. No one had given me answers for that, and I'd been afraid to ask. I wanted to know, but I also didn't. Sometimes knowing can make the anxiety worse, like getting a shot. If you find out at the last minute, you won't waste time worrying about it before hand. Only, I still worried. I was making myself crazy with all the back and forth of emotions and thoughts, and my birthday approached quickly.

I released another big sigh, overwhelmed by it all, and I felt Dad shift in his seat. I wasn't intentionally trying to make him feel bad. But with every little noise or gesture, he seemed more and more displeased. Guilt sucked. It wasn't his fault that I'd never been the kind of girl to make friends easily. The new school was nice, but he knew I struggled to find my place, as usual.

We pulled up in front of the school, and Dad forced a smile. "I know it's been rough, kiddo. I'm sorry. We never meant to put you through all of . . ." He paused and gestured around him. ". . . this."

I shrugged. "I'll survive." I reached over and gave his arm a squeeze. "It'll just take some time for me to adjust to . . ." I mimicked his gesture. ". . . this."

He chuckled. "All right, sweetheart. You'd better get to class. I'll talk to you tonight."

I nodded and stepped out of the car. I shut the door and glanced up at the large brick building in front of me. My teachers were nice enough, and there were a few students that I kind of liked. The only person that had really made an effort to befriend me was Miranda Saunders, a very kind girl with platinum blond hair, porcelain skin, and a perfect, heart-shaped face. She stood a good four inches taller than me as well. She was the kind of girl that it would be easy to be jealous of, if she weren't so sweet.

I pushed through the doors and saw her standing next to my locker. As usual, she was dressed impeccably in designer jeans, a gorgeous blue sweater, and uncomfortable-looking wedge shoes that added unneeded inches to her height. She looked like she had just stepped off the pages of a fashion magazine.

"Oh, hey, Zoey!" Her wide smile greeted me. "Did you study for that English quiz Mr. Zander is giving us today?"

I tried not to laugh. "I did. How about you?"

I pulled books out of my locker while pretending not to watch her reaction.

"Of course, although if I don't do well, I may have to ask for tutoring." She grinned.

I couldn't hold back my laugh this time. "I knew it! You are totally trying to find a reason to stay after class."

Her expression changed to one of horror, as if I'd insulted her. "Me? Whatever makes you think that?"

I turned to face her. "How about because all you ever do is talk about how hot Mr. Zander is and how you wish he were younger, or you were older?"

Miranda batted her long lashes at me. "I will admit to no such thing." She smirked and sighed. "But I will admit he's fun to look at."

I shook my head. "True, but it's still disturbing."

She gave me a wink and then turned her head in the direction of our classroom. "We should get going."

I picked up my English book and followed her. I'd only glanced down a moment when I ran into something warm and solid.

I raised my head to see a Havenwood Falls T-shirt at eye level. It covered what felt like an impressively muscled chest. I felt myself blush at my blunder and looked up into the exquisite face of one Jordan Woods.

Jordan was an Adonis in blue jeans. His shaggy blond hair, bright blue eyes, and chiseled jawline pulled me in every time I set eyes on him. I felt my nerves kick up a notch.

"Oh, gosh. I'm so sorry. I should have been watching where I walked." I hoped I wasn't mumbling, since I tended to do that when I got nervous. I could almost hear the blood rushing to my face as I blushed.

"No problem." He looked me over for a moment. "Aren't you the new girl? Zoey? Your dad runs the pawn shop now, right?"

I nodded, suddenly losing my ability to speak. I'd never actually spoken to Jordan face to face before this, but I'd silently worshiped him from afar.

"Cool. Well, I guess I'll see you around. Have a nice day." He smiled at me and continued to his first-period class.

It took a moment for me to breathe. That smile almost melted my knees. When I took my next step, my legs shook a bit, and suddenly Miranda stood right next to me. "He's cute, huh? You should totally flirt with him."

"Me?" I squeaked. "I struggled to complete a sentence just now. Flirting will be impossible."

"Don't let him fluster you. He's only human, like the rest of us." She smiled, but it didn't reach her eyes.

"Sure, like the rest of us." I didn't say more. Instead I walked to class and pondered the fact that I didn't know who was human and who wasn't. *Shouldn't I sense something? Would this be one of those things that develops after my birthday?* I really hoped all this started making sense soon. I felt as if I were losing my mind, and I was sure an insane dragon wandering Havenwood Falls was the last thing anyone needed.

~

THE CLOCK slowly ticked away as I watched from my desk in the back of the room. Lunch was minutes away, and I was more than ready. I'd overslept and skipped breakfast, so I paid the price. It felt like my stomach was devouring itself, and if I didn't eat soon, it would growl so loud that everyone in class would hear it. Thankfully, most of the other students were engrossed in their history books and showed no indication that they'd heard the smaller rumblings coming from my stomach. I tried to focus, but I just couldn't get into the Civil War at that moment. My preoccupied mind struggled with everything else, and I couldn't concentrate. I had so many questions.

How many of the kids around me are supernatural, too? What if I do something wrong and get in trouble with the Court? Am I in danger from any of the other supernatural beings that live here? Is my mom safe, since she's human?

The bell rang, and I slowly gathered my books. I still ran these questions through my mind when Miranda hooked her arm through mine.

"Ready for lunch?" She sounded chipper as always.

"Yes, so ready. I'm starving." I groaned.

Arm in arm, we walked to the cafeteria. She placed her lunch box on the table, and I frowned.

"Do you have something against cafeteria food? You always bring your lunch." I teased her, although I did wonder if there was something about our school lunches that she wasn't telling me.

"No, not at all. It's just that I'm on a special diet. Food allergies and all that."

"Oh, okay. You'll have to let me know what they are so I don't accidentally give you something you can't have." The thought of making my best friend, really my only friend, sick, worried me. I'd never forgive myself if I accidentally hurt her.

She smiled and waved me away. "It's all good. Now go get your lunch and get back so we can chat."

I stuck my hands in the pockets of my jeans and strolled over to the lunch line. It moved quickly, and I arrived at the food trays in no time. I watched the line worker place pizza in the middle of the plate, then set a fruit cup and salad on the sides. She raised her eyes to mine and asked, "Milk?"

I shook my head no. "Water will be fine."

She nodded and handed me a bottle of water along with my food tray.

I'd almost made it back to my seat when I noticed Miranda appeared as if she were about to be sick all over the table. I rushed over to her, setting my tray aside so it wasn't in my way.

"Are you okay? You don't look well." I put my hand in hers, and it felt unusually cold.

"Yeah, I just think my lunch isn't agreeing with me." She raised a hand to her mouth and covered it.

I grabbed the thermos she'd been sipping from to inspect the contents. Miranda reached for it, but wasn't fast enough to get to it before I did. I sloshed the contents around inside.

"What is this, soup? Is this one of your food allergies?" I tilted the insulated thermos to get a better look.

"Uh, yeah. My lunch must have gotten tainted." She reached for the thermos again, and I handed it to her, spilling a little on the table. I grabbed a napkin to wipe it up and then froze.

"Miranda, is that what I think it is?" My eyes grew wide as I looked into hers.

She put the lid on her thermos, stood, and grabbed her things. "I gotta go."

I stood, too, forgetting all about my pizza and salad. Shoot, I don't think I could have eaten anyway. Not after what I just saw.

I gave the table a quick swipe with the napkin before I followed her out of the cafeteria, down the hall, and into the girls' bathroom. She ducked into a stall and quickly slammed the door.

"Miranda, you can talk to me. I promise to be open-minded," I said quietly.

"I don't think so," she said, just before I heard her start to puke.

I waited patiently until she had purged it all from her system. She flushed and opened the door, then jumped when she realized I was still there.

"You didn't have to wait," she muttered.

"I know, but I wanted to." I smiled at her.

Miranda turned on the water and washed her hands.

I moved to stand beside her. "I can keep a secret. I'm getting good at that, actually. I may even have a big secret of my own." I gave her a wink, hoping it would encourage her.

"You do?" Her voice sounded hopeful.

"I do." I placed a hand on her arm. "So, let's make a deal. You tell me yours, and I'll tell you mine?"

She nodded. "Okay." She took a deep breath. "My lunch is probably what you thought it was. Except that it wasn't my usual. Mom must have accidentally put her lunch in my thermos by mistake."

"You don't drink the same . . . uh . . . stuff?" I didn't know if I could get the word blood past my lips just yet. I ducked my head down to be sure no one else occupied the stalls behind us. I knew it wouldn't do to have someone overhear our conversation.

Miranda dried her hands. "No, I'm very particular about my meals. They must be from animal sources. I don't like the taste of . . . well, the usual sources."

I raised my eyebrows. "So, you're like the vegan version of your kind?"

She chuckled. "Yeah, something like that."

"That's pretty cool," I said. I still thought it was gross, but it didn't surprise me that drinking human blood would upset her. Her kind nature wouldn't allow for anything else.

She smiled at me. "Thank you. I'm glad we're friends, Zoey." She pulled me in for a hug.

I hugged her back. "Me, too, Miranda."

Holy crap. My best friend is a vampire.

CHAPTER 4

$\mathcal{M}$iranda leaned against the sink and crossed her arms. "My mom and I are both vampires. I'm kind of a freak, in more ways than one. My mom had a short relationship with the man that fathered me. Once she found out she was pregnant, he bolted, so I've never met him. What makes all this unique is he's a vampire and changed my mom before I was born . . . before they found out about the pregnancy. As a rule, vampires aren't supposed to be able to sire children, at least that's what I've heard, so he became irate, accusing her of cheating on him. She'd been changed, but I was born this way. I'm not the norm."

She sighed. "I'm also kind of an outcast because I prefer animals over the blood bank stuff." She frowned. "The others of my kind do their best to avoid me." Her voice held a hint of sadness and I couldn't help but place my hand over hers.

"They don't know what a great person they're missing out on." Great, I'm turning into my mother.

She squinted her eyes at me in suspicion, but I sensed a teasing tone to her voice. "Get that line from your mom?"

I laughed. "Was it an obvious mom-ism?"

She nodded. "It was. And I've heard it a million times from my own mother."

We both stood in silence for a moment, then I spoke up. "Maybe they actually know what they're talking about now and then."

Miranda nodded again. "Well, the plus side is I'm pretty popular with the humans in the school. It's mostly just the vamps that have labeled me a pariah."

I let out a huff. "Yeah, well count yourself lucky. I can't seem to get anyone, humans or otherwise, to give me the time of day, unless they are picking on me." I paused and looked at my best friend. "Why are you so nice to me?"

She reached out and put a hand on my shoulder. "How could I not be? You exude kindness and compassion, Zoey. I knew the moment I saw you that you were special."

That made me smile, and blush a little. "Thank you. I think that's the kindest thing anyone has ever said to me."

"You deserve kindness."

I didn't know how to respond to that, so I changed the subject. "You've haven't heard my secret yet. It's only fair."

Miranda's eyes lit up. "Yes! Tell me!"

I took a deep breath. This would have been the first time I admitted my secret to anyone, but since Miranda had a secret of her own, I felt safe with her. I still worked to push the words past my lips. "I'm not human, either."

She shrugged. "I figured as much. I know you aren't a vampire, so . . ." She waited for me to fill in the blanks.

"I'm a frost dragon." I tried to mask the insecurity in my voice.

"A dragon!" she squealed.

"Shhh!" I hissed. "Not so loud."

"Sorry." She bounced up and down. "But that's just the coolest thing I've ever heard."

"With all the supes that live in this town, that's the coolest thing?"

She chuckled. "I've always been fascinated with dragons, so I might be a little biased. A frost dragon? So, you breathe ice instead of fire?"

I nodded. "Something like that."

"Awesome," she whispered beneath her breath. Miranda's eyes widened. "Oh my God, Zoey! You have to meet Bale! He's a dragon shifter, too! He's not a frost dragon, but still . . . you guys would probably have a lot in common."

I shook my head. "Not yet, Miranda. I recently found out myself, and I'm doing all I can to hold it together right now. Maybe after the dust has settled."

Miranda nodded. "I get it. There's a lot to adjust to."

She placed her hand on my arm in a gesture of support. It was good to know, though, that there were others kinda like me. And to have a friend like Miranda.

THE REST of the day went by quickly. Since I'd skipped lunch, I managed to keep my hunger at bay by quickly choking down some pretzels I'd bought from a vending machine between fifth and sixth periods. Miranda felt much better and even a little giddy after I'd told her my secret. She thought being a dragon was great, although I couldn't verify or deny that for her either way, since I hadn't actually experienced it yet.

We were walking to our last class of the day, when a girl I didn't recognize shoved me into a wall and knocked the books from my hands.

"What hole did you crawl out of, freak?" She growled the words at me.

I glanced up into her face and saw a lot of anger and hatred. It was nothing unusual for me—this was just a repeat of my past school experiences.

Miranda's voice came from my left. "Leave her alone, Katy. She isn't bothering anyone."

Katy turned her glare on Miranda. Her dark, short-bobbed hair swung as she stepped closer. "Who's gonna make me? You?"

Miranda closed her eyes, and Katy smiled. Katy must have thought she frightened Miranda, but in reality, I believed Miranda worked to control her temper. She gave off a vibe that reeked of danger.

I placed a hand on Miranda's arm. "It's okay. I'm not hurt." I turned to Katy. "I'm Zoey Mills. It's nice to meet you." *Kill them with kindness, right?*

"I know who you are. I've heard all about your family. You aren't welcome here." She put a finger in my face. "If you knew what was good for you, you'd move away—all of you." With that, she stomped away. I watched her retreat and tried to understand what my family had to do with anything.

I turned my face to Miranda's and whispered, "Is it possible she knows? Is she supernatural, too?"

Miranda shook her head. "She's human, but her dad is one of the few in town that know of our existence. He's not supposed to speak of it, so I'm wondering if she overheard something she shouldn't have."

"About my family?" I squeaked.

"Well," said Miranda, "you are the newcomers in town. A little place like this . . . there will be talk. Granted, it's usually in the form of your usual gossip, not about what species someone is."

I nodded. "Well, whatever she heard, she must not have liked it. I'm not a stranger to bullying or people thinking I'm odd, but it would have been nice to go a bit longer before it started up."

Miranda's smile held sadness. "We won't allow her to push you around, Zoey. I promise."

I nodded, thankful for someone willing to stand by me. I pulled her in for a hug and wiped a tear from my eye. "I don't know why I'm so emotional. I thought this kind of thing wouldn't bother me anymore."

She squeezed me and bent down to help me gather my books. "Let's get to class and get this day over with."

THE FOLLOWING DAY, the school buzzed with talk of something called the Cold Moon Ball. It was a large celebration that took place every year during the Cold Moon. That seemed cool, especially since this year the Cold Moon and my birthday landed on the same day: December third. I took a flier from a stack sitting near the entryway of the school and scanned the information. I was shocked to learn that the dance itself was a ball held in my grandfather's house, a charity event people flocked to. To be honest, I didn't see my grandfather as the charitable type. But it appeared to be something everyone looked forward to, if the excitement surrounding the announcement was anything to gauge by, so I guess his grumpiness didn't scare off everyone in town.

A shout caught my attention, and I turned to find a freshman named Marty glaring at an older student named Gary. Marty had been hanging chess club posters on the main bulletin board, and it seemed that Gary had been hassling him.

Gary shoved Marty, so Marty shoved back.

In one swift move, Gary put Marty in a headlock. "Stay out of my way next time, you little jerk."

Marty struggled. "Let me go!"

Everyone witnessed the aggressive behavior, but did nothing.

Jordan Woods jogged past me as I watched in dismay. "Gary, leave him alone. Don't you have better things to do, man?"

Gary sent Jordan an angry scowl. "Mind your own business, meathead. Marty and I are just having a little fun."

Jordan stepped forward and grabbed Gary's arm. "Let. Him. Go."

He now stood nose to nose with the bully.

Gary released Marty, and the freshman hit the floor as he began to gasp for air.

"Maybe I should let you take his place," Gary snarled.

I moved closer, wondering if I could somehow help, but also knowing that being the new girl in school, my help may not be appreciated.

Jordan crossed his arms. "If you think you're big enough, then go for it."

Gary stared at him for a long moment, then spit his gum on the floor in front of Jordan. "You're a waste of my time."

He turned to leave.

"Keep in mind that Marty, and any other student at this school, will also be a waste of your time. If you bother them, you bother me."

Gary adjusted his jacket and pretended not to care about Jordan's threat. "Whatever." He gave Marty one last glare before strolling down the hall, away from the snickering students.

As someone who'd been bullied most of my life, I appreciated what Jordan had done. Marty had Jordan on his side, and Gary wasn't likely to pester him again. I was going to step up and help pick up the posters Marty had been hanging, but Jordan beat me to it. He gathered the posters and helped Marty to his feet.

"You okay, buddy?" Jordan asked, dropping a hand on Marty's shoulder.

"Yeah, I'm good," Marty mumbled, embarrassment coloring his cheeks.

Jordan handed all but one flyer to Marty. "Chess club, huh?"

Marty nodded silently.

"I've never learned to play chess. If I join, will they teach me?"

Marty nodded once more.

"Is it hard?" asked Jordan.

"Not once you learn the pieces." Marty's fingers flipped the edge of his poster stack nervously.

"Can you teach me? I'd love to at least know the basics before I start playing against anyone." Jordan's expression was sincere.

Marty's eyes lit up. "Sure! I'm free just about any time after school."

"Awesome." Jordan clapped Marty on the back. "I'm looking forward to hanging out with you." He folded the flyer and put it in his back pocket. "See you after last period."

Marty walked away with his head held high and a smile on his face. True joy formed his expression.

My heart thumped wildly in my chest. I'd already thought Jordan was cute, but this made him angelic. He came across like a knight in shining armor. Except in this weird scenario, I was the dragon he'd normally expect to slay, not fall in love with. I groaned at the thought of him finding out my secret. I turned and stuffed the Cold Moon Ball flier inside one of my notebooks.

"Hi." A familiar voice spoke softly near my ear.

I looked up to see Jordan smiling at me.

"You gonna go to the ball this year?" he asked.

"I . . . I don't know. I'm just now learning about it." I tried not to let the butterflies in my stomach make my voice shake.

"It's pretty fun. We go every year." He chuckled. "I'm surprised you don't already have the inside scoop, seeing as your grandpa runs it."

I smiled. "Yeah, you'd think I'd know all about it already."

"You should definitely go." He continued to smile at me.

"Okay, maybe I will." *Am I flirting? Oh God. I'm actually flirting.*

His grin widened. "Maybe you should go with me. I mean, I'm an old pro at this. My mom has been taking me since first grade. I can show you around the event and help you learn the history behind it, if your grandpa hasn't already explained it to you."

I bit my bottom lip. "Yeah, that might be fun."

He looked down at his shoes, then back up at me. I thought I detected a slight blush. Adorable. "Great, it's a date then." His smile was wide. I nodded, and he waved as he began to walk away. "Talk to you later, Zoey."

"Sure," I mumbled.

Within seconds, Miranda appeared at my side. "Oh my God! You are going to the ball with Jordan? That's so awesome!"

My mouth fell open. "How did you know? He just asked me. And how are you always next to me so quickly?"

She smirked and looked around, then leaned in. "Vampire. We're fast and have great hearing. It's awesome, until you hear a fight. Or your parents doing it in the next room."

"Ew!" I laughed.

"I know. Some things you can never un-hear." She shuddered.

I smiled again. "Have I told you how much I adore you, Miranda? 'Cause I do."

She flipped her blond hair off her shoulder and stuck her nose in the air regally. "Of course you do, daahling. Everyone adores me." We both burst out in laughter.

∾

I RODE through the rest of the day on a cloud of happiness. Not only did I have an amazing best friend, but I had a date. With the cutest boy in school, no less. A small part of my mind wondered if it was some kind of cruel prank, but I couldn't let fear or negativity cloud my ability to at least attempt to have fun.

I said goodbye to Miranda on the front steps of the school as her mom pulled up to the curb. My dad had texted me to say he was running late, so I decided to hang out on one of the benches at Cook's Corner Park across the street—a nice quiet little spot under a tree that provided a magnificent view of the block but still gave the feeling of privacy. The park itself was beautiful, with vine-covered arches, stone paths, and a bronze fountain as the centerpiece. I couldn't wait to see what it was like in the spring. The spot I'd chosen allowed me to leave the snowball fights and noisy students behind, and I could imagine settling down in this spot with a good book when I had some free time.

I sat with my back to the large elm tree and pulled my phone from my pocket. The signal was really spotty at the moment, but I could kill time with a solitaire game. I'd just made my first play when I heard voices from behind me.

"Oh look, it's Zoey the emo girl," snarled Katy.

I frowned. *Not now. Not when everything else today had been so nice.* I turned around on the seat and saw Katy and two of her friends standing there.

I didn't like confrontation, so I tried to think of ways to keep this encounter from going south. "Hi. Am I in your spot? I can move if you'd like me to." I tried to form a friendly smile.

"Oh, I'd like you to move all right. All the way back to where you came from in Freakland." Her smile was cruel and sinister.

I stood to walk away, and one of her friends ran around me to block my path. "Where do you think you're going?"

I looked up at her. She was several inches taller than me and quite a bit larger overall. If I had to guess, I'd say all three of these girls were athletes.

"Listen, I don't want any trouble." I tried to sound polite.

Katy stepped next to her friend, further blocking my path. "Then maybe you shouldn't be flirting with Jordan Woods."

"Jordan?" I asked. "I barely know him. I've only talked to him a couple of times."

"But you're going to the Cold Moon Ball with him," Katy said.

"Well, he did ask me today, and I said yes." I paused. "Is he your boyfriend? If so, I swear I didn't know."

"No," scoffed Katy. "He's not my boyfriend, but don't get any ideas that he's yours, either. You don't belong here, and you don't belong with him."

I frowned. "Listen, I don't know what I did to make you upset with me, but if you'd—"

Katy interrupted me with a hard slap to the face. Stunned, I didn't know how to react. I'd been called names, screamed at, and teased mercilessly, but I'd never been physically assaulted before.

Katy laughed. "Did I smack some sense into you? Or do I need to do it again?"

Her friends laughed, and I took a moment to catch my breath. My face stung, and I worried her attack had left a mark. I closed my eyes, trying to control my emotions. My eyes began to burn as the tears filled my lashes. *I will not cry in front of her. I will not give her that satisfaction.*

I turned around to wipe my face, knowing that she and her goons were just as likely to strike with my back turned. I didn't care. I had an intense need to rein in my slowly building anger. Anger and heartbreak were emotions familiar to me, but this time something felt different. My hands began to shake, and when I opened my eyes, the world seemed slightly dimmer. I glanced down at my still trembling hands and saw my fingernails begin to grow into claws.

My hearing instantly amplified, and I could hear the three girls whisper behind me.

"What a crybaby. She should run home to mama," said one.

I heard another breathe out a shaky sigh.

Katy chuckled. "Let's give her something to really cry about."

The crunch of snow sounded the alarm that Katy was moving. I heard the sounds of something being picked up and then more crunching. My instincts kicked in, and I ducked just as a large pebble-filled snowball flew past me and hit the tree. I stood, ready to turn and defend myself, but terrified of what I might do. I started to panic. *Not here! Not now!* I knew my dragon was once again trying to protect me. I appreciated it, and to be honest, a part of me wanted to see these girls running away in fear, but I knew this was not the right answer. Not at this time. Not when I didn't yet know what I was capable of or how to control it.

Salvation stepped up in the form of my father. "What seems to be the trouble here, girls?"

I closed my eyes and forced my hands to relax, slowly feeling my claws retract.

Katy spoke for the group. "Nothing, just having a snowball fight."

I heard the other girls murmur in agreement.

"Ah, well, I think it's time we all moved on, don't you?" His calm voice had an edge to it that held anger as well.

The three girls said nothing as they walked away. Dad placed his hands on my shoulders. "Are you all right, sweetheart?"

I nodded, but couldn't yet find my voice.

"Are you sure?" He turned me to face him.

I looked up, letting the tears spill down my cheeks.

He gave me a small smile. "I see you've had a new experience with your dragon. I'm just sorry it happened at the hands of those horrible girls."

I nodded. "I'll be fine."

He pulled me to him and wrapped his arms around me protectively. "Yes, you will. You'll be better than fine."

I hoped and prayed he was right.

AT DINNER THAT NIGHT, Mom asked me about the incident with the girls.

"Do you really want me to rehash it?" I asked.

"I don't want to know about the girls. I want to know about you. What happened to you? Did your vision turn cloudy?" Concern laced her voice.

"It did for a little while." I picked up my spoon and tried to use it as a mirror. "Do my eyes look weird or something?" I gasped and dropped the spoon. "Did they change like Grandpa's did?"

Dad nodded. "A little, but they are normal now. My vision always becomes cloudy just before my eyes change. It happens quickly now, but in the beginning, it was a slower process."

At that moment, I was so glad I hadn't turned around during the assault. My eyes already seemed a little odd to people, with their mostly gray coloring. I could just imagine what Katy would have said or done if she'd seen dragon eyes instead of human.

"Once your vision clears, it becomes very sharp. You can see for miles, most of the time. Your hearing is also intensified." He smiled, giving me the impression he enjoyed that aspect of being a dragon.

"My hands . . . my fingernails changed, too." I held them up, as if they could still see the evidence of claws that had retracted hours ago.

Mom frowned. "Did those girls witness any of this?"

"No, I kept my back turned to them." I put a forkful of macaroni and cheese in my mouth.

"Good. Glad to hear it." Her brows furrowed, causing the slight wrinkles she often complained about to deepen.

Dad looked at Mom. "It's okay, Bianca. She has a good head on her shoulders. She has the instinctual dragon wisdom. She'll handle things in the right way." Dad gave me a wink and took a bite of his own macaroni and cheese.

"I'll do my best." I tried to sound enthusiastic for Mom's sake. Dad was excited, Mom was worried, and I was completely confused and overwhelmed.

"So, I assume that is just a small part of what happens when a human changes to a dragon?" I tried to sound nonchalant, although I really felt like wigging out.

"Yes. You were experiencing the beginning stages of that change." He gave me a sad smile. "This should be something you are excited about, like a rite of passage. But instead we live in a world where we have to hide these things."

I nodded again, feeling a lump in my throat. I wasn't sure I wanted to be excited about being a shifter. Especially if my being different painted a large target on my back.

Maybe this explained why Grandpa was so grumpy all the time.

CHAPTER 5

"The ceiling needs painted." That was the first thing I said to myself as I opened my eyes Saturday morning. I didn't know why that thought popped into my head, but as I gazed upward, all I could think about was the dingy white color. Maybe this was how my brain tried to find something totally mundane to focus on. Goodness knows I'd had enough excitement to last me for months. I'd hoped to sleep in, but groaned when I turned my head to the side and saw the clock said seven a.m.

I had planned to spend my day relaxing with a book and otherwise doing a whole lot of nothing. I could have still followed through on that, so I stretched and shuffled to my bathroom. I flipped on the light and glanced at myself in the mirror, then I screamed.

Mom and Dad were in my room within moments.

"Are you okay? Where are you? What happened?" Dad shouted.

I stepped out from the bathroom and saw Dad with a baseball bat, ready to do battle. "This happened. What is this?" I asked as I held up a handful of hair.

Dad lowered the bat, and Mom's mouth formed the word "oh" without actually saying it.

"That's probably one of your special traits," Dad said as he walked toward me. "I think it looks kinda cool." He touched my hair. "Isn't this all the rage right now?"

I rolled my eyes. "It's popular to color and highlight your hair all kinds of crazy colors, yes. But I'm not sure this is the same thing." I stepped back into the bathroom and gazed at my reflection. My raven-black hair now had streaks of iridescent white dispersed throughout. The contrast was almost blinding. I turned my head and noticed that the light sparkled off the white strands. It reminded me of a pearl, with the subtle colors chasing the light as I moved.

Mom stood in the doorway. "It's rather beautiful, once you get over the shock."

I nodded. "Yeah, I guess." My mind reeled with the mockery that would come my way at school on Monday. At least I had the weekend to adjust to it. "Do you think I could dye it back to black?"

Dad's voice carried from my bedroom to the bathroom. "You could try, but my guess is that it won't take."

"Oh joy," I said. "One more reason for me to stand out."

Mom smiled at me. "One more thing that is uniquely you and completely breathtaking."

I had to refrain from rolling my eyes yet again. She was my mom. She had to say stuff like that. Instead I smiled back at her.

"Thank you." It's the only response I could muster.

By the time lunch rolled around, I'd found myself sitting in a booth at Whisper Falls Inn, thanks to my mom's orchestrations of a "surprise" visit from my best friend, who screamed with delight when she saw my hair. My black hoodie was my *new* best friend now. I would never take it off again.

"Take off that hood, Zoey!" Miranda whispered at me loudly, for the third time.

"No way," I growled. "I'm not ready to showcase this mess to the whole town. I'm still getting used to it myself."

Miranda crossed her arms and tapped her fingers with impatience. "It looks freaking amazing. I might see if my hairdresser can replicate it."

"You lie," I muttered.

"Seriously." Miranda crossed her finger over her heart. "I'm a little jealous actually. I'm usually the first one to try new styles, but Mother Nature helped you scoop me on this one."

I couldn't help but grin a little. "I don't know . . . it's just so different. Not remotely subtle. And it happened overnight. Last night I went to bed with normal, boring hair. Today . . ."

"That's part of why it's amazing. You can't help but gaze at it, like a work of art." She reached across the table that sat between us and squeezed my hand. "Now lower your hood."

I played with a small strand of dark hair that had escaped my hood. "I don't know. I'm not ready for the stares, even if they are because people think it's cool. I don't like being the center of attention."

Miranda started to say something else when Michaela, the inn owner, arrived with our food. She sat back and waited until my plate and both of our glasses were settled on the table, then took a sip of her drink. "Yum. I love this place. Thanks to Michaela, they always have my favorite drink here. She's a vampire, too, and prefers the same food source I do." Michaela winked at us before she strolled back into the kitchen, and Miranda smiled at her. "Your mom was right to suggest I take you out today. You've gotta come out of your shell a little more, and I'm just the girl to help you do it."

I groaned. "I've been an antisocial freak all my life. One afternoon with you isn't going to change that."

"No." She played with her straw. "But it will help."

I shook my head.

"Eat up. We have a full day ahead of us." She pulled out her cell phone, and I heard the clicking sound as she typed.

"Now what are you doing?" I asked.

"I'm texting my mom. I'm letting her know we are going to be in town the rest of the day and that I'm using the credit card." She flashed me an excited grin.

"I'm doomed." I pouted as I shoved a French fry in my mouth.

∽

WE WALKED out of Callie's Consignments with two formal gowns in tow. I wasn't sure how I felt about the upcoming ball, but knowing that I'd be there with Jordan, I was willing to step out of my comfort zone a bit.

"You could have shopped at Dress Perfect. I wouldn't have minded at all." I felt bad that Miranda chose a consignment dress when she could have had something custom made. I, on the other hand, couldn't afford something custom and wasn't about to let her pay for it.

"No way. I love this dress!" She held up her garment bag. "I've had dresses made before. Looking with you will always be much more fun than standing around for a fitting."

I smiled. "It was fun."

"Now we need jewelry." She jumped up and down in excitement.

"Oh, I have plenty of that. In fact, you can raid my stash and see if there is anything you like."

"Really?" Her eyes widened. "You'd do that?"

I shrugged. "Why not? I can't wear it all."

"But . . ." She hesitated. "How does your dragon feel about that?"

I shrugged again. "It doesn't have a say. The human side of me is more dominant where that is concerned." I wasn't totally sure what my dragon did and didn't want, but I knew it wouldn't be upset with Miranda over borrowing a little jewelry.

"Well, if you're sure, that'd be awesome!" Her smile was infectious, and I couldn't help but smile back.

We walked to her car and placed the dresses in the back seat. After she locked up, we walked toward the shop next to Madame Tahini's—the business my dad ran for my grandfather. It seemed comical, now that I knew our secret. Wouldn't people freak if they knew that dragons owned Simple Treasures Pawn Shop?

"Is your dad working today?" asked Miranda.

I shrugged. "I'm not sure. I think so."

Her grin became mischievous. "Let's go see all the stuff people have pawned."

I laughed. "It's not like we're gonna find a hidden stash of gold or someone's deep dirty secrets."

"You never know. You can learn a lot about a person from their possessions." She gave me a sly wink.

She was right. But I wasn't sure we'd know what items belonged to whom, so it likely wouldn't do us much good. I had just reached for the door when it opened, and the bell above it tinkled loudly.

"Well, hello, Zoey. I was just coming to see you." My grandfather gave me a slight smile and leaned on his ancient cane.

"Hi, Grandpa." I turned to motion to my best friend. "Have you met Miranda Saunders?" It seemed rude not to introduce her.

He turned his gaze on her, and his look was shrewd. For a moment, I feared he would be rude. Then he spoke.

"It's nice to see you, Miranda. How is your mother?" His expression and voice both indicated his sincerity.

"She's very well. I'll tell her you asked about her. Thank you, Mr. Mills." Miranda was every bit the polite young lady she should have been.

I decided to break the brief silence. "So, why were you coming to see me?" I hoped it was for something good.

I noticed real, deep emotion behind his eyes. "I wanted to give you this. It seemed like an appropriate gift for your sweet sixteen."

He placed a large, flat velvet box in my hand.

I glimpsed up at him. "Wow, thank you, Grandpa. Do you want me to open it now?"

He nodded.

I looked at Miranda, then back at the box. The hinges were old, and the lid raised slowly as I lifted the top. Nestled inside soft blue velvet sat the most beautiful necklace I'd ever seen. It held a dainty silver chain connected to a stunning stone that was also encased in silver. Specks of colors glinted up through the glossy exterior.

"It's an opal. It was your grandmother's. She wanted you to have it." His voice hitched ever so slightly as he mentioned Grandma Christine.

"How is that possible? Grandma Christine . . . I mean . . . I never had the chance to meet her. How could it be for me?" It seemed hurtful to bring up the fact that my grandmother had passed on long before I was born, but I didn't know how else to ask the question that buzzed around in my brain.

He smiled at me. "Grandmas have a sixth sense about things." He glanced at Miranda and appeared to struggle with his next string of words. "Trust me. This was meant specifically for you." He patted my shoulder. "And it'll match perfectly with your new hair color."

I felt my eyes go so wide, I feared they'd pop out of my head. How did he know? I'd firmly pulled the hood back up after trying on the dresses, so my hair remained covered. "Thank you, Grandpa. It's lovely."

He glanced down at the necklace and smiled once more. "Yes, it'll be perfect. You should wear it to the Cold Moon Ball. That's a very special day for all of us, but especially you." He nodded at Miranda and then hobbled his way around the corner and out of sight.

"Close your mouth, Zoey. You'll catch bugs in there. Wait, do dragons eat bugs?" Her expression became thoughtful.

I turned to face her. "No, we don't eat bugs . . . as far as I know." The thought almost made me gag.

"You know, he's right. That necklace is a perfect match to your new highlights." She smiled brightly.

"Not helping," I muttered.

She nudged me and laughed. "Come on, Zoey. I promise, your hair is amazing. This necklace is amazing. *You* are amazing. Give yourself some credit."

Speechless, I pulled her in for a hug.

～

MONDAY MORNING ARRIVED way too soon. By the time I went to bed Sunday night, my anxiety was in a full-blown tizzy. I had convinced myself that the change in my hair would only paint a larger target on my back. I'd slept fitfully, dreaming of an odd mixture of dragons, jewelry, bugs, and bullies.

As I walked up the steps to the school, I'd convinced myself I'd be crying in the bathroom by noon. I pushed through the doors and instantly tensed, waiting for the onslaught. Instead, a decent-sized crowd gathered around someone, all of them talking and laughing. No one even noticed I'd arrived.

I decided to take advantage of that moment and sneak to my locker undetected. Just as I'd reached the combination lock, I heard Miranda yell my name. I froze, then slowly turned around.

Miranda pushed her way through the group, and they all followed her. I looked at her and dropped the backpack in my hands. Miranda was all smiles as she stepped in front of me.

She put an arm around me and looked at the rest of the students surrounding us. "Doesn't it look amazing? We decided to both go super contrasty so it'd show up better." She smiled at me. "Right? We had so much fun getting our hair colored together."

The shock hit me hard, and I couldn't respond right away. Miranda's beautiful blond hair now had dark red streaks blended in. It looked really cool, to tell the truth. Everyone else seemed to be loving it.

A chorus of voices expressed that they liked mine as well, then the bell rang, and we all scattered to our classes. Miranda and I both took our seats near the back of Mr. Zander's class. I couldn't keep my eyes off my best friend.

I leaned closer to her and whispered, "What did your mom say about your hair? Did she hate it?" I really hoped her mom had a sense of humor.

"Who do you think did it? When I told her that you were self-conscious about your new look, she was all for the idea." She looked for the page number written on the chalkboard.

"I can't believe you did this." *Mind blown.*

"Don't be silly. This is what best friends do." She patted my arm. "I knew you were worried about it, so I figured if they were gonna mock it, they'd have to mock us both. But see, I told you. Everyone loves it."

Mr. Zander interrupted us. "Zoey and Miranda, anything you'd care to share with the class?"

"No, sir," I said meekly.

"Sorry, Mr. Zander. It won't happen again." Miranda smiled at him.

He went back to writing on the chalkboard, and we went back to our textbooks. I snuck one final glance at Miranda. I'd been right. It wasn't even second period, and I was in tears, but not for the reason I'd expected.

CHAPTER 6

*M*iranda and I sat in our usual place at lunch. We were chatting along happily when someone approached our table and stood directly in front of me. I raised my eyes to see Kai Reynolds. His six-foot-tall football physique cast a formidable shadow over my fish sticks and tater tots.

"Zoey Mills." He crossed his arms in front of him.

"That's my name." I tried to smile. Kai was kind of intimidating, and at that moment, he reminded me of my grandfather. He was also very attractive, and I couldn't tear my eyes away from his face.

"We should talk," he stated.

Miranda frowned at him. "Kai, why would you need to talk with Zoey? You don't know her."

"True, but I know *about* her." His emphasis sounded like a warning.

I looked at Miranda. She sighed. "Sit down, Kai."

He pulled out the chair in front of him, took a seat, then leaned forward on the table. "I hear you're going to the Cold Moon Ball with Jordan Woods."

"I am." I'd decided over the weekend that there was no reason to deny it, despite Katy's bullying. I didn't want Jordan to think I wasn't excited about going with him.

"You should reconsider," said Kai.

"Why?" Miranda blurted out the question before I did.

He focused his golden-brown eyes on her and raised a dark eyebrow.

"Oh lord. Really? Tell me you're kidding." She shot him a glare.

He leaned back in his chair. "Mixing with humans is never a good idea."

"What?" I squeaked. I looked at Miranda, and I'm sure she saw the horror on my face.

She held up one hand. "I didn't tell him. Some supes just know."

"Are you . . ." I didn't know how to phrase the question.

"I'm like Miranda," he stated.

"I see." I really hoped one of these days I'd be one of those that "just know." I was tired of all the surprises.

"If you really want to go to the ball with someone, I can take you." He didn't crack a smile.

Miranda leaned forward. "Wow. That's a convincing way to ask a girl out. I'm surprised your flowery words haven't melted Zoey right here in her seat."

He glared at her, then moved his gaze back to me. "If not me, we can find you a suitable date, but I think we'd suit well."

My heart beat rapidly. There was something about him that kept me riveted. It was more than just his looks, but I couldn't put my finger on it, and I couldn't seem to escape it.

Sanity reentered my brain. I shook my head. "No, thank you. I've already told him I'd go with him. And for the record, I don't care if he's human or not. I like him."

He stared at me for a few seconds, then shook his head in disgust. "You're just like your dad."

I stood. "Thank you," I whispered loudly. "My dad is a great man, and I'm proud to be his daughter."

Miranda stood and put her arm around me to show her support.

Kai frowned. "You'll regret this, Zoey. It never ends well with humans."

I shrugged. "It's my mistake to make."

I didn't truly believe it was a mistake. My mom and dad were perfectly happy together.

He smirked at me. "Whatever."

He stood and walked away. I struggled to tamp down the disappointment I felt when he dismissed me so easily. *Why do I care what he thinks?*

I turned to Miranda. "What was that all about?"

She sighed and motioned for me to sit back down. She took her chair as I sat in mine. "So, Kai is a bit of a speciesist. He thinks, at the minimum, that supernaturals should only associate with other supernaturals. If he's being particularly snobby, he'll insist that most supernaturals should stick to their own specific species." She paused a moment and glanced across the room to where Kai now sat with his friends. "I think he might like you a bit, though, and would bend his species rule if you showed interest in him."

My heart lodged in my throat once more. He was so different than Jordan. Arrogant, self-assured, with a sensual vibe surrounding him. It pulled at me, and I hated myself for feeling that way.

"If that's how he talks to girls he likes, I'll pass. My grandpa is the same way, which is why he and my mom don't talk much." I hoped I sounded more convincing than I felt. I looked at my lunch, but found I'd lost my appetite.

"Either way, don't let him bother you. Only a small group in town feel the way he and your grandfather do." She took a sip from her thermos, and I wondered how my life had gone from dull to complicated so quickly.

ONCE HOME FROM SCHOOL, I sat in my room and thought about the upcoming ball and my birthday. While I didn't truly believe what Kai said earlier in the day, it did plant a seed of doubt in my mind. I wasn't expecting marriage or anything, but I did hope that Jordan and I could at least give dating a shot.

Kai was an enigma. I understood my attraction to Jordan. He was cute, kind, and everything I'd ever thought I wanted in a guy. But I had no idea why Kai had become a contender for my feelings. I'd never been one of those girls that chased after the bad boy, and he was very much a bad boy.

"Ugh." I groaned, shaking off the frustration as I moved to my bed and sat down. I grabbed the ornate jewelry box from my nightstand and placed it in my lap so I could study the maze of lines on the top, as I had so many times before. This time, when I traced the lines with my fingers, they moved.

"What the heck?" I watched in disbelief as the metal changed shape. "I knew this was special. I knew it!" I couldn't contain my excitement.

Once the pieces stopped moving, I noticed an empty circular spot in the center. I leaned closer to get a better look and grandma's necklace, which hung around my neck, gravitated to it like a magnet. *No way! It couldn't be!*

With great care, I reached behind my neck and unclasped the chain, letting the pendant fall completely into the center of the lid. The lines on the top moved around once more, and a small compartment in the side popped open.

"Whoa. The necklace is a key."

I pulled the compartment drawer the rest of the way out and found a letter inside. With shaky hands, I removed the paper and unfolded it. The fragile parchment had yellowed with time. After placing the jewelry box on the bed, I carefully straightened the letter out in my lap.

Dear Granddaughter,

I know this will come as a surprise, but I knew you would be the one to own the box and the necklace. How did I know? Well, let's just say that not all fortune tellers are frauds. Speaking of which, please tell Madame Tahini thank you for her wisdom and advice. Without her, I would not have known to write you.

While I do not know your name, I do have a somewhat detailed description of what you look like. You are almost at your sixteenth birthday, and lots of changes are ahead. Some have already happened; others are yet to come. Embrace who you are, little one. Be proud of your heritage. You come from an extensive line of Icelandic Frost Dragons who once roamed the earth in mighty droves before the human population vastly increased. We are still a noble species with much to offer those around us. Most of us are wise beyond our years, although at times, I wonder if your stubborn grandfather isn't the exception to the rule. We possess amazing gifts as well. Some are universal; others are unique to each dragon. You'll learn what yours are as you mature.

Never fear, little one; you are stronger than you know. Never back down from doing what is right, and always act in kindness and compassion. This will never steer you wrong.

Take great care with this necklace. Opals are known for their magic properties, but this one is extra special. It contains a spell that will help you control the emotions that come with growing up as a shifter. It will also help you with any specific needs you may struggle with. What those will be, I can't say—only the stone knows. Some days you'll feel like more of a dragon, others you'll feel more human. Eventually both sides must coexist in harmony if you choose to stay in Havenwood Falls. That's a choice only you can make, once you're of age. Choose wisely, my granddaughter, and know you are loved.

Grandma Christine

P.S.: I love the white in your hair. Never change that.

"Whoa. This is too much to handle." I carefully placed the letter on the jewelry box and moved it to my nightstand. I closed my eyes as I flopped myself back onto the bed. It blew my mind to think my grandmother knew a lot of what would come to be. Her words sunk into my heart and warmed my soul. A tear slid down my cheek as I realized that I missed her, and I'd never even met her. But she seemed to know me, and I think we would have gotten along wonderfully.

My grandfather was a totally different story. I didn't know how to take him. I believed that Grandma served as a cushion that softened Grandpa's blows. But now she was gone, he was angry, and I was sure I had missed a vital part of that puzzle.

CHAPTER 7

*A*larm. Clothes. Breakfast. The following day started out fairly normal. Well, as normal as it can be for someone who was half dragon. I did my best to keep my head down, focus on work, and not be noticed. I'd just stepped outside the school doors when Jordan approached me.

"Hey, Zoey." He smiled, and my insides began to melt.

"Hi, Jordan." I did my best to look confident and return his smile.

He slipped his arms through his backpack and shifted the weight so it rested on his shoulders. "I like the new hair color. It's . . . unique."

I couldn't tell if he really liked it, or if it was simply kindness on his part. "Thanks. I wanted to try something different."

"You succeeded. It looks great on you." He continued to smile at me, and I tried to focus less on that and more on his words.

I looked down at my feet for a moment, hoping the rush of heat to my cheeks would quickly subside. "I'm glad you like it."

He stuck his hands in his pockets. "So, I was wondering if you had any plans tonight?"

I shook my head. "I don't think so. I'd have to check with my parents to be sure."

"Would you like to grab pizza with me? I thought we could go to Napoli's." He appeared to be a little nervous, and it was endearing.

"Yeah, sure. That'd be nice." I struggled to keep the tremble from my voice. I had to play it cool. It wouldn't do to scare him off before I even had a chance to know him.

"Great. I'll pick you up around five thirty then, if that's okay."

I nodded. "That'd be perfect."

He turned and jogged down the steps while I stood there, grinning like an idiot.

I reached up and ran my fingers over my grandmother's necklace, which brought me comfort. Maybe it was the connection to my grandmother. Or maybe the spell contained in the stone. I didn't really know what brought about the soothing of my soul. All I could be sure of was that the necklace and I were fated to belong to one another.

My dad pulled up in front of the school, and I quickly made my way to the car. After strapping in, I wasted no time in finding out the evening plans.

"Are we doing anything special tonight?" I kept my voice casual.

"Just the norm. Why? Have plans?" He grinned at me.

"I do, if it's okay. Jordan asked me to grab pizza with him tonight." I pressed my lips together, trying to contain my enthusiasm.

"Ah, I see. Sounds fun. Do you need a ride?" He kept his eyes on the road.

"No, he's picking me up," I said as I dug through my backpack to be sure I'd packed my geography homework.

"Glad to hear it. It'll finally give me a chance to do the protective dad routine I've been practicing since I learned you were gonna be a girl." We pulled up to a stoplight, and he rubbed his hands together like a villain from some corny superhero show.

"Dad, please. Don't embarrass me." I felt sure I'd expire from utter humiliation if he did anything crazy.

"Me?" he asked, his voice full of surprise and innocence.

"Yes, you." I pointed a finger at him. "You love pushing your dad boundaries. I can deal with the dad jokes, but antics like cleaning a gun in front of my date is too far."

He shook his head. "I don't even own a gun, sweetheart. I do, however, own knives. Lots of knives."

"Dad . . ." I said in warning.

He laughed the rest of the way to our street. I, on the other hand, contemplated the logistics of running away from home.

~

JORDAN and I sat in a booth at Napoli's with a large cheese pizza between us. I'd debated how I should dress, but after a long argument with myself, the sensible side of my personality won, and I opted for a clean pair of jeans and a nice, but not too fancy blouse. Jordan had changed as well and looked amazing in his jeans and blue polo shirt.

"This pizza is so good," I murmured just before taking a bite of my second slice.

"It's the best." He took a bite of his own and winked at me.

"You said you've lived here all your life. Do you like it?" I thought that a safe place to start a conversation about his life.

"Yes and no. Like all small towns, it has its pros and cons." He took a sip of his cola.

"Football team, lots of friends . . . I'm gonna guess the good outweighs the bad. You've got it made here." I teased him, but his eyes were somber.

"Don't be so sure. School isn't everything. We've discussed moving a couple of times, but it never worked out. I used to get frustrated by that, but now . . . Well, I'm glad I'm still here."

I tried not to blush. "I'm glad, too."

He reached across the table and took my hand in his. "I know we don't know each other very well, but there is just something about you that I'm drawn to. You're not like most of the other girls here."

Dude, you have no idea. "Oh, I'm pretty average. Nothing special about me."

"See, there's where you're wrong. Besides being unusually pretty, there is something about you that I can't put my finger on. Something deep on the inside that is dying to come out." He rubbed his thumb over the back of my hand, and goosebumps raced down my spine. If he only knew how close to the truth he really was. Yet I'm not sure he could ever know. Kai's words pricked at the back of my mind. His face invaded my thoughts, and I had to push the image away.

"I know that sounds like a tacky pickup line," he said, "but it's the honest truth. I don't know how else to explain it."

"Thank you. That's very sweet." I hoped my face expressed how much his words truly meant. I didn't feel so much like an outsider in that moment.

"I've gotta hit the restroom. I'll be right back." He scooted out of the booth and headed to the back of the restaurant. I'd just taken another bite of pizza when Kai sat down in Jordan's seat.

"I've warned you about Jordan. Why won't you listen?" He was annoyed, and the frown he wore was severe.

I reached up and touched my necklace. "No, you told me it was a bad idea, but you never really said why."

I was really getting tired of people trying to tell me what to do. I crossed my arms and stared him down, begging my emotions not to betray me. They didn't listen. My skin prickled with awareness as Kai reached across the table and placed his hand over mine.

His voice changed and became tender. "You will never have the normal life he'll expect. Things will happen. You'll change." He leaned back against the seat. "How are you gonna explain the first time you change into a full-blown dragon in front of him? Think he'll just laugh it off?"

I shrugged. "I don't know, Kai. It's not like we're engaged. We're just hanging out. Take a Xanax and calm down."

"My, you're certainly becoming outspoken," he sneered.

"How would you know? Outside of my secret, you know me even less than Jordan."

His eyes bored into mine. "I'm giving you fair warning. End it. You should be with me. Don't make this harder than it has to be." He stood and walked away as if he hadn't just threatened me.

"Jerk," I muttered as I looked back down at my pizza and tried to slow my fluttering heartbeat. He was correct about one thing—I did suddenly gain an attitude that wasn't my norm. I didn't know where this confidence came from, but I liked it. The necklace again? Possibly.

I wished the necklace could tell me why Kai and Jordan both appealed to me, and which one was the correct choice.

Within minutes of Kai leaving, Jordan made it back to our table. "Sorry I took so long. I also had to call and check on my mom."

"No need to apologize. I think it's great that you care for her so much. Is she ill?" I hoped I wasn't being intrusive.

"Uh, yeah . . . sorta. She wasn't feeling well when I left earlier." He seemed to have lost interest in his pizza.

"Do you need to be with her? I don't mind if you need to go." I'd be disappointed, but family was important.

He fidgeted in his seat and began to look uncomfortable. "I don't want to go, but I should probably check on her in person."

I nodded. "Sure, we can try this again later. And there is always the ball." I smiled to reassure him that I wasn't in the least upset.

"Thank you." He quickly left his seat and went to the register to pay the bill. While I waited, the waitress came over and boxed up the remaining slices of pizza to go.

He returned, I picked up the box, and we walked side by side to his car. We'd just buckled up when his cell phone buzzed. He pulled it out and frowned. "Hey, do you mind if we make a quick stop before I take you home?"

"No, not at all." I couldn't help but be concerned by the way his face drained of color.

He put the car in gear, and we sped down the street toward the south end of the town square. It wasn't a far drive, but we arrived at our destination faster than I'd have thought humanly possible.

We pulled up to Building B in an apartment complex called Havenwood Village. He slammed the car into park and turned to me. "Stay here. I'll be right back."

Before I had a chance to respond, he bolted out the door and took the steps two at a time. I saw him enter an apartment with the number 204 on the door. I sat quietly waiting, when I heard a loud crash. I forgot all about his request to stay, and I bounded up the stairs after him.

When I pushed open the door to the apartment, I found Jordan hunched over a woman lying on the floor. He sat her upright. Blood dripped from her mouth, and a bruise covered her cheek.

"I'm here, Mom. I'm here," he soothed as he pulled her close to him.

"Jordan? Is everything okay?" I wanted to help, although in truth I felt totally helpless.

His eyes snapped to mine. "No, thank you. I thought you were going to wait in the car." He sounded a little angry.

"I was, but then I heard a crash, and it worried me."

His eyes drifted to a spot on the opposite wall where the remains of a lamp lay in pieces.

"It's nothing I can't take care of." Ice laced his words, and I realized I was completely out of place. I was an intruder, and he didn't want me there.

"Okay, sorry. I'll just go back downstairs." I turned and carefully made my way down the steps and to his car. I struggled with the idea of waiting on him or calling my parents. In the end, I settled on walking home. As I crossed the town square, I spotted the gazebo. I was drawn to it, and before I realized what I had done, I found myself seated just inside the latticework.

The chill in the air surrounded me, yet once again I found I didn't really need a coat or my hoodie, though I wore it anyway. Normally, I'd have been shivering by now. This dragon trait made me immensely grateful in that moment. I hated being cold.

Jordan's red Toyota slowed to a stop at the curb across from me. He got out and cautiously walked toward me. I wasn't sure if I should be worried or mad. He behaved like a jerk back there, and I only tried to help. Kai's face flashed in my mind, and I pushed it away for the second time that night.

Jordan reached the railing and leaned against it. "Hi."

I looked up at him, a frown creasing my face. "Hi."

I had no enthusiasm left to give at the moment. First Kai, and now this. I was tired.

"I'm sorry about that back there. I'm not used to . . . I mean, not many people know about . . . that." He fidgeted and kicked the tip of his tennis shoe in the dirt.

"I won't tell anyone. I'm not a gossip." It hurt that he might not trust me.

"I know. It's not that." He stepped up onto the wooden flooring and walked to stand beside me. "Can I sit?"

I motioned to the empty spot beside me.

He perched his butt on the edge and crossed his legs out in front of him. "My dad hits my mom. I can't stop it."

I could hear the distress that admission caused him.

"I'm so sorry, Jordan. I don't know how you'd stop something like that. Can you call the police?" I hoped I wasn't asking a stupid question.

He shook his head. "The first time I did, Mom lied and told them that she'd fallen down the stairs. She had bruises on her arms from where she'd tried to block his blows. That was just a minor one." He sighed. "She wouldn't press charges or tell the truth, so I knew it was a waste of time after that."

"Why not?" I asked, then realized I probably knew why. For the same reason I didn't want to pursue Katy and her friends after they hit me. I feared it would only get worse.

"She loves the jerk. And I think she's afraid he'd kill her once he got out of jail." He turned to me with tears in his eyes. "He will, ya know. He'll kill her. And me, too. He's only hit me once, and that time my mom lost it on him, but it didn't change anything. Now I work to keep the peace as much as possible. I can tell when he's had a bad day, so I check on her if I'm not home. She didn't answer the phone, so I knew something was wrong."

My heart broke for him. I couldn't imagine living in that kind of environment—seeing someone you love hurting someone else you love. No one deserved that.

I reached over and took his hand. "Don't feel guilty. You are doing all you know to do." I swallowed. "If you ever need someone to talk to, or just want to get away for a bit, feel free to call me. It'd be a privilege to be there for you." He nodded, but I wanted more. I wanted a smile. "Wow, now who's using the cheesy pickup lines?"

He smiled then, and my heart almost stopped beating. I did that. I caused that beautiful smile in a sad moment.

He sat back on the bench a little and adjusted so he faced me, then he leaned forward, and before I knew what happened, he kissed me. At some point, I must have closed my eyes, because I had to open them to look into his.

He smiled and ran a finger down my cheek. "You really are amazing, Zoey. I'm so glad I know you."

I shivered at his touch. "I'm glad I know you, too." This time I closed the gap between us, and I had the first real, heart-stopping kiss I'd ever experienced.

CHAPTER 8

*J*ordan continued to kiss me. A thrill ran through me as his lips touched mine over and over. His hands began to roam over my body, and while I liked his touch, I knew this pushed the limits for a first date. I kept my eyes closed and pushed his hands to my back, where they belonged. He moved them to explore my body once again, this time with more force, and my eyes flew open to protest, then I screamed.

I wasn't kissing Jordan. I was kissing Kai! His seductive smile and bedroom eyes pulled me in. I didn't want to want him, but I did. He put one hand in my hair and pulled my head back, giving him access to my neck. He kissed lightly, and I couldn't stop the groan that escaped my lips.

He moved to my ear and whispered, "See, Zoey? See how it could be between us? Don't fight it."

Knocking interrupted yet another passionate kiss. He pulled back and whispered, "Go away."

The knocking continued, so this time I repeated his words, but louder. "Go away."

"Zoey? Are you up yet? We have a busy day ahead of us."

Mom? Why is Mom here?

The knocking became louder.

I bolted up in bed and rubbed my face. Mom knocked on my bedroom door again, then opened it.

"You need to get around, sleepyhead. We have so much to do before the Cold Moon Ball tomorrow." She winked at me, then closed the door behind her.

A dream? Oh, thank God it was a dream. The tension drained from my body. I really hated that I'd dreamed about Jordan and Kai had forced his way in. Jordan and I had only gone on the one date, but it felt like I had cheated on him. We weren't officially an item yet, so cheating wasn't really an issue, but after last night's kiss, I'd hoped there was a future for us. If only I could get Kai out of my head.

I quickly dressed and went to the kitchen to help. Everyone worked on prepping for the celebrations that would follow on Sunday. Even my mom jumped in on the action by baking pies for the huge meal that preceded the ball.

The doorbell rang just as I had intended to ask Mom what she needed me to do.

"Saved by the bell," I quipped. Then I yelled down the hall as I walked to the front door, "I'll get it."

I swung it open to find Aunt Jetta standing on the other side.

"Hey, kiddo! How are you?" I hadn't even said hello when she pushed her way in and started touching my hair. "Oh my gosh. This is gorgeous! I wish my hair would have done this."

I laughed. "Yeah, it's been an attention-getter, all right."

She hugged me and looked down into my face. "Seriously though, how are you? Are you handling all this change okay?"

I nodded. "For the most part. I'm learning to be okay with it."

"I'm glad to hear it. Would you like to have a girls' day out—just you and me? It would let us get acquainted better." The excitement in her features rubbed off on me, and I realized I really did want to go.

"I would, but I feel like I should help with the Cold Moon stuff." I tried to hide my disappointment. I liked Aunt Jetta. She oozed fun from every pore.

"Nah, don't worry about that. Everyone has it covered. And since tomorrow is also your birthday, I thought it'd be good to do something special today. Something I think you need to see."

"Oh, okay. Let me check with Mom." I turned to see Mom walking up behind us.

"Yes, you should go. Aunt Jetta will take good care of you, and I'll see you back here tonight." She wiped her hands on a dish towel.

"Seriously? You don't want me to work and learn all about the process of doing for others?" My sarcasm did not go unnoticed, but it did surprise me how easily she was willing to let me off the hook.

"Seriously. You've learned that plenty. It's not every year you get a Cold Moon Ball and your sixteenth birthday all in one day. There are other lessons to learn today." She looked at Aunt Jetta, and it felt like an unspoken message passed between them.

"Okay then," I said. "What do I need to wear?"

Aunt Jetta smiled. "Something very comfortable and loose."

Loose? Well, this should be good.

I jogged to my room and quickly changed into a pair of sweatpants, T-shirt with hoodie, and my favorite tennis shoes. In less than ten minutes, I had returned to the doorway with Mom and Aunt Jetta.

"Okie dokie. I'm all set. Teach me, oh master," I said with a mock bow.

Aunt Jetta chuckled and motioned for me to exit the doorway before her. I did, but not before turning to give my mom a big hug. "I love you," I whispered.

"I love you, too," she whispered back and planted a kiss in my hair.

WE'D BEEN HIKING up the side of a ridge in the woods outside of town for almost an hour. My legs grew tired, and I realized how badly I needed to start a cardio routine of some kind. Aunt Jetta moved ahead of me with ease.

"Hurry up, slowpoke. I have something cool to show you." She waved me forward.

I huffed in annoyance. "I'm coming."

She waited until I reached the spot where she stood and let me catch my breath. "Look."

I raised my eyes, and my mouth fell open. Before me stood a gorgeous waterfall—three, actually. They weren't tall, not like the great falls the town was named for. The water had partially frozen, but I hadn't noticed the cold. Again, my dragon kept me comfortable. With each day, I started to like my dragon more and more.

"This is called Small's Falls. Isn't it beautiful?" Aunt Jetta placed her hands on her hips and gazed at the falls with a fondness in her eyes that I'd not previously seen before.

"It is beautiful. Is this a special place?" I studied her face.

"It is. Very much so. How did you know?" She moved next to me and put an arm around me.

"The look on your face. You seem happy to see it." It embarrassed me a little to admit I was so in tune with her expressions. It seemed odd to be so familiar with her, considering I didn't know her that well.

"It will soon be a special place for you, too." She gave me a brief squeeze before she stepped aside. "Follow me."

I stretched a moment, then fell in step behind her. We walked in silence, the only sounds being the occasional animal running to avoid crossing paths with us, or the crunch of leaves and frost under our feet.

As we approached the falls, she stopped, clearing the overgrown path in front of her. "Wow, it's been a while since anyone has been here. We'll be changing that."

I watched her pull dead vines and various small branches out of the way as we walked. We stopped, and she pointed out a very narrow outcropping of rocks that trailed down the small cliff connecting to the falls. She stepped out onto one, and my heart stopped.

"What are you doing? That looks dangerous." I felt my anxiety creep up, and I reached to touch my opal, then realized I'd left it at home. I feared losing it in the mountains.

"It's okay, Zoey. I know the steps don't look like much, but not everything is as it appears. Come here." She motioned for me to take her hand.

I slowly approached her, and she grasped my hand in hers. "Do you trust me?"

Fear robbed me of my voice, but I also felt sure Aunt Jetta would never put me in danger. I nodded.

"Good. Hang on to my hand tightly." She squeezed my hand for reassurance. Before I knew what happened, she yanked me toward her and down on the ledge.

My heart felt like it'd leapt into my throat. I looked down at the tiny ledge we stood on, only it wasn't tiny. It was more like a landing than a ledge. Plenty of room for both of us.

"See? It's an optical illusion. You can't see the steps until you're right up on them." She winked at me.

"Cool." I gazed down to see several larger steps that led all the way to the bottom of the falls.

"Okay, ready to see something really awesome?" Her enthusiasm once again spread over me.

"I am." I still reeled a little in shock over the freaky stairs, but I did my best to push past that.

I followed her to the bottom, where we were close enough to the water to feel the occasional splash. She turned to me and took my hand once more, leading me to a door-sized opening in the rock. She pulled a small flashlight from her pocket and clicked it on. With two quick steps, she moved inside and was completely swallowed by the darkness.

"Aunt Jetta? Where'd you go?" I willed myself to remain calm. "I can't see you."

As if by magic, her arm thrust through the darkness. "Take my hand again. It'll make sense once you're inside."

I grabbed hold of her with both hands and let her lead me through the curtain of inky blackness. It surrounded me like a thick obsidian fog, and then suddenly we were in a small cave, her flashlight illuminating most of the room.

"How . . . I mean . . . I couldn't see the light from outside." I moved my gaze from the room to the dark doorway.

"It's witchcraft." She wiggled her eyebrows up and down at me, and I rolled my eyes.

"No, really," I said, "how does it work?"

"I wasn't kidding. It's witchcraft. The Luna Coven has helped us keep this cave a secret. It's all ours." She gestured around us. "And you haven't even seen the best part."

"Really? It's our cave?" I walked closer to her.

"Yep. Let me show you the main room." She shined the light in the direction of a larger opening, and from where I stood, I could see tiny specks of light.

"What is that?" Curiosity won out over fear, and I moved forward.

Aunt Jetta walked right behind me. We passed through the opening, and she pulled out a lighter. She held it up, and that's when I saw the torches lining the wall. I watched her light each one until the entire room became bathed in a flickering amber light.

Once more, she shone her flashlight on the opposite wall, and it sparkled. "Go take a closer look," she urged.

I slowly walked forward while she kept the light focused in front of me. When I reached the wall, I extended my hand and ran my fingers over the rough texture. It was comprised of dirt and rock, but something else pushed through—something embedded within.

"That's kimberlite." She watched me as I ruffled through my memories. I'd heard that name somewhere before, but I couldn't place it.

I turned to look at her. "I don't get it."

"Diamonds. Kimberlite contains diamonds." She spoke calmly, but I could see the elation in her eyes.

"No way!" I hopped up and down a bit. "We own all these diamonds?"

"We do. How do you think we pay for our lifestyle? The pawn shop hasn't been *that* lucrative. Although to be fair, your Grandpa Mills was a whiz with investments. So, he's probably earned as much as we've pulled from this cave."

"Whoa." I couldn't believe its beauty.

"There's more." She motioned for me to follow her once again.

We approached another opening and stepped through. She lit a few more torches while I stayed in place. When she lit the last one, she turned to me. "Ta da."

I looked around and gasped. "This cave is *huge*."

"It is. And look at that end." She pointed in a direction, I didn't know which since I'd lost my bearings inside the cave, and I walked toward it, noticing a light at the end. The closer I approached, the lighter it became. I could also hear water running.

"We're behind the falls?" *Way cool!*

"We are," she said. "And again, no one can get in here. Just us dragons."

"People don't stumble upon it by accident?" I asked.

"A few have, but the spell protects it. All anyone else can see is a small, dark, and empty cave. Pretty cool, huh?"

I nodded. Beyond cool. Simply amazing.

She sat down on a large rock. "Humans have learned to avoid it all together. The water is fatal to them."

"So. Cool."

She motioned to me to join her. "Zoey, we need to talk."

That phrase is never good.

"Okay." I made my way next to her and sat down.

"Being a dragon shifter can take some getting used to. The hardest part is making the transition from human to dragon. It's something you have to practice the first few times." She reached down and clasped my hand. "It's not as scary as it sounds, but it's not something you can just practice out in the open. This cave gives us plenty of room for that."

"Oh. So, this is our training space." I suddenly worried about the pain that might be involved in shifting. It wasn't something I'd considered before.

"Yes, exactly. I brought you here today to practice." Her tone held excitement.

"What?" I jumped up. "I'm not ready for that. My birthday isn't until tomorrow." I started to panic again.

"Sweetheart, you could have shifted anytime you wanted to this past couple of weeks. You just didn't know how." She clasped her hands in front of her.

I looked at her and took a deep breath. "Does it hurt?"

She shrugged. "It can be a little uncomfortable for your human form, but nothing you can't handle. I promise."

I nodded, still a bit apprehensive. "Okay."

"Let me help you. I'll explain how you do it, then I'll change. You can follow me."

I nodded again.

"So first, you take off your clothes, unless you want to be without wearable clothes when you return to your human form." She started stripping, and I focused my view on the dirt in front of me. "Zoey, don't let this embarrass you. It's part of the process. Animals don't wear clothes, and they aren't embarrassed to see each other. You shouldn't be, either. At least, not in this instance." She folded up her clothing and placed them on the rock she had just sat on. "Now look at me."

I looked up and tried to focus on her face. Even though I shouldn't have been embarrassed, I was.

"Think of your dragon. Talk to it. Allow it to come forward in your mind. Once you've freed it in your thoughts, you'll be able to free it physically, too. Now watch."

She stood back and closed her eyes. Within moments she began to change shape before my eyes. She groaned a little, but it didn't sound like she suffered. Her hands became huge claws with long talons while her arms morphed into muscular legs that jutted out in front of her. Her legs followed a similar pattern. Her head thrashed back and changed from the face I was now familiar with to one of a giant, fierce reptile. A crown of thorny looking scales wrapped from one side of her jaw to the other. Powerful wings poked out from her shoulder blades, and her tail grew to almost the length of her body. Aunt Jetta's scales were white with a blueish tint to match her eyes. Snout to tail, she had to be forty feet long and twenty feet high. She opened her mighty jaws and I saw the gleam of enormous teeth. Some were smooth like fangs, while others featured a serrated edge. She was beautiful and terrifying all at once.

I took a few steps back, and she gently placed her monstrous head in front of me. I reached out and touched her snout. "Aunt Jetta?"

She snorted, and frosty air rushed from her nostrils. I recognized it, as it looked like the same stuff I blew on my burn that fateful day I learned about my true identity.

She blinked one large, pale blue reptilian eye at me and gave my hand a small nudge.

I instantly felt less afraid. "Okay, I'll do it."

I stood back and took off my clothes, trying to concentrate on anything but the fact that I was naked in a half-frozen cave. I closed my eyes and tried to imagine what my dragon might look like. A vision began to form in my mind. A white dragon with iridescent scales stepped forward and bowed to me. I bowed back and reached forward to touch it. It lowered its head and allowed me to stroke its magnificent crown.

"Are you my dragon?" I asked. It nodded its head. "Will you promise to keep me safe?"

It nodded once again.

I stepped closer and wrapped my arms around its neck in an embrace. I could feel the affection my dragon had for my human form, and all my fears dissipated. In seconds, we were melding together. I felt my muscles and bones expanding and pulling, but it wasn't horrible. Along with a little pain, it felt like finally getting a good stretch after a long nap. My bones creaked slightly, and I felt some popping.

When I mustered the courage to open my eyes, I was looking up, only slightly, at my Aunt Jetta. She spoke to me, and I felt relief that we could still communicate in this form, albeit telepathically.

"You're beautiful, Zoey. One of the most beautiful dragons I've ever seen." She pushed her head against mine and rubbed our cheeks together.

"Am I?" I wished I had a mirror.

"How do you feel?" she asked.

"A little weird, but good. Really good." I felt like smiling, although I had to assume that I couldn't physically smile. Maybe human Zoey smiled for me, somewhere inside.

"Do you feel like getting some exercise?" She stamped her feet for emphasis. "I'm dying to stretch out my wings."

"Can we do that? I thought you said we shouldn't be seen outside of the cave." I wiggled my wings a little, testing how they felt. I could only move them minutely, thanks to the now cramped space in the cave.

"That's true. But we have one more trick up our sleeves. Camouflage." She lifted one front leg and pointed a claw at the falls at the end of the cave. "We can exit that way."

She lumbered past me, and I awkwardly followed, still getting used to walking on four large legs. She pushed her head through the water of the falls and then back inside, shaking the water off like a dog would after a bath. "We're good. We'll step out into the water, then I'll show you how to trigger your camouflage."

She pushed her way through the falls, with me close behind her. We both sat in roughly knee-deep water. Well, knee deep for a twenty-foot-tall creature. I glanced down at my rippled reflection in the water. As she'd said, beautiful. I now stared back at the dragon I'd envisioned in my mind. My coloring was pure as snow, with iridescent scales that matched the streaks in my human form's hair. My eyes were more a marbled grey and contained even less blue than my human form did. My crown of horns mimicked Jetta's, but was smaller, as was the rest of my sizing. I turned my head and opened my jaw, inspecting the copious number of teeth that now filled my mouth.

"See? You're stunning." She stepped a bit closer. "When you're a full adult, at age twenty, you'll be the same size as I am. You're not all that far from it now. I'd estimate you're close to sixteen or seventeen feet tall."

I looked back at my reflection in awe.

"So," she said, "to hide within your surroundings, simply scan the area around you and mentally choose a camouflage. Your body will do the rest."

She stepped onto the bank, and I followed her. She glanced around us, then disappeared. But she wasn't completely gone. I could sense her and see little things that gave her away, but I felt sure that was another perk to being a dragon. We could still see each other, for the most part, but others couldn't.

I followed her lead. I didn't feel different, but when I looked at my claws, they appeared transparent. I could still see them, yet I couldn't. It felt surreal.

Jetta stretched her wings out and sighed in bliss. "It's been so long." She shifted her head toward mine. "Are you ready for more?"

I couldn't help but be excited. "Yes. Totally."

"Good. Let's fly."

CHAPTER 9

$\mathcal{I}$ followed Aunt Jetta to a higher altitude, practicing my camouflage techniques along the way. I could shift from dead leaves to snow, to trees, to water, and back again. I could even make one part of myself resemble the trees, while another part of me looked like the ground. I loved it. We were totally undetectable, outside of the sounds we made as we traversed the mountainside. Even then I was surprised at how nimble we could be for such large creatures. We weren't nearly as noisy as I'd expected we'd be.

We reached a cliff, and she stopped to face the open air that stretched out in front of us. I could see the entire town from where we were perched.

"It's beautiful," I whispered.

"It truly is." She turned her head toward me and pushed her forehead to mine in an affectionate gesture. "I hope you'll give it a chance, Zoey. Havenwood Falls is an amazing place, once you settle in."

I nodded as I pulled my face from hers.

"I'd miss you if you left, but I'd also understand." Aunt Jetta spoke softly in my mind. "Your grandpa can be a tyrant when he doesn't get his way. He can make life very difficult, if he chooses to."

"I have no plans to leave. Not at the moment. I guess time will tell."

"Good." She nodded in front of us. "Then let's get a closer look." She moved to the edge and stepped off into nothingness.

My breath hitched as I waited for her to reemerge in my sightline. Then suddenly she appeared, hovering just above me, flapping her beautiful wings with a grace I could only hope to achieve.

"It's easy," she yelled. "Just step off and flap your wings. Instinct will take over."

Falling terrified me. I moved to the edge and looked down. It had to be hundreds of feet to the bottom. I felt my claws dig into the earth of their own will, grasping at anything that would pull me from the edge. Instead, I'd managed to mangle the earth beneath me until it gave way, and I fell.

Screaming as I plunged to the earth, I frantically tried to remember what Aunt Jetta had instructed. The wind rushed past my face, and my eyes couldn't focus as dirt, rocks, and trees passed my vision at a breakneck pace. Without effort, my wings extended fully, and I flapped them in a panic. It wasn't elegant or delicate, but it kept me from colliding with the rocks below.

I slowly rose into the air, trying to gain my bearings while I worked to smooth my rhythm. Aunt Jetta swooped down beside me, then shot back up into the air like a rocket, her body spinning like a top as she passed through the clouds.

I wanted to do that. I wanted to soar and dive and swoop. I flew up to where she'd disappeared and hovered in place as I searched for her. "Aunt Jetta! Where are you?"

She glided next to me, as if she were swimming in the air. "I'm here, sweetie."

"I want to do all of that. All of it!"

She laughed. "You will, just follow my lead."

She pointed her head down, tucked in her legs and pulled her wings tight against her back. She bolted like a rocket.

I repeated her motions, and in seconds, the ground rushed up to meet me. It was exhilarating! As we neared the ground we both extended our wings, and they worked like a parachute, slowing our descent. We flapped a few times, and once again we were rising about the trees.

I continued to lift, letting all my stress and worries slip away. This brought peace. This was heaven. I lost track of time as I practiced gliding across the sky, enjoying a freedom I'd never felt before.

Aunt Jetta landed on an outcropping of rocks, and I settled in beside her.

"It's an amazing feeling, isn't it?" she murmured.

"It is. It's my new favorite thing." I couldn't keep the awe from my voice. I reveled in this newfound ability.

"Something you need to know, Zoey. Don't lose yourself too much as you fly. If your dragon gains too much control, your human side may never return."

I blinked several times as I tried to comprehend what she meant. "I might stay a dragon forever?"

"Only if you truly choose it. And in this day and age, sometimes it seems the better choice. But never forget that there are wonders to your human side, too. Things you would miss, and people who would miss you."

I nodded. "I promise to be careful."

"Good." She stretched her wings once more. "We should probably head back. Tomorrow is a big day."

My TIME with Aunt Jetta yesterday had been amazing. I'd learned that shifting back required a similar process as before. I had to embrace my alter ego each time.

December third had finally arrived—my sixteenth birthday and the day of the Cold Moon Ball. Everyone ran around like mad, setting up for the various festivities that would begin around dinner time. I helped my dad set up the tables inside the Annex, which is where the party began. It was a large sandstone complex comprised of three connected warehouses. The Market building was used as a community hub on Saturdays and showcased the best the area had to offer from local farmers and artisans. The middle building was the Theater. It was open in the front, and the back half housed a large screen and stage for movies, concerts, and plays. My personal favorite was the Art Museum. I enjoyed looking at the array of talent that enriched our small-town lives. Paintings, pottery, quilting, and jewelry were just a few of the items on display. I also reveled in the historical pieces that gave the public a glossed-over glimpse into the community's origins. A majority of the town turned out for this festival, so all three warehouses would be opened to accommodate the residents of Havenwood Falls.

After everyone was fed, the schedule then listed games and socializing in the square, followed by a parade of wagons leading up to the ball held in Mills Mansion.

Dad and I were in the Market area of the Annex, while Mom helped set up in the Art Building.

"Dad, when did you learn what your unique dragon gift was?" I handed him a chair.

"Well." He sat the chair down and turned to face me. "If I remember correctly, it was on my sixteenth birthday. That's roughly when it happens. Have you not discovered yours?"

I shook my head. "I keep thinking I'll wake up with some amazing revelation or ability. So far, nothing." Odd that I found that fact disappointing, considering it terrified me days ago.

"Don't worry. It'll happen when you need it to." He began to unfold another table.

"What does that mean?" I pouted a bit.

"It means that when you need that specific ability the most, it will surprise you." He continued to work.

"And that'll happen today?" I wasn't sure what to think of that piece of news.

"More than likely, sweetheart." He eyed some townsfolk approaching to help with tables and nodded in their direction.

I looked over and waved, then turned back to him. "I guess we'll have to finish this conversation later."

Why do we always seem to get interrupted just when the conversation is getting good?

"Absolutely." He winked at me.

I continued to set up chairs until every empty spot at the tables had a seat. I kept my mind on more pleasant things, like Jordan. I'd relived that kiss in the gazebo a hundred times since it happened. It was more thrilling than shifting and magical necklaces. It felt much like flying. Every time I thought of it, a tingle ran all the way down to my toes. As for Kai, I did my best not to think of him. His memory brought emotional chaos and confusion.

I looked forward to seeing Jordan at the dinner and ball. He was handsome in everyday clothing, and I could only imagine how fantastic he'd look in a suit. I was lingering on that mental picture when Miranda's voice interrupted my daydream.

"Zoey! I'm so excited!" She grabbed my arm and squeezed.

"Hey, what's up?" I tried not to let it show that she'd almost scared me witless.

"Guess who asked me to save a dance or two for him at the ball?" Her voice squeaked out a high-pitched sound.

I looked at her for a moment as I tried to figure out who could possibly make her this wound up. "Mr. Zander?"

She screwed up her face in disgust. "Ew, no. That'd be icky. He's old enough to be your dad."

"My dad? Why not your dad?"

"My dad is *really* old. Like, great-great-grandpa old, if I understand my mother correctly." She stuck her hands in her pockets.

"Oh yeah. I forgot about the immortality thing. My dad's older than you'd guess too, but not that old." I sighed. "Wait, I thought you had a thing for Mr. Zander?"

"Oh, he's nice to look at, but realistically that's about it. I need someone my own age . . . who won't go to jail for dating me." She giggled, and I had to join her. It was kind of absurd, once I gave it some consideration.

"Okay, so who is it then?" I couldn't think of anyone she'd shown specific interest in.

"Kai Reynolds." She beamed.

My eyebrows raised so high, I feared they'd disappear into my hairline. "Kai? The Kai that threatened me?" My brain screamed, *The Kai I've dreamed about?* No way I would admit that one out loud.

"Yes, same one." She sat on one of the chairs I'd just set up. "He's not all that bad when you get to know him. I've always thought he was cute. Besides, keep your friends close and your enemies closer." Her smile held a hint of mischief.

"Wait . . . what are you planning?" I sat next to her. "You don't really like him, do you?"

"I do, but I don't trust him. I'm not above using him to keep tabs on him." She waved a hand in front of me. "I know. I know. It's not the moral thing to do, but I think he's up to something. I don't want him ruining your big night. So, after a generous amount of flirting with him, he asked me to dance with him at the ball." She rubbed her hands together for maximum effect. "He will fall prey to my charms and drop all his devious plans."

"I'm not doubting your charms, Miranda, but what if it doesn't work?" I hoped she didn't take insult at my question.

She shrugged. "Then we'll have my cousins drag him off and keep him occupied."

I laughed out loud at that. "Oh, Miranda. You're such a joy in my life."

She sighed dramatically. "I'm glad someone appreciates me."

I grabbed her hand and gave it a squeeze. "Oh, you have no idea. I don't know what I'd do without you."

I LOOKED in the mirror and fidgeted.

"Honey, you look beautiful. Stop fretting." Mom kissed the top of my head.

"I just don't want to embarrass myself." I turned my face to see if my hair was all still in place. Mom had curled it and piled it on top of my head, leaving a few ringlets to frame my face. Crystal-tipped bobby pins held it all in place, making my hair shine like the inside of our cave. I had to admit that my raven hair, with the unusual pearl-like streaks, looked fantastic all curled up.

"You won't embarrass yourself. You will be brilliant. Jordan will take one look at you and be knocked off his feet." She adjusted the bodice of my gown a little.

I tried not to blush. "You think?"

"No, I know. Now, time for the finishing touch." She slipped my grandmother's opal necklace around my neck.

The pendant felt cool against my bare skin. It matched very well with the light blue strapless gown I wore. The taffeta had a similar ability to shift colors with the lighting. I felt like Cinderella going to the ball. I only prayed it didn't end with me running away like a coward and leaving a trail of clothing behind me.

Mom adjusted her own dress, then placed a hand on my arm. "Ready?"

I nodded, we grabbed our coats, and I followed her outside to wait for Dad. We didn't have to wait long. He pulled the car up front, and we carefully seated ourselves. I did my best to keep the seatbelt from crushing my bodice.

In a few minutes, we were at the Annex and finding our seats at the table. Jordan had not yet arrived when we took our place, so I saved him a spot next to me.

The servers began to tend to each table. Plates were piled high with turkey, potatoes, beans, salads, and what looked like every dessert imaginable. I wasn't sure I'd ever seen that much food in my life. At first, I worried that this was an extravagant waste when there were so many in need, then I noticed something I wasn't expecting. People from all walks of life were present. Regardless of financial or social standing, everyone mingled together over a free meal and the joy of giving. It warmed my heart to see so much goodwill. Especially knowing that most of the time, various sects of the supernatural citizenry preferred to avoid each other.

I scanned the crowd, but didn't spot Jordan or his family. I wasn't totally sure his mom and dad would even attend, given their tense relationship. Then I saw them. Jordan's mom looked lovely in a pale yellow dress. Her makeup was impeccable, and her bruises were well hidden. It made me mad that she had injuries to hide in the first place, but at least she could attend and enjoy herself. Jordan stood close by, talking with . . . Katy.

My heart dropped to my stomach. She was cute, I couldn't deny that. She had more friends than I did as well. But surely Jordan wouldn't ditch me for her. He'd already committed to attending the celebration with me.

I saw Katy lean in and whisper something in his ear. He smiled and shook his head. As he turned to talk to his mother once more, Katy's gaze landed on me, and the satisfied smirk on her face caused me to see red. She obviously wanted to make me jealous. Sadly, it was working.

I turned my attention to my dad as we finished our meals. *It's okay*, I told myself. He'd find me soon.

As I picked at my dessert, I felt the hairs on the back of my neck stand to attention. I knew before I looked who I'd find standing behind me.

"Hello, Zoey." Kai's voice was deep and smooth, rubbing a balm over my wounded ego. I turned to see him standing with his hands in his trouser pockets. He wore a black tuxedo and looked like he'd stepped off the pages of GQ. I closed my mouth so I wouldn't openly gawk at his gorgeousness.

"Would you care to join me for a game of croquet? They have it set up across the street." He smiled down at me, and I had to remember to breathe.

I pulled my gaze from his and glanced around the tables once more. Jordan seemed to have disappeared. He could be in another part of the Annex, but why hadn't he sought me out yet?

"Sure, why not," I stammered as I stood. I moved to gather my plate, and he stopped me.

"They have people who will clean up afterwards." Kai took my hand and hooked it through his arm, then led me out the doors. We strolled in silence as we traversed a couple of blocks to the town square.

My fingers tingled where my skin touched the fabric of his jacket. I tried to ignore the sensations, but it was as if he sensed I wanted to pull away, so he hugged me closer to him as we walked.

"It's a lovely night. Almost as lovely as you," he murmured as we strolled across the grass.

I felt the heat rush to my cheeks. "Thank you, that's very kind."

"Nothing kind about it. I'm simply telling the truth." He passed the game of croquet that was already in progress.

"Wait? I thought we were going to play—"

He cut off my sentence with a finger to my lips. "Shh . . . let's just enjoy each other's company for a while."

My senses heightened. Something felt wrong. Something had been off from the moment he first spoke to me. I just couldn't place it. The attraction I felt still lingered, but it was engulfed in a veil of danger. My instincts urged me to get away from him.

"Kai, I should get back. I need to speak with my parents before the parade begins." I backed away.

He followed me, a grin pulling up the corners of his lips and exposing the tip of his fangs. "What's your hurry, sweet Zoey? We haven't had a chance to really get acquainted yet."

I shook my head. "You don't want to know me. I don't know what you want, but it isn't me."

He took one more step, and as I moved to avoid him, my back hit a solid object. I looked around to find myself up against a large tree, inconveniently hiding us from the view of many in the square.

Kai put his arms on either side of me. "Oh, but it is you I'm interested in. You're special, Zoey. And those of us who are special should stick together." He leaned in close, and his gaze captured mine. I felt locked in that stare. My limbs refused to move. He put one hand behind my neck and pulled me close to him, then pressed his lips to mine. For a moment I relaxed, reliving the dream I'd had, then my mind screamed at me to run. This felt too familiar. We'd done this before, yet I knew we hadn't. *That dream! He did something to cause that dream!* I pushed at his chest, but he barely moved. My next instinct was to bring my knee up as hard as I could. He froze, then backed away, squatting a little as he stumbled backward.

I turned and ran.

~

THE FEW GAMES that had been set up on the square were scarcely occupied. Not too many people were willing to brave the colder air outside of the Annex, but there were a few who donned their coats and took part in the fun.

I ran toward them, praying Kai wasn't following me. I stopped near a bean bag game to catch my breath when a stray bag flew right into me, knocking me off balance and into the person next to me, who then spilled his punch all over my dress. I froze in place, surveying the damage to my skirt. My beautiful blue taffeta had been drenched with pink splotches.

I closed my eyes. "I will not cry. I will not cry," I whispered to myself over and over. When I opened my eyes, Katy and her two minions stood in front of me.

"Oops. I'm so clumsy. I'm so very sorry, Zoey. I ruined your dress, and the ball hasn't even started yet." Katy pouted as she spoke loudly, assuring bystanders heard her apology. "Here, let me help you get cleaned up."

She grabbed my arm, and her friends gathered behind me and gave me a not-so-gentle push. They rushed me over toward the Annex, but once we were out of sight, they shoved me over to the gazebo.

"I warned you, freak." Katy glared at me. "You have no business here or with Jordan. And now you're cozying up to Kai, too? What a hussy."

I stepped back from them and touched my opal, letting its soothing influence rush over me. "You do realize that my grandfather runs this shindig we're attending tonight? That my family is one of the founding families of Havenwood Falls?" I put my hands on my hips. "If anyone doesn't belong, I'm guessing it's you. And you hate that. Kai and Jordan are both interested in me, and you hate that, too. You're a jealous hag."

Katy bristled. "Oh, you think you're so high and mighty because you have the Mills name? But your family are a bunch of thieving, back-stabbing freaks, and you should all be run out of town."

"What?" I asked. "What the hell are you babbling on about?"

She stepped closer to me and pointed a finger in my face. "Your grandfather and his crappy investment advice cost my family everything. We lost our vacation home, our nicest cars . . . everything that was important to me."

"Oh lord. That's what all this is about?" I rolled my eyes. "You need to get a grip, Katy. You obviously don't know how investing works. Nothing is ever a sure thing. Haven't you paid attention in economics?" I sighed. "I don't know what advice your family did or did not take from my grandfather, but I'm hardly responsible for that."

An angry sound formed in her throat, and for a moment, I thought she would attack me.

"Have you paid attention tonight? Did you notice Jordan has avoided you the entire evening?" She smiled sweetly, but it was full of venom. "I told him all about you. He wants nothing to do with someone like you."

"And just what did you tell him?" I waited.

She glanced at her manicure, as if the conversation bored her. "I told him how you use people to get what you want, then discard them. I told him that you thought he was beneath you because his family isn't in your social circles. Do you know what he said?" She batted her eyes innocently. "He said he'd only asked you out because he felt sorry for you. The new girl in town that no one liked. He's such a nice guy that he wanted to help." She fanned herself dramatically. "He's a keeper for sure. Too bad it won't be you he chooses when it's all said and done."

My blood boiled. *It couldn't be true, could it?*

"I think that's quite enough, Katy." Aunt Jetta stood just behind me. Then I saw Miranda step up next to her.

"Oh good. Another Mills freak. Why do you all look like you belong on *The Addams Family*?" Katy sneered.

Aunt Jetta stepped around me. "You haven't begun to see freak, sweetheart."

Katy opened her mouth, but snapped it closed again. Her confused expression told me she hadn't expected an admission of our freakishness. It took some of the sting from her barbs.

Miranda walked up to Katy, almost nose to nose, and stared into her eyes. "You know, Katy, you keep using the word freak, but if you really knew the truth, you and your greasy gremlins there would crap . . . your . . . pants."

Katy stepped back, her eyes as wide as saucers. I placed my hand on Miranda's arm.

"She's not worth our time. Come help me clean my dress. We have a ball to attend."

We all three turned to walk away, but Katy managed to muster one last burst of courage, and she grabbed my arm.

"Don't you turn your back on me when I'm speaking to you, freak!" The rage in her voice mingled with desperation. She had lost her power over me, and she knew it.

I pulled her close to me, my dragon granting me a strength in my grip that Katy couldn't escape from. My voice came out low and had a slight growl that mingled with the syllables. "If you ever touch me, or any of my friends again, I will not only end you, but I'll end your entire family."

I felt my eyes flash, and my vision blurred for mere seconds before returning to normal. I'd give her a glimpse of what she was dealing with. Not enough to get me in trouble, but enough to make her wonder what she truly saw.

I released her wrist, and she backed away quickly, blindly groping at her friends' jackets as she pulled them with her. She didn't utter another word as they all three turned and scampered away.

"Worst birthday ever," I complained as we stood in the bathroom of the Annex and rubbed my skirt with a wet paper towel.

Aunt Jetta kissed my forehead. "It's been eventful, but I promise you that my sixteenth was much worse. Remind me to tell you about it sometime."

"It's not over yet. You may find yourself defending that title before the night is up." I groaned. "Is this coming out?"

Miranda moved her face closer to the material. "Probably as good as it's gonna get."

I tossed the towel in the trash and dried my hands.

"You know," Miranda said, "for a few moments there, I understood why my kind eat people."

Aunt Jetta laughed. "Yeah, it's tempting sometimes, isn't it?"

I looked up. "Did dragons ever eat people? I know the fairy tales always make us out to be man-eaters."

"Some did, but I think that's more the style of the fire-breathing kind. As a general rule, frost dragons didn't. We preferred to live in peace." She looked in the mirror and adjusted some strands of her hair that the wind had misplaced. "We've pretty much always been more about fish, seals, etc. The old country was full of that stuff." She applied a fresh coat of lipstick. "That doesn't mean that frost dragons haven't ever eaten someone, though. It's totally possible." She smirked.

"No, thanks." I said. "Katy's so spoiled, she'd taste bad."

Miranda laughed. "No doubt."

Aunt Jetta exited the bathroom and held the door open for us. We left the building and rushed back to the area near the square where everyone stood waiting for the parade to start.

"Are we really gonna ride in those all the way to Grandpa's?" I asked, pointing to the row of wagons pulling into place.

"Sure are," Aunt Jetta said.

Miranda grabbed my hand. "Come on. Let's grab a seat on the outside. I hate riding in the middle."

As we neared the horse-drawn wagons, I noticed that each one had built-in bench seats and could hold quite a few people. Miranda and I were helped up, and we settled into seats near the front. Aunt Jetta waved to us as she climbed into a nearby wagon to sit with a friend of hers.

"Do you really think Jordan is just taking pity on me?" I didn't mean to blurt out the question at that moment, but it had been bothering me.

"I don't." Miranda placed her hand over one of mine. "I've never known him to be that heartless. Kind? Yes. Shallow? No."

"So why do you think he's avoided me all night? I haven't even gotten so much as a hello." My heart broke at the thought.

"I'm not sure, but my guess is he isn't intentionally ignoring you." She glanced around the square.

I shrugged. "I hope you're right."

She gave my hand another squeeze, and in that moment, the horses began to pull us out of town and up toward Havenwood Heights.

People chatted all around us as I took in the scenery before me. It was lovely. Businesses were lit up for the celebration. Various celestial ornamentation mingled with Christmas decorations. Once we reached the residential areas, the lights changed to solely those of the Christmas variety. The soothing clop of the horse's hooves, the snow, and the lights all gave me the illusion of serenity. It didn't last long, but I treasured what I could get.

We pulled up in front of Grandpa's house, and my eyes immediately went to the stone dragons. Grandpa Mills stood at the top of the stairs, watching the wagons arrive. Once everyone had unloaded, he picked up a bullhorn to speak. I had to stifle a giggle, knowing he could growl loud enough to shake the ground beneath us all.

"Welcome to my home, everyone! Please enter and let us dance and give thanks to the gods for the protection of our lovely little town." He lowered the bullhorn and handed it off to a man standing nearby. Then he hobbled inside, and people began to follow. A lady took our coats as we passed through the entryway.

Soon we were standing in a large ballroom at the back of the house. Once again, my breath caught, as I was taken aback by the beauty of the room. There were crystal candelabras everywhere, each one of them holding six lit candles. A large skylight graced the ceiling and allowed a perfect view of the moon. The only artificial light present came from two small chandeliers at each end of the room.

One wall had been lined with tables loaded down with drinks and appetizers. Each table had a large vase of fresh cut flowers.

I leaned into Miranda. "Where does he get fresh flowers this time of year?" I asked.

"I'm told he flies them in from all over the country." She seemed unimpressed by that detail.

The music started, and I turned to face her. "Weren't you planning on charming the grouch out of Kai?"

I debated telling her about my encounter with him earlier. Maybe if she kept him busy, he'd leave me alone. I knew she could handle herself if he stepped out of line.

"Oh yeah, I guess I should find him. Will you be okay?" She looked concerned.

"Yeah, I'll be fine. If I need reinforcements, I'll let you know. Just . . . don't take any crap from him." I gave her a smile and a light shove toward the dance floor. She turned to wink at me and then began her search for Kai.

I stood to one side and swayed with the music while others spun around on the floor.

"Would you like to dance, birthday girl?" I looked up to see my father, hand stretched out for mine.

I nodded. "That'd be nice."

He led me to the middle of the floor, and we began a country dance that I recognized from gym class. We'd been taught several dances especially for the ball.

"I'm sorry we haven't done anything big for your birthday. This celebration has kept us all busy. I promise to make it up to you." He spun me around and then back to him.

"It's okay, Dad. I know it's been crazy." I stepped back two steps, then forward two steps.

"It's your sweet sixteen, but I have a feeling it hasn't been so sweet."

I shrugged. "It could have been worse."

Dad stopped and turned around. I saw Jordan standing behind him. "Mind if I cut in?" he asked my dad.

Dad smiled. "Sure thing." He bowed to me before he walked away.

Jordan grasped my hand in his and placed his other at my waist. "How are you liking the festivities so far?"

"How am I liking it?" I couldn't believe he'd asked me that. "Well, outside of having punch spilled on my dress, being bullied by three jerks, accosted by . . . never mind who it was, and my date ditching me all through dinner, it's been peachy." I couldn't keep the sarcasm from my voice.

He stopped. "I'm sorry, Zoey. I didn't mean to abandon you. It's just . . . something happened, and I couldn't get to you until now."

I pulled my hand from his. "Yeah. No problem."

I walked away from him and toward the double doors that led to the backyard. Without stopping, I pushed through them, letting them swing shut behind me. I glanced around and remembered Grandpa had a huge garden to the right, so I walked the path until I was surrounded by evergreens and hedges. That's when I heard the commotion.

"Dad, you've gotta stop this. You're being ridiculous." My dad's voice echoed loud and clear.

"Don't tell me what I have to do, boy. This is my home." He shouted, but not like he had the night we had dinner with him. It sounded human.

"Daddy, I'm a grown woman. I can wear what I want." Aunt Jetta's voice was completely devoid of emotion.

I silently made my way to the edge of one of the larger hedges and peeked around it.

Grandpa pointed to my aunt's leather dress. "That is not a gown. It looks like something out of some smutty catalog. And your tattoos are completely visible."

"My dress is completely appropriate for this occasion. It covers all my naughty bits." She smiled as his face turned red at the mention of her naughty bits. "And my tattoos are part of me. They go where I go."

"It's a fine day when my own daughter has less respect for me than my human daughter-in-law," he grumbled.

"Well, see? You've been wrong about her all this time," Aunt Jetta said. "She's actually an amazing person, but you won't take your blinders off to see it."

"She's human!" Grandpa Mills growled.

"She's my wife." Dad's tone held a warning.

Grandpa turned to Dad. "And now your own daughter is chasing after a human boy. This is your fault, Tristan." He pointed a bony finger at my dad.

I'd heard enough, and I stepped out. "What is wrong with you people?" I shouted. "Why can't you get along for more than five minutes?"

Suddenly, Kai and Miranda came pushing through the hedges behind me. Kai looked at me, then Grandpa. "I'm sorry, sir. I tried."

Miranda hauled off and punched Kai in the gut. He doubled over. "That's for conspiring against my best friend, you jerk."

My heart broke. "Grandpa? *You* were trying to keep me from Jordan?"

He had the decency to look guilty. "Honey, he's human. It'll never work. I forbid it!"

Tears filled my eyes. "It's been a horrible day already, but to find out that my own flesh and blood worked out a plan to break my heart is more than I can bear. And on my birthday, too."

My vision blurred. I turned and ran back the way I came, running straight into Jordan. *Great. Can my luck get any worse?*

CHAPTER 11

I swiped at the tears on my cheeks as Jordan stood in front of me.

"Zoey, let me explain. Please." He held his hands out to me.

I stepped back, not wanting him to touch me. "Fine. Explain."

I crossed my arms and waited for him to say something—anything—that would make me feel better. At the same time, I wasn't sure if I could trust him. He did ignore me most of the night. I tried to push Katy's awful words from my mind.

"My mom came tonight. She hasn't in recent years, but it was nice to see her enjoy the celebration for once." He smiled for a brief moment. "Then Kai told me he needed to speak with me. The next thing I knew, he'd locked me in a closet in the Annex. It took almost an hour before someone heard me yelling and let me out."

I frowned. "I'm so sorry, Jordan. Kai is a deceitful jerk, thanks to a directive from my grandpa."

"Your grandpa? Why would he do that?" He looked as confused as I expected him to be.

"It's hard to explain." I couldn't very well tell him the truth.

"Okay." He paused. "Well, when I finally found my mom, Dad had shoved her into the car. He was drunk and yelling at her. Accusing her of flirting with all the men around her." He shook his head.

"Nothing was further from the truth. He's just so jealous, he can't see straight, especially when he's had too much to drink."

"Oh no. Is she okay?" I worried she'd been beat up again.

"Yeah, she's fine. My father, on the other hand . . ." He sighed. "I managed to get her away from him, and a friend of hers is looking after her. I punched my dad, and his head hit the trunk. It knocked him out cold. He's currently sleeping it off in the car."

"You're wrong about that, son." An angry voice spoke from the shadows, then the man I assumed to be his dad stepped forward. He looked at me. "Is this the little hussy you've been lusting after? They're all the same, son. They aren't worth your time."

"You don't know what you're talking about. Zoey is a lady. Mom is a wonderful woman. If you were sober for more than five minutes a day, you'd know that."

Mr. Woods stepped forward and raised his hand.

"No!" I yelled and instinctively stepped in front of Jordan.

Mr. Woods stopped and looked at me. "Stay out of this, or you'll get what's coming to you, too."

Jordan pulled me to his side. "You won't touch her."

Mr. Woods shook his head and chuckled. "She must be something in the sack to make you stand up to me."

Jordan threw a punch. "Do not talk about Zoey like that. She's the most honest, loving, and kind person I know. She deserves respect, and you will give it to her." His voice held years of pent-up anger.

"Ha! I don't think so, boy." Mr. Woods rubbed the spot where Jordan had hit him. "Ain't a female in this world deserves respect from a man."

He lunged forward and tackled Jordan, knocking me to the ground, as well. I hit with a hard thud and felt something pop in my ankle. I cried out in pain.

My grandfather's loud and menacing voice broke through the chaos. "Thomas Woods. You take your hands off that boy right now."

Mr. Woods sat on the ground, straddling Jordan, smacking him in the face. "This is my son, old man. I'll discipline him however I please."

"No, you won't." The sound of my own voice startled me. It was me, yet it wasn't quite me. I could hear the subtle growl of my dragon filtering through.

Mr. Woods took a step back.

Grandpa pushed forward and glared at Mr. Woods, then looked at me. "Do you see how they behave? This is what you want to shackle yourself to?"

Kai spoke up then. "Despite my orders from your grandfather, I'm still very interested in you, Zoey. I'd be honored to save you from yourself."

Enough was enough. The anger and frustration I'd buried pushed to the surface, and instead of tamping it down, I gave it free rein.

"I am not a toy to play with! Nor am I a servant to be bossed around. I will make my own decisions, and none of you will tell me how to live my life." I hobbled forward, my ankle causing me to wince in pain. "You!" I pointed at my grandfather. "How dare you decide what's best for me. You ignored me for over fifteen years. You have no right to expect a say in my future now." I shook my head. "Manipulating my feelings for your own ridiculous prejudices is beyond despicable. You are a mean, selfish old man. What other miseries have you inflicted in my life?"

Grandpa growled. "I do what I must for this family."

"Oh really? Like exiling your own son because he fell in love with an amazing woman? Ignoring your grandchild? Torturing your daughter because she lives life to the fullest? That's how you help them?" I scoffed. "I'd hate to see what you'd do if you didn't care."

Jetta stepped forward and gave me a slow clap, the look on her face full of appreciation.

I turned to Kai. "You had the gall to not only pretend to like me, but I'm pretty sure you used some of your . . . gifts," I spoke the word as if it caused a bad taste in my mouth, "to manipulate my feelings for you. Dreams? Really? That's low. I have zero attraction to you now, and I'm quite sure I never did." I leaned closer, putting my weight on my good ankle. "Oh, and if you ever put your hands on me again, I'll make sure you sing soprano for weeks."

Jetta snorted as she held back her gleeful laughter. I knew she enjoyed watching me dole out the tongue-lashings that were long overdue.

I turned to Jordan. "I like you, Jordan, but there are a lot of things you don't know about me. Things you'll have to accept if you want to be a part of my life."

He nodded. "I can handle that."

I shook my head and fought back the sadness that began to overtake me. "I'm not sure you can."

Mr. Woods stepped forward. "See? She's worthless, son. Walk away while you still can."

Jordan's rage flared again, and he swung at his dad, this time missing. His father threw a punch and knocked Jordan to the ground, blood oozing from his lip.

I stepped forward, this time ignoring the pain, and grabbed Mr. Woods' jacket. "Don't you ever hit him or your wife again."

He gasped, and it was then that I realized I'd lifted him high enough off the ground that his feet were dangling.

I put him back on solid ground, then shoved him away. He staggered, then lunged at me. My father and Aunt Jetta grabbed him on either side before he reached his intended target.

"Jordan, what would you like us to do?" my father asked.

Jordan blinked. "Do?"

Aunt Jetta nodded. "We can put him in jail."

Dad's grip on Mr. Woods' arm tightened, and the man winced. "Or . . . we could banish him."

Aunt Jetta smiled. "That would work."

Grandpa muttered something under his breath.

"Banish?" Jordan looked completely confused.

"We can send him away. He'll live out his life peacefully, if he so chooses, and never bother you or your mother again," Dad answered.

Jetta released Mr. Woods and pulled Jordan aside. She whispered to him, out of earshot of his father. I assumed she was giving him further details on the exile they suggested.

After a couple of minutes, my nerves were stretched thin. My ankle hurt, and all I wanted to do was get away from everyone. I hobbled to the line of trees behind Grandpa's house.

"I need to be alone," I shouted as I slowly walked away. "Don't bother looking for me."

"Zoey, can I come with you?" Jordan asked.

I froze. *Do I want his company?* I wasn't sure. Tears rolled down my cheeks, and I swiped at them, trying to hide the evidence of my heartache.

"If you like," I murmured, unsure if he could even hear me. I limped forward into the forest until I reached a large log. The pain became intense, and I knew I couldn't make it where I wanted to go. The cave.

I sat down, and tears fell once more. I brushed them away before I pushed my skirt aside and rubbed my sore ankle. Jordan walked only a few feet behind me. He'd been following in silence, allowing me my privacy until I was ready to address him.

As I continued to rub my ankle, the pain began to subside. I had no idea what had happened, but it felt as if it were healing. I was astonished at what appeared to be happening before my eyes.

"Can I sit?" asked Jordan.

I blinked up at him, trying to clear my head. "Sure."

He scooted close to me and reached for my hand. "I don't know what's going on, but you can trust me, Zoey. I would never turn away from you."

I chuckled with self-deprecation. "You say that now."

"No, I mean it. There is nothing that you could say or do that would scare me off." He gave my hand a squeeze.

I looked into his eyes, and the decision was made. I would tell him and let the chips fall where they may.

"Jordan? I'm a dragon."

CHAPTER 12

*J*ordan laughed awkwardly. "Right."

"I'm not kidding." My expression was solemn.

"How is that possible? You look human to me." The timbre in his voice indicated he still thought I was joking.

"I'm a shifter. I'm half human and half dragon." I stood. "I can show you, if you like."

His eyes narrowed. "Um . . .okay." Obviously, he was still skeptical.

"Turn around," I ordered. "I have to undress before I change."

His eyebrows shot up. "Do I have to?" his tone teased.

I couldn't help but smile a little. "Yes, you have to. My dad is a dragon, too, and if he thinks you saw me naked, he might be tempted to eat you."

Jordan shrugged and turned his back to me, moving his legs to the other side of the log.

I reached back and unzipped my dress, letting it fall and pool at my feet. My shoes were next, along with my undergarments. I stepped back into the darkness and picked a somewhat open spot to transform.

"You promise you won't freak out?" I shouted from my hiding spot in the shadows.

"I promise," he yelled back.

I summoned my inner dragon and let her take over. Popping,

cracking, stretching—sensations I was becoming accustomed to took over as I left the human Zoey behind.

I stepped forward as quietly as possible, then put my muzzle close to Jordan's back and snorted. Frost covered his back, and he shivered.

"Hey, no throwing snowballs while my back is—" He turned around and froze. "Oh, dear God." He scooted back off the log and landed on his butt in the frost-covered leaves.

I placed my head on the log and looked at him, hoping he could see that I meant him no harm.

"Zoey?" He stood and took a cautious step forward.

I gave a slight nod, then closed my eyes, not wanting to see the fear on his face that I knew would be present.

I felt a hand rub my nose. "Unbelievable," he whispered.

I opened my eyes, and Jordan smiled, awe and wonder filling his eyes. "Wow. I knew you were amazing, special. But this . . . I hadn't even scratched the surface."

I blinked, letting a tear fall. He leaned forward and placed his cheek up against me. "I care about you, Zoey. This doesn't change that."

I closed my eyes.

He reached out and touched the opal that miraculously still hung from my giant neck. "Please, come back to me. You're beautiful like this, but I'd like to talk."

I slowly raised my head and moved to look at where my clothes still lay.

Jordan noticed the pile of fabric. "Do you need me to turn around again?"

I nodded once more.

He turned his back and said, "Let me know when it's safe to look again. I don't want your dad eating me."

The human side of me chuckled, although I think through the dragon it came out as an odd growl.

I closed my eyes and summoned my human form. I felt myself shrink and compress. In moments, I once again became sixteen-year-old Zoey Mills. I quickly grabbed my clothes and shimmied into them, leaving only my gown to be zipped.

"Okay, I'm dressed," I said as I walked up behind him.

Jordan turned to me and reached forward to cup my cheek. I was still terrified. *How could he be okay with this? At best, he can't possibly see a future for us as a couple.*

He leaned forward and kissed me lightly on the lips. "It's cold out here."

I nodded. "It is. You need your coat."

He glanced at me. "Do you need one? You don't seem to be cold at all."

I shrugged. "I'm not. Perks of being a frost dragon."

"Huh. That's cool," he said.

I looked at him. "Was that a pun?"

He chuckled. "Not a good one."

I laughed, too. "True."

He shivered again.

"Maybe we should get you back to the house," I suggested.

"I'm okay. I want to stay here with you." His teeth were starting to chatter.

"It's hard to talk if you die of hypothermia. Let's go back. I promise to stick around and talk."

He nodded and grew somber.

"Are you okay?" I asked.

"Yeah, just thinking about my dad." He sighed.

"I understand. Did my dad explain banishment?"

He nodded. "Sort of. I didn't understand it fully, but it sounds better than going through this hell over and over."

"What did you decide then?" I asked.

"I told him to do whatever it took to make it stop. If that meant erasing his memory, or whatever it was, I'm fine with that. My mom would be heartbroken, but she'd get over it. Her heart will heal faster than her bones." His mouth formed a grim line.

I put my hand in his as we walked back to my grandfather's house.

~

JORDAN, Aunt Jetta, Miranda, and I sat in front of the fire at my house. Dad had dropped us off at home, and Mom had made us all hot chocolate, so we sipped it as we talked.

Aunt Jetta happily filled Jordan in on the basics of our species, relishing all the unique attributes of being a dragon. He was captivated.

"Of course, we aren't supposed to share this secret with humans, unless we have valid justification. You can never tell anyone. Ever. Do you understand that, Jordan?" Aunt Jetta's eyes bored into his.

Jordan nodded. "Absolutely. I'll take it to the grave."

Aunt Jetta's lips turned up into a devious grin. "I have no doubt about that. I like you, kid, but if you spill this information to anyone you aren't supposed to, I'll eat you for breakfast."

Jordan's eyes widened. "I read you loud and clear."

"Smart guy," Jetta said as she patted him on the back.

"So how does the whole dragon relationship thing work?" he asked. "Do you look for someone just like you?" He paused. "I'm sorry. I don't know how to ask this without sounding stupid."

I understood. "You want to know how we choose a life partner?"

He nodded.

I reached up and caressed my necklace, amazed I still had it. It's like it changed with me when I shifted. "Well, I guess like everyone else. We find someone we like and if things work out, then there ya go." I suddenly felt much wiser than my sixteen years. *Thank you once again, dear dragon.*

Aunt Jetta held up her hands. "Don't look at me. I haven't found it yet."

Mom set down her mug and smiled. "Yes, that sums it up." She looked at Jordan point blank. "And Jordan, if you really like Zoey, there is nothing to stop you two from being together."

His eyes filled with emotion. I recognized it as hope. "Really?"

Mom nodded. "Absolutely. It worked out okay for me."

"Whoa," he said. "You're not a dragon, either?"

"Nope. I'm as human as you are."

He looked at me and reached for my hand. "I'm willing to try if you are, Zoey. I really do care about you."

I blushed a bit. "That'd be nice."

My dad walked into the room and ruined the moment. Jordan dropped my hand. Dad's expression was grim. "Heidi Bennet was seen fighting with her boyfriend at the ball. She ran into the woods and hasn't been seen since. They're organizing a search party. I told them to call me when they were ready to head out."

Mom and Aunt Jetta exchanged worried glances. A human in the woods at night is never a good combination, especially in Havenwood Falls.

"Jordan." Dad sat down in a chair across from us. "Can I speak with you a moment? It's about your dad."

Jordan went pale. I took his hand in mine once more as a show of support. Jordan swallowed and nodded.

Dad cleared his throat. "Your dad is fine. I flew him to a wooded area just outside of Grand Junction. Then gave him explicit instructions to forget about his family and Havenwood Falls."

Jordan frowned. "Does he know?"

Dad nodded. "He does now."

"But, won't he tell everyone?" Jordan asked.

Dad grinned. "Who's gonna believe a guy that's slobbering drunk?"

"What about when he's sober?" Jordan asked.

"Not a problem, either. As I told you before, this town has a special ward on it. Once you leave Havenwood Falls, you only have a certain number of days to return or you forget you were ever here. Your dad won't remember his life here. And it's not likely he'll ever stumble back in. This town has a way of keeping itself hidden."

Jordan bit his lower lip, and I assumed it was all sinking in.

"He'll never harm you or your mother again. And as for employment, I've already offered your mom a job at the pawn shop. It's not the best pay, but it'll help until we find her something she likes better."

Jordan's eyes filled with tears of appreciation. "Thank you so much, Mr. Mills. I can't begin to explain the service you've done us."

"No need to thank us." He smiled and leaned forward to give Jordan's hand a firm shake.

I looked at my dad. "What about Grandpa?"

He scratched his head. "He's a stubborn old man who's stuck in his ways. He's angry and will still be someone we must contend with. We'll just have to keep working on him."

I frowned.

"Don't let him bother you, Zoey. You gave him some real food for thought tonight. I imagine he'll be stewing on that for a while."

"Sounds promising," I said.

"Oh," said Dad. "Are you okay? I noticed you were in pain earlier, after Mr. Woods pushed you."

I lifted my leg and pulled my skirt up to expose my ankle. "It was weird. I sprained my ankle pretty bad when I landed. When I got to the woods and sat down, I rubbed my ankle, and it started to feel a bit better."

Dad and Aunt Jetta exchanged glances.

"What? What does that mean?" I asked.

Aunt Jetta leaned toward me. "Were you crying by any chance?"

I thought about it. "Yeah, I was. But only a little."

"Did you happen to get tears on your ankle?"

"Maybe from my hands?"

Aunt Jetta smiled. "That's your unique gift, Zoey. Your tears have healing properties."

"That's a wonderful gift, but keep it a secret," Mom said. "Other supernaturals would kill to get their hands on your tears."

Dad's face was somber.

"Why?" I asked in alarm.

"There are several things about dragons that have magical properties. For some, it's their scales, others their blood, and most rarely, their tears . . . and these are just some of the reasons a dragon would be killed and harvested. I'm not trying to scare you, just inform you of the dangers of not being discreet." He looked pointedly at

Jordan. "Her life could be at risk if you were to leak this to anyone. Do you understand that?"

Jordan nodded. "Yes, sir. I would never put her in harm's way."

"Glad to hear it. Now, let's get out that birthday cake we never ate. How does that sound?" Dad rubbed his hands together in glee. He loved cake.

Mom brought in the cake and I blew out the candles. They sang Happy Birthday to me, and for the first time in years, I felt I belonged. I felt strong and capable. I could withstand anything life threw my way. I could stand up for myself and be proud of who I was.

My awesome aunt, my amazing parents, my best friend, and possibly the love of my life were there by my side. What more could I ask for? Best. Birthday. Ever.

～

ABOUT THE AUTHOR

Since childhood, Amy Hale has been creating exceptional stories that summon a whirlwind of emotions and inspiration unto the reader. She loves creating characters and worlds from nothing but her imagination and a few glasses of wine. Her love of the written word has not only resulted in her writing some of her readers' favorite adventures, but has also manifested itself in the form of book hoarding. She's convinced it's not a sickness.

She debuted her first fiction novel in 2015, after retiring from thirteen years of non-fiction writing for various online entities. For the last couple of decades, she's also carried the titles of Laundry Goddess, Chef, Butt Wiper, Soother of Temper Tantrums, and in more recent years, Moderator of Sarcastic Eyerolls and Sass. She resides in Illinois with her husband, as well as two grown children who claim they are never moving out. Regardless, they are the center of her universe, although her cat believes otherwise.

If she had any spare time, she'd love music, photography, watching Mystery Science Theater 3000 with her family, and long rides on the back of her husband's motorcycle.

Learn more at authoramyhale.com.

ACKNOWLEDGMENTS

I first must give thanks to God for this amazing path He has put me on. I am nothing without Him.

I owe an unfathomable debt to my husband John. He has been patient with me as I chase this amazing dream. He has given me strength when I felt like giving up. He has showered love on me when I was at my worst. I am blessed to have you by my side, dear husband. I love you!

I'm thrilled to be a part of the Havenwood Falls family. Many thanks to Kristie Cook for inviting me to join this amazing and talented group. I also appreciate the help and guidance you've given me through this project, Kristie. Love ya, dear friend!

I want to send some huge thanks my Havenwood Falls sisters E.J. Fechenda, for the use of Willow, and Michele G. Miller, for letting me borrow the Annex. They were perfect additions to my story!

Mad love for Regina Wamba for giving my cover the perfect look. I couldn't have envisioned anything better!

I owe a million hugs to my friend and partner in crime Terri Wilson. Thank you for keeping me calm and organized when I felt anything but.

To my Havenwood Falls family, which grows every day, thank you for being so supportive of me. Your enthusiasm, brainstorming sessions, and loving encouragement have meant the world to me. I'm excited to see us all build this amazing world together.

Thank you to the readers, who have kept me striving for excellence. Your reviews and comments have helped me improve and grow my craft. Thank you for spending time with me and my characters.

AWAKEN THE SOUL

BY MICHELE G. MILLER

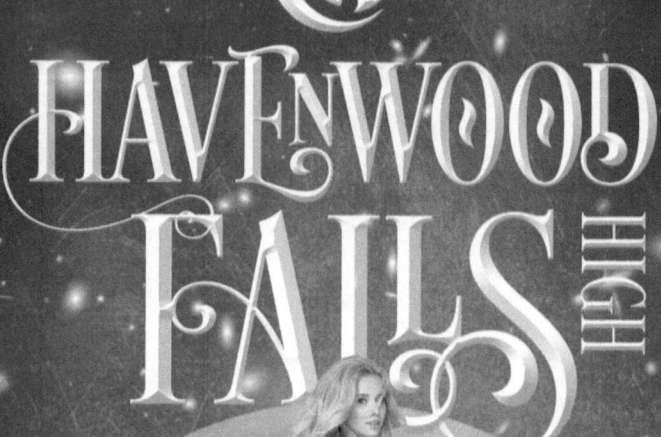

Havenwood Falls High

Awaken the Soul

MICHELE G. MILLER

~ A Havenwood Falls Young Adult Novella ~

OTHER BOOKS BY MICHELE G MILLER

<u>From the Wreckage Series – Coming of Age Dramas</u>

From the Wreckage

Out of Ruins

All That Remains

West: A POV Novel

After the Fall - Austin's story (New Adult Suspense)

Into the Fire – Dani's story

<u>The Prophecy of Tyalbrook Trilogy – YA Fantasy Romances</u>

Never Let You Fall

Never Let You Go

Never Without You – Coming 2018

<u>Individual titles</u>

Last Call – New Adult Romance

CO-WRITTEN WITH MINDY HAYES

<u>Paper Planes Standalone Series – Sweet Contemporary Romances</u>

Paper Planes and Other Things We Lost (YA)

Subway Stops and the Places We Meet (Adult)

Chasing Cars and the Lessons We Learned (New Adult)

Nothing Compares 2 U, novella - *10 Things I Love About You Anthology* (New Adult)

To Angie for giving Viv and Breckin names.
To Jo for helping give them life.
Thank you, ladies.

HOLD ON FOR YOUR LIFE

BRECKIN

*W*hite.

Everywhere I look. Pure, undiluted, untouched. Colorado in December.

Banking left, the tip of my wing disturbs a snow-laden pine bough, scattering ice crystals. The mountain forest is peaceful this late in the afternoon, though the threat of a storm lurks in the gray sky. A gust rolls in from the north, and I snap my wings, letting the airstream guide my path toward home.

How long will this peace last? This morning's message from Elias served as an eerie reminder of my time limit. Four months. Tucking my wings, I shift, free-falling toward the ground, dodging trees as I dart in and around the woods. Freedom. I arch skyward, shooting high above Mount Alexa. The ground, the falls, the trees—they are blemishes on a snowy white canvas.

A scream penetrates the peace. I twist, levitating among the clouds, my gaze narrowing on the ground far below.

The crimson trail, smeared for yards before the dense forest covers the evidence, is hard to miss.

Blood. Thick, human blood.

This is Havenwood Falls—it's not an abnormal occurrence in the forest. But . . .

I dive, lured by a scent that burns my nostrils and confuses my senses.

I'm on the ground within moments of her scream. Her keening death cries prick at my skin, sending an unfamiliar sensation skittering up my spine and across my wings. Angry snarls join her moans. I should leave, yet I press on—following the blood trail. The creature drags her instead of making a clean kill. Most shifters kill, rather than play with, their food. I maintain distance, preferring to remain in the good graces of the other supernatural beings within Havenwood Falls. Angel or not, minding my business keeps the peace. History has proven this. The world is a better place when all creatures, good and evil, play nice together. That type of thinking will be my downfall in four months, if I'm not careful.

An unnatural calm claims the still woods, and my senses sharpen. I move forward as an ache builds up in my chest. Her cries diminish, but her scent strengthens. It's familiar. The spicy combination of ginger root and mint. I duck beneath low branches and break through thicker brush, my steps quickening as I track them. Another growl disturbs the woods, and I pause. Twenty feet ahead, a shadow of fur and menace crosses my path—retreating. The feeling in my chest intensifies like a fist crushing my heart.

Ginger, mint, and something—more. They inundate me as I maneuver around a thick tree and come to a stop.

She is bathed in blood. Her long golden hair spreads around her head, a silken halo on a snowy pillow of white. From my vantage point, I cannot see her face, but her scent—her perfume—gives her away.

Vivienne Freeman.

And above her lifeless body, he is ageless and brings with him the kiss of death. A reaper. His corporeal existence remains unseen to the human eye.

Her name begs to be spoken. A kick to the gut, it is an urge unlike any other. The image of her, two desks in front of me in chemistry for the past few months, is superimposed on the gruesome scene before me. The wisps of hair framing her face, her elegant profile, the way she hunches over her desk while she works. Movement breaks the memory. The reaper's swirling mixture of light and dark extends toward her face, and a thread of black touches her forehead reverently. The perceived intimacy compels me across snow and blood, my wings bared as a warning to this angelic host.

"Leave her be."

Reapers have no affiliation with Heaven or Hell. They're vessels of Death. Wardens sent to usher souls from this life into the next. I've had limited interaction with others of my kind, but I know about egos. I'm the son of an angel, with a human soul, thanks to the woman who gave me life. One of the Nephilim. In hierarchy alone, I win.

Dropping to my knees, I take in Vivienne's shredded jacket and blood-soaked clothing. Her face matches the snow—pale, deathly. Her lips colorless. Her heart? My hand presses against her chest. The pulse is faint, but it beats. Barely.

The reaper hisses as a ripple shocks the air, shattering the calm. His cloaked form floats back as though pushed by the disturbance. He turns, and his piercing blue eyes hold my gaze. *She is mine, son of angels.* His voice does not speak for human ears. He has no body, no face—only a mist-like outline and blue eyes.

"She isn't dead." My hands rip at her clothing, searching out her injuries.

Her heart beats. He can't kill her. Reapers don't kill. They reap souls once the earthly bodies die, nothing more. I can save her. Grabbing my sweatshirt from where I keep it tucked into my waistband when I fly, I staunch the flow of blood from her wounds. The fabric soaks through immediately. A call to medics won't help. She'll be dead in minutes.

As though he's read my mind, the reaper reaches out once again, straining for her. This is Death. I have no part in it. I barely know Vivienne. She's a classmate, not even a friend. A beautiful girl I've known my entire life, but who has never been impressed by me or my antics.

"Don't take her." The words pour from my lips as the falls pour through the rocks of Cooley Creek. "Can't you spare her? Does she have to die?"

My questions are futile. Reapers don't decide these things. There is a larger plan. We all merely follow it. My fists slam the ground. Why can't I walk away?

She is special, the reaper speaks in my mind, soft and low. *Lovely. Her soul was meant for more.*

He rambles like someone in awe. His little, obsessive words click through my head. *I want, I want, I want,* he murmurs. *So special. So different.*

Rage builds within my chest as his chattering continues. Spots flash in my vision, and my stomach hardens as bitterness coats my tongue.

"She is mine!" I shout the statement within my soul and out of my lips.

No. She is mine, son of angels.

Low, guttural anger rips from within, snapping my control. My hands burn as my muscles bunch and flex, and the world around us dims, blackness snuffing out the afternoon sun. Shadows grow long, branches creak, and the reaper drifts away once again.

I mock his pitiful presence. "Yes, I *am* the son of an angel. I do not cower before a warden of Death."

"You are a boy," the reaper says aloud, his shroud waving in the wind as the heat consuming my hands creeps up my arms.

The light of a thousand fires burns at the tips of my fingers pressed against Vivienne's wounds. *Heal her.* I call upon an ability I possess, but have never tapped into. My teeth grind in my tight jaw.

The reaper's hisses are nonstop. He is furious. I'm saving his prey, taking his prize. His electric eyes flash as he lowers to the ground and assumes an upright position, hovering above the snow. He remains nothing but spirals of mist, taking the loose shape of the classic specter of Death humans are used to visualizing.

A cold touch shocks my side, and I flinch. *Vivienne's hand.* It slides down my bare ribs, searching for purchase. Her fingers curl around a belt loop of my black jeans as her back arches off the ground. The intensity in my palms grows, and pain contorts Vivienne's features. Her brows draw above her eyes, her mouth forming a voiceless scream as a dribble of blood coats her bottom lip. Her free hand digs into the snow. Her suffering torments me, and yet I hold tight, healing her as she writhes. Her heels scrape against the wet ground as her legs bend and stretch. She's missing one running shoe.

Then it's done.

The light dies. The weak, gray sun reappears.

Vivienne's eyes flutter, offering little glimpses of watery blue nirvana before they close, and her head falls to the side.

With a smug grin, I lift my gaze to the reaper.

I want her, he says with his mind, his eyes.

My lip curls. "You can't have her."

I will. His black head tilts, a subtle nod, then he's gone.

The forest awakens, the calm of death no longer holding life at a standstill.

My coarse breaths come quickly, my pulse racing as I gather Vivienne close. Leaning over her, I press my lips to the frozen edge of her ear. "It's okay. I've got you. You're safe."

Her heart beats, strong and steady.

My muscles relax as I survey the forest. It's nearly nightfall. The temperature dropped rapidly in the last several minutes. The air is ripe with the scent of the gathering storm. It's a mile, possibly two, north. Tucking my ruined sweatshirt between our bodies, I search the ground for evidence of what transpired here. Her blood is everywhere, but nothing else. The storm will cover the blood from human eyes, although the scent will drive the supernaturals in town crazy. Nothing to be done right now. I need to move Vivienne someplace warm.

Cradling her close, I leap into the air and snap my wings wide. I'll take her to my house, clean her up, and make sure she's okay. I'll figure out my next move after that.

Unanswered questions bombard me. *What happened in the forest? Why did I react with such savagery? Will the reaper be back? Should I worry? Tell Elias? Speak to Father?* No. I won't call upon him. I have four months, six if I can convince him to let me finish out school, before I take my place at his side. His or another's—the decision has yet to be made, and I need all the time away from him I can get.

My forehead lowers, pressing to Vivienne's temple as my hands tighten their grip. Her lips have regained a pink, human tone. I inhale a shaky breath as the emptiness, the nothingness, I've lived with disappears. She replaced it in an instant. Her scent fills me. Her warmth, her life, digs into my soul with gripping talons, anchoring in and refusing to let go. These emotions are unexpected and unwanted. I've never felt much of anything for anyone.

Is this feeling human or angelic?

~

THE FIRST SNOWFLAKES appear before I reach home. Staying low, I fly above the tree line and cloak us from sight as we soar over Havenwood Heights. If I were alone, I'd be home already, a perk of angelic birth, but Vivienne is vulnerable. Especially in her current state. Her pulse remains strong, her heartbeat steady, but her color is pallid. She lost too much blood, and I don't know how my healing abilities work. *Should I take her to the medical center? Her mom works there, but what would I say? Maybe I should bring her home?* The feathers between my shoulder blades twitch. *Yeah, I'm not a fan of that idea either.*

We land on my back deck, and I head straight for the nearest guest room. Forcing my arms to cooperate, I release Vivienne onto the bed as I shift pillows beneath her damp head. I carefully work off her bloody jacket, ruined shoe, and wet socks. She's dressed in athletic gear —thick, waterproof running pants, a sweatshirt, a thermal—and it's all ruined by blood. She'll have to forgive me for the skin I see as I rip at her shirts. Her side is injury free. Smeared blood and mottled bruising the only proof anything happened.

Clenching my jaw, my fingers slip into the waistband of her pants and work them down her hips. At the sight of her running tights, I release a relieved breath. I leave them on—they're clean, dry, and modest. When I finish, I sweep the dirty comforter away and cover her with a thick blanket. My fingers linger at her temple as I brush her hair from her face. Her skin is warmer. And soft. So damn soft. It's an effort to remove my hand and leave the room.

Once in my room, I swipe my hands through my hair and curse. Even from across the house, she tugs at me, wanting me to return. I press my palm to my chest as though I can press her out. *What is going on?* I change into clean sweats and a T-shirt, splash my face with cold water, and head for the kitchen, my thoughts on making Vivienne something warm, when my cell goes off.

The screen flashes: Elias.

"Hey man," I answer nonchalantly.

"Hey man?" Accusation laces his words.

Crap.

"Your silence is telling. What happened?"

Did he notice it, too? The bizarre shift in the air, the release of my abilities, the reaper's presence? "To what are you referring?"

I stick a milk-filled mug in the microwave.

"I've suspended service for the night. Should I come over? Or call your father?" he asks meaningfully.

"I used my abilities." I slam a cabinet shut. "It was unintentional."

A tirade of colorful curses serenades me. "Tell me what happened."

"I don't know." I chew on my lip and contemplate my words. "There was a reaper."

Okay then, forget a well-thought-out explanation. Let's lead with the biggie.

"A reaper?" Elias repeats. "Who died?"

"No one."

"No one?" His breath hitches. "You healed? Why in the hell would you do that?"

His anger raises my hackles. "Because I can."

"Breckin."

"Don't lecture me, Elias. I need to go. I'll explain everything later." I end the call and toss my phone on the counter.

When I return to Vivienne, she's on her side with one hand resting beneath her cheek and the other clutching a down blanket to her chest. The thick bedding swallows her. She's tiny, a foot shorter and seventy-five pounds lighter than me. The weight of her in my arms lingers.

Splotches of red mar her fingers and smear her chin. Leaving her drink on the bedside table, I head toward the bathroom and return with a warm washcloth. I'm aware of each swipe of the cloth, like I'm washing my own hands. Vivienne sighs and flinches when I set her hand down and rub her jaw. A whimper releases from her throat, making me pause.

She brushes her chin against her shoulder as she shifts restlessly. Her forehead creases as she fists the blankets and draws the edge to her mouth, tucking her face in before settling down.

The wind howls as a thick veil of white comes down fast outside my windows. I move from the edge of the bed to a chair across the room, my heart slowing as hers does, and I wait. There's nothing more I can do.

BAD DREAM

VIVIENNE

*S*lapping at my bedside table, my hand searches for the incessant vibration dragging me unwillingly from sleep. Finding my cell phone, I fumble with the screen, bringing the device to my ear. "Hello?" I clear my throat and repeat myself when the word barely passes my lips.

"Viv? Where have you been?" Mom's voice sounds far, far away. I blink rapidly, clearing the sleep from my brain. "Were you asleep, honey? I've been calling all evening. Are you sick?"

Her questions come in quick-fire succession, and I struggle to keep up while sitting. Rubbing my aching temple, I peek at my cell for the time. Midnight. What the heck?

"Uh . . . no. Or, yeah. Yeah, I was sleeping. I'm not sick. Just tired."

There's a pause. A shift on the other end. "You didn't call after your run. You know you're supposed to let me know when you get home if I'm not there. I was worried. Especially with this storm raging and the disappearance of the Bennett girl."

Heidi Bennett. She went missing last weekend, during the Cold Moon Ball. The adults around town are freaking out, but consensus at school is she probably had a fight with her boyfriend, or parents, and will show up in a few days. I work my head side to side, stretching out the kinks as I wait for her to say more.

"Viv? Are you sure everything is okay?"

"Mmmhmmm," I hum, focusing on a shadow lurking beyond my window. The hair on the back of my neck stands. I never leave my blinds and curtains open, especially at night. Living on the first floor of an apartment complex doesn't offer a whole lot of privacy. Plus, the guys across the way are pervs. "Yeah. I'm fine. Sorry I didn't call. I laid down. I guess I fell asleep."

After your run. Her words register belatedly, and my pulse picks up.

"Okay, sweetie. Go back to sleep, and I'll see you when I get home in the morning."

I nod, then remember I'm on the phone. "Yeah, okay, have a good shift. Love you."

"I went for a run," I say to the empty room after the call ends.

The snow outside reflects the bright winter moon and casts long shadows across my small bedroom. Sinking into my blankets, I pull my comforter over my bare shoulders. *Wait. Bare shoulders?* My hands run over my body. *What am I wearing? Running tights and a sports bra?* Kicking into a sitting position, I draw my knees to my chest.

I went for a run. I . . . Tears prick my eyes.

A dark flash hurtles at me. Pain. Blood. My throat closes. *No. It was a dream. A nightmare.*

Hurrying from my room, I search for my clothing. My jacket, pants, shoes, any of the gear I normally wear running. I flip on lights, search closets, the hampers, the washing machine. My heart plays the beat of a thousand drums.

A low, animalistic snarl fills my ears. A cool touch. An urgent voice. My knees give way, and I crumble to the floor, dizzy and spent. *Why can't I remember anything? What am I missing? Nothing is right.* I crawl to the couch and pull myself up, drawing a throw over my body. I need sleep. Maybe I am getting sick.

The view from the couch to my bedroom window is unhindered, and there—beside the pine outside my building—is a shadow.

My eyelids grow heavy as I peer across the apartment. A shadow in the form of a human.

I pry my eyes wider, my temples pounding. A shadow with amber eyes.

I should be scared by a shadow outside my window in the middle of the night. I should call 911, I should scream, but I don't. I'm not afraid. My mind calms as my frantic heart settles. With one last sleepy effort, I search out the shadow, catching a wavering glimpse before everything falls dark.

~

"You're bloody crazy, Viv." Zara blows into her cupped hands as she shifts from foot to foot.

"Are you being British again?" I laugh as I walk the steps from my window to the pine for the third time. My gaze searches the ground for something—anything—that proves someone stood out here last night. "Which Austen movie did you watch yesterday?"

"It wasn't Austen. It was a documentary on the royal family. It was brilliant."

"You're mad." Though I'm teasing, I can't help but go into character and pull out my British slang.

"Well done." Zara's tone and accent come out a bit Mary Poppins. Her fascination with British culture knows no end. We've spent thousands of hours watching, listening to, and studying British entertainment. "But, I would argue I am not the one here who is insane, my dear Viv."

"I know what I saw. Someone was out here last night."

"And in your apartment, stealing your clothes?" She steps into the snow and works her way to my side. "There is nothing here. Even if you did have a Peeping Tom, there would be no evidence. It snowed all night. You're not going to find a fresh set of footprints. You've watched too many crime shows."

Why did I bother telling her?

Zara tugs her knit hat over her ears, smooshing down her thick, dark hair. "Can we go inside? I'm freezing and you don't have a jacket on."

"That's because I can't find my jacket," I remind her.

"Did you tell your mum?"

Grabbing her arm, I lead her toward the apartment. "Tell her what? That someone robbed me of my running gear? That I'm seeing things?"

I'm positive something happened yesterday. Something bad. Something dangerous. I rack my brain for any semblance of what it could have been.

A smattering of needles prick across my shoulders, and I pause, my gaze scanning the parking lot, looking for something, sensing it. Other than the kids building a snowman by the building across from mine, the complex is quiet.

"Mom's already giving me a hard time about running alone since Heidi went missing. If I alert her to anything out of the ordinary, she'll start making me spend all my free time at the medical center with her."

"Good point." Zara weaves her arm beneath mine. "Let's go. We can drive over to Backwoods and buy you a new coat before the movie."

～

"THIS IS NOT how I intended spending the last of my birthday money," I complain as I dig for my wallet and hand most of my cash to Willa Kasun, who smiles sympathetically from behind the register.

"The fact that you still have birthday money from last April is telling, my friend," Zara, the spendthrift, says with a shake of her head.

The snap of a shopping bag opening draws me from my pouting. "Oh, actually, can you remove the tags so I can wear it?" Willa's dark brow arches. "I lost mine, and it's a bit chilly out there without one."

Zara nudges my shoulder, an inelegant snort jerking her shoulders. "She's so daft. She'd misplace her arse if it weren't attached."

Daft? I mouth, giving my so-called best friend a fixed look.

Willa's lips twitch as she pulls out a pair of scissors, cuts the tags, and slides my new jacket across the counter with the receipt on top.

"Thanks. See ya." I toss a wave as she gives me her canned "Thanks for shopping at Backwoods Sport & Ski."

Shoving Zara toward the exit, I hiss, "Way to go, Z. She probably thinks I'm a complete idiot."

Zara giggles and stops at a sunglass display. She slides a gaudy red and gold pair on and poses. "Whatever. No one thinks you're an idiot. We go to the same school; she knows you're Ms. Academia. Plus, she shared a womb with Kase. She most certainly knows an idiot when she sees one."

"Oh my gosh, shut up." I swallow back a giggle and search the immediate area, clamping down on her arm. The Kasuns own this store. Their dad is sheriff, their older brothers are deputies, and Kase—while not the sharpest pencil in the box—is well-known and well-liked. "Besides, I know for a fact you're smitten with him."

"Smitten?" Zara's light caramel skin flushes as she smirks. "I am not smitten. He's hot, I'll give him that, but after that mess with Ana? No, thank you. I'm staying far, far away from him."

"You have excellent self-preservation skills. They may be over, but Ana would rip your head off if she thought you were after him."

A deep chuckle nearby stops me. I turn, blood creeping up my neck at being overheard, but there's no one there. The store's busy enough, locals and tourists alike flipping through the racks of ski gear and sporting goods, but not one of them pays us a bit of attention. No smiles, no curious eyes. I adjust my scarf, pulling it around my neck as goosebumps appear across my skin.

"Pizza or burgers?" Zara asks as we step outside and I shrug into my jacket. I lift a shoulder, my mind occupied with the eerie sensations crawling over my skin. Everything within me screams in warning, and like last night, nothing is right.

"You said burgers, right?" she prods and bats her large Bambi eyes.

It's a standing joke—what's for dinner? Zara works at Napoli's. She always wants Burger Bar when we go out. I prefer Napoli's, probably because they prepare me special orders since they're used to me hanging around. Shaking away the pall hanging over me, I agree to burgers. I'm in no mood to argue.

"Burgers it is." She swings her keyring around her index finger and heads for the parking lot. I glance back at the store one last time before following.

There are a few cars parked at the drive-in bays outside the Burger Bar, but the inside is packed. The crowded booths and occupied tables aren't a surprise. Some of the girls from school wave us over and share their booth.

Living in Havenwood Falls is like living in a fishbowl. We breathe the same air and walk the same paths daily. We see the same people at every restaurant, movie showing, and festival. It's the second Saturday of the month—movie night. It's been a Havenwood Falls tradition since long before my birth. It began as a summer ritual, a family-friendly movie in Danzan Park, but once the Arts Council renovated the old mining warehouse—adding a stage and theater—the city extended the showings to year-round. Havenwood Falls, known for strange occurrences and more festivals than days of the week, is heaven for a people watcher like me.

Dipping my fries in a pile of peppered mayo, I half listen to the girls chat about their day on the slopes while my gaze flits over the crowded restaurant. I'm entertained by the guys at the next table as they jostle one another over a ketchup bottle. No need to question why I've never seen them with dates. Poor immature fools.

Across the restaurant, Nikki Morris fusses with her perfect hair and makes faces at her phone. I can't tell whether she is taking a selfie or using the camera as a mirror. The new kid, Max Cooper, arrives, and she straightens, plastering on a glowing smile and lowering her cell. I'm happy they're still dating after all the mess she's been in lately. They're both insanely good-looking, like many of the people in Havenwood Falls, and popular. I turn my head, my gaze sliding past holiday decorations covering every vacant spot in the restaurant, before they stop on a vaguely familiar face. He's propped against the wall next to the entrance with a menu in his hands, but his eyes aren't reading the daily specials. They're firmly set on me.

Intensely charged blue orbs framed by dark lashes and a pale face — *Wait.* I blink nervously. My eyes and mind play tricks on me. I don't know him at all, yet my pulse ratcheted up the moment I spotted him. Flickers of memories tickle the back of my mind, knocking and asking to be let in.

My lungs deflate, each breath more difficult than the last, the longer he stares. I grip the table, my fingers curling around the metal edge, as a chill creeps up my spine. He pushes from the wall, and I lurch forward.

Zara jumps, her hands grabbing the cup of water I knocked over. "What the hell, Viv?"

She pushes my shoulder while across the table, the others shift baskets and throw napkins on the mess I've made.

"Sorry. I don't know what happened. I—"

"You were totally eye screwing that guy, that's what happened. Who is he?" Zara nudges my side again. "You're soaked. Get up, you loon."

"I'm—" *Soaked?* Cold moisture seeps through my jeans, and I look down as water dribbles off the table into my lap.

"Yep, I'm wet," I say lamely, sliding from the booth.

"What guy?" the girls ask in tandem as their heads swivel in the direction of the door.

He's gone.

"Viv?" Zara touches my hand at my side. "Are you okay? You're shaking."

My head nods of its own accord as I will my trembling to cease and look over the restaurant. People laugh, people eat, everything's the same. Except for the guy, who is no longer by the door. I tug at the sleeves of my sweater.

"I'm fine. Um, I'm gonna go to the bathroom. I'll be back."

Faint voices tap at the back of my head, like gnats flying around on a summer day. They buzz and swoop close, only to retreat—taking whatever secrets they hold with them. The sensation makes me dizzy as I round the corner to the bathroom and pull up in time to miss bumping into Scarlet Howe. Scarlet smiles and holds her hands up like

I'm a robber as I apologize and press against the wall so she can pass. I take three steps backward and turn for the door handle when someone grabs my wrist and yanks me into the bathroom.

"Don't scream," a voice says as the light flicks on in the single-person restroom, and he spins my back to the wall.

My scream dies when I see Breckin Roberts standing over me, his face so close his breath caresses my cheek. My entire body lights up like a Christmas tree. A spark of something—awareness?—slips across his face, and his head cocks to the side. Gosh, I could stare at him all night. I want to. Just stand right here and look at him.

"You need to come with me." His tone leaves no room for questions, so of course, I scoff.

"Are you high? This is the girls' restroom, Breckin."

"I need you to come with me," he says again, as if I didn't hear him the first time.

"You want me to come with you? Is this your way of asking me out?"

What a ridiculous question. Breckin Roberts would never ask me out. Breckin doesn't ask anyone out. He skulks in corners as girls flock to him. Not that I've been watching him or anything. I attempt stepping sideways, but his palms slap on either side of my body, caging me. Something within me springs forward, reaching for him.

"Did you see him?" Breckin dips his head until our eyes are level, which is a feat, considering our one-foot height difference. Any attempt at words dies on my lips. "Did you?"

The urgency in his voice stirs the gnats to circling again. My eyes burn. *The blue eyes, the dark presence.* My jaw trembles. Where is this fear coming from?

"Hey." Breckin scans my face. "I've got you." He rubs the length of my upper arms, his touch light.

Time stops.

It's okay. I've got you. You're safe.

"What? What did you say?" The echo of a growl haunts me.

Breckin tilts his head, his teeth tugging at his bottom lip. A phantom pain slashes across my side as the image of a hand clawing at snow breaks through my mind. Gasping, I clutch my stomach. "I need to go."

I push at his chest, my words a mere whisper as blood pounds in my ears, but he stands his ground.

Breckin shakes his head, his golden-brown hair falling over his flawless face. "I can't let you go, Vivienne."

His tone is one I've never heard from him. This is Breckin. He usually drawls every syllable he says as though he couldn't care less about what he's saying or to whom he's speaking. I've always had the impression that he's honoring us with his words when he speaks. This is different. This is authority.

DON'T CLOSE YOUR EYES

BRECKIN

*T*he color leaches from Vivienne's delicate face as her shoulders roll forward, making her appear tinier than she is. She drops her head, her long hair forming a curtain and closing her face off from my gaze.

"What happened yesterday afternoon?" Her voice cracks as she wraps her arms across her stomach. "What did you do to me?"

The moment I touched her and pulled her into the bathroom, I longed for more. More of her skin beneath mine, more of her scent, more of her presence. A spark ignited. Desperate, my fingers tangle in her blond strands, pushing them back. "I don't know what you're talking about."

Vivienne grabs my wrist, holding my hand to the side of her head.

"You're lying." Her head remains bowed as her gaze lifts until she stares at me through thick, dark lashes. My thumb brushes her temple as she speaks. "Something happened to me. You were there. That guy —" She cocks her head toward the restaurant. "He was there. I feel it. I know it."

"Viv—"

"Tell me the truth, or let me go." Fear clings to her words the way perfume clings to her body. Her fear takes root deep within me, urging my angelic side to protect her. Her scent, though . . . that damn minty ginger scent. It digs into my soul and makes me oh so human.

There are rules in Havenwood Falls. Rules governing the supernatural. There are rules with Father. I fear his rules more than the Court's.

I speak the truth regardless.

"You were attacked." My arms drop as I move back a half step.

"Attacked?" Uncertainty clouds her face. She wets her lips and swallows. "By what?"

Bear, dragon, mountain lion, wolf—you name it, it could have attacked her. A shifter or an animal with no supernatural tendencies. *Sure, Breck, while you're at it, why don't you scare the hell out of her and mention vampires, demons, and witchcraft, too?*

"If I had to guess, I'd say a small bear." Cubs aren't too scary. It's reasonable.

"A bear? In December?" She scowls.

"Right. Maybe a wolf or fox? I didn't see it. I heard you scream, and by the time I found you, it was gone and—" My explanation ends there.

"I was out for a run. I didn't see it." She tugs at her sweater sleeves, pulling them over her fists. "I don't remember anything. I just, I woke up and—" She clears her throat, changing her tone and line of questioning. "I screamed, and you just happened to be nearby?"

"I was." Her nose scrunches as a dubious little twist of her mouth appears. I raise a brow. "You're not the only person who enjoys exercising in the woods, you know."

"So, what did you do?"

There's no escaping the ego that tugs a smile across my lips. "I saved you."

She inhales through her nose, her shoulders lifting as a hand moves to her side. Her fingers brush her ribs where she was injured. "My clothes?"

"Ruined."

The door knob jiggles behind Vivienne's back, followed by two knocks. She steps away, glancing at me before looking to the door. I still—waiting for her next move.

"Someone's in here," she says after a moment, and I release a relieved breath.

She's not running. It's a start. The reaper is nearby. His imprint, much like Vivienne's fear, is detectable in the air—a unique marker with the sole purpose of notifying other angels of Death's presence. He is nearby, and he shouldn't be. He should have left Havenwood Falls, or moved on to the next soul in need of reaping. He shouldn't be lingering around Vivienne. The way he looked at Vivienne, the possessive hunger in his gaze . . . Anger spreads across my shoulders, and I roll them, forcing my wings to remain concealed.

Vivienne closes the gap between us, her head tilting back. "Why did you save me?"

If only I knew. "Why wouldn't I?"

"We're not friends, Breckin. Granted, we're not enemies, but you've never given me a reason to believe you're the knight-in-shining-armor type."

"But I've given you a reason to think I'm not?" Her comment affects me. I'm not one who is affected by humans. It matters none to me, yet I ask for clarification anyway. "That's what you think of me?" She moves back, her head high, her eyes searching for answers she will not find, and I move forward. "You know so little of me, but you think I'd leave someone for dead in the woods?"

Her feet still. She sways, her jaw dropping. "I was dying?"

The answer is in her head. It's all there. Hints of the afternoon, still frames of the horror. They wait for her to recall them fully, because swiping her memory didn't work as it should have. The moment she looked through her window last night and her eyes connected with mine, I knew it hadn't worked. I was cloaked. She shouldn't have seen or sensed my presence. She heard me laugh at her joke at the store. She felt my presence when I should have been invisible.

She awakens emotions and instincts I've never known. Something happened between us yesterday. I need answers, which means speaking to Father or Elias. And that means having her come with me, because I'll be damned if I'm leaving her out in the open for a reaper to stalk.

"Was I dying?" she asks for a second time, her hand grabbing a fistful of my shirt.

My gut twists. "You were basically dead, Viv."

Her head shakes, refusing my words, as her lips tremble and tears form on her dark lashes. "I don't understand. I don't—"

My wings tear at my back, itching for release, and I grit my teeth, holding myself together. "Come with me, and I'll explain."

"I can't walk out of here with you. I have friends out there, waiting. I'm supposed to go to the movie festival tonight."

She's right. It's not as though most of the people out there don't know me. The place is filled with kids from school and other locals. There's no reason Vivienne and I couldn't be friendly, but I'm not friendly. It's not my MO, and her friends would question her endlessly. The fewer questions, the better. I could cloak us, and we could walk out of here together, but that would still leave her friends guessing.

My mind grapples for a solution. "Doesn't your mom work night shift at the clinic? Is she working tonight?"

"Yeah. She's always on shift, since Dr. Nance died."

"Good. I want you to go out there and tell them you don't feel well, and you're going to see your mom. Tell them to go to the movies without you. I'll wait here for a minute, then sneak out and meet you by the front door."

Vivienne twists her hair over her shoulder and backs into the door. "This is crazy. You're crazy."

"Trust me."

Forcing my hands not to reach for her, I wait as she considers my request. I sense her fear and hear the anxious beating of her heart, but beneath that is more. There's an acceptance, a light, hiding behind the darkness.

She cocks her head and grabs a strand of hair, twisting it. "You'll explain everything?"

"Everything I can." Not a total lie.

Agreeing, Vivienne peeks into the hallway before giving me a look over her shoulder and slipping out the door. I immediately make myself invisible and follow. Skirting around tables and patrons, I head for the exit, all while keeping an eye on Vivienne and her friends. My sensitive hearing picks up their conversation.

"I got sick in the bathroom," she says weakly as she stands at the end of the table. "You guys should go to the movies without me. I'm gonna go see my mom."

"I'll drive you over." The offer comes from Zara, who's already sliding out of the booth. She holds Vivienne's jacket out to her.

"No," Vivienne says with too much force. "I mean, it's practically next door. I'll walk. It's fine. Plus, if I have the flu, I don't want you to get sick."

"Viv?"

"I need to go," Vivienne interrupts, grabbing her bag and cell phone. "I'll text you."

A chorus of goodbyes follow as she heads my way, and I slip out the door before she reaches me, shifting back to visible and smacking into two guys from school.

"What the hell, Breckin? Where did you. . ." Their words fade as I grab their arms, implanting an alternate memory and sending them on their way as Vivienne appears.

A rush of energy washes over me at the sight of her. It's exhilarating and confusing as hell. Most days, the two entities that make up who I am are separate, but more and more, my angelic side takes over. As my divine abilities strengthen, my humanity fades.

Vivienne makes me human.

She bites her lip when she spots me, then glances back over her shoulder, and my chest expands. I've all but lost the ability to feel over the past few years. Father hates humans—except when he wants them for satisfying his basic desires. He's deemed them useless. It's an attitude I picked up. I assumed my angel side felt indifference. It doesn't. Not with her.

"You okay?" I ask, holding out my hand.

She lifts the strap of her bag over her head, bringing it across her chest, and shoves her hands in her jacket pockets as she looks about.

It's Saturday night, and the drive-in and parking lot are full of people coming and going. The reaper's presence remains strong out here.

"Where's your truck?"

Dropping the hand I'm still holding out to her like a fool, I turn and head around the back of the building. "We don't need it."

"We don't need—" Vivienne's boots crunch the gravel and snow as she follows. "Where are you going? Breckin?"

I duck behind the fence hiding the restaurant's dumpsters.

She grumbles low, too low for human ears, but I hear every word. "What am I doing? Breckin Roberts graces me with his attention, and suddenly I'm swooning and following him into dark alleys, taking his word as gospel. I'm mental, truly mental."

"Breckin?" she hisses, coming around the fence.

"Hold on tight," I warn, and Vivienne screams as my arms go around her waist and we jump into the air. Her face tucks into my neck, a second scream vibrating against my skin as her feet kick at the air.

"Viv, it's okay. I won't let anything happen to you." My hand shifts up her back, pressing her closer to my chest. "By the way, I don't believe that qualified as an alley, and you're not mental."

Vivienne moans. "We're . . . we're . . ." She whimpers again, her anxiety skyrocketing.

"Flying?" I provide helpfully.

She whines.

"Open your eyes, Vivie," I tease, slowing our ascent. Her head shakes beneath my chin, and I chuckle at her mumbled plea. "I already said you're not crazy, and no, you're not dreaming. You're safe, I promise." Lowering my lips to her ear, I whisper, "Open your eyes."

Her arms tense—one around my neck, the other around my back. Her hand moves dangerously close to the joint of my wings and spine as she adjusts her body and lifts her head. Her face is a hair's breadth from my lips as her chin tips up and her eyes open. Fear reflects at me.

"You're wearing some sort of jet pack, right? I've seen those invention shows. The military make them, and rich people buy them as toys. You're rich, your dad travels the world . . . he brings you expensive toys—" Her high-pitched rambling draws another smile to my lips. If she'd stop talking, she'd hear the beat of my wings against the air. She continues.

"Don't drop me, Breckin. I'm not sure I'm a fan of this. I prefer driving. You have a cool vehicle, a classic even. Couldn't we have driven? Can you put me down? I mean, can we go back down?" I shift, turning my body under hers as we head east, toward my house. Vivienne squeals, squeezing her eyes closed. "No, no, no. What are you doing? How high are we? Please tell me this is a nightmare. This isn't real. You're not here, I'm in bed—"

I kiss her.

It's a simple brush of my lips against hers—one I must rip myself away from, because *holy hell*, I want more—but she shuts up.

"Was that not real?" I ask, winding my leg around her calf and locking her closer.

Her jaw works back and forth. "It couldn't have been."

We glide on the wind, my wings beating once every twenty feet. "Why not?"

She draws a shaky breath, her hand shifting at my spine, her nails digging into my skin as she clutches tighter. Her lips form a silent O.

"You're shirtless," Vivienne accuses.

It took her this long to notice? Removing my shirts when I fly is a must, unless I want to shop for new clothes every time my wings make an appearance and rip them in two.

"I am." She tilts her head, though she still doesn't look down. "I'm not wearing a jetpack, either. All you have to do is look beyond my face, and all your questions will be answered."

"Oh, I highly doubt that." Wry humor clings to her words. Catching her bottom lip with her front teeth, her eyes slide left and go wide. I still, allowing her a good look at my wings. Her chest expands with her deep inhale.

"They're real," I say preemptively. "Not some expensive toy my father bought me."

"You have wings." The rhythm of her racing heart tugs at my

angelic senses. My palm aches to press against her chest, to memorize the song each beat creates. Blood rushes to her face, and I grin.

"You like them."

Her head whips around, her blush deepening. "They're beautiful," she admits. "But I don't—"

"Crap." A dark shadow circles a hundred yards behind us. I should have caught his presence sooner. Vivienne has me off my game. "Close your eyes and hold on tight."

I push her head to my chest and bank left, flying toward Mount Alexa and over the falls. We pick up speed as I lead the reaper away from my house and the town. The Court of the Sun and the Moon would not look favorably on a Saturday night fight between angels in the square. Searching out a spot, I locate a small clearing in the trees deep in the forest, near the northernmost ridge, and land.

Vivienne's legs give out as her feet hit the snow. I loosen my hold, giving her room to stand on her own.

"What's wrong? What is it?"

I push her toward a wide tree. *How do I explain what she needs to know?*

"He's here," Vivienne says as her cold fingers clutch my bicep. Her sharp intake of breath tells me she's putting pieces together. "He has wings, too," she says, looking over my shoulder.

Deep rolling laughter sounds behind me. I turn and face the reaper, who's taken the shape of an unfamiliar teenage boy.

My hand tightens around Vivienne's. "You can't take her."

"Can't I?" His eyes flick over our heads. A snap reverberates through the forest as branches twist and break above us. We dodge to the right as a pile of snow and bark land in our footprints.

"You would kill her?" That's not allowed. Reapers do not determine death. He risks the wrath of a guardian angel; he risks the wrath of *me*. Fury builds. "You do not want to play with me, reaper."

He slinks forward. "You stole her from me."

I push Vivienne behind me. "And I would do it again."

FALLEN ANGEL

VIVIENNE

*A*ngels growl.

This little tidbit pops into my mind as the man with glowing blue eyes snarls.

Angels.

At least, I suppose that's what Breckin is—an angel.

The ground spins, and I focus on the dark wing sheltering me. My wide eyes follow the copper-tipped feathers to where they connect with Breckin's spine. They were iridescent in the moonlight, but in the shadows of the woods, they're inky black perfection against glowing skin. The impulse to stroke them is maddening.

"You cannot protect her forever, son of angels."

Breckin's wings twitch.

I slide closer, touching his lower back as he laughs. "Now, I'm sure you're familiar enough with our kind to know your challenge will not be taken lightly."

Cringing at Breckin's snide tone, I step sideways for a better look at the angel threatening us. Breckin's wing blocks me, extending like a wall. My stomach flutters at his protectiveness. *This is not the Breckin Roberts I know.*

"She is such a pretty thing. Do you plan on making her your toy?"

Breckin's muscles flex beneath my fingertips, as a hair-raising snarl vibrates in his chest. "Do you plan on dying today, reaper?"

There's the Breckin I know. Why am I suddenly finding him hot? Well, he's always been hot, but now he's Channing Tatum wearing a welding mask hot.

The other angel grunts. I lift on my toes, but Breckin is too tall, and his wings are too effective at blocking my view.

"What is your allegiance, boy? A son of angels in love with a human? They will kill you once they find out. I will take her soul from you soon enough."

A gust sprays fine snow as my breath catches. *In love with a human? My soul?* Breckin steps forward, allowing me a glimpse of this other angel. His wings, smaller and lighter in color compared to Breckin's black ones, stir the air. He levitates before us, and his wings still, as though he was merely waiting to catch my gaze. When he does, it's as though he sees through me. His eyes hold me captive.

"Do not let the half-breed taint that soul of yours, my sweet."

"Who are you? What do you want?"

Breckin grabs my wrist. "Vivienne."

I stop. I've stepped in front of Breckin—and don't recall moving.

"Soon enough." The dark angel smiles. Cool, finger-like strokes cross my mind—caressing, invading—and I stagger back, my hand against my forehead, as he shoots into the sky.

Transfixed, I stare after him, anticipating his return. Moonlight, stars, and wisps of clouds hover above the trees. No shadow angel. No blue eyes.

"Viv?" Breckin cuts through my haze. He cups my shoulder, and tingles race along my arm.

"What is this, Breckin?" My sanity hangs by a thread as questions tumble forth. "You're an angel? He's an angel? He wants to kill me? Tried to? How did you steal me from him? What's going on?"

"You're shivering." Breckin steps forward—his wings lowering and folding closer to his body—as I move back.

"I'm fine. Answer my questions."

"I will, once you're warm."

I can't see his face in the shadows of the trees, but I can read his voice. He's concerned, which is funny, considering his lack of clothing. "You're shirtless."

He releases a strangled laugh, shaking his head. "Yes, I am. I'm also not prone to hypothermia."

"Because you're an angel?" I prod.

Breckin sighs, his warm breath sending a puff of smoky air between us. "Part angel, yes."

Part angel. *Half-breed.*

I sniff, my nose running, thanks to the cold. Flexing my stiff fingers, I look about. We're high on the mountain. The air is thin, the trees scarce, the wind gusts consistent— how did I not notice this before?

Taking advantage of my preoccupation, Breckin's wings surround me, drawing me near as he bridges the gap between us. He's taller than me. Tall enough for me to fit under his chin as I walk into his arms and press my cheek against his unnaturally warm skin. My fingers lock behind his back, and he leaps at my icy touch. His dark wings envelop me—a Breckin cocoon, of sorts—and an overwhelming mix of tranquility and trepidation washes over me. Being in his arms is so right, yet I'm terrified. Not of him, or what he is—but of what's happening. I fight the pull coaxing me to stroke his wings as his feathers ruffle. His hands shift on my back, one low and one high, his fingers slipping under the hair at my nape and holding my head against his chest.

"Please don't drop me."

"I've got you."

A rush of cold air hits me, stealing my ability to reply, as we shoot into the sky.

This time I'm brave enough to turn my head and open my eyes to the world below. The lights of Havenwood Falls glow. It's a cheery, lit-up town in an otherwise dark canyon of mountains and trees. Mathews River shimmers from one end of town to the other, and beyond. Cars dot the streets, moving slowly from work to home, from homes to stores. From here, the moonlight turns the flecks of gold in

Stuart Fountain into glowing dancing fairies. The gazebo in town square is a beacon thanks to all the Christmas lights wrapped around it. My world is so small, so peaceful from this vantage point. Breckin's wing shifts into my sightline, and with a deep breath, I understand: my world is nothing like I thought.

~

WE CIRCLE THE TOWN TWICE—"TO assure we're not being followed," Breckin says tightly—before descending to a snow-covered deck. Breckin's house is a completely updated and remodeled historic Victorian located on the corner of Fairchild and Eleventh. Not exactly the most private spot for a family of angels. The fence around the yard is a stone wall and iron bars. Anyone who passes by can see us standing here. I would have expected them to live up in the woods on a private lot, or in Havenwood Heights. I've passed this street hundreds of times. How did I not know he lived here?

"You're not worried about people seeing you?"

Breckin shrugs as his wings disappear before my eyes, and he pulls his shirt from where it's tucked into the back of his pants and draws it over his head. "Humans don't see us like this."

"I see you," I counter, leaning this way and that for a glimpse of his back as his shirt covers his skin.

Amber eyes lock on mine. "I let you."

My argument dies, my breath catching at the cocky arch of his brow. I allow Breckin to lead me inside, his fingers warming mine. He pushes a hand through his hair, releasing deep sighs as we walk through the richly decorated—and unusually dark—house and down a set of stairs. He flips a switch, and we end up in what might as well be called an apartment in his basement. A living room, complete with a stone fireplace, a huge projection screen, and dark leather couches and chairs, fills the right side. An eat-in kitchen and bar fills the left. On the far end of the room is a second sitting area with two doors on the far wall. I make out the end of a bed through one and spot a sink—obviously a bathroom—through the other. Biting my nails for the sole purpose of ensuring my jaw hasn't dropped to my knees, I turn and gawk at the rest of the basement: built-ins, a full-sized pool table, an old-fashioned arcade game, and a bar-height table with chairs in the corner.

"I think this place is bigger than the apartment Mom and I live in."

"My house?" Breckin asks, leaving me standing at the bottom of the steps.

I laugh at the excess laid out before me. "No, your basement."

The fireplace flares to life with the flick of another switch, and Breckin straightens. "Sorry," he says uncomfortably.

My eyes wander the room. No Christmas tree, lights, presents, or stockings. The upstairs was dark and unfestive as well. Christmas is in two weeks. "Don't you celebrate the holidays?"

He's an angel—isn't Christmas a pretty big deal to them?

Breckin's mouth twists, his shoulder sort of popping up in a half shrug as he looks around. He seems indifferent. I should have kept my mouth shut.

"Sorry, that's not my business." I hug myself, and my teeth chatter as a shiver works from my toes to the top of my head.

Breckin grabs a throw. "You're freezing. Take off your shoes and jacket and come sit by the fire."

I wiggle my toes in my boots. They're ice, despite the thick wool socks I wear. The fire looks delectable, but I stand fixed at the base of the stairs—uncertain. Searching my bag, I pull out my phone as Breckin remains beside the fire, his face impassive.

"I won't hurt you."

My eyes lift from my cell.

"You're safe, Vivienne. He won't come here, and I won't hurt you," he repeats.

"I know." I sigh, like I'm surprised the words came from my lips.

Breckin shoves his hair back, his right eye narrowing thoughtfully.

"That sounds ridiculous, doesn't it? After tonight . . . I don't think I truly *know* anything, but . . ." I pause. My fear and hesitation aren't rooted in what he is, or isn't. We've lived in the same town and gone to the same school all our lives. He's got an ego, he causes trouble occasionally, but he's not a bad guy. And he isn't someone I've ever been afraid of. Still, my heart races as nerves dance in my stomach. I'm terrified of letting down my guard. Terrified of my thoughts, my feelings. *Feelings? Where did this come from?*

"I trust you. I'm just—" My shoulders lift when I can't articulate properly.

"Freaked out? Scared as hell? Considering a mental institution?" He says it with such calm—straight-faced, mouth drawn—I can't prevent laughter from bubbling up.

"Well, thank goodness." My fingers fumble with my jacket as my hesitance melts away. "It's nice to know I'm not the only one who thinks I'm crazy."

Breckin's poker face slips as I untangle my bag from around my neck and set it on the floor. I shrug out of my jacket, kick off my boots, and inhale deeply before daring to move forward.

He holds the throw blanket out as I near him and the plump chair he's angled toward the fire. "You're not crazy, Vivienne."

That's debatable. "First things first." Accepting the blanket, I sit and pull my knees to my chest, covering my legs and feet. "I should text Zara so she doesn't call my mom."

"Good idea. Are you hungry? Thirsty?" He crosses the room to the kitchen as I type out a vague text. My gaze flits from the keyboard to his back, unable to not look for evidence of the wings hiding in there somewhere. *Do they hide? Are they magic? Invisible?* "Ask whatever you want."

My head snaps up. Breckin's face reflects in a mirror running from floor to ceiling behind the wet bar. He watches me stare at him. My cheeks burn. Hitting send on my text, I drop the phone to my lap and drag the throw to my chin. The fire works its magic, the flames warming my frozen toes.

"I'm not sure what to ask," I admit, after a moment of watching him watch me.

He pulls two water bottles from a mini refrigerator, his mouth twisting. "You've been watching my backside—"

I choke. "Uh, watching your wings. Not your backside, thank you very much."

"Yes, my wings. That's what I meant, Vivie. I didn't know you had such a dirty mind."

I gape at his smug grin. His tease draws my ire at the same time his calling me Vivie draws goosebumps over my skin. "I do not have a dirty mind."

As if testing me, he twists the lid from his water and drinks half of it—a knowing smile on his perfect face when he's done. Darn my eyes for staring. I face the fire and bite the inside of my cheek.

Breckin sets a bottle of water on the table by my chair and takes a seat on the couch. I peer into the fire, watching the flames leap around the ceramic logs, the blue glow from the gas flickering at the base.

"I like real fires better," I say for no reason, other than to break the silence, my eyes not leaving the fireplace. "There's no snap, crackle, and pop to a gas fire. No faces in the burning logs."

"Faces in the logs?"

"Yeah? Don't you ever stare at the flames? At the way the embers and burnt logs burn into creatures?" My breath catches. Creatures, like demons and dragons—that's what I usually see in a fire. Scary fairytale type things I never considered real, like angels. Now I'm unsure.

"The one upstairs is real. I brought you down here because the lack of windows is safer."

I work up the nerve to face him, to ask my questions. "Safer from what?"

He's sitting on the edge of the couch, his forearms resting on his thighs. He flips his water bottle between his knees and regards me.

"You said you would tell me everything if I came with you. What happened yesterday? Why do I need to be in your basement? Why do I need safety?"

His head falls. "I'm sorry. It's my fault you're in this position."

"Why would this be your fault?"

Yesterday was a normal day. Zara dropped me off after school. I ate a snack with my mom, then changed to go for a run while she got ready for work. She dropped me at my usual trailhead at the base of

Mount Alexa, and I started jogging. For the past three years, I've followed this route—jogging for several miles. Yesterday something happened. Something different.

"You said I was attacked, that you heard me scream. But I have no memory of it. I have no physical injuries." I shake my head, challenging everything he told me.

"You have bruises," he says softly. "On your ribs."

"How would you—"

He sinks into the couch. "Because I took your clothes off, Vivienne. I carried you back to my house and undressed you and made sure you were okay before carrying you home."

My sports bra and running tights. Half my clothing was missing. My shoes were missing. My breathing accelerates, the possibilities filling my mind.

"You were covered in blood. I saw it from the air and . . . it's not the first time I've seen a wild animal attack while out flying, but . . . but I followed the trail. Something drew me down to earth yesterday. Something made me track you."

My fingernails dig into my palms as the blood drains from my face.

"Whatever it was ran off. All I saw was a flash of movement as I came through the trees and saw you lying there."

"No." My feet slip from the chair, dropping to the floor with a thud as I sit forward. "No, that's not right. Blood from where? I'm not injured. I'm fine." A tear slides down my face.

"I'm an angel."

He's no longer cocky and full of egotistical pride. He says those three words as if they're nothing—like reciting the day's weather or answering a simple question. My palm covers my mouth.

It *is* the answer.

He's an angel. He called the other a reaper. *A reaper.*

"You said I was dead. He said you stole me from him." Images flash through my mind. *The rip of claws at my side. The darkness hovering, the pain of a million suns consuming my body, the amber eyes—*

Breckin's eyes—filled with worry. My cheeks are hot with tears. "Breckin?"

"You were moments from death. He was here to take your soul. You were supposed to die." His pain-laced voice cuts me deeper than knowing the truth.

But I didn't die. My wounds were healed.

He nods, somehow knowing my thoughts and confirming what I know to be true. "I healed you. I brought you back."

PIECES

BRECKIN

"*A*ngels aren't supposed to interfere in Death's work." I slide to the far end of the couch, putting myself directly across from her. "I won't apologize for it. I couldn't let you die, Viv." Leaning forward, I pluck her hands from her lap.

She's in shock. Her shoulders slumped, her jaw slack, her hands limp in mine. Her eyes seem far away, staring past my face, but I tell her everything. I start at the beginning and explain exactly what I saw when I landed in the snow and found the reaper over her. What he said. How I responded. Finished, I lean closer, my head bobbing around until she meets my gaze.

"I won't let him take you, I swear." My fingers tighten their grasp.

Her face undergoes a kaleidoscope of emotions before she wets her lips and speaks. "On the mountain, earlier . . . he said something."

He said a few things. "Yes?"

"He said you were a son of an angel in love with a human." Her gaze slides left, as her cheeks color. "Is that true?" she asks, returning her ice-blue stare to mine.

"There isn't an easy answer to your question."

"Then the answer is no." She pulls her hands from mine and sits back.

I nearly growl. My hand clutches her blanket-covered knee,

because it's the closest thing in my reach, as I lean in, bringing my face inches from hers. "No. The answer isn't that simple."

Our eyes lock and hold in a battle of wills before I remove my hand and give her space. "We barely speak, Vivienne. Would you believe me if I said I was in love with you?"

Her hair dances around her face as she shakes her head. "Of course not."

"But you're angry?"

Her mouth opens, then closes, her head turning to the fire once again as she exhales deeply. If I knew what love was, if I knew how to decipher the emotions she's brought to life in the last twenty-four hours . . . the reaper might be right.

"My mother died giving birth to me, did you know that? My father wasn't around much. I had nannies."

Sadness clouds her eyes. "I remember the nannies."

Sure she does. Kids asked me all the time why I had a 'new mom' every few years. That's what happens when your nannies sleep with your angel father—they don't last long.

"He isn't the easiest, uh . . . person, for lack of a better word. Feelings are weakness. That's what I was raised to believe."

"What do you mean?"

How do I explain the supernatural world to someone who's never known it? "There's a hierarchy amongst angels. Good versus evil. The righteous versus the sinners."

She fidgets in the chair, pulling her legs up. "I know the Bible."

"Then you know angels aren't fat, happy toddlers painted on ceilings. We're warriors, fighters. My father isn't half blood, he's Divine. A Dominion." She works to understand, but her expressive face gives her away. She's lost. My titles and explanations make no sense. Why would they?

"He isn't good." I let my revelation sit for a moment. "And I'm not supposed to be good either."

Unexpectedly, she huffs a light laugh. "What in the world does that mean?"

"I tell you my father is a Dominion angel of sin and you laugh?"

She laughs louder, her fingers going to her lips. Does nothing unnerve her? She's extremely calm, considering she's learned about angels, reapers, and her own near-death experience tonight.

"No, you told me he wasn't good. That is a far cry from . . . what did you call him? A Dominion angel of sin?"

"They're pretty much the same thing. Just different levels of bad, I suppose."

Technicalities. I'm playing a game with words, and Vivienne knows it. Her face twists into the chastising grimace.

"Different levels of bad?" Her shoulders shake with laughter. Her brows knit together, and her smile falters as she inhales sharply. "Is that who the reaper meant, when he said they'd kill you? Was he talking about your father?"

And now she understands the hierarchy of angels. There isn't much loyalty.

"No. My father won't kill me." Not because he loves me as his son. He wants me for what's to come. Rubbing my forehead, I stretch my neck from side to side. "Honestly, I don't know what the reaper meant. I healed you. I interceded where I shouldn't have. There are those who would have a problem with that." *And those who would take issue with me telling her about us to begin with.*

"Are you in trouble?" Her forehead wrinkles as she chews at the edge of a fingernail. "What can they do to you?"

Her concern sparks something within me. The pressure in my chest returns, the talons digging in again. "Of all things, you're worried about me?" I'm astonished.

She snatches a strand of hair and wraps it around her finger. "You saved my life."

I reach for the hair, rubbing it between the pad of my thumb and index finger. "And I'd do it again. I'm not worried about the consequences. The reaper doesn't realize who I am. Who my father is."

Her hand covers mine, dragging it from her hair as she holds my gaze. "What about me?"

What is she asking?

"What happens to me in this whole situation?"

My cell phone buzzes, saving me from replying. I stand and fish it from my pants pocket. It's Elias. I hold a finger up to Vivienne and wander toward the kitchen.

"Hey." I refrain from saying his name to protect his identity. He's been a resident of this town as long as I have. He runs a business, eats, shops, and plays in the same places the rest of us do.

"What the hell did you do tonight? I'm hearing chatter. You know there are eyes everywhere in this town, Breckin."

Damn supernaturals. "The reaper I told you about, he's hanging around and making threats."

"Threatening you?" Elias' voice drips with anger.

"Me. And Vivienne."

Elias growls, and Vivienne's eyes go wide. He'd cause an avalanche if he were up in the mountains.

"Fine. I'll see what I can find out. We shouldn't have a reaper lurking around unless he's doing his job. I was told she saw you both. The Court won't like that. Erase her memory."

"I can't." I turn my back to Vivienne and lower my voice. "It doesn't work on her. I tried last night. Plus, I need her to know everything until I take care of this. I can't keep her safe if she doesn't know."

"It's not your job to keep some human girl safe. You've got bigger decisions to make, Breckin. Your father will be home soon. He'll expect your allegiance."

"I've got four months."

"Breckin," he warns.

"See what you can find out about the reaper and keep Father and the Court away. I'll protect her no matter what, but I could use your help. Please."

"Feeling a bit possessive, are you?"

I look at Vivienne in the mirror. "I'm feeling a whole lot possessive."

"Of course you are. You're an angel, and angels don't like others messing with what belongs to us."

"Thanks, man."

The call ends with Elias promising me a message as soon as he has information. Vivienne stands, and I turn with a shrug. "There's a lot I can't tell you. Things about Havenwood Falls you're not allowed to know."

"There are other angels here?" she asks as she walks across the living room. I nod. "You're protecting them from me?"

"Not exactly, but I suppose in a way, yes. The less you know the better."

"The reaper called you a half-breed like it was a dirty word. Why?"

"Angels weren't created to reproduce with humans. They should have been happy in Paradise, but they weren't. They wanted more. It was forbidden and caused dissent." I rub the back of my neck. "It's really an issue thousands of years in the making."

Her head bobs in understanding. I'd expected more questions.

"What are you feeling possessive over?" she asks, nodding toward my phone as her lips curve seductively. I doubt she knows she's doing it. She's always had this alluring innocence about her.

"I'm two parts of one whole. I'm human, but I'm also angel. My angel side has staked a claim."

She inches forward. "Staked a claim?" Her brow lifts. "On me?"

"It's what the reaper sensed. I don't control my angelic emotions as well as I should. I didn't mask my feelings yesterday, or tonight."

She stops an arm's length away and looks at the floor. "Why did you save me? Would you have stopped for anyone?"

No. I witnessed vampires kill a few months ago. I did nothing. Why was yesterday different? I don't have the answer, but I'd like one. I debate her questions too long. Vivienne clears her throat and crosses her arms.

"You just did, is that it? For no reason?" Her voice trembles. "I don't remember much, but it was quick. Something knocked me down, and there was indescribable pain. That's it. That's all I recall. I should have died. I should have died, but you saved me, and now here I am."

I cave, the human and the angel. Her emotions, her fear—it's too much for me. Snatching her by the waist, I pull her into my arms. "It wasn't for no reason. There's something about you. I should have flown right on by, but something hooked me." My nose burns with the memory. The smell was foreign. "The scent of your blood, something . . . it called to me. I didn't have a choice."

I shake my head, frustrated at having so many questions, and so few answers. Vivienne grimaces. "Is there something wrong with my blood?"

The answer to that would open a whole new can of worms. One issue at a time.

"There's nothing wrong with you or your blood. I'm sorry. I know this is a lot to take in. Trust me, I'm afraid I killed you by saving your life. I thought I could erase your memory, and everything would go back to normal. I didn't expect a psycho reaper or these feelings."

Her eyes light up. "I thought feelings were a weakness?"

"As a human, they are. They make you soft. As an angel, though . . . the angel is smarter than the human. He's enamored with you. I can't do anything about that, and I will protect what's mine, Vivie."

She leans into me, her hands settling on my hips. "So you *are* staking a claim."

"How does that make you feel?"

She glances down, before raising her eyes to mine. "I like it when you call me Vivie."

Her body against mine ignites desire, and I curl my fingers into her sweater as my wings beg for release. "Do you?"

She nods with a smirk. My head lowers; my lips find hers, brushing a quick kiss before drawing back.

Vivienne's hands slip up my chest, wrapping around my neck and tugging me back. Her lips toy with mine, pressing small kisses back and forth over and over but never drawing me in. My pulse accelerates, and fire ignites in my veins, spreading quickly. Vivienne yelps as I pick her up and plop her on the kitchen counter behind us.

She leans back when I move to kiss her again. "Angel strength?"

"That, and you're five foot nothing." I wink and move between her knees, happy she's somewhat level with me.

"We can't all be perfectly built angels."

I'm perfectly built? I study her. The delicate, heart-shaped face, her pouting lips, her silky hair, the graceful ballerina limbs on her petite frame. Anyone with a sinister mind could snap her in two without breaking a sweat. I brush my knuckles across her cheek, my fingers sliding into her hair and moving it from her face. "Everything about you is perfect. Too perfect for me."

We meet halfway. Her mouth opens, allowing me a small taste. I mold my lips to hers, and her socked feet hook around my thighs, drawing me closer.

"What is happening between us, Breck?" she asks as her fingers lose themselves in my hair. "What is this?"

There's so much confusion written on her face. I feel it, too.

"I don't know."

It's the most honest thing I can say. A switch flipped last night when I healed her. No, before I healed her. Things changed when I heard her scream. I know plenty of shifters. I'm aware of how they find mates. Angels don't have mates, we don't imprint, but I swear to the maker, this girl imprinted on me. On all of me—the divine side, as well as my soul.

DEMONS AT THE DOOR

VIVIENNE

I toss and flip to my stomach, hiding my head beneath a pillow as thumping bass rattles my headboard. Why do the neighbors insist on blaring their music on the weekends?

Three raps at my door wake me further. "What?" I whine, my feet flailing like a kid having a temper tantrum.

"Hey, sleepyhead, you getting up?" Mom pops her head in.

"Sleepyhead?" I roll to my back, and my eyes focus on Mom's jeans and sweater. "What time is it?" She typically sleeps until after lunch when she works nights. Why is she up this early? Even her blond hair is fixed in a no-fuss braid, instead of her usual work ponytail.

"It's after noon. I thought we could go to lunch and do a little shopping today."

After noon? I push up from the bed, and a wave of nausea hits me.

"I can't believe you're still sleeping. You're usually the one waking me on Sundays. Did you and Zara stay out all night partying?" She steps farther into the room, no real accusation in her words. She knows us better than that, but . . . I clutch my stomach.

"Viv?" She's across the room and pushing back my hair, the back of her hand on my forehead before I can blink. "Are you not feeling well?" She turns my face to hers. "You're pale, but not feverish. You look tired."

"I must have picked up a bug at school. I'm okay, just a little green."

She leans in, her light eyes searching. "Well, shoot. We need to Christmas shop."

"You go then. I can take care of myself." Fear settles around me. I pull a pillow to my chest.

"I'll shop tomorrow. How about I make my famous grilled cheeses and we find a good movie to watch?" She pats my knee as I nod. "I'll start lunch."

She crosses my room, grabbing a dirty cup from my dresser before turning. "You must have been tired to fall asleep in your clothes. You haven't done that since you were six," she says with a smile, pulling the door closed behind her.

My head spins, and I grab my hair to keep it in place. *My clothes?* I'm wearing jeans and a sweater. I bolt for my bathroom and lose the meager contents of my stomach.

We spend the afternoon watching movies on the couch. This is a normal Sunday for us, but everything feels wrong. I check my phone, re-reading the text I sent Zara last night:

Decided against going to the clinic. Went home instead, feeling okay but tired. Enjoy movie night and I'll see you Monday.

I recall the Burger Bar. I have a vague memory of snow and being cold. A flash of fire—and nothing else. No memory of texting Zara. No memory of coming home. Mom laughs at a scene in our third romantic comedy, and I tuck my legs closer. My chest is empty, like something is missing. I close my eyes as they burn with tears. Whether from my raging headache or because of the gaping hole, I can't be sure. *What is going on with me?*

～

BY THE TIME Zara arrives outside my apartment building Monday morning, I've run through every scenario imaginable. Maybe someone slipped drugs into my food Saturday night? Maybe I'm crazy. Maybe

I've been sucked into some alternate universe, like in the last book I read.

"Your carriage, my lady," Zara shouts through the open passenger side window as I lock the apartment and hurry to the car.

I toss my backpack over the seat and jump in. "You're letting all the heat out."

"Feeling better?" she asks as I buckle my seatbelt and get situated.

I consider confiding in her, then swiftly change my mind. *What would I say?* I keep seeing her standing beside me outside my apartment window, calling me paranoid. *When was that?* It must be recent, and yet I can't recall. *Nope. I can't tell her.*

"All better." I switch the air vents to warm my gloved hands and change the subject. "Tell me about the movies."

Zara gasps as she shifts into drive. "Girl. I finally confirmed it with my own two eyes. Graysin Ravenal and Everett Weston are dating."

"I thought we'd already confirmed that."

"It was rumor. Now we can mark it down as fact. They are so freaking gorgeous together. I kind of hate her. I want an Everett of my own."

"Z, he's gotta be pushing thirty."

"Twenty-eight," she corrects. "I think I need an older man. I'm sick of the boys we have to pick from at school. They're ridiculous. Saturday night—" I bend over, re-tying the laces on my boots as Zara complains. "—then a bunch of the guys from the football team started shoving each other and screwing around. I swear, they act like wild animals. How they get dates is beyond me."

"They're all tall, dark, and gorgeous." Tossing my hair, I sit up and look out the front windshield.

Zara sighs. "Ain't that the truth."

I should remind her how she sat on the knee of one of those football players, flirting wildly during lunch Friday. My mouth opens to do just that when a dark figure captures my attention. We're stopped at the light at Eighth and Main, and he's leaning against the side of Pyntz Butcher Shoppe looking like sin—all pale skin, jet black hair, and dark clothing.

"Z, do you see him?" I grab Zara's forearm, my gaze fixated on the guy. "Across the street."

"Who? Mr. Emo?" The light changes, and we pull forward. "Isn't that the guy from Saturday?" She squints as we turn onto Main with the traffic and pass a sidewalk width from him.

From Saturday? Vibrant blue eyes flash, and my stomach drops. Too afraid to turn in my seat, I check the side mirror. Sweat peppers my forehead as he watches us drive away. My body goes cold.

"He's creepy." I force my eyes to stop looking.

Zara pshaws. "Creepy? I thought you two were going to need a room after the way you stared each other down the other night. Then he disappeared and you left—" Zara inhales sharply, slapping her palm against the steering wheel. "You liar! You didn't get sick, did you? You left with him."

"What? No. Are you kidding? I don't even know him." I twist, looking for the stranger over my shoulder. It's cold and not yet eight in the morning, making him easy to spot on the mostly vacant sidewalk.

"Well, he must be stalking you then, because that's the guy from the other night. You should totally talk to him next time you see him. He's hot." Zara's finger jabs my side as I watch the object of our conversation.

He walks quickly—too quickly. I do a double-take, surprised at how close he is. He removes his hand from the pocket of his long black coat, and my head fills with visions of him pulling a gun and shooting, like some gangster. Instead he lifts his hand to chest level and moves it from left to right. Strange, but nothing like a shootout.

Chiding my ridiculous imagination, I turn back to the front. "Z, I think I'm—"

"Watch out!" Zara screams. Her hands grip the steering wheel as the car jerks and skids along the ice-painted road.

Car horns blare, my seatbelt locks across my chest, and someone shouts, as a city tour bus stops, sideways, five feet from my door.

"You girls okay?" a voice asks, followed by tapping on the window. Words fail me. My body shakes. Zara's curses fill the car, as do her thanks. "Vivienne? Zara?"

At the sound of my name, I look up and find Mr. Zander from school jiggling the handle to my door, his face concerned. My hand reaches forward and unlocks the car door, pushing as he pulls it open.

We're an hour late for school by the time Sheriff Kasun finishes with us. No one was hurt, nothing damaged.

"I swear, Viv. Our light was green. The bus driver wasn't paying attention." Zara yanks the school door open, the heat welcoming after standing outside.

"We're fine. I'm not mad." I check my watch. "Let's hurry and get excuse slips. The bell's about to ring."

"You're not mad, but I am. He could have killed you," she says, her face still devoid of color as we walk toward the administration office. "How are you so calm? That bus barreling toward us won't stop flashing through my mind. That's my second near miss this semester! I'll have nightmares for weeks, and you probably want to stop riding with me."

I stop walking and push her to the edge of the hallway. "Look at me." She does, and her eyes glisten with unshed tears. "That thing with Willa was all on her. Not your fault. Neither was this. We're both safe. We're safe, Z," I repeat, hugging her as the class bell sounds. "Come on."

We secure tardy slips from the office and head separate ways. I duck my head and attempt maneuvering the crowded halls of Havenwood Falls High without being stopped. A few students drove around our near-wreck this morning, their faces gawking like typical rubberneckers, which meant the whole school was aware before first period. Not in the mood for discussion, I slip into chemistry instead of hanging in the hall as I normally would. Three other students are already in their seats as I walk down my aisle.

Electricity shocks my wrist, and I gasp, twisting to find my arm in Breckin Roberts' grip. My pulse accelerates.

"Sorry." Breckin removes his hand, balling his fingers into a fist as he leans back and looks up at me. I stare as undecipherable whispers nag at the back of my mind. "Rumor has it you and Zara Shannon almost collided with a bus this morning. You okay?"

There's an edge to his voice as his eyes search me from head to toe like he's checking for injuries.

"I'm fine, thanks." I drop my backpack to the floor and lower into my chair. *What was that?* Breckin and I have barely spoken since elementary school. He defended me from a few jerks in town freshman year, but other than that . . . The sensation of being watched crawls up my spine. The knowledge that Breckin's eyes are fastened on my back sends me scooching down until my neck presses against the back of the chair and my butt hangs over the seat edge. *Thank goodness I'm short.*

I close my eyes and replay everything from this morning. Those blue eyes penetrate the thick layers of fog surrounding my mind. *I know him. I do, but how?*

More students walk into class, their laughter and conversations making me an outsider. A few people say hi. I offer vague smiles as the seats around me fill up.

"Hey, Viv. I saw Zara in the hallway. You two must have had a guardian angel watching over you this morning, huh?" Zal Purser asks as she tugs on the turquoise beads around her neck.

I half fall out of my desk, my heart rate accelerating as I lurch into a sitting position. "What did you say?" I ask, my voice unfamiliar to my own ears.

"I said you must have a guardian angel looking out for you."

Angel. My head whips toward Breckin. He's watching, his amber eyes narrow, his jaw tight. *Guardian angel. Blue eyes. Angel, angel, angel . . .*

Dark spots fill my vision. I sway in my seat, grasping at the edge of my desk, when a hard body presses against my shoulder and arms wrap around me.

Heat blows around my cheek. "Vivie?"

Vivie. The lock unlatches, and memories rush in. The animal attack, the reaper, the bathroom at Burger Bar, Breckin's kisses. I suck shallow breaths, recalling the danger, the warnings. The way the reaper waved a hand this morning and how a bus almost killed me.

"Breck!" I turn into his chest and grab his shirt. "It was him. The bus, this morning . . . I know it was."

Then I see his hands at my waist as he lifts me onto a counter at his house and his smile as his lips descend on mine. My gasp is audible. *Saturday night. He erased my memory?*

Someone calls our teacher as Breckin rubs my arms and helps me stand, supporting most of my weight.

"Vivienne?" Heels click against the floor as she nears.

"I'll take her to the office. She's still freaked out about this morning," Breckin offers, his voice take-charge and firm.

Breckin grabs my bag and escorts me from class. My eyes focus straight ahead, ignoring the curious glances, especially from friends. They're probably wondering when Breckin Roberts and I became close enough for me to cling to him as though my life depends on it.

The hall is empty, the bell having already rung, but neither of us speaks as he ushers me down the corridor and around a corner, where he opens a door and pulls me inside. We're in a janitor's closet, the scent of bleach and bathroom soap overwhelming.

His back to me, he rubs his neck with an exhale as he leans forward and rests his forehead against the door. His hunter green thermal clings to his shoulders and back, and I stare, searching for the wings I now remember. He twists around, remaining against the door, his mouth tight as he shoves his hands into his pockets.

"Why?"

"Are you okay?"

I snort at his insane question. "Am I okay? Where should I start?" Breckin's mouth opens, and I forge ahead. "We kissed. I thought it meant something, but you erased my memory—"

"Vivie?"

I look past the tenderness in his eyes and continue. "I mean, I suppose that's no different than not getting a call back after a date, right? If you were human, I guess that's what this would be—a one-time, never speak to me again hookup. One could argue you were doing me a favor. Taking away my memories is nicer than letting me linger over what happened."

"That's not what happened." Anger flashes across his face as he steps away from the door.

I move, kicking a mop bucket of dirty water. "No? How often do you do this anyway? No wonder I've never heard tales of you with girls. Do you erase every idiot's mind once you have a taste?"

His snarl, purely angelic, scares the hair straight up on my neck. "Vivienne." He grabs my arms, and my back bumps into the shelves stocked with toilet paper and paper towels. Two rolls fall to the floor as Breckin presses close. "You are *not* an idiot, and I didn't erase your memories. Didn't you hear me Saturday night when I told you I was staking my claim? Yesterday was hell for me. And this morning—" His hands move to my face, holding me tight as his forehead touches mine. "When I heard about the accident, it took all my strength to stay away. I figured it would seem odd if I showed up."

My hurt evaporates with his words. I grip his wrists. "I'm not supposed to remember you, am I?"

"You're not." Although his voice is serious, his lips tug into a smile.

"Who erased my memory, Breck?"

His mouth opens, then closes as he chooses his words. "Another angel."

"The one you spoke to the other night?" He nods. "Why?"

"Because if we're not careful, this will become about more than a reaper."

MY IMMORTAL

BRECKIN

*U*ncertainty clouds Vivienne's eyes as my words sink in. This is insane. I'm torn by the return of her memories. I want to take her mouth right here in this closet and drink her in until kissing her erases the fear that buried me this morning when I heard about the accident. At the same time, I want to rage at my angelic abilities until I figure out why they don't work on her. Why does she remember?

Her exhale teases across my face as her hands wrap around my waist. "I don't want to forget, Breck."

The panic in her blue eyes infuriates my protective side. My hand slips around her neck and tucks her head under my chin. "We're trying to keep you safe."

"From the reaper?"

"Among other things," I say vaguely. "And his name is Sebastian, by the way."

She pulls back. "He has a name? How do you know it?"

Might as well tell her what I know, but not here. Not now. I brush her hair back with a smile. "I'd rather not have this conversation in a janitor's closet at school."

"After school, then? Will you tell me everything?"

Everything I can, I say in my head as I nod.

~

THE DAY DRAGS, and not seeing Vivienne after we part doesn't help. Her messages do, though. She texts me little tidbits about each of her classes, which keeps my brain from exploding with worry until, at last, the day ends.

She blew off my request to meet at her locker, saying she knew where I parked. It bruised my ego, her not wanting me to wait for her. So here I am, leaning against my Bronco and waiting, somewhat impatiently, for her to come to me. The moment her voice cuts across the noise and reaches me, my muscles relax. Cars, music, and hundreds of students crowd out of the building, yet her voice stands out among them all. My soul breathes a sigh of relief. She's surrounded by friends, a warm interested smile on her face as she listens to Macy Blackstone talk about her weekend. Macy's a witch hunter. How would Vivienne react if she knew? What would she think if she knew about the shifters, vampires, and mages who control much of this town? There's so much she doesn't know, so much I can't tell her.

Macy leaves with a wave, and Vivienne scans the lot. A spark ignites within, like the flick of a match, when her blue eyes find me. This girl consumes me. My soul tugs like it would rip itself from my body to reach her side.

My soul?

Vivienne toys with a strand of hair, twirling it as she smiles and nods at her friends, while her eyes remain locked on mine. I straighten and move around the hood. I need her to come over here. Now.

At my movement, she steps down from the curb. "I better go," she says over her shoulder.

"You're not riding home with Zara?" asks Scarlet.

Vivienne hesitates, her steps slowing as mine quicken. Spinning her back to me, she answers, "No. I'm . . . um, I've got another ride today."

I catch the confused look on their faces. Vivienne rides with Zara every day. We don't have to be friends for me to know this. It's a small school, a small town. Everyone knows. The same way everyone knows

Zara drops her off, then heads to Napoli's, where she does her homework, eats, then works the dinner shift until ten.

Gazes shift between Vivienne and me. "With who?"

"Me," I answer for her.

Vivienne twirls, finding me standing in front of her. I don't watch her friends, but I imagine their faces are about as stunned as Vivienne's.

"Hey," she says breathlessly, her lips curving into a deliciously shy smile.

"Hey, yourself." I draw her backpack from her shoulder and swing it onto mine. "You ready?"

Her face flushes as I slip her hand into mine.

"They're staring, aren't they?" Vivienne asks when I look back.

"They're not the only ones." Half the departing students track us by the time I open the passenger door.

Vivienne's hand goes to her hair, twirling again as she tugs the other from my grip. "Great. What are we going to tell people?"

I toy with the zipper on her jacket, my need to be close growing by the second. "Tell them we're going out."

Vivienne's head falls back, her shout of laughter taking me by surprise. Inside, my soul growls, ordering my hand to take hers again. It's damn needy today.

She makes a face. "Like they'll believe that."

She's right, though not because people wouldn't believe I'm attracted to her. She's beyond beautiful. She has plenty of admirers, but I've never been on that list. I've never been one to single out any girl. I go to parties, hang out, and flirt, but holding hands and making a public declaration? I've never done that.

My fingers curl around her wrist, pulling her hand from her hair and using it to draw her closer. Her lips part, and I take advantage, capturing them in a quick kiss.

"Now they will," I say as I pull away. I look around. Sure enough, we've made a scene.

"No," Vivienne whispers as her fingers take my chin and bring my attention back. She slides her hand down around my neck, applying pressure and drawing me to her mouth. "Let's be sure they get the picture."

Her words awaken the need I have for her. Her scent—the deeper underlying scent of her soul—fills my head, and I'm drunk on her. She tempts my human soul and fires up the angel within. She wants me as much as I want her. Whatever this is between us, it is not one-sided. We're so connected, I meet her lips move for move. She shifts right; I shift left. She sucks my bottom lip; I tighten my grip and bite hers. We're lost in each other, in the middle of the school parking lot.

"I think that'll do it." I chuckle at the gawkers pointing and whispering, when we manage to separate. Vivienne releases a giggle in her throat and heaven help me, my desire builds again. Swallowing hard, I move from the open car door. "Let's go to my house."

With an apologetic grin on her face, she waves to her friends as I close her door. Once I'm in the vehicle and buckled, I turn in my seat. "I'm sorry if that was out of line."

Vivienne's face scrunches. "Kissing me?"

"Yeah. In front of your friends and all. I couldn't help myself."

She bites her lip, her eyes flicking to her lap. "I know the feeling. The moment I spotted you, I had this ridiculous desire to run across the parking lot. Is there something about your angelic heritage that lures women in?"

My hand slides across the seat and finds hers. "Have I lured you in?"

"That would be crazy, right? I can't be falling for you, Breck, I know nothing about you."

"You *know* the most important thing about me," I counter, interlacing our fingers.

She scowls, although it's ruined by the smirk that follows immediately after. "I meant, the things couples share when they're falling in love. Your favorite foods, movies, music. The normal things."

It's my turn to scowl. I shake free from her hand and start the car. "Right. 'Cause being part angel is definitely not normal."

Shifting into gear, I grip the steering wheel as an odd mix of emotions flows through me. *She isn't rejecting me. She kissed the hell out of me two minutes ago, for everyone to see. So why am I let down by her comments on love? Why the hell am I acting like a girl? Get your crap together, Breckin.*

"No," she says after a long moment of silence. "Being angel is not normal, but neither is falling for one."

"But, you just said—"

"I'm falling for you, Breck. It's not reasonable, and it makes no sense, but I know it like I know my own name. I know it here." She taps her chest.

Her soul.

With my foot firmly on the brake, I lean across the cab and kiss her hard. "Vivie," I say against her lips, my hand gripping the back of her head. "I feel it, too."

Her hand touches my cheek as she pulls away. "That's why the reaper wants me, isn't it?"

I still.

"He sensed your feelings, he said he would take my soul away from you, he told me not to let you taint it."

She's right.

Our bond is through our souls. *Soul mates.* It makes perfect sense.

And it's exactly the type of thing that would drive a reaper crazy with power.

I hold her gaze. "It doesn't matter what he wants. He's not getting it."

"You sound so confident."

"I'm an angel, Vivie." She cracks a smile. It's small, but it's there, and it lights up the dark corners of my being, and breathes life into me. She's changing me with every look, touch, and smile. I'm hers. "Tell me about this morning."

My hand holds hers all the way home as she explains what happened with Zara and the reaper, Sebastian.

"And you're sure it was him? You said you had no memories before you saw me in chemistry." I turn onto Fairchild and pull directly into our drive, waiting as the garage door opens.

"I'm certain. When I saw him, I had this immediate reaction. I didn't have to know why I knew him, there was just something off. Something that made me wary. And after—" She doesn't finish. She shakes, like she's working a shiver through her body.

We pull into the garage, and I cut the engine. I pump her hand in mine as she reaches for the door. "Wait. Stay there."

Hurrying around the Bronco, I make sure the garage door closes all the way before opening her door and extending my hand.

"You're a gentleman? Who knew?" She teases as she jumps down from the jacked-up seat with an "umph."

"I'll find you a stool."

Her fist connects with my abs, then flattens, rubbing where the punch landed when I grunt. "Oh, sorry. I didn't mean to hit you so hard."

"Aw, you're cute, tiny girl. You think your little baby punch hurt me?"

Her palms slap at my stomach, pushing, as she walks around me. "You know there is such a thing as being too cocky."

"Not for an angel." I wrap her in a bear hug from behind, inhaling her scent. *Intoxicating.* She melts into me, her back molding with my chest until we're one.

She sighs and hooks her hands around my forearms. "I'm scared."

"I know you are." As if I can infuse her with my courage, I squeeze tighter. "I won't let anything happen to you. He can't kill you, it's against the rules." Then again, he isn't playing by the rules anymore.

She turns, her eyes skeptical. "What about today?"

"He wanted to scare you. Or me. Sebastian is playing a dangerous game." *One that will end with him ceasing to exist if he threatens Vivienne again.*

"This is too much. I don't think I can deal with this. Maybe I don't want my memories, maybe I—"

"It's too late." I clasp her to my chest. "Memories or not, he knows who you are and *what* you are to me. He's not going to stop."

"So what do we do?"

Hunt Sebastian down and end him. Vivienne's fear prevents me from saying the words. "We go inside. We take an hour to eat and think about anything other than Sebastian. Then, we call my uncle."

I head for the door, but her hand yanks me back when she doesn't follow. "Breck?" Her fingers tighten around my hand. "What am I to you?"

My eyes scan the frailty of her. This delicately beautiful slip of a girl who claimed my soul and is taking possession of my heart.

"My soul mate."

SOMEONE TO YOU

VIVIENNE

"**Y**ou have an uncle?"

I follow Breckin into the house, and this time we stay on the main floor. He points to the stools sitting at the kitchen counter, telling me to have a seat as he raids the refrigerator. *Seriously?* He throws words like soul mate around, then drags me into his million-dollar kitchen and offers me a snack? *How did this become my life?*

Soul mate. My mind refuses to process his words. I'm numb.

"Sort of. We're not related, but he's the closest thing I have to family."

"Is he the one who erased my memories Saturday night?"

A jar of nacho cheese slides across the pristine marble counter as he shuts the refrigerator. "Yeah." He moves to a pantry the size of my bedroom and grabs a bag of chips.

"And what does he think of all this?" I prod, when he doesn't elaborate.

"Chip?" He pops the lid from the jar, dipping a blue corn chip into the sauce.

"Breck?"

"Vivie?" His brow arches. I force back a reply at his flippant tone.

"What does your uncle think of this?" I wave a hand between us.

"You can ask him when he arrives." He stretches across the counter and holds a chip out. "Eat."

"Did you just order me to eat?" I bristle, taking the chip without thought.

"Order is a strong word." He dips another. "I asked."

I cross my legs and square my shoulders, taking a breath. "You most certainly did not ask."

The corner of his mouth tugs up. "Are you mad at me for trying to make you eat something?"

The chip he handed me drops to the counter, the glob of fake cheese smearing yellow across the gorgeous white. "I'm mad at you for ignoring my questions and yes, for trying to make me eat."

"You're not hungry?"

"Oh my gosh. That is not the point, Breckin."

My flustered outburst is met with a flirtatious grin. It takes all my willpower to remain across the four-foot kitchen island from him. *This boy makes me crazy.*

Exasperated, I lean back. "Do you always get what you want?"

"Yes." There's no shame in his answer. I clamp my jaw.

My weak soul dances at his cockiness as my independent mind theorizes ways to knock him off his high horse. As though he knows exactly what I'm thinking, he smiles and tilts his head, his amber-flecked eyes pinning me to my seat. His intense gaze sends heat creeping up my neck. I wipe my palms on my thighs as Breckin's entire face transforms. A tight mask of concentration takes over as he straightens his back and breathes with precision—his chest rising and falling slowly.

Something teases across my mind, and I jerk back, gasping for air.

Breckin blinks, his face relaxing as a small scowl appears.

I grip the counter and watch him closely as the feeling withdraws. "What did you just do?"

His scowl deepens.

"What did you do, Breckin?" My stool clatters back as I stand. Fists form at my sides.

Breckin wipes at his forehead with a curse. "I'm sorry."

He hurries around the counter, and I step back, unnerved by his actions. His face falls.

"Vivie?" Breckin lifts his hands in a silent plea for forgiveness. "I'm sorry. I shouldn't have. I was trying to use compulsion. I never—"

"Compulsion? To make me eat?" I spit the words at him.

"You argued with me."

That's his excuse? "I'm sorry? I argued with you?"

"No, that's not what I meant. I mean, it is, but—" He scratches his head. "I wanted you to eat. You were arguing, and it made me wonder if I could—"

"Oh. My." Swallowing, I groan and walk away, needing space. Halfway across the kitchen, I turn back. "You arrogant angel. You think you can order me to eat and sit and stay. That I won't ask questions? Do you want me to blush and giggle while following you around like the other girls do?"

Breckin's shoulders shake as his lips quirk.

"Are you *laughing* at me?" I ask, the urge to punch him strong.

His face goes blank.

"Don't ever try it again, Breckin," I order, nearly stomping my foot.

"I won't. I promise. I would never try to control you, Vivie. I was curious if it were possible. Since erasing your mind didn't work."

"I mean it, never again. It's horrible. Like spiders crawling around in my mind. Sebastian did it, too. I hate it."

Breckin stiffens. "Sebastian was in your head? When?"

His tone kills my anger. "Saturday night. I don't know if he was *in* my head, but it felt the same."

He pulls his cell from his pocket, holding up a finger when I ask what he's doing. Tugging on my sleeves, I fold my arms across my chest and wait.

"We need you." His eyes stay on mine as he nods. "Nope. She remembers everything." There's a pause as he listens to the person on the other end of the line. "Okay. Yeah." After a few vague, one-word answers, the call ends, and he sets his cell on the counter. "Can you stay for dinner?"

"If I say no, will you try to force me?"

He blows out his cheeks. "No, Viv. I'll never try to compel you again."

"Damn straight you won't." Breckin cracks a smile. "Of course I'll stay. He's coming?"

"He is, in about two hours."

My pulse kicks up a notch, my nerves fluttering to life. Breckin pushes the stool I kicked back to the counter and comes toward me. His hand touches the bottom edge of my sweater, tugging it. I take a step toward him as he takes another toward me.

"I'm truly sorry." His hand brushes my cheek as it wraps around my head. "I know this is a horrible excuse, but . . . everything feels different with you. It's new territory. My curiosity got the best of me."

I hook a finger through his belt loop and pull us closer still.

"Different how?" My voice is husky and broken. My soul, or whatever it is within me that seems to want him, flutters.

"I've compelled humans before, to forget what they saw, or to get what I want." I frown, and he grimaces. "It's easy with them. A touch or a look and a thought, and they do what I need. You don't work that way. My abilities don't work on you at all. It's . . ."

"Freaking you out? Scaring you? Making you consider a mental institution?" I repeat his own words.

"Frustrating as hell," he says with a short laugh. "And all of those other things. Hopefully, Elias will have answers."

"Elias?" There's one Elias in town that I know of. Elias Jamison, the owner of Havenwood Falls Ski-Ventures. Besides transporting thrill seekers up the mountains on ski runs, he does life-flights for the clinic. Mom has spoken of him a few times, but I rarely see him around town. *He's an angel?*

"I can tell by your face you're making the connection, and I'm sure you have questions, but I have a favor to ask." *Questions? Only about a million of them. Elias Jamison is an angel.* I've never felt anything strange around him. I've never . . . unless my memories have been wiped before.

184

"Vivie." Breckin's finger tilts my chin. "You're thinking way too hard."

Counting to three, I inhale and release a deep breath. Breckin grins.

"Can we just chill for a bit? Have a snack and talk until he gets here? About normal things?" Breckin asks, with hope in his voice.

"About normal things?"

"Yeah. Like your favorite food, movies, and music. You know, the stuff people learn when they're falling in love with each other."

I stretch up on my toes. "I think I heard that somewhere before."

Even at my tallest, my lips are nowhere near his. He presses a kiss to my forehead, understanding my hint. Well, somewhat understanding, since I wanted his lips on mine. Mildly placated, I drop to the flats of my feet. I must frown, because Breckin chuckles and hauls me into his body, his arms solid against my back as he lowers his head.

"I know your soul. I want to know the rest of you, Vivie. I want to know everything."

The anticipation sends giddy sparks through my body. "Everything? That might take a while."

Two inches from my lips, he pauses. "Then let's start with the important things."

I wet my lips. My body is a firecracker waiting for the fuse to reach the explosives. Everything tenses as a smile forms. "Easy. I'm wildly attracted, and attached, to an angel."

A deep growl fills his chest, rumbling through his entire body as his eyes darken and arms tighten.

"Would you kiss me already?" I half ask, half order.

The explosives ignite.

We've moved to the basement, Breckin preferring the safety of being underground to the open windows of the main floor, when Elias arrives.

"He brought pizza." Breckin smiles, giving my leg a tender squeeze before leaving me on the couch and moving to the kitchen. I rest my arms on the back of the couch, my gaze following him. "Enhanced smell," he says at my dubious stare.

Enhanced smell, senses, vision, and hearing. He's my own superhero. I track the noises above. It's obvious from the way Elias parked in the garage and entered the house on his own that he is considered family. When his heavy steps hit the wood of the staircase, I stand and straighten my hair and sweater.

Breckin sends me a wink, I take a breath, the stairs creak, and then Elias appears.

Elias Jamison is what most would picture when thinking about a Colorado mountain man. He's stout and burly. Half a foot shorter than Breckin's six-two, he's got the shape of a bodybuilder and the dark, wiry beard of an outdoorsman. He plops the boxes in his hand onto the counter and turns my way.

"Vivienne," he says, with the type of gravelly voice rock stars envy. His bright blue eyes look me up and down.

I open my mouth, but did words come out? I try again. "I don't remember you from Saturday. You were here, right? You erased my memory." It's not hello, but the questions have built up.

His full mouth cracks a smile. "Breckin told me you were a curious one."

My gaze shifts to Breckin, who lifts his brows as if daring me to deny it.

"Well, you know. It's not every day a girl comes under attack from reapers and falls for an angel." I attempt a nonchalant shrug, but Elias's black look freezes the humor on my lips.

"Falls for?" He glares at Breckin.

Oh. Oh, crap. I should have kept that to myself. It popped out, my lovesick heart and soul not seeing anything wrong with how I feel. Sebastian's warning hits me. *A son of angels in love with a human? They will kill you once they find out.*

"It's not his fault." I hurry to the end of the counter, putting myself between them. "We're not in love or anything. He's—"

"Viv." Breckin grabs my shoulder and pulls me into his side. "It's fine. He wouldn't hurt me. Or you."

Elias's gaze volleys between us, his face thoughtful. After a moment of tense silence, he wipes a hand across his face and through his hair, lifting his baseball cap, then replacing it before he finally releases a long exhale.

"Soul mates."

Hearing the word from Elias's mouth is confirmation. Breckin squeezes my shoulder.

"How do you know?" I ask, when neither of them speak.

"His pull toward you Friday night. The fact that neither of us could erase him from your memories. The look in his face. And yours." Elias huffs a light laugh. "I've seen many teenage girls wear the same head-over-heels-in-love look, Vivienne. I've never seen it on Breckin."

I have a head-over-heels-in-love look on my face? My cheeks warm. *He does?* I can't help but glance up at Breckin.

"You're right," Breckin says, smiling down at me. "She's totally falling head over heels in love with me."

I punch him.

KNOCKING ON HEAVEN'S DOOR

BRECKIN

*W*e sit around the fire, our pizza—from Napoli's, Viv's favorite—on the coffee table before us, and take turns filling Elias in on every detail of the past seventy-two hours. Vivienne describes her feelings in such detail, I find myself taking her hand in mine on more than one occasion. The fear she felt when she woke Friday night after I left her. The not knowing what happened but feeling so off.

"It made me feel sick, Elias. Whatever it is you did when you wiped my mind. Don't do it again," Vivienne says, chiding him like a parent.

"That would be the soul mate connection." Vivienne's brow lifts, and Elias clarifies. "It is extremely powerful. Most consider it a gift given by the maker to fulfill the order of things."

Vivienne's eyes grow as they flit between us, her mouth gaping.

"In human terms, it means we were matched to fulfill our destiny," I provide helpfully.

Or not so helpfully, judging by the way her stunned face swings my way.

"Destiny?"

"C'mon, Viv. Don't tell me you don't believe in destiny? That people are put in places to make things happen, or sometimes bad things happen to good people because they need to learn a lesson that will bring them to something better?"

"I think you've been scrolling the internet for motivational memes," Vivienne says. Elias clears his throat, cutting off a low chuckle. She shrugs at him before returning her attention to me. "I don't know what I believe in. Maybe things happen for a reason. Maybe it's coincidence."

I face her on the couch and take her hands. "We're not a coincidence, Vivie."

Elias' face sobers as he sits forward and speaks. "A soul mate is forever, Vivienne. No one can take him from you or you from him. That is why you felt sick when we tried to wipe your memory. Your soul fought for what your mind forgot."

She releases a sigh. "Why? What purpose is there in giving Breckin me as a soul mate?"

Her mouth turns, a small pout forming. I cup her face in my hands. "Hey. Are you kidding me? You and your beautiful soul, and all the amazing things you do? I remember the campaign you started in third grade for the buddies bench on the playground after that new kid cried because she didn't have any friends, and you were so upset because you didn't know she was alone. Or what about all of your volunteer work? The food drives in town square, the tutoring you do?"

Her eyes glisten. "How do you know about those things?"

The truth hits me. "The real question is how did I ignore what's between us for so long? I've watched you for years. I've watched you, and I hoped that one day you'd look at me and give me the time of day. Sebastian was right about you being special. I'm the one who doesn't deserve you."

Leaning forward, she kisses my cheek and hugs me. "You have to say that. Your soul is connected to mine."

"Yes, because it was made for me," I say, hugging her quickly, then pulling back and looking in her eyes. "Whatever the reason, Vivienne, we were put together, and we will remain together."

"I still say you got the short end of the stick." She pats my cheek playfully as she stands and bends close to my ear. "I won myself a hot supernatural who can fly me all over the world. You got a tiny human who can't drive and sings off-key." She winks.

Elias regards her with a touch of amusement and a whole lot of admiration as she excuses herself. He waits until the bathroom door closes before speaking his mind.

"This is dangerous, Breckin. You know that, right?"

I drop the confidence I've held all afternoon. The moment I put it all together, the moment I knew we were soul mates, I realized we were screwed.

"What am I supposed to do? We can't erase her memories of me. I can't compel her. I tried—it did not go well. Is it because of the soul mate bond?"

Elias crumbles a napkin and leans back in his chair. "Like I said, she retains her memories because of the soul bond, yes. The compulsion, though?" He scratches his beard. "She said Sebastian tried, and it didn't work with him either. Maybe something happened when you healed her. Maybe it's something else, but compulsion is the least of your concerns right now."

I stare into the fire. Three days ago, my biggest worry was dealing with Father after my birthday.

"What will Sebastian do with her if he gets his hands on her?"

"The soul mate of Hamon's son? What do you think?"

I curse.

"Your father has enemies. She would be a nice bargaining chip."

"He wouldn't care. He doesn't care about me or what I do, as long as I join his ranks."

Elias laughs. "You don't think your father will find power in this? Breckin, there's something about her. Something different. She's not quite human."

The moment I smelled her blood, I had the same thought.

"I've met her mom. She's human."

Elias shifts, his face thoughtful. "What do you know of her father?"

Nothing. No one in town has ever mentioned Rachel Freeman having an ex-husband or Vivienne knowing her dad. I shrug.

"Her mom came home after college expecting. He was never in the picture. I'm not even sure her mom knows who he is," Elias says as his hand runs over his jaw.

My gaze snaps from the flames to Elias. "What makes you say that? How in the hell would you know anything about her family, anyway?"

"Breckin, the Freeman family has lived in Havenwood Falls for a long time. I've been here a long time. I know things."

"Is this about the Court? Are they involved with Viv somehow? I know what they do to people who anger them. I don't want her involved with them, Elias. She's—"

"I'm saying I'm an angel who has been here a long time for reasons other than you. I did speak to Ric about Vivienne's attack, though."

"The sheriff? Why?" The Court of the Sun and the Moon doesn't rule over us as angels. Their magic simply can't compare to our power. Elias has worked with them to keep peace, but why involve them with this?

"A girl went missing a week ago, Breckin. Whatever attacked Vivienne could be behind her disappearance. We can't keep the information secret."

"And what if it was something else? Something to do with us, or Vivienne specifically? What if the Court comes after her? If she isn't human, they will—"

"Breckin," he says my name sharply, reining my fears in. "Ric is trustworthy. We may need the Court's help eventually, but for now we can handle it on our own. He's agreed to let us deal with things as long as it stays among our kind." He watches my face and continues. "She was right to ask what the point of her being your soul mate is, by the way. There's a reason you were brought together. There always is."

I stand. I want to scream. I need to fly, to think. My wings want release. They want the freedom of the open sky.

"Go." Elias leans forward and jerks his head toward the stairs. He knows me well. "Take a moment, calm yourself. I'll watch over her."

I could use it. A flight to work off some energy. Watching over Vivienne the last few days, even when in secret, has left me no time to breathe. My hand goes to my back, intending to yank my shirt over my head, but the sound of water in the bathroom stops me.

"No. I can't run away from this, even for a little while." I lower my voice. "Whatever I have to do to protect her, Elias."

He tips his head. "We'll need to end him."

"Then we end him."

Vivienne steps out, smoothing her hair into a high ponytail, and looks up. She catches me watching and smiles. My wings settle, my restlessness calming. She does that. Only her.

"I was thinking about what you said, and I realized something," she says as she crosses the room, and I twist on the couch to get a better look at her. "I watch you, too."

"You do?"

Her eyes shift from Elias to me. "You sit in the back at assemblies. You tap your fingers on the edge of your desk in chem like you're playing a song in your head, and you glared at me in middle school every time I caught your eye. I thought you hated me."

It clicks. "And you stopped talking to me," I recall as she returns to my side on the couch.

She lifts her shoulder and frowns. "I cried." Her hand covers her mouth. "Oh my gosh. I'd forgotten about it, but I did. I went home and cried to my mom because Breckin Roberts seemed to hate me, and I couldn't figure out why."

I push back my hair and inhale deeply. *I hid from her.* I spent most of the summer between sixth and seventh grade travelling with Elias. We came back, and when school started, I saw Vivienne in the hallway and nearly threw up. My stomach dropped and shook, like I was in a space shuttle. I'd chalked it up to a crush when it didn't stop after a week. Every time I saw her, I felt crazy.

I look at Elias. His mouth forms a small grin, and his eyes shine with suppressed laughter. "You knew," I breathe.

Vivienne's head whips to my "uncle."

"I suspected."

"Suspected? For how long?" I ask.

"From the first time you met."

Vivienne gasps, and I fish her hand out from the sleeve of her sweater and interlace our fingers. "Tell us."

Elias's grin drops. "I wasn't there. You were with a nanny at the time, Kathy I think it was, and she said you two went for a walk at the park. Vivienne and her mom were there. She gushed on and on about how inseparable you two were. It could have been two toddlers just playing, but—"

His eyes narrow meaningfully, and I pick up what he wasn't saying. *He knew. He knew she was different.*

"You think we were always connected, then?" Vivienne asks.

"I think you were. Like I said, soul mates are forever. Somehow you two were able to ignore the attraction. I imagine it was easier to resist because you'd felt it from such a young age."

Vivienne and I share a glance. There's no denying the attraction anymore. And there are no easy answers when discussing things pertaining to destiny and creation.

"If you suspected we were soul mates, why didn't you say something to me that first night? You made me think we could fix everything by erasing her memories." *Why is he keeping things from me?*

Elias scratches his beard and blows out a long exhale. "I hoped I was wrong. I wanted the memory erasure to work, Breckin. I didn't want to see either of you put into this situation."

His eyes meet mine, and they're filled with words he will not speak. *This will be trouble.*

He warned me that first night, but I thought he was worried about my healing her, or my exposing myself. No, he's worried for us. I give him a nearly imperceptible nod, letting him know I understand.

Vivienne clears her throat and shimmies—like she's shaking off a pall. "So, Elias. An angel who runs a business flying people on high adventure ski courses. It almost feels like an inside joke."

I choke on the sip of water I just took. For his part, Elias just leans back and snorts, his eyes watching Vivienne again with a gleam that I can only think of as pride.

"It *was* a joke. In a way."

Vivienne laughs lightly. "In a way?"

"Elias can't fly, Viv," I explain, unable to keep myself from wincing. An angel's wings are irreplaceable. They are their own life force. They speak their own language. How Elias manages without his has always amazed me. Vivienne's face contorts. I can read the questions she's too afraid to ask in her expressive eyes.

"It was years ago, a fight with things best left unsaid, for now," Elias says.

Unsaid, for now. Hopefully, unsaid forever. I don't want to have to tell Vivienne about all of the scary things that lurk about this world. She hasn't asked about other creatures, whether from fear or preoccupation, and I'd love it if she never had to find out. *Wishful thinking, Breckin.*

There's a sadness in her eyes as she looks at Elias. "I'm sorry." She offers him a warm smile.

He accepts her smile with one of his own. "It's not so bad. The business keeps me in the air, and I get to keep an eye on this delinquent."

"So that's how you ended up in Havenwood Falls? Breck's father asked you to watch over him while he's out doing . . . things?"

"Things?" Elias laughs, but agrees.

But that's not true. Elias was in Havenwood Falls way before I was born. He was here before he lost his wings, if I remember correctly. Why *did* he settle here?

THE HIGH-PITCHED SCREECH of Vivienne's window opening draws a smile to my face. Leaning against the tree outside her apartment, I maintain my focus on the parking lot and sky and wait for her to speak.

"You know I can see you even when you try to cloak yourself, right?"

She never disappoints. We've done this all week. I wait for her feisty little jabs like a hungry man waits for dinner. The scent of her freshly washed hair invades my space, and with a last glance around the complex, I turn and walk closer.

"Your neighbors will think you're crazy if you keep yelling outside at nothing."

"Breckin, go home and sleep. He's not here. It's been four days, and we've seen nothing."

She props her elbows on the sill and leans farther out. Taking the end of her wet hair, I wrap it around my fist and cloak her with me. "I don't sleep," I tell her, not for the first time. "And I want to be here. I feel better when I'm near you." I breathe her in before capturing her mouth with mine. She tastes like cinnamon toothpaste.

"Then come inside," she says against my lips, her tongue running over my bottom lip.

"That's not a good idea, Vivie." Her mom is at work, and the desire between us is too strong.

"It's a great idea, Breck." Her hands go around my neck, as though she can yank me in through her window.

Tucking my wings tight against my body, I climb into her room, shutting and locking the window before pulling the curtains closed. I still at Vivienne's proximity, my back to her.

"I'm not sure which I find more beautiful. You or your wings," she says softly for my ears only. Her finger grazes the edge of my left wing, and my breath hitches. She's never touched them. No one has. I close my eyes, yearning for her touch, my feathers straining for it. She moves to the curving slope at the top.

"I am an angel. I am not beautiful." My voice is as gravelly as Elias's. I fist her curtain as her entire palm pets down the length of my spine. The baby fine feathers twitch.

"You are my angel, Breckin Roberts, and you are beautiful to me."

I move quickly—grabbing her body and pinning her on top of her bed—with an angelic passion and need I've never known. Vivienne gasps, bucking against me as her eyes sparkle.

"You. Are. My soul."

Her leg hooks around my calf. "Do you know how badly I've wanted to touch them?" she asks with a breathtaking smile.

"You are my soul, Vivie," I repeat, lowering my face to hers and brushing her cheek and jaw with my nose, inhaling her scent. "I'm connected to you like no other."

She trembles beneath me. "I'm connected to *you* like no other."

I release her wrists from over her head. Pushing up, I brace myself with one hand and run my palm across her smooth skin. I've kept information from her all week, and I've run out of time.

"You're frowning. What's wrong?" Her warm fingers travel over my ribs and pull me down on top of her.

Pulling my wings in, I flip us over and hug her tightly. "I need to tell you about my father."

She lifts her head, her eyes scanning my face before she scrambles from my arms and sits beside me. I push myself into a sitting position. "Elias had to tell him what was going on here."

"Okay."

I blow out a deep breath. "You know he's not good. He's fallen, Viv. Thousands of years ago, there was dissension in the ranks, and it led to war."

"Among the angels?" Her eyes dip to my chest, and she leans over and tugs my shirt from where I keep it tucked in my belt. She arches a brow as she holds out the shirt.

"Yes, among the angels," I confirm as I slip the shirt over my head. "They were divided, some turned. The stories I've been told come from one side. Or I suppose, two—my father and Elias. They tell the same one, though. Mostly. They were thrown out of Heaven—many angels were—and for a while, they worked to gain their favor back, but when nothing happened, they fought. My father turned, and now leads other lesser angels in tempting humans to stray. It's his job to turn people away from living a good and righteous life."

"You're not your father, Breckin." She takes my hand when I stare at her with confusion. "You told me you were supposed to be bad. You're not."

"No, but I'm expected to declare my allegiance to him when I turn eighteen. I'm supposed to join him."

"And if you don't?"

Man, I love her strength. I hold her gaze as I admit the worst-case scenario. "He could end me."

"End you?" Her head shakes slowly. "You mean kill you?"

"Elias says he won't. Although he's never shown much fatherly care, he has some feelings for me. More than likely he'll force me, or make my life hell, until I relent."

"I don't understand. Can't you just live? Have some sort of neutrality? Go to college and be with me?"

I'd like nothing more. Vivienne's blue eyes fill with tears, and I hook her by the back of the neck and press her head to my chest. "I could try, but eventually I'll have to pick a side. Peace won't last forever."

"Why are you telling me all this now?" She swipes at her wet cheeks as she draws back.

"In order to keep you safe, we have to end Sebastian. Only one thing kills a reaper. Death's scythe, which, unless you have a direct line to him, we're not getting our hands on." Vivienne's hands go to her head. "But, I learned something before I came over. If a reaper is in a host body, as our guy is, then an angel blade will do him in."

"Where do you find an angel blade?"

My finger slides over her damp hair, taking a thick section and twisting it. "From my father."

READY, SET, LET'S GO

VIVIENNE

"So, are you ever going to talk to me about Breckin Roberts?"

My grip loosens on my curling iron, the metal coming way too close to my ear, as Mom pops her head around my bathroom door as I'm getting ready for school.

"Gosh, you scared me!" I unwrap a curl and set the iron on the counter. "What are you doing home this early?"

"I have seven months before my only child goes off to college. I figured if I wanted to spend any time with you, I'd have to come home before you left for school."

Guilt sucker-punches me. "I'm sorry."

She picks up the curling iron and steps behind me. Drawing a chunk of hair from my scalp, she sets about curling it, just as she did when I was younger. "You haven't been running, you haven't stopped by the clinic to help file. This boy must be pretty special for you to give up all of your normal activities."

"He is," I admit, meeting her gaze in the reflection of my bathroom mirror. "Do you need me at the medical center? I can come in."

"Not if you'd rather hang out with Breckin, sweetie."

See your mostly working mom or hang out with your newly found soul mate? What a choice. I fuss with the front of my hair, searching for pieces in need of the curling iron, as I carefully consider my answer.

"What if I bring him by?"

Her light brow arches. "Introducing him to the parental unit? Is he that special?"

My eyes roll as I smirk. "Mom, you know Breckin. You know his . . . Elias—"

"His Elias? Is that a term you kids are using these days that I wouldn't understand?"

"Elias Jamison. He's Breckin's unofficial uncle. We ate dinner with him. He's really nice."

Her face changes. A thoughtful and far off look glazes over her eyes. "Yes, he is nice. And yes, I know them both, but not all that well. I'd love it if you brought Breckin by the center. I'd like to get to know the boy who's convinced my normally rigid daughter to drop her schedule for an entire week."

"Rigid daughter?" I scoff. She raises her brow again, a silent "Are you going to dispute it?" and I give in. "Aren't you the one who poked at me for not having enough fun?"

"Not too much fun, Viv," she says, and I inhale deeply at the censure in her tone.

This week has been a whirlwind. My usual "rigid" schedule, as Mom calls it, fell to the wayside. My daily running was replaced by making out with an angel. My evenings helping Mom file charts and eating dinner with her at work were replaced by dinner dates in front of a fire with Breckin. Four afternoons spent doing our homework together, and getting to know each other, on a level other than the angelic, soul mate level.

"It's a good thing you raised me right." I turn and pilfer the curling iron from her hands. "He'll be here soon. Let me finish getting ready. How about we come by tonight? A Friday night date with my mom at a medical center? How could he say no?"

"Say no to a night with the Freeman girls? He couldn't." She slaps my butt on her way out the door.

~

I have so many questions. Breckin and I need to talk before Mom jumps on him and interrogates him tonight. If he agrees to go. I should have asked on the way to school, but I chickened out. I should have said something before he left me at my classroom door, but my stomach fluttered and my senses swam as he kissed my cheek.

I've put off letting them meet because I was worried she would see just how strong my feelings for him are. She knows me too well. Now, before they meet, I need to sort things out. Things I put off because I was too frightened of the answers. If Breckin is my soul mate, what does that mean? We're seventeen. We're in high school. This isn't normal, being this attached to another when you're not even sure of yourself.

And he's an angel. He won't age much further—he's immortal. Will I be a creepy old woman passing the man I love off as my son, then grandson someday? I will grow old and die and leave him behind. My stomach turns. Am I thinking of a future with Breckin? Am I in love with him? Our souls are so in sync, it clouds all other feelings. It could be love, but it's too soon to go there. Soul mates or not. Isn't it?

"Buck up, cupcake. You'll see lover boy again in one hour." Zara knocks the back of my head as she takes her seat beside me. We've spoken less this last week than we have our entire lives. "You two are the real deal, huh?" Her words are dipped in resentment.

"Jealous?"

Zara snorts. "Of your hot boy toy? Totally. But I miss you more. He's gonna have to give you up. At least occasionally—shared custody?"

I smile. Just like with my rigid schedule and mom, I've disappeared on Zara this week, too. With a rogue angel out to get me, it can't exactly be helped, but she doesn't know that.

"Eat lunch with us, and we can work out arrangements."

"Really? He'll share you?"

Never. Breckin's words—*You. Are. My soul*—roll through my head. I flash a coy smile. "What makes you think he's the needy one?"

"I've never known you to be clingy, Viv."

"That's because you've never known me to be in love."

Her face changes from wide-eyed shock to worry. *Why did I admit that? Was I not just questioning my feelings? I'm an idiot, because I know darn well what my feelings are.*

"You think you're in love?" Zara scoots her chair halfway into the aisle. "Viv, I don't want to see you get hurt. I know there's some sexy appeal to Breckin Roberts, but he's *Breckin Roberts.* Don't get your hopes up."

She means well. I push the leg of her chair with my foot, sliding her back toward her own desk. "I love you, Z. Everything will be fine."

If she has more to say, she's denied the chance by the start of class.

Halfway through AP Lit, my cell vibrates. I covertly slip the phone from my pocket.

Breck: My father is at the house. I have to go see him.

Me: Now? I'll come with you.

My heart races as I wait for his reply. He's taking too long. Why? A glance at the front of the room verifies I'm not being watched. I type again.

Me: Breck?

Breck: You can't. I need you to stay here. Stay in the building and with someone at all times, okay? I'll be back in time for chem.

I can't? Irrational worry, or maybe it isn't irrational considering what he's told me about his father, hits me.

Me: Will Elias be there?

Again, his reply takes too long. I lean down and grab my backpack, half determined to run for the exit. Beside me, Zara hisses, drawing my attention. Her brows dip over her eyes in a silent question. I shake my head and mouth, *I'm fine.*

Breck: Elias is there, Vivie. I'll be fine, I promise. I'll see you soon.

The remainder of class is a blur. Within moments of Breck's last text, dread hits me. I rub my chest, the emptiness I felt after he and Elias attempted erasing my memories coming back full force. Elias said I'd get used to it—the way my bond calls to Breckin's when we're not in close proximity. I'm empty, and he's not even two miles away.

Two sharp knocks on the classroom door stops us in the middle of reading a passage from *Heart of Darkness.*

"Sorry for the interruption. May I see Vivienne for a moment please?"

The pencil I'm doodling with stills as I look up. The assistant principal wants me? She lifts a hand and waves me over, before ducking back into the hall. Sharing a curious glance with Zara, I slip my cell up my sleeve and stand. The reading continues before I've left the room.

AP Lit is at the end of a hallway on the first floor of the school. To the left are exit doors with colorful posters advertising the Yuletide Ball tomorrow night, and to the right is a long corridor of closed classroom doors, and the Assistant Principal's back, as she walks away.

Am I supposed to follow her? What about my things?

The exit doors behind me open, a shock of cool wind and a beam of light shining into the hallway.

"Hello, pretty one." His rasping voice sends tendrils of fear curling up my spine.

THIS IS WAR

BRECKIN

 e stands in the middle of the living room, beneath the arched ceiling and before the burning fireplace, the owner of this house and my life. Or so he thinks.

"Father."

He does not turn. I didn't expect him to. "Breckin."

His profile is the same. The same face I've known my entire life. The face of a man who could be my brother. Thousands of years old and he looks like a frat boy right out of college. He looks like me, but looks are deceiving. Father isn't a college boy. He isn't harmless.

"Well?"

And he isn't patient. Leaving my wings out, I step farther into the room, nodding at Elias, who leans against a wall, arms crossed over his chest, the glare he wears for Father's sake firmly in place.

"I am told you healed."

I nod. His profile glows orange from the fire. I catch the way the muscle in his cheek flinches, and the silence grows.

"Where is she? This girl worth saving? I smell her on you. I smell her in this house."

My eyes flick toward Elias. His head moves a fraction, a slight shake as his pale eyes lower. I hold my tongue.

"You dare ask for my help, but you choose not to speak to me?" He finally turns his full attention to me. His amber eyes, more red in tone than mine, flash with irritation. "Do you know what you did, by interfering? Did you think your actions would go unnoticed?"

"I didn't have a choice."

"No?" He steps closer. "You risk notice, son. You have one choice in your existence: gain strength until you join me."

"That's a choice?" I scoff, anger unfurling in my chest. "I will not let her die. And if you don't help me keep her safe, you will be the one with a choice."

"Breckin." Elias pushes off the wall, his tone a warning, but it's too late. I opened my damn mouth, and I need to play it through.

"Do you think I'm stupid?" I ask them both. "I know you sense what she is to me. I know you know how important she is, not only to me but to you."

A slow grin works its way onto Father's face. "Perhaps there is more of me in you than I thought."

"Perhaps." I nod. "Or perhaps I'll do whatever it takes to make sure Vivienne is safe."

He stiffens, his head snapping toward Elias. Something passes between them. Elias lies for me all the time. *Does he know? Does he suspect Elias' true allegiance has been with me since the day he was forced to watch over me?*

"Yes, I imagine you will," he says after a moment, turning and tucking his inky-black wings close to his large frame. "This reaper, Sebastian. He disobeys his laws by remaining here. He lost his invisibility, thus making him dwell in a host. His existence is forfeit because he threatened my future."

"Thank you."

That is what I expected. He will say it is for me, for what I will bring to his leadership when I pledge my allegiance to his ranks. But I'm not fooled. He's curious to figure out why the Creator gave me a human soul mate. A human I'd known and been around all my life. I'd always understood bonds to be undeniable, and ours feels that way now, but why didn't it before? Why did it take her near death for the bond to click so strongly? I check the clock on the wall. First period ends in two minutes. "I promised her I'd be back in time for our next class. I don't like leaving her alone."

"I will meet her."

My wings bristle at his command, and I swallow hard. He isn't using his abilities on me, but he could. He could compel me to do his bidding any time he wants. It's what makes this all so damn difficult. "Eventually."

My pocket vibrates. Father cocks his head, his eyes following as I pull out my cell and answer.

"Zara?"

"Is Viv with you?" Zara asks breathlessly through the phone.

"What? Why?"

"Breckin, I'm aware of your reputation. You don't play by the rules, but Viv does, and if you—"

"What the hell are you talking about, Zara? Where's Viv?" I interrupt.

"She was called out of class, and she never returned. I grabbed her stuff and went to find her in the office, but they acted as though they had no idea what I was talking about. I figured you'd bribed them or something, since neither of you are in chemistry, where you should be."

"I had a family issue and had to leave campus. She was probably worried and is on her way here. I'm sure it's nothing. I need to go."

"Okay, but—" I end the call, shoving my cell in my back pocket and looking at Elias and Father.

Sebastian has her. She wouldn't have left campus. A growl rips through my chest as I swing at the nearest lamp, the glass shattering as it hits the wall.

GAME OF SURVIVAL

VIVIENNE

I can't breathe. We fly at such a pace, I cannot find a way to take in air without it being forced into my lungs. My eyes burn, and my skin pulls from the pressure being exerted. It's like the force of a roller coaster, but infinitely more powerful. I tuck my head into Sebastian's leather coat, hating the inferred intimacy, as I hang on with every ounce of my strength, praying he doesn't drop me from the sky to my death.

When I fear my body will be ripped apart by the wind, we slow, and his arms loosen.

I scream.

Opening my eyes, I cringe and duck as we fly through the dense forest along the rocky slope of a mountain. Are we still in Havenwood Falls?

His arms release me, and I slip. "No!" My hands and arms hold tighter, my legs stretching around his. "What are you doing? Don't drop me, please!"

My head jerks back, his fingers digging into my scalp.

"Can't you fly, pretty one?" His blue eyes shine as he laughs.

I peer over my shoulder at the ground below. Rocks. Jagged, loose, snow-covered boulders cover this section. I beg, tears pouring from my eyes as I climb his body, working to maintain my hold. It's no use. My muscles tire quickly, my sweat-covered palms slipping as we weave between trees. The moment my legs lose their connection with Sebastian, I anticipate the fall. Closing my eyes, I whisper Breckin's name. I picture Mom sitting at home, wondering what happened to her only child. I picture Zara and all my friends—will they find my body? Will I be another missing person like Heidi Bennett?

My eyes meet Sebastian's. "I don't want to die. Please?"

A smile graces his supernaturally perfect angelic face as he grasps my wrists and pries me away—as simple as plucking a piece of lint from his shirt—dropping me.

I have one moment to scream before I land hard and roll, coming to a stop when my arm cracks against a snow-covered rock. The snap of bone in my forearm sends pain throughout my entire body. The sound vibrates in my teeth. Biting my lip so hard I taste blood, I scramble into a ball and search the sky. *Where is he? Where did he go?*

The swoosh of wings is nearby. I push to my feet and run.

Tripping over limbs, tearing through bushes, and slipping on ice, I play hide and seek with an angel in the sky. His laughter trails me, and his shadow mocks me, never straying far from where I am. My toe snags a limb, and I pitch forward. I twist in time to save my arm from impact and slam head first into a thick pine. Warmth oozes down my face as white flashes behind my eyelids. It hurts. My broken arm, my weak legs, the throbbing in my head. Red drips to the white snow, and I lift my hand to the wound.

"Breckin?" I whisper his name, praying against all hope he hears me as the reaper lands.

Sebastian's shadow blocks the sun. His mottled gray and cream wings remain fanned out, like any moment he'll take off again. He's proud of what he's done—victory wreaths his face. But what is my cost?

"I knew you were special the moment I was sent to reap you. Death's orders are always the same, but for you . . . they were different. Your blood told the story. It has been thousands of years."

"What do you want with me?" I drag myself backward, my hand searching the ground for a weapon as I go.

"Had he left you to me, your soul would be free. I never considered doing anything but my job." He walks forward, keeping his distance as I push backward. "But he is the son of an angel," Sebastian says with distaste. "He interfered. He broke the laws, and he opened my eyes to what you are. What you can be."

Bile rises, burning my throat as the world spins. "What am I?"

The question barely passes my lips when snow flies, and Breckin lands, his body crouched before me. The muscles in his back flex, ready for a fight as his wings stretch out, taking up twice the space as Sebastian's.

"You," Breckin peers over his shoulder, "are my soul."

He scans me, verifying I'm relatively unscathed before focusing on Sebastian. My shoulders shake with relief. Using the tree at my back, I work into a standing position. Dizziness swamps me. I clutch the pine, my face pressing against the rough bark as I work to remain on my own two feet.

"You dare take her from me?" Breckin growls. "This will not end well for you, reaper."

Breckin leaps into the air, throwing himself at Sebastian, a flash of movement to my already blurry vision. The ground shakes, and thunder-like sounds echo through the forest as their bodies connect. Sebastian soars backward, twists, then launches at Breckin.

They fly through the forest, breaking branches and tumbling trees like dominos. Tangled limbs land on the snow a few feet from my position. I cringe as Sebastian punches Breckin, but Breckin returns the punch as though it was nothing. Back and forth they struggle. They're indestructible beings, fighting a cage match neither looks to win.

"Will she join you?" Sebastian drawls when they part, stalking each other. His blue eyes look past Breckin. "Will she turn her back on her calling for you?"

My stomach drops. Phantom butterflies within my chest flit about, tugging me toward Breckin while, at the same time, holding me back.

"You don't know?" Sebastian laughs. "He didn't tell you."

Is he talking to me or Breckin? My question goes unasked as Breckin's wing lifts, blocking my view, and more voices shout from above.

"Vivie, move back," Breckin orders above the others.

Breathing through the pain of my broken arm, I hide behind a tree. My legs refuse to move farther.

A moment later, a hand cups against my mouth as an arm wraps around my waist from behind.

"It's me," Elias says, picking me up off the ground and swiftly moving away from the fight.

"Elias? No. Help Breck. Where are you going?" I claw at his hands. His grip tightens, and I kick at his feet as he runs farther into the forest. He can't fly—we won't go far—but he runs with speed. Breckin's voice fades into the background, and my soul shreds, ripping a sob from my chest. Fear consumes me. "Elias, please. What if something happens to him?"

"His father is here," he pants, an edge to his voice. *Is that bitterness?* Elias thinks of Breckin like a son. It's in his tone. "Hamon will take care of the reaper. Breckin is fine. I need to move you to safety."

His words make sense, and he is attempting to help, but my body doesn't listen. I have no control over my reaction. My legs kick, and my head butts against his chest as I flail. A deep-seated knowledge that Breckin is being threatened has awakened, and my soul fights to return to her other half. Elias curses as I lean forward, throwing him off balance, and his arms loosen. Taking advantage, I punch at his arm and jump free of his grip. It was a mistake.

Falling to the ground face first, I land on my stomach, and black, all-consuming pain rips across my arm. Moisture and warmth immediately cover my skin. My sleeve is soaked in blood. I roll to my back, screaming in agony as I push the sleeve up. A bone protrudes through the skin.

"I'm trying to protect you," Elias hisses, falling to his knees and reaching for me. I flinch. Elias' face changes, his worry wiping away and leaving an unreadable mask. "I'm sorry, Viv," he says gruffly.

My head shakes. "I need Breck, please," I beg, willing my limbs to move, to run back toward the faint sound of yelling, but the pain is too much. My muscles lock.

"Everything will be okay," Elias says, lifting his arm. Everything goes silent.

WHEN IT'S ALL OVER

BRECKIN

*M*y father, an avenging angel full of malice and power, is a jarring sight as he lands in the snow between Sebastian and me. I risk a glance at Vivienne and find Elias dragging her away. Relieved, I focus on Sebastian.

"Hamon." Sebastian nods in deference.

Father glances my way. His mouth twists as he takes me in. I spit blood on the ground, aware the look I'm receiving is because of my weakness. My energy pulls, healing the wounds Father frowns down upon.

"You challenge the son of an angel, reaper?" He questions, his words full of distaste.

"I defend myself. Your son interfered with my job—"

"My son saved his soul mate," Father interrupts. He tucks his wings and moves forward. "You are inferior to us in every way. Did you think you could win something from me?"

The reaper's eyes go wide. His jaw slackens as he looks around the forest. Elias and Vivienne are gone. Father stands before him with an angel blade at his waist, and I'm ten feet on his other side. He's trapped.

He leaps into the air, but it's too late. Father grabs his ankle and throws him to the ground like a sack of grain as I rush forward.

Sebastian scrambles back, but Father is a blur. The divine, even fallen ones, are more powerful than lesser angels, and before I can blink, Father has the reaper from behind, pulling him into a standing position.

"You damned her," Sebastian says between gritted teeth, glaring as he claws at Father's arm. "You should have let her die."

"How? How did I damn her?" I shout as Father jerks back, choking the reaper. "What is her calling? What do you know?"

Sebastian grunts, his lips parting, but his words never exit. My father's arm arcs around his shoulders, and the glow of an angel blade flashes as it slices across his chest.

"No!"

Sebastian's eyes glow, flaring wide, before closing as he crumbles to the ground, leaving the remains of the human host he inhabited before us.

"Why did you kill him?"

"Your soul mate was hurt." His gaze flicks over my shoulder. The snow is red with blood. "Find her and send Elias back."

My jaw clenches as I study him. There will be time for explanations later. Leaving him behind, I grab my phone and jump into the air in search of Elias and Vivienne.

"Your battle skills need work."

I turn at the displeasure dripping from Father's words. I'd assumed he'd be gone a while, taking care of the mess with Sebastian—even he answers to someone. Or so I thought.

Controlling my contempt, I nod. "There hasn't been much need for fighting here."

He killed Sebastian, with a simple slice to the chest. It was nothing for him, but it'll cost me everything, eventually. Including Vivienne.

"There will be." He walks to the opposite side of my bed and looks down at Vivienne's still form. She's a mess, with her knotted hair and dirty, tear-streaked face—but she is beautiful. And she is mine. I tense as he reaches for her now healed arm. The primal urge to challenge him for the audacity to touch her consumes me. Father or not. My face must tell the story, because he pauses, withdraws his arm, and inhales deeply. My teeth grind.

"You will prepare. You will train." His eyes never leave her face. "If you plan on keeping her."

Is that a threat?

"I have until April," I remind him needlessly. He can't bind me to his ranks until I turn eighteen.

"I can send fighters here."

"No." I stand, disliking the advantage he has with me sitting by the bed. "Thank you," I say, merely to appease him. "We'll be fine. I'm sure he told no one about her." *Other than you, of course.*

He doesn't realize I know. He assumes Elias is useless at anything other than watching over me, because he no longer has wings. Elias— the Dominion angel who ended thousands on both sides of the war between Heaven and Hell—a glorified babysitter. How does he not see it? Elias is the one who told me the reaper knew exactly who I was the day I healed Vivienne. Elias is the one who found out what Sebastian did with that knowledge.

The reaper went to Father and cut a deal.

When Father ordered me home this morning, I should have known. Vivienne's capture at school, the way Sebastian toyed with her in the woods—it was all planned. The only part that didn't go the way I, or the reaper, expected was the part where he met his end at the tip of an angel blade wielded by his supposed ally.

His betrayal doesn't bother me. Father isn't trustworthy. I've known this for years. His loyalty is to himself and himself alone. Sebastian wanted out of Death's servitude. He wanted a larger role in the things to come. I understand the reaper's motive. What was his?

"Why did you kill him before he could answer my questions? What do you know?"

Vivienne stirs, and Father cracks his neck, his eyes narrowing before he steps back.

"You have until your birthday. Elias will keep me informed of everything here," he says, ignoring my questions. I reach for Vivienne's hand, already dismissing him.

"Breckin, you owe me her life."

He's out of the room before I can speak, but his words send flames of anger through my veins. *I owe him her life? Yes, he saved her. Does he think he owns her, too? Will he use her to rein me in? Will he use me, to get his hands on her?* Vivienne's thumb rubs against mine, and I refuse to taint this moment with one more thought about his motives.

"You healed me." She licks at her lips and blinks several times. "Where were you when I broke my leg skiing two years ago?"

Pushing her hair from her face, my thumb smooths over the cut in her brow as I sit on the edge of the bed.

"Yes, I healed your arm and a pretty nasty cut on your forehead, but you still have some minor cuts and bruises." I place a kiss on her forehead and linger, my lips hovering over hers. "And probably a bit of a headache, thanks to Elias."

She turns her head to the right and winces. *Yep, there's the soreness.* "Are you hurt?"

Warmth floods my chest at her concern. This human girl could have been ripped to shreds by Sebastian, and she asks about me?

"Angel, remember. I heal myself."

"Elias hit me?" She confirms more than asks.

"You weren't cooperating, and I needed to get you away from the fight," Elias says from the doorway. His presence confirms Father is gone. I sit up. Kissing her can wait.

"I'm sorry, Vivienne. I'm sure Breckin can take away the pain."

She offers me a crooked smile before turning toward him. Her jaw drops. "What happened to your lip?"

"*He* hit *me*." Elias points out, his fingers touching the split lip. "Then he warned me if I healed myself, he'd do it again."

Vivienne's blue eyes flick between the two of us, then she bursts into laughter. Grabbing a fist of her filthy, blood-stained sweater, I pull her into a sitting position and wrap her tightly in my arms. I kiss her temple, my soul quieting for the first time since it found her a week ago.

I GET TO LOVE YOU

VIVIENNE

"*W*ho could have predicted Breckin Roberts would lose his heart to a lass like you?"

"Gee, thanks, Z." My hip bumps hers as we watch Breckin walk across the overly decorated school gym for some drinks.

She giggles. "Every time he looks at you, I blush. You two are in so deep."

She has no idea. "The decorating committee outdid themselves. I barely recognize this place."

"I know, right?"

Trees twinkle throughout the gym. Everywhere I look, there are balloons, ribbons, and fabric in white and silver. Giant snowflakes and glittery stars cover the walls and hang in doorways and around the stage, where a DJ plays music. When Breckin asked me to the Yuletide Ball yesterday afternoon, I thought he was teasing.

~

"I PROBABLY SHOULD HAVE ASKED before my soul imprinted on yours, but do you have a date for the Yuletide Ball tomorrow?"

We're snuggled on his couch watching a movie, my head on a pillow in

215

his lap as his hand combs through my hair. The Christmas lights Breckin weaved around the mantle earlier in the week wink at us. Elias left an hour ago to work a little angel magic at the school so my attendance reflects an early dismissal due to illness. Breckin's father is gone, and except for a brief description of what happened on the mountain, neither Breckin nor Elias will tell me much of what went down.

I roll my head and look up at Breckin. "The ball? No, I don't have a date. There's a group going stag, and I'd considered it, but that was . . . before."

"Do you want to go?"

"Right. Like you want to go to a school dance." I laugh and roll back to my side, focusing on the movie.

Twenty minutes later, Breckin's hand stills in my hair again. "Vivie?"

"Hmmm?"

"I want to take you to the dance tomorrow night." My heartbeat accelerates. "Nothing about being with me is going to be normal for you. I want to give you normal. School dances, prom, ice-skating at the park—"

I fly into a sitting position. "Wait. Are you asking me to prom?"

Breckin laughs, his hand taking mine and weaving our fingers together. "I'm sorry it's not some crazy social media–worthy request. I could plan one, if you need that."

"Are you kidding? All I need is you. And normal is overrated, Breckin." I pull his face to mine. "By the way, my mom is expecting us at the clinic for dinner tonight."

"That's reasonable. I should formally meet my girlfriend's mother."

"Yeah, you should," I agree, kissing him soundly.

"MAY I HAVE THIS DANCE?" Breckin's lips tickle my ear as he steps up behind me, his hand curling around my hip.

I take the cup of punch he's holding for me and turn into his chest. "You dance?"

"Drink, and come find out." He winks and walks by, continuing to the edge of the floor and slipping his hands into his pockets. Waiting.

I take one sip and set the cup on a table. Zara is already on the floor, along with everyone else we've been sitting with, but I don't care about them. Right now, it's me and my angel.

His eyes sparkle as I join him. My hands slip between his waist and arms, and press his back, bringing him closer. He keeps his hands in his pockets, a smile playing on his lips. I'm wearing four-inch heels, and still he looks down at me. *So not fair, but I love it.* I hold his stare.

After a moment, he caves, and I'm wrapped in his arms. His unnatural heat sears through my gold velvet dress, warming my skin. His chin rests on top of my head as he inhales deeply.

"Ginger and mint," he says with a touch of humor. His lips kiss my hair, before he pulls back. "That was how I knew it was you that day. I smelled ginger and mint, and I knew."

I press my cheek to his chest. "What happens next?"

I didn't mean to ask, but the questions linger. Sebastian's words won't let go of me. He said I had a calling. He questioned if I would stick with Breckin. He insinuated Breckin knows more than he's telling me.

Breckin inhales deeply. "We live. We celebrate being seniors, and we do all of those things normal couples do."

"Breck."

"Vivie." His fingers dive into my hair and tilt my head back. "I have found the one whom my soul loves." He quotes a Bible verse, as though every answer we need lies in those words. "We were not put together to be torn apart. I don't know what comes next. I wish I did."

I close my eyes and push away the uncertainty. He's an immortal angel. He can think that way. I'm not sure I can—I almost died once. He has until his birthday—four months—before his father returns and he's forced to join him. *What then?* I shiver, and Breck shushes me, like he knows where my thoughts turned.

Shifting, he lifts me at the waist and hoists me to face level. "All I know is that you are my soul. I will do whatever it takes to keep you and to call you mine."

Hugging his neck, I touch my forehead to his. "I have found the one whom my soul loves," I repeat as my lips touch his.

Our paths collided eight days ago, but our souls were destined for each other. Our future chosen long before we were born. *That* is what I know. How? There's no explanation, but deep within, something sings when it sees Breckin Roberts. And when I close my eyes, it tells me our story is far from over.

EPILOGUE

ELIAS

"*Y*ou ran out of the house yesterday," I call over my shoulder. He didn't make a sound, yet I know he's here.

"Oh? Did you miss me?" Hamon asks, and I turn. He leans against the open door to my hangar, his legs crossed at the ankles and his arms crossed at his chest.

I close the lid to my toolbox and adopt my own pose of insolence, propping my hip against my work bench. "Hardly"—I snag a rag and wipe the grease from my hands—"your son might, though."

"Breckin hates me."

"Do you blame him?"

"No." Hamon straightens, pushing his hands through his hair and stretching his neck from side-to-side. "You kept things from me, Elias."

His voice is filled with a deep-seated weariness. *How much are his alliances requiring of him these days?*

"I'm doing what you asked all those years ago," I say, recalling another night, seventeen years ago, when he also appeared in my hangar.

~

JUNE 2000

. . .

THE ECHO of footsteps in my hangar stills my hand. He's been missing for months, but I can't look at him—my anger is too strong. Yet, I have news.

"Phaedra's descendent had a child."

He stops walking. "A girl?"

"Aren't they always?"

"The father?" he asks as he rolls his broad shoulders back.

The question hits a nerve, a reminder of my failure, and I don't reply.

"You have watched over her line for two hundred years, but this you do not know?" He sneers.

"I was dealing with the mess you made, Hamon. I left her unprotected."

Stretching his neck from side to side, he steps farther inside, his wings bristling in the light breeze. Months gone and that's all he wants to know? His inability to speak of Phaedra's descendants aggravates me, but his unwillingness to ask about Breckin sets my blood to boiling.

I don't hide my irritation. "You have no other concerns?"

"Is her child the same as the others?"

"Human? Yes, she seems to be."

He stuffs his hands into the pockets of his dress slacks and releases a long exhale. "And Breckin?"

It's about time.

"Obviously, he is half angel. He is healthy." One of the Nephilim, not something Heaven likes having around. "The woman I hired seems nurturing. You should stay in Havenwood Falls for a while and spend time with him. He is your son."

"He is nothing. You'll watch over him as you do Phaedra's blood, and when he comes of age, he'll join the ranks."

I clench my jaw. "You will let him choose, though. Won't you?"

"The way we chose?"

Always this.

"We had a choice, Hamon."

"We were given less choice than man. We were locked out of Heaven."

Inhaling through my nose, I close my eyes and pray my words sink into his blackened heart. "There is time for redemption. You can change your ways. The wars will never stop. You can be on the right side."

"Tell that to Phaedra."

Everything comes back to Phaedra. I swipe the wrench I was using before Hamon arrived from the table.

"A demon killed her," I remind him needlessly.

"Because she was powerless."

We've had this fight for years. It is still pointless. I turn my back and return to working on my copter. Hamon's steps resume, and I peek over my shoulder, finding him walking to the open doorway. Leaving already.

"What is the child's name? Phaedra's blood?" He asks at the entrance.

"Vivienne."

His head bobs as his wings stretch out. "Watch over her. Watch over them both," he says as he jumps into the air.

I RETURN to present day when a grunt escapes Hamon's lips. "I suppose we should have expected this." He pauses, and I twist the rag and wait. "Them. Vivienne and Breckin," he finishes almost reluctantly. "More punishment—"

"Maybe it's His way of righting a wrong. His apology," I interrupt.

"Nothing good can come of them being together. What is she? A human with angelic ancestry? Something else?"

"She is your son's soul mate, and she is Phaedra's great, plus a few, granddaughter. She is family, Hamon."

"She is a complication. She will make him weak."

Like Phaedra made you weak? He has to be thinking it. It's in the way his muscles flex and tense. He's angry, because he sees himself as he was years ago.

I toss my rag down and meet him halfway across the hangar. "Stay in Havenwood Falls. Be his father and help me figure out what this all means."

The suggestion pulls a long sigh out of him, before he turns toward the exit. "I have a job to do, and so do you."

"Hamon?" He's leaving as he always does. Ignoring the salvation that knowing his son could offer him. Ignoring the forgiveness Breckin brings.

Hamon's dark wings spread wide as he stops. "I'm not ready, Elias."

"I'll watch over him, then. I'll watch over them both, until you are, old friend."

Without a response, Hamon leaps into the night, his wings an ebony shadow against the snow-covered trees as he leaves Havenwood Falls.

Breckin and Vivienne's story will continue in July 2018.

ABOUT THE AUTHOR

Michele writes novels with fairy tale love for everyday life. Romance is central to her plots, where the genres range from Coming of Age Fantasy and Realistic Fiction to New Adult Romantic Suspense. She is the author of the bestselling *From the Wreckage* series and co-writes the Paper Planes series with author Mindy Hayes.

Having grown up in both the cold, quiet town of Topsham, Maine, and the steamy, Southern hospitality of Mobile, Alabama, Michele is something of an enigma. She is an avid Yankees fan, loves New England and being outdoors, and misses snow. However, she thinks Southern boys are hotter, Alabama football is the only REAL football out there, and sweet tea is the best thing this side of heaven and her children's laughter!

Her family, an amazing husband and three awesome kids, have planted their roots in the middle of Michele's two childhood homes, in Charlotte, North Carolina.

Website: http://www.michelegmillerbooks.com/
Email: authormichelegmiller@gmail.com
Facebook: https://www.facebook.com/AuthorMicheleGMiller
Twitter: https://twitter.com/chelemybelles
Pinterest: http://pinterest.com/chelemybelles/
Instagram: https://instagram.com/chelemybelles/

ACKNOWLEDGMENTS

I'm so grateful to the people who support me through the book process and life:

My husband and kids deal with me forgetting laundry, dinner, carpool, emails, and the list goes on. How they put up with me I'll never know!

My amazing crew of readers, bloggers, and friends on Facebook and "in real life" keep me sane. You make this solitary life a little less solitary, and a lot more lifelike. Thanks to **Mindy Hayes, Jessica Surgett** and **Jo Pettibone** for providing feedback on this story when it was new, sparkly, and still being fleshed out.

My core reader group over on Facebook, **Mindy and Michele's M&M's**: Thanks for being a sounding board when needed, book pimps when needed, and friends always.

To the Havenwood Falls family: This group continues to grow, but their generosity, creativity, and enthusiasm for this project astounds me. I'm so lucky to be able to write, and collaborate, with these amazing creatives.

More specifically, thanks to these ladies for creating and sharing your characters with Viv and Breckin:

Randi Cooley Wilson: Graysin Ravenal, Everett Weston, and Zal Purser

Kallie Ross: Scarlet Howe, Willa, Kase, and Ric Kasun

Kristen Yard: Nikki Morris and Max Cooper

Amy Hale: Mr. Zander

And of course, a final HUGE thank you to Kristie Cook for

creating Havenwood Falls and making this all possible. I am in awe of your business savvy and ingenuity.

BOUND BY SHADOWS

BY CAMEO RENAE

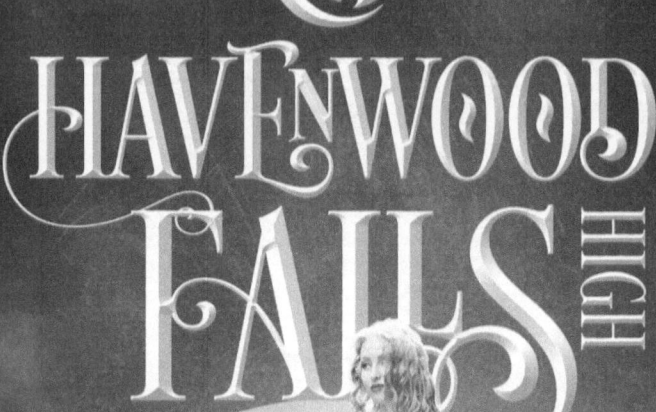

HAVENWOOD FALLS HIGH

Bound by Shadows

USA TODAY BESTSELLING AUTHOR

CAMEO RENAE

~ A Havenwood Falls Young Adult Novella ~

OTHER TITLES BY CAMEO RENAE

The Hidden Wings Series (Complete Series)

Hidden Wings

Broken Wings

Tethered Wings

Gilded Wings

Wings of Vengeance

Midway Series (Hidden Wings Spin-Off)

Guarding Eden

Saving Thomas – Coming Soon!

The After Light Saga (Complete Series)

ARV-3

Sanctum

Intransigent

Hostile

Retribution

In My Dreams Duology

In My Dreams

In My Reality

This book is dedicated to all those who embrace their weirdness.
Keep life interesting and entertaining.
Keep it real.

CHAPTER 1

Change was coming. I not only knew it—I felt it. Not just because New Year's was a few days away, but because of the newly gained sense I'd acquired when I turned sixteen a little over a year ago. So I wasn't hugely surprised when the doorbell rang in our quiet neighborhood on an uneventful Saturday night.

"I'll get it," I said, placing the last clean dinner plate in the dish drain, then wiping my hands dry on a dish towel.

My dad's watchful eyes were on me as I strode for the door. He was overprotective, and although I felt suffocated at times, I understood. It'd been just the two of us for as long as I could remember.

My father had chosen our neighborhood in New Mexico because it was safe and filled with dozens of cautious, watchful eyes. Especially the pair that belonged to the old lady across the street who moved in a few weeks after we did. She used to babysit me when I was younger, but not since I turned sixteen and pleaded with my dad that I was old enough to watch myself.

Old Ms. Gingrich—the Grinch—was a stiff and nosey woman who smelled of mothballs and strong herbs. She was strict and watched me like a hawk.

I wouldn't have been surprised if she was the one who rang the doorbell, hunched over, her wiry white hair in a tight bun, with some odd request for my dad. It happened so often, I wondered if she was going senile and thought he was her son.

As I reached the door and pulled it open, it wasn't the Grinch who greeted me, but two unfamiliar faces.

The first was a pretty woman with pale skin and short brown hair. The man standing next to her was tall with broad shoulders, dark brown hair, and chocolate eyes specked with gold.

"Can I help you?" I asked.

"Eris?" His eyes widened like he knew me. As he stepped forward, I stepped back.

He knew my name. How?

His strong scent wafted to my nose, woodsy and musky. A powerful smell for a powerful-looking man. I couldn't help but stare at him. There was something oddly familiar I couldn't put my finger on. The woman, I was sure I'd never seen before.

Footsteps pounded behind me. "I'm sorry, but we don't accept solicitors here," my dad said firmly.

The man's eyes moved to my dad, still filled with recognition. "Piers?"

My father stepped in front of me, pushing me behind him—a defensive move. Then, he went quiet as he took in the man's face.

"Garrick?" His expression twisted.

"It's been too long," the man replied.

The two of them collided in a hug, and I stood there feeling a mixture of surprise and confusion. My dad never hugged anyone like that, with so much emotion and intensity.

"Where the hell have you been?" my dad asked, grabbing the man's shoulders. "All this time, I—I thought you were dead."

"Dad?" I asked, trying to make sense of what was going on.

"It's okay, Eris," he said, turning toward me. "This is your long-lost uncle Garrick."

"Wait. What?" I gasped. "I have an uncle?"

"Actually, you have two," Garrick replied. "But I'm the handsome one." He winked, then laughed, turning his attention back to my father.

"Dad, why didn't you tell me?" I never knew I had other living family members.

My dad shook his head. "I'm sorry, Eris. There is so much I just can't remember."

"Piers, I know this is a huge surprise, and believe me, I understand." He turned to the woman. "This is Lyra Beaumont. We're here because—well—it's a bit complicated." He looked at the woman and ran a hand through his thick, dark hair. He was having trouble explaining their reasons for being here, frustration written all over his face. "We've come with bad news of a close family member."

"Is it Barney? Is he okay?" My dad's face went pale.

I assumed Barney was the "not as handsome" uncle.

Garrick shook his head. "No. Barney's fine. We're here about your son, Piers."

My father's eyes narrowed, then he glanced back at me, his expression unreadable. I shook my head and looked back at the man claiming to be my uncle. I didn't have a brother. That was the kind of thing someone didn't forget.

"Garrick, I don't have a son," my dad replied.

Garrick slowly reached into his pocket and pulled out a paper, then offered it to my dad.

Tiptoeing, I peeked over his shoulder to see an old photograph that had been folded in half, but I immediately recognized three of the faces. My dad, my mom, and me. But I was much younger. And there was someone standing next to me . . . a boy with his arm over my shoulder. I could see the resemblance. He had the same golden-brown hair and the same shaped eyes as me, only he was a foot taller and looked a few years older.

"You have a son, Piers, and if you let us in, I'll explain why you don't remember him."

My father paused, looking at the picture. I could see the tension in his jaw. "How did you get this?" my dad snapped, holding the picture up. "Is this a fake?"

Garrick held up both hands in front of him. "It's real. I assure you."

"Why, after all this time, would you show up and tell me about a son I don't have?" A deep guttural growl erupted from my dad's chest. "What the hell is going on?"

"Piers, I promise we'll explain," Garrick pleaded, turning to Lyra and giving her a nod.

Lyra quickly waved her hand in front of my dad and whispered a single word. I couldn't hear the word, but after she spoke it, my dad took a shaky step back. He shook his head, his eyes blinking rapidly several times.

Then, it was as if a switch had been flipped. His entire demeanor shifted, and his harsh expression was replaced with what I could only describe as understanding.

Could it have been magic?

I was no stranger to magic. Ever since we moved into this house, I could do things no normal kids could do. Like move things with my mind. My first real encounter was when Dad and I were sitting at the dining table eating breakfast. I was tired, and he'd asked me to pass the syrup. In my mind, I willed the syrup to move, and to mine and my dad's surprise, it did. He was not only shocked but immediately concerned and warned me —repetitively—to never, ever use my magic in front of anyone else.

And that wasn't all. Once in a while, whenever I felt really sad or frightened, a glimmer would appear—a small, bright ball of light, about three inches around, and when it came close, it radiated warmth. At first, I was afraid of it, but every time it appeared, it made me feel a lot better. Less . . . alone. I also learned that no one else could see it. So it had become my secret. A glimmer of hope and light that would come whenever the world around me felt dark.

My dad stepped aside, allowing my uncle and the woman into our living room.

"What's the news you came with?" Dad questioned, his arms crossing over his chest. I could see the muscles in his biceps tighten. He was ready to defend us, if he had to.

"I will tell you, but first, Lyra needs to perform a simple ceremony to reverse a memory spell that has been placed on both of you. Once she finishes, it will be much easier to explain."

"Memory spell? What the hell is that?" My father's arms lowered, and a growl rumbled deep in his chest. Garrick stepped back with his hands up in surrender.

"Piers, you know me. You've known me your entire life, and *you* agreed to this spell when you left Havenwood Falls, knowing full well what the repercussions would be."

"Havenwood Falls?" My dad shook his head.

"Yes. Think about it." Garrick approached my dad slowly, carefully. "There is a large chunk of your life missing. That chunk were the years you lived in Havenwood Falls with Aurora and your children. When you left, a memory spell—which is automatically placed on everyone who leaves the town—caused you to forget."

My dad shook his head. "I don't understand what you're saying, but I swear . . . if you do anything that will harm my daughter—"

"I know," Garrick said, his hands still raised. "You just have to trust me, Piers. Let Lyra do her thing, and we can talk after."

"Please, take a seat," the woman said, gesturing to our brown leather couch. She wasn't wasting any time, but I didn't sense any negative vibe from her. That was one thing I could pick up on in most people—if they had good or bad intentions—and my intuition was usually right. I guess my dad didn't feel anything negative either, because he gave me a nod and took a seat on the couch.

Lyra stood in front of us while Garrick paced slowly behind her. "I need you both to relax, close your eyes, and try to clear your mind," she said.

Right. Easier said than done with the gazillion unanswered questions they'd just thrown on us. And the fact I'd just learned I had relatives. Living relatives.

I leaned over to my dad. "Do you trust them?"

His eyes found mine. "I do. I have a feeling they're here to help and not harm."

I nodded, then leaned back. My dad took my hand, which helped me relax a bit.

"Wait a minute," I blurted, my eyes popping back open, finding Lyra. "Is this safe? Our minds won't be scrambled or altered in any way, right?"

Lyra grinned. "It's perfectly safe, dear. I promise there won't be any scrambled minds. I'm just removing a spell. That's it."

"Okay." I sighed loudly, wondering what kind of memories were hidden from me for who knows how long. "Let's do this."

As I closed my eyes, the woman began to chant. As she continued, I focused on the words, relaxed into them, and soon felt a gentle buzz in the air. My head felt tingly and light, like a weight was being lifted. Then, after a few moments, she stopped.

I opened my eyes and found her walking back toward Garrick.

"Is it done?" he whispered.

"Yes, the spell has been removed," she spoke softly. "It might take a while, but they should start to remember things soon."

"Thank you," Garrick replied with a nod.

"Wait," I blurted. "The memory spell—what exactly is it used for and why?"

Garrick sat on the loveseat across from us, his hands folded in front of him. "When you and your dad left Havenwood Falls, the memories of the place, the people in it, and everything that happened there were suppressed. Think of it as a type of amnesia caused by the spell. For me to explain why I've come, we needed to remove that spell. Lyra," his eyes traveled to the woman, "is a witch from Havenwood Falls, and one of the few trusted to reverse it." His eyes darted back and forth between my dad and me, watching us with great anticipation. Then, he clapped his hands together loudly. "So . . . is it working?"

My dad exhaled, pressing his face into his palms.

I was surprised he wasn't saying anything. He normally questioned everything. Why was he so quiet?

He finally sat forward and looked at Garrick. "Right now, all I have is a massive headache." He stood from the couch and began to walk toward the kitchen.

"Where are you going?' I called after him.

"To take something for this throbbing pain in my head."

"Just give the spell some time," Lyra said after him. "You've been gone for quite a while. It might take a bit to unravel all the memories. It's different for everyone."

My father returned a few moments later and plopped down next to me, his elbows pressed against his knees, the picture in his hands. His eyes were narrowed, studying the faces.

We all watched him in silence.

"I've had this emptiness inside I couldn't explain. A hole of sadness I could never fill," he murmured. "Now I understand where it came from. It was the place the memories once were. Memories of them." His finger traced over my mom and the boy in the picture. Then, he quickly swiped a stray tear that escaped his eye and trickled down his cheek.

I'd never seen my dad so shaken, so . . . emotional. He was strong, physically and emotionally, and not once had I ever seen him cry.

"I'm sorry, Piers. What Lyra just did will reverse the spell and return what was hidden these past seven years," Garrick explained, his brow furrowed.

My dad nodded, then closed his eyes. His head fell back onto the couch.

I waited again, for some lightbulb to click on in my mind and all my memories to flood back. But there was nothing. As time ticked on, doubt and frustration set in.

Just before I was about to say something, my dad's head snapped forward, and his eyes went wide, blinking away an invisible fog. He stood from the couch and stared at the man standing in front of him. I saw something in his eyes. Something I couldn't explain.

"You okay?" Garrick asked.

My dad nodded. "I remember."

CHAPTER 2

$\mathcal{G}$ arrick stood and hugged my dad. "It's great to have you back, brother."

Brother. As they stood together I could see how strong the resemblance was. They had the same features, the same dark hair and gold specks in their dark eyes.

But what about my brother?

"Dad," I spoke, and they went quiet. "Is it true I have a brother?"

His eyes met mine, and there was a short pause before he answered. "Yes, Eris. It's true."

My chest constricted and ached to the point of bursting. He'd forgotten about his son. His *son.* And not only his son . . . *my brother.* How could he allow himself—allow *us*—to forget something so important?

"Why did we forget him?"

"Eris," Garrick cut in, but my mind and the room were spinning. "It was necessary—"

"No!" I yelled, fisting my hands so tightly, my nails cut into my palms. "This is kind of a big deal. Why would anyone want to make me forget that I have a brother? For the past *seven* years I never knew he existed." I could barely breathe, my body shaking as I looked at my dad. "Why did we leave him?"

"Your brother refused to leave Havenwood Falls, and the entire family agreed. We had his best interests at heart," Garrick answered again.

"His best interests?" I snapped, my eyes glaring at him. "How old was he when we left?"

"We recently celebrated his nineteenth birthday."

Nineteen? I quickly did the math, my eyes narrowing on my dad. "You left him when he was twelve? You let *him* make the decision to stay and were okay with it?"

"You don't understand, Eris," Garrick added. "Your brother was troubled at the time, and despite it seeming like an irrational move, we all knew it was the right decision. He's had a good life. I assure you. It just wasn't safe for him to leave with you, and you'll understand why soon."

I couldn't speak, my body shaking. I felt violated. They'd taken something away from me, and I'd had no say in it.

"What's his name?" I didn't want to wait for the damn memories to return to find out.

"Camden," my dad answered. "His name is Camden."

Hot tears filled my eyes and spilled down my cheeks. *Camden.*

"Eris," Lyra spoke softly. "The memory spell is not specific to any individual. Every person, whether a resident or visitor of Havenwood Falls, will not remember the place or anything that happened there once they leave. It's a safeguard."

"A safeguard? For what?"

"Havenwood Falls and many of its residents are *special* and need to be protected," Lyra replied, glancing at Garrick. He nodded in affirmation.

I sighed, claiming defeat. They weren't going to tell me anything else.

"Piers," Garrick said, placing his hands on my dad's shoulders. "The reason we came is because Camden is injured."

"How? What happened?" My father's voice was strained.

"We don't know. He's in a coma, and we believe it's tied to a spell.

Some kind of dark magic. The mages are working on it, but as of now, he's unresponsive."

Mages. Dark magic. A memory spell to make us forget the place. *Special?* Just from those few words alone, I knew Havenwood Falls wasn't a normal community.

"Do you have any idea who did it?" my dad asked.

"No. But the sheriff is investigating. Hopefully we'll have something or someone soon."

I was still in shock and disbelief. I wanted answers—firm answers I could grasp on to—and the only one to give them to me was . . .

"Dad? What happened in Havenwood Falls that made us leave?"

My dad walked up and put his arm around me, then sat me back down on the couch. "Havenwood Falls was a place we lived with your mother and brother. It's the place you were born, Eris. But something horrible happened. Something I couldn't stop." Tears welled in his eyes, and I could tell he struggled with telling me everything. Telling me the truth. "Soon, I will be able to explain it all to you, but not right now. All you need to know is there were things that happened in Havenwood Falls that forced me to leave and take you with me. Promises I made to your mother. And of course, things I wanted to forget." His head lowered. I could tell that most of his memories had returned. But mine still hadn't. *Why?*

My dad had kept one single picture of my mother, which was framed and placed on our living room mantel. It had been the only evidence I possessed that proved she existed. So many nights I stared at that picture, memorizing the lines of her face. She was beautiful and had so much life in her golden-brown eyes. She was laughing, the sun beaming just as bright as her smile, her golden hair shimmering. When I closed my eyes, I could almost see her and often imagined what it would have been like to have her in my life. How different it would have been.

My dad told me she'd died giving birth to me. He'd handwritten it on the back of the picture.

Aurora Witheridge-Blaekthorn – Beloved wife

Died giving birth to daughter.

But that wasn't true. In the picture Garrick brought, she was there, and I was about nine or ten.

I jumped up to grab her picture from the mantel when my dad pulled Garrick to the side. He tried to talk softly, but I could hear him clearly.

"I'll need to make arrangements for Eris before I leave."

I turned, aghast. "Arrangements? No, Dad. You are *not* leaving me here."

"Eris," my dad exhaled. "There are things in Havenwood Falls that can—"

"Hurt me?" I huffed. "Dad, the world is filled with things that can hurt me. I'm not a child anymore. I'm seventeen. And, besides, you've taught me how to defend myself." He knew that was true. "Dad, please. You can't leave me here. You can't keep me from seeing my brother."

I turned to Garrick and hoped he would help plead my case. "I think she should come, Piers. She might be able to help."

"No. Absolutely not!" my father growled. "I don't want her involved in any of the family issues."

"Piers, you can't keep her away forever. It's in her blood."

"What's in my blood? What aren't you telling me?" I demanded.

"I said no," my dad snarled and walked away. "Besides, she has school work."

"Dad, it's winter break and besides . . . I'm homeschooled," I rebutted.

He wasn't going to budge, so I had to come up with something else. If anyone could change his mind, it was me. I knew him best, and I knew what it took to play his heartstrings. If I could get him thinking, then maybe, I'd have a chance.

I followed him into the kitchen. "Listen, Dad. You have a son in a coma. I agree, you need to go and be with him, but you'll be leaving me here for days, maybe longer, under the supervision of an old woman. What if something happened? You wouldn't be here to protect me. Besides that, I just found out I have a brother who is in a coma. I *need* to be there, too."

Garrick joined us, leaning against the kitchen entryway. "She'll be safe with the family, Piers."

I twirled back, and Garrick winked at me. At that moment, I liked him. I had an uncle who was on my side, and it felt good.

Lyra also stepped in and added, "We can put wards up around your property. She'll be safe as long as she stays within the boundary. Besides, I agree with Garrick. It's better for her to be surrounded by family, and I think it's time—" She stopped.

"Time for what?" I asked. My dad's eyes narrowed.

"To meet your family." She smiled.

I knew that wasn't what she had been about to say, but I took it, because they were pushing for me to go.

My father had taught me everything I needed to know about self-defense and how to use weapons, but there was something about me he didn't know. A secret I'd kept from him, different from the magic I had when I was younger.

Ever since I'd turned sixteen, strange things started happening to me. Things I couldn't explain.

My sense of smell, taste, and hearing were heightened, and I could see extremely well in the dark. Not only that, I felt strong—*really* strong—and could move heavy things with no problem. At first, it terrified me, but I knew that if I told my dad, he'd freak.

He was the kind of dad who would rush to the drugstore and buy a ton of medicine if he heard me cough.

The thing was, since the changes started a year ago, I never got sick. Not once. So, I kept the changes to myself. Besides, I didn't want anyone else to know. They wouldn't understand. I'd read enough books and watched enough movies to know what would happen if I went to a doctor. I'd be tested—poked and prodded—and then they'd give the ultimate answer: "I'm sorry, Mr. Blaekthorn. We don't know what's wrong with her." Then there'd be more experiments, only to get more unanswered results. Nope. I wasn't a damn lab rat.

So, I embraced my oddities.

I knew, deep inside, nothing was wrong with me. Actually, I felt like everything was right.

With the new changes, I was also having a recurring dream of a woman, tall and beautiful, with long golden hair and honey-colored eyes. And with her, always at her side, was a beautiful golden-haired wolf. She would kneel and embrace it, pet its thick fur, and sing sweetly to it, lulling the wolf to sleep. When her eyes found mine again, she would smile, and the dream would end.

I had no idea what the dream meant, but I always felt so peaceful when I would wake after it. It happened so often, I felt like I knew the woman. She looked a lot like my mother, but she wasn't her. She was older, and I often wondered if she was my estranged grandmother. The woman I was told left after my grandfather died, without a word.

Another knock on the door made me stiffen. This time, my dad went to get it.

"Ms. Gingrich," he said, and I sighed.

"Is everything all right?" she asked in her old, craggy voice.

"Yes," he replied. "My brother stopped in for a visit."

Her head peeked in, and Uncle Garrick waved to her. "Oh, I didn't know you had a brother," she said, her eyes narrowing.

"Well, you never asked," he chuckled, then stepped outside for more privacy. It didn't matter. I could hear him even if he whispered. "Ms. Gingrich, I'd like to ask a favor."

"What is it?" she asked.

I was just about to rebut when he said, "I'll be taking Eris with me out of town for a bit, to visit the family. Would you mind watching over the place while we're gone?"

"Of course," she replied, patting his hand. "But you watch her well, Piers. Keep her safe."

"I will, ma'am. And thank you."

She nodded, then wobbled away.

Internally, I squealed.

My father had agreed to me going, but with strict rules. Mess up, and he'd drive me right back to New Mexico to stay with the Grinch, no questions asked. The utter seriousness on his face gave me no choice but to willingly agree.

Within a few hours, we were packed and ready to leave. Outside were two large, identical black trucks. To my surprise, Uncle Garrick had a Chevy Silverado 4x4, just like my dad's. I guess the Blaekthorn brothers were a lot alike.

Before we left, I saw Ms. Gingrich talking to Lyra. Lyra handed her a pamphlet, and then walked away. That was odd.

By the time we hit the highway, it was a little after midnight, and I fell asleep.

I dreamed of my brother. We were both younger, around the ages in the picture Uncle Garrick brought, and were playing in the snow. Behind us was a two-story log cabin with gray smoke billowing from the chimney. On the porch, my mom and dad sat with two steaming mugs in their hands, watching us. My father looked so much younger and stress-free. Smiles adorned their faces as they chatted and laughed with each other. I could see the love in their eyes, every time their eyes met. A look I'd never seen in my father's eyes.

Camden threw a snowball, hitting me directly in the face, and I stood there, stunned.

"Get him back, Eris!" my mother yelled. Her eyes were wide and kind, urging me to fight back.

I bent and gathered snow in my gloved hands, packing it into a tight ball. As soon as I threw it, Camden ducked, and I missed. Mom and Dad set down their mugs and ran out toward us. A family snowball fight began. Me and Mom against Camden and Dad.

My mother's laughter was beautiful. Like a ray of sunshine on the cloudiest day. We were laughing and screaming, chasing my dad and brother all around the front yard, throwing snowballs, tackling each other, making snow angels, and having a blast.

"Eris," my dad said, nudging me awake softly. "You okay?"

"M-hmm," I hummed. "Why?"

"You were making sounds in your sleep. Were you dreaming?"

"Yeah," I breathed, my heart still aching at the new memory. "I think my memories are starting to return." I was glad they hadn't come all at once. I wasn't sure if my heart could take it.

"That's good," he said.

I sat up and yawned, stretching my arms over my head. "Where are we?"

"In Colorado."

"How long have we been driving?"

"Almost seven hours," he said, his eyes tired. "I'm hoping we'll arrive soon."

We were still following Uncle Garrick's truck down a winding, narrow, bumpy road. A rocky cliff was on one side, and it looked like a sheer drop on the other. Snow lined the sides of the road, and I found myself white-knuckling the truck's grab handle.

"Haven't you learned to trust my driving yet?" he asked with a smile.

"On a normal road, yes. But in the middle of the boonies, on a road with snow, possible ice, and a death drop . . . my faith is being tested."

Dad laughed out loud, and it was a wonderful sound. I hadn't heard him laugh much since we moved to New Mexico.

He took hold of my hand. "Change is coming, Eris," he said, his eyes still on the road ahead. "But we'll get through it together, like we always have."

I turned to him and smiled. "I know we will, Dad . . . like we always have."

CHAPTER 3

a little after eight in the morning, we pulled in front of a
building with a sign on its front that read "Havenwood Falls
Medical Center." It looked like it was once a one-and-a-half-story
home that had been renovated, and was painted white with blue
trim.

Lyra waved goodbye and headed to a car in one of the stalls. Two
men, who looked like they could be related, met my dad and uncle
outside of the facility. Uncle Garrick extended his hand to the older
one, who was wearing a flannel shirt and jeans.

"Sheriff Kasun," he addressed him, then nodded to the other,
dressed in a police uniform. "Conall."

"Eris, why don't you go inside," my dad instructed. "We'll be
right in."

It was cold outside, so I happily obliged.

As I stepped into the facility, I saw a girl around my age sitting
behind a desk to the right, flipping through a magazine. She was
pretty, with long black hair, hazel eyes, and a nose piercing. "Hi. How
can I help you?" she asked with a smile.

I swallowed and walked up to her. "I'm here to see my brother,
Camden Blaekthorn."

She gasped, her eyes widening as she took in my face. "Your Cam's sister, Eris." I was a little taken aback she knew who I was, but nodded. "Gosh, you've, like, totally changed since the last time I saw you."

I studied her face, but didn't recognize her.

"You, don't remember me, do you?"

I shook my head. "I'm sorry."

"Hey, it's fine. I suppose you'll, like, remember all the details later, huh?" She grinned, tapping the side of her temple with her finger. "My name's Taylor."

"Nice to meet you, Taylor," I said.

"I bet the family's glad you're back," she added.

I shrugged. "I haven't seen them yet."

"Oh." Her eyes flitted to a chart on her desk. "Well, I'm sorry about your brother. I hope they, like, find out what happened to him soon." She leaned over the desk and pointed to my left. "He's in room number two. Take a right around that corner, and it's down the hall on your left. The nurse practitioner checked on him like ten minutes ago, so you're free to go in."

"Thank you," I said.

"Good luck." She smiled. "And it's good to have you back."

I nodded and smiled back, then began my journey down the stark white hall. My heart hammered harder and faster with every step I took, a mixture of anxiety and excitement welling up inside of me.

The place smelled sterile, a mixture of bleach and lemon cleaners.

Then, I spotted a small black number attached to a door. *Two.* Taking in a few deep breaths, I placed my hand on the knob and paused. My feet were frozen, not allowing me to step any farther.

Just do it, Eris, I urged myself.

I took in one last breath, then turned the knob and pushed the door open.

A young man lay on a bed, eyes closed, chest steadily rising and falling. Wires were attached to him, monitoring his heartbeat. The steady spikes on the monitor appeared to be strong.

I studied his profile, his features so foreign, yet so familiar. Flashes of memories, once stolen from me, started to return. But they were from when we were much younger.

I still wanted to know why we'd been separated and all memories of him erased. They said it was to protect the town, but there had to be more. My dad left this place for a reason. What was so important that a father would leave his son? What happened here in Havenwood Falls that made us leave seven years ago?

I made a silent promise to myself, and to my brother, that I'd help to find out what happened. Even if I had to look myself.

Judging by the photo, Camden had completely changed. He wasn't a boy anymore. He was a young man. He looked muscular, his body a lot longer, his face thinned out, his nose strong, and jaw more prominent and stubbled with facial hair. I wondered if he would have known me if he saw me. Because if I'd seen him in New Mexico, even if he stood right in front of me, I would have never guessed he was my brother.

"*Who* are *you*?" A deep, sensual voice rumbled behind me, making me jump.

I turned back, but had to look up at the figure standing behind me.

Good God, he was gorgeous, around my age, with a strong jaw and straight nose. His hair was dark brown and unkempt, like he'd raked his fingers through it a few times. He was tall, at least six-one, with broad shoulders and defined muscles under his almost too-tight shirt.

But it was his eyes that captured me. Beneath the long, dark lashes were the most beautiful hazel eyes rimmed in gold.

Where did he come from? I hadn't heard anyone walk down the hall.

A devilish grin grew on his full lips, and heat rushed to my cheeks. Quickly, I turned away, arms crossed over my chest, hoping that if I ignored him he'd go away.

"Are you Cam's new girl?" he questioned.

I gasped, pivoting back to him. "Excuse me?" I shot him my best evil eye. But it did absolutely nothing, only made his full lips turn up even more—lips I wasn't sure whether I wanted to punch or to know what they felt like pressed against mine.

Wait. No! What the hell was I thinking?

He stepped closer, his right hand braced against the doorframe, blocking me in. "So, where has he been hiding you?" His voice was low and seductive, his eyes sweeping down my body and back up until he met mine.

"Who the hell are you?" I sneered, wanting to smack that adorable grin right off his face.

"I'm Cam's best friend, Rylan. Rylan Gilles." He held out a hand to me, but I didn't take it. I exhaled and turned my attention back to my brother.

"Well?" he pressed.

"Well, what?"

"Are you going to tell me your name?"

"No."

Laughter rumbled behind me.

I didn't know this guy and wasn't here to make a new friend. All I wanted, was to see my brother.

I heard him take a step closer and could feel his body heat radiating against my back. I twisted my head toward him. "Haven't you heard of personal space?"

His eyes narrowed as he tucked his hands into his jeans. "You're feisty."

"Well, you're rude."

"I like feisty."

"I'm sure you do," I exhaled. "So why don't you go somewhere else and find a feisty girl who gives a damn." He didn't respond, so I glanced back. "What?"

"Nothing." His eyes narrowed, studying mine, but he still had that damn snarky grin.

My dad's voice echoed from down the hall.

"Over here," I called, hoping to squash this awkward chatter.

"Hey, Rylan," Uncle Garrick said as they stopped near us. "How's Cam doing?"

"Nothing's changed," Rylan replied. "Vera said you'd gone out of town, but wouldn't tell me why."

Uncle Garrick smiled. "Well, this is why." He threw an arm around my dad's shoulder. "Rylan, I'd like you to meet my oldest brother, Piers. Cam's father."

"Wow," Rylan exhaled, extending his hand. "It's a pleasure to meet you, sir." My dad took Rylan's hand and shook it firmly.

"Piers, Rylan has been staying with me and Vera," Uncle Garrick explained.

I stayed tight-lipped but listened intently.

"He came wandering into Havenwood Falls about six months ago, after he lost his family. He and Cam became close friends, and when Cam told us about his situation . . . we couldn't help but take him in." He slapped an arm around Rylan's neck. "He's a good kid, and a big help around the property and the store."

"It's nice to meet you, Rylan," my dad said, using his cautious voice. I could see his eyes carefully studying Rylan's face.

"And," Uncle Garrick's hand landed on my shoulder, "Rylan, this is my beautiful niece, Eris . . . Cam's sister."

There was a sparkle in Rylan's eyes as he glanced at me. "It's a pleasure to meet you, *Eris*." His head angled, giving me a broad smile, revealing straight, white teeth.

God damn it. Why did he have to be so damn handsome *and* cocky?

We must have held each other's stares for some time, because my dad cleared his throat. Rylan turned away first, and I exhaled a breath I wasn't aware I was holding.

"I'm sure my brother has a set of rules for his household," my dad started, and my stomach began twisting. My dad glanced at me, and I knew exactly what he was going to say next. The same thing he told every boy he thought showed the slightest bit of interest in me. "But I have one very important rule for you. My daughter is off limits." It wasn't only a command; it was a warning.

"Yes, sir," Rylan answered with a nod of his head. He then glanced at me, and I shrugged, quickly turning away.

"Good, then," my dad said. "Now that we're all on the same page,

I need to see my son." He stepped around me and headed toward my brother. I tried to follow, but my feet were still frozen.

Uncle Garrick stepped forward, patting Rylan on the shoulder. "I'll see you at home." He then followed after my dad.

Twisting my head back one last time, I saw a smile broaden on Rylan's face, making the gold around his eyes shimmer brighter. He leaned close, his scent refreshing and attractive, a mixture of pine and fresh air, and what I thought the forest might smell like after a rainstorm.

"I'll catch you later, cupcake," he whispered softly into my ear, the heat of his breath brushing against my cheek.

"Don't call me cupcake," I growled. And before I could say anything else, he winked and walked away, chuckling, as if my dad's words meant nothing. As he exited, my body relaxed.

What the hell was wrong with me?

I turned my gaze back into the room. My father was leaning over my brother, whispering words into his ear, holding his hand. My heart ached as I finally stepped inside and closed the door.

CHAPTER 4

There was a knock on the door a few minutes later. A man walked in and shut the door behind him. He was of average build, with salt-and-pepper hair and navy-blue eyes. He tucked a pen into his white lab coat and walked up to my dad, extending his hand.

"You must be Piers Blaekthorn," he said. "It's nice to meet you. I'm Dr. Underwood."

My father took his hand and shook it. "Nice to meet you, Doctor. Do you know what's happening to my son?"

"We're not entirely sure. The mages believe it's a spell, and because my own healing abilities don't seem to work on him either, I'd have to agree. It's a dark spell that is keeping him in a deep sleep, and he hasn't been responding to any treatment. But Garrick told me about what happened to your wife. Do you know if—"

"Wait," my dad interjected, holding up his hand. He then turned his attention to me, and his eyes softened. "Eris, could you please wait outside for a moment?"

"Why?" I was confused. Was what happened to Camden connected to my mom?

"Please, honey." His eyes begged. "There are things we need to discuss privately."

"If it's about Mom and you know what happened, I think it's time you told me."

"I will, sweetheart," he said, his fingers brushing the side of my cheek. He stood in front of me, laying both hands on my shoulders. "I promise, when we're done here, and I know more, I will tell you everything."

"Everything?" I questioned.

"Everything."

"You promise?"

"Yes, I promise."

"Okay," I sighed, giving in.

He leaned forward and kissed my forehead. "Thank you."

I guess waiting a little while longer was better than nothing. I knew his memory was still returning too, so I didn't want to push him.

"I can take her home," Uncle Garrick offered, his eyes finding mine. "Your aunts Vera and Lydia are there and very excited to meet you. They've been going on about how great it will be to have another female around."

My dad's brow raised at me . . . a silent question to see if I agreed. And I did. I was glad to learn I had two aunts. Maybe they knew my mom. And maybe they would have some information about her to tell me.

"When you're done with the doctor, text me," Uncle Garrick said to my dad. "Lyra said she was going to register you with the Court of the Sun and the Moon, but I'll try to get a hold of her daughter, Addie, about putting on your tattoos. Maybe she'll be able to swing by the house later."

"That'll be great," my dad replied, his voice strained.

"Wait. Tattoos?" I said a little too excitedly, knowing my dad would never let me get one.

"They're temporary. For visitors," Uncle Garrick explained.

"Why?" I asked. "That's an odd thing to give visitors."

"This town is . . . well, not your normal town," Dr. Underwood added.

"Yeah, that's what I've been hearing." I exhaled.

Uncle Garrick's phone chimed. "Come on, princess," he said, glancing at his phone. "Aunt Vera wants me home. Something about a clogged pipe." He sighed and rolled his eyes. "I'll take you to your place, so you can unpack, or rearrange your room, or do whatever it is you want to do."

"We have our own place?"

"Of course you do." Uncle Garrick took my hand and led me out of the room. "We have cabins on the outskirt of town, where we run our business."

I glanced back at my dad before the door closed, his eyes sad, his body tense as he turned to the doctor.

What was really happening? I hoped he could find answers soon. I needed them as much as he did.

As we drove in silence, Uncle Garrick finally spoke. "Hey, Eris?"

I knew the tone. It sounded so much like my dad's voice when he was preparing to offer a "helpful" speech.

"Yeah?" I answered.

"I know this is a huge change for you. But we're all family, and you and your dad were meant to be here with us. I understand why your dad left and took you away from here. It was a hard time for all of us, but I really believe things will be better now that you're both here."

"You know what happened?"

"Yes." He sighed, deeply. "But that's not a story for me to tell. I'm sorry. I know your dad will explain everything soon, but I know it's overwhelming for him too. Everything he wanted to forget, all the negative memories, especially of the loss of your mother, has come back to him all at once. Just give him a little time to process it all." He placed his large hand over mine. "Okay?"

"Okay." I looked out the window and watched the tall pine trees pass by.

"It's good to have you back, princess."

"Thanks." I wondered if they all had their own nicknames for me.

In no time, we pulled down a road that headed toward the mountains. On the left was a large building, with a sign on the front that read "Blaekthorn Lumber & Supply" around a logo of a howling wolf with pine trees. The entire building was decorated with icicle lights and other Christmas decorations.

"That's our family store," Uncle Garrick said, pointing toward it. "I'll give you a tour later."

"Wow, it's big," I murmured, more to myself. "I like the logo. Are there wolves in the forest?"

He laughed and glanced at me. "Yeah, there are definitely wolves that roam around this area."

"Oh," I replied. Dad would probably give me a weapon before I went sightseeing. "So, where do you get all the lumber?"

"Right here, on our property. One day we'll show you the operation. How we chop the trees, load them, and take them to our mill, where we strip and cut them into lumber."

I was impressed. "How big is the property?" It must have been huge to process a lot of lumber for a lumberyard. I also knew it took years and years to grow a tree.

A smile widened on his face. "Big enough. You'll soon learn about how things work here at Blaekthorn Lumber, but I think it's best if you and your dad, once he returns, sit and discuss more important matters first."

I nodded. His words brought nothing but more confusion, and made my head throb.

We traveled down a graveled drive, with manicured shrubs and greenery lining the path on either side, and beyond that, lots and lots of pine trees.

I imagined the drive filled with blooming flowers during the spring and summer. But it was winter now, New Year's Eve, and remnants of a recent snow lined the sides of the drive. The sky was brightening, but still gray and cloudy and cold.

Maybe I'd get to see snow fall before we left here. It didn't happen often in our small town in New Mexico.

Soon, three large log cabins came into view, each separated by at least a half-acre. They were beautiful, with snow-covered mountains as a backdrop. Pine trees in each of the front yards were covered with

Christmas lights. I could barely see them now that the sky was brighter, but knew they'd be gorgeous at night.

The cabins were built the same—two stories, with front stairs that led to wrap-around porches. These were *not* what I had expected when Uncle Garrick said cabins, but then again, I recalled the picture and the dream I'd had, and they were exactly the same.

We pulled up to the house in the middle, where Uncle Garrick's truck idled. "Well, this is it. Welcome home, Eris." He handed me a key and patted my hand. "Cam has been staying here for the last few years, when he's not at our house for food, but we've made sure he kept the place clean. Your room is upstairs. I'm sure you'll know which one it is as soon as you see it. Your aunt Vera bought you some new bedding and girly room stuff, and said she can take you shopping later in town if you needed anything else."

"Thank you." I tried to smile, but wasn't sure if I was ready.

"Did you want me to walk you in?" he asked.

"No, I've got this," I said with feigned confidence.

"All right. When you're ready, come over. My house is that one." He pointed to the cabin on the left when his phone chimed. "Your Aunt Vera just texted. She'll have breakfast and coffee ready when you arrive."

"That sounds great. Thanks again." I grabbed my bag, and as soon as I slid out of his truck, a cold breeze bit every exposed area on my body. I shivered, ready to take Aunt Vera up on shopping for some warmer clothes, if I was going to be here for any length of time.

As he pulled away, I stepped up the stairs, stairs I probably ran up and down countless times in my past. My heart hammered, and I suddenly wished my dad was here. There were buried memories I had of this place, and I hoped they didn't come with some horrors.

Putting the key into the door, I twisted the knob and pushed it open. The inside was nice and open. To the right was a large kitchen with all the amenities, even a large potted poinsettia. Behind the kitchen was a dining area, and to the left was a family room with plush brown couches, a fireplace with a fire already crackling inside—most likely thanks to one of my aunts—and a large screen TV. In one corner was a large, real Christmas tree, beautifully decorated, but losing some of its needles, which were scattered on the ground under it.

Everything was rustic, logs and hardwood, with brighter rugs and curtains. The décor was warm and inviting, and gave me a real homey feeling.

Directly in front of me were stairs leading to the second floor. I headed up to find my room, starting with the room directly at the top of the stairs.

Turning the knob, I pushed open the door and clicked on the light. There was no doubt it was Camden's room. The décor was dark, with lots of blacks and deep reds. It was clean and somewhat organized, which I didn't expect. His walls were covered with rock posters and girls in bikinis, which, I guess, I did expect.

I was about to turn around and leave when I noticed something peeking from behind his pillows. I walked over to his bed and moved them. His headboard had four deep gashes, claw marks, marring the wood.

What the hell had happened?

I ran my fingers along them, and they were rough. Maybe he carved them out with a knife.

I didn't think he'd appreciate me being in here without his permission. But I also wondered if there was something here that could help me find out what happened.

On his dresser were a couple of pictures in frames. I picked up the first one, of Camden and Rylan sitting in front of a campfire roasting marshmallows. They were laughing, and it made me smile. I wondered what kind of a person my brother was—was he kind and fun to be around, or was he a jerk?

There was another picture of him on a ski slope with a snowboard in his hand. Next to him was a pretty blond girl. They were standing side by side, each with an arm around the other's waist. Another broad smile adorned his face.

In these pictures, he looked so happy, and the big question lingered in my mind. Why didn't he want to come with us? Why did he want to stay?

Placing the pictures back, I turned to find my room. I headed down the hall to the door closest to Uncle Garrick's house. As soon as I opened it and stepped in, there was no question it was mine, but I felt like I was walking into a toddler's room. The walls were a pale pink, reminding me of cotton candy. They must not have been painted since we left.

Then, I noticed the bedding and the matching curtains.

Oh. My. God.

The comforter was pink and covered with images of *cupcakes.* The pillowcases were cupcakes, and so were the throw pillows. One had the word "sweet" written on it in silver sequins; the other had sprinkles and a cherry. Not to mention the matching cupcake curtains.

Internally, I groaned. Rylan lived next door and probably saw Vera come home with all this stuff. Hence, the "cupcake" nickname. Oh, God. I would never hear the end of it.

The carpets were a dark brown, like chocolate, and super soft. On one wall was a dresser, and on the other, a closet and another door.

Opening the door to the adjacent room, I found a bathroom— again, fully stocked with everything I needed. It was awesome, but I moaned at the décor. More cupcakes. The carpet next to the tub was a giant freaking cupcake. And the shower curtain—pale pink with cupcakes across the center. *What the . . . ?*

Aunt Vera had OCD—obsessive cupcake disorder.

The sound of a rumbling engine had me exiting the bathroom and peeking out my bedroom window. A motorcycle pulled into Uncle Garrick's driveway, and I watched Rylan's tall, muscular frame slide off the bike and pull off his helmet. Even from behind, he looked hot. Especially his butt, and the way it filled out his jeans.

After raking his fingers through his thick hair, Rylan's head twisted in my direction, his head lifting, his eyes finding my window. A broad smile rose on his lips, and then . . . he waved.

I snapped the curtain shut and pressed my back against the wall. *Crap!* He caught me. How did he know I was watching? Did he know this was my bedroom?

The thought of him helping my aunt decorate my cupcake room was disconcerting.

Slowly peeking back out a small crack in the curtain, I watched him enter the house. My insides twisted, realizing he was going to be there when I went over for breakfast.

He was going to be trouble.

CHAPTER 5

*A*fter taking a shower and changing into my warmest clothes, I walked next door and nearly froze to death. How the heck could Rylan ride a motorcycle in this frigid air?

As I knocked on the door, my stomach somersaulted, over and over. For me, these were brand-new family members. Most of my memories still hadn't returned, and I was beginning to wonder if they would.

As soon as the door opened, I was squeezed tight by a woman I assumed to be Aunt Vera. She was beautiful, tall and lean, with long brunette hair and deep green eyes. "Eris Blaekthorn. Look at you," she said in a Southern accent. "You're all grown up, and so beautiful," she gushed, holding my face in her hands. "You look so much like your mother." Her smile was refreshing. "Come inside, you must be freezing."

"Thank you," I said.

She took my hand and led me into the kitchen where it was warm, and there was a huge spread of pancakes, bacon, sausages, hash browns, fruit, muffins, and coffee.

"Here ya go," she said, handing me a plate, pushing me toward the food. "You must be famished."

I wasn't gonna lie. "I am." It all looked yummy, so I decided to take a little of everything.

"Welcome home! I hope you like your bedding," she added. "There weren't many choices in town. It was either the cupcakes or a huge rainbow with clouds."

"I like the cupcakes," I said with a smile, sitting at the dining table.

"Well, good," she chimed. "I liked the cupcakes too. I thought the chocolate ones went perfectly with your carpet."

"They do," I agreed, trying to sound thankful. "Thanks again."

"Cupcakes?" a familiar voice sounded. "I love cupcakes."

I turned to see Rylan jogging down the stairs, freshly showered. He was in jeans and . . . shirtless. His upper body was still wet, glistening, and it looked as if God himself might have chiseled that chest. Tight skin. Muscles. Perfection.

A tribal tattoo covered his right shoulder and bicep.

"Rylan, put your shirt on," Aunt Vera puffed. "We have a guest."

"I see that," Rylan said before he stretched a shirt over his head. I watched in awe as his muscles flexed as he slowly pulled his shirt down.

Holy hell.

Before he spotted me gawking, I snapped my head to my plate, attempting to spear a stray strawberry.

"Rylan, this is Eris, Camden's sister," she introduced, plating a fresh batch of muffins from the oven.

Rylan's eyes met mine, with a sparkle in them. "Yeah, we met at the medical center."

Walking over to the counter, he grabbed a plate and piled on bacon, eggs, sausages, and pancakes. Then, he headed in my direction and sat directly across from me.

He winked, and I instantly felt self-conscious, wondering if I had food on my face or in my teeth.

"Rylan, how is Cam doing?" Aunt Vera asked. "Have they found out anything yet?"

"Nothing yet," Rylan replied. "But Sheriff Kasun and his pack have been investigating. Hopefully, the mages can find a cure soon."

"I hope so too. I've been worried sick. I'll drop by this afternoon," she said.

"What did you mean by pack?" I asked Rylan. "And aren't mages sorcerers?"

"Oh." Aunt Vera turned with a bewildered look on her face. "He meant officers, and I guess you could say the ones helping are like shamans. Healers."

The phone rang, and my aunt stepped out of the kitchen.

Rylan leaned across the table to grab the syrup, which was right in front of me. "Hey, cupcake."

"Don't." I scowled, which made him chuckle.

His head cocked to the side. "I thought you liked cupcakes."

"I do. I—" He was getting me tongue-tied, so I changed the subject. "You could have asked me to pass the syrup."

"And miss a chance to get closer to you?" he purred.

I narrowed my eyes, glaring at him, but my stomach had butterflies slam dancing inside. He picked up a piece of bacon, his eyes locked on mine, and he bit it. Damn him. And damn the way he made eating that piece of bacon so freaking sexy. He knew it too. *Jerk.*

Aunt Vera returned to the kitchen.

"Where's Uncle Garrick?" I asked.

"Oh, that was him. He'll be here shortly. He had to run over to the warehouse because they had a big order and needed his help."

"They should have told me. I could have helped," Rylan said.

"Oh, it's already done. Garrick just needed to operate the loader, and you know how much he loves driving that large machine," she said, turning with a grin.

"Hello?" A voice called from the door.

Aunt Vera shuffled toward it, wiping her hands on her apron. "Lydia, come in!"

"Is our princess here?" a high voice squealed.

In walked a pretty, blond woman of medium build, with bright red lips and large boobs. She peeled out of her long coat, revealing a sundress with brightly printed flowers all over it.

How could she not be cold?

Aunt Vera tipped her head toward me. "She's having breakfast with Rylan."

I heard Rylan chuckle under his breath, then I turned to watch Aunt Lydia enter.

"Eris, darlin'. Look. At. You," she gushed, clapping her hands in front of her. "You're a vision. Isn't she a vision?" Aunt Lydia also had a Southern accent, much stronger than Aunt Vera's.

I stood as she walked over, and she pulled me into a bear hug. My cheek pressed firmly against her chest, and I caught Rylan trying to swallow a laugh.

"I'm your aunt Lydia," she finally said, setting me free. "I used to change your diapers when you were just a baby." Another chuckle from Rylan. "You'll get to see your uncle Barney soon. He's been out chopping trees or God knows what else. I swear, if I didn't promise him food and some good lovin', that man would live in them woods."

"Lydia," Vera scolded, her eyes widening.

"Oh, Vera. Look at her. She's not a child anymore. Are you, Eris?"

"No, ma'am," I answered, feeling childish, and didn't dare glance up to see Rylan's expression.

"You'll also get to meet your cousins, Weston and Drake. They're over at a friend's house playing video games." She sighed. "I haven't seen much of them over winter break, but told them they had to come home this afternoon for our New Year's Eve barbecue."

She walked over to Rylan and gave him a hug. "I see you've met our resident hottie," she said. "He doesn't have a girlfriend yet. Well, at least none we know of." Her eyes narrowed on him.

Rylan shook his head. "No ma'am. No girl, *yet*." As he spoke the last word, his eyes met mine, making my face and insides heat. *Jerk*.

"Lydia," Vera scolded. "No matchmaking in this house. Piers will go full wolf on you."

I laughed. "Full wolf?"

They both looked at each other. "Oh, it's just a saying. Means he'll shred her to bits."

"Yes." Lydia laughed, slapping a hand on Rylan's shoulder. "Eris's daddy is wildly protective. We like you, Rylan, and your handsome face. So, don't go making googly eyes at her or make her blush in front of him," she warned, pinching his cheek.

This time *I* laughed as his nose crinkled.

"I'll keep that in mind," he said, his smile widening. "At least on my part."

"Eris, don't mind your aunt Lydia," Vera sighed, finally grabbing a plate. "She doesn't have a filter, and speaks whatever is on her mind."

"Don't worry." I chuckled. "I'm used to it. My dad doesn't have a filter either."

Breakfast was eventful. Both aunts asked me a ton of questions about growing up in New Mexico, and although there wasn't much interesting to tell, they hung on every word. Much to my surprise, so did Rylan.

"So, Rylan, what are your plans for the rest of winter break?" Aunt Lydia asked, popping a grape into her mouth.

"I'll probably ask the Kasuns if they need any help with the investigation."

"That's great. I'm sure they could use it. The sheriff and the Court have been extra busy this winter break, especially with that teenage girl who went missing . . . Heidi Bennett. Did you know her, Rylan?"

"No, but everyone in school was talking about her disappearance. It's almost been a month."

Aunt Lydia shook her head. "That's so sad. I hope they find that poor girl. Maybe she left and didn't tell anyone." Her eyes narrowed as she turned to Rylan, "Do y'all think Camden and Heidi's cases are related?"

"I don't know," Rylan replied. "They are totally different, but could be. Something strange is going on, that's for sure. I hope they find out what it is before anyone else goes missing or gets hurt."

"Yes, no going off into the woods alone," Aunt Lydia said, sipping her coffee.

"What happened to Camden?" I asked. "I mean . . . who found him and where?"

Rylan set his fork down. "A guy named Rusty found him in the woods and brought him into the medical center. He said he found him unconscious."

I nodded, wondering how it happened. "Where did he find him?"

"On the other side of Cooley Creek, which runs between the Blaekthorn property and Havenstone," Rylan replied, pointing east. "His body was found a few miles behind Havenstone. Right on the bank of the creek."

"Thank God for Rusty," Aunt Lydia sighed. "Who knows what would have happened to Camden if he hadn't been on patrol?"

There were stomps on the porch outside, and then we heard, "We're home!"

The door swung open, and Uncle Garrick, my dad, and another man with a full beard stomped in.

"Well, well, look what the wolves dragged in." Aunt Lydia laughed. Both women stood and headed over to the men. "Piers, aren't you a sight for sore eyes," Lydia said, hugging him tightly. My dad hugged her back.

"It's good to see you too, Lyd," he replied, his voice tired.

"Piers," Vera squealed. My dad picked her up and twirled her. "It's good to have you back. I can't believe how grown up Eris is. She looks so much like Aurora."

A sadness washed over my dad's face as he looked at me. "Yes, she does. And it's good to be back."

"Did they have any new news about Cam?" Lydia asked.

"No. Nothing yet," Garrick replied.

"Well, go get something to eat before you all waste away," Vera said, waving the men to the table.

"Princess!" The man with the beard exclaimed, smiling broadly at me. He looked like a muscular lumberjack. He had to be my uncle Barney, because he danced toward me with his arms wide open.

I stood to greet him, and when he reached me, he wrapped his large arms around me and squeezed me so tight I thought I was going to explode.

He was taller than both my dad and Uncle Garrick. His arms were as big as tree trunks, and his chest was solid as rock. He smelled like fresh-cut wood and earth, and when he hugged me, his beard tickled my forehead.

"Barney, let the girl breathe!" Aunt Lydia exclaimed, smacking him on his arm.

He let go with a hearty laugh. "Princess, you look as pretty as your mother. Thank God," he said, nudging my dad.

Dad glanced at me and smiled. "Hey, I contributed to half of her looks."

"Yeah, I can see that. She definitely has your ears and neck." Another boisterous laugh burst from Uncle Barney's gut. My dad first growled at him, then joined in with his laughter, which was infectious.

I was happy to see my dad with his family, smiling and laughing. For so long it'd just been the two of us, but it seemed like he was falling right back into this world. Although it was still a world without my mom.

I wasn't sure if any of the others noticed the slight sadness behind my dad's eyes, but I did. I knew him best, and also knew that being here was bringing back both good and bad memories.

While Aunt Lydia and Vera chatted with my dad, helping to fill his plate, Rylan stood and leaned toward me. "Catch you later, cupcake," he whispered, then took his dish and walked to the sink.

"Where are you off to, Rylan?" Aunt Vera asked.

"I need to run my bike to the Havenwood Falls Garage. It's making a weird noise, so Joshua said he'd take a look at it for me."

"That's mighty nice of him," she replied. "Well, be careful. There might be ice on the roads."

"Will do," he said. He glanced my way and winked before slipping out the door.

When he left, I felt a little sad and wondered if he'd escaped to avoid conversation with my dad. If I was him, I would have.

Aunt Lydia stood. "Eris, your aunt Vera and I need to run into town a little later. We need a few more supplies for the New Year's party tonight. Would you like to come with us? We can show you the town, and maybe get you some warmer clothes?"

"I'd love that." I immediately turned to my dad for affirmation.

"Yes, that's fine," he said. "As long as you stick with your aunts. No going off on your own." He gave me his very stern, serious look.

"I won't," I said.

"Eris, we have a lot to discuss," he added. "You ready to go home?"

The room instantly quieted. I stood and took my dad's and my dishes to the sink. "Thanks for breakfast, Aunt Vera. I'm glad I got to meet all of you . . . again," I said, and they all laughed.

I followed my dad outside.

"Hey, remember we're having a New Year's Eve party at our house tonight," Uncle Barney called after us. "We're gonna have a barbecue, fireworks, and I got a brand-new guitar."

"We'll be there," my dad said, then took my hand. "You ready?"

I took a deep breath and exhaled. "Yeah. I'm ready."

"Good, because it's time for you to learn the entire truth."

Even though a few memories had returned to me, I knew there were still things hidden without the spell. Like how my mom died, why I was taken away from this place, and why Camden was left behind.

I was anxious, but glad I was finally going to get some answers.

CHAPTER 6

The walk back to our cabin was short and brisk, but the cool air was enlivening. Walking up the steps to the porch, my dad paused and turned around to glance at me. I gave him a nod of affirmation and realized it was the first time he'd been back here since we'd left seven years ago.

He unlocked the door and pushed it in, then stood in the entry a few moments before he strode into the kitchen, toward the fridge, and opened the door. It was fully stocked.

Grabbing a bottled water, he twisted the top off and slid onto one of the barstools at the counter, then patted the stool next to him.

My heart thrummed inside my chest. Answers. I was finally going to get answers.

"Have all your memories come back yet?" I asked.

He took a swig and nodded. "Most of them."

"Mine haven't."

His eyes met mine. "They will. You were young when we left, so there might be things your mind won't remember."

I nodded. "What happened to Mom?"

He placed his bottle of water on the table and folded his hands together, staring blankly at the poinsettia in front of him.

Then he began. "Your mother was special. She was not only

270

beautiful, but she was brave and smart. And she loved her family fiercely."

My heart swelled at the thought. "How did you two meet?"

A memory must have flashed before him, because he blinked it away and took another sip of water.

"Before I explain anything else, there are things I need to warn you about. Things you might not fully understand or even believe in."

"Dad, just tell me," I sighed. "I promise . . . I can handle it."

A grin rose on his lips as he swiveled his chair to face me. "Your mother was a woman of magic, and she came from a long line of magic."

"Magic as in—"

"Witches," he said. "Your mother was a very powerful witch, as were her mother, grandmother, and great-grandmother. Her father— your grandfather—was a hunter." I was still trying to process the witch part when he added, "A werewolf hunter."

My eyes narrowed on him. "Werewolf hunter?"

I thought he was joking and started to laugh, but his face hardened.

Oh my God. He was serious.

I swallowed a lump in my throat. "Did he catch any?"

He turned away from me, his elbows resting on the counter. "Yes, he did. He was responsible for killing a mother and her thirteen-year-old son while they were out hunting for food one night. He shot the mother with an arrow, and when the son refused to leave her side, he shot him too."

"My God," I gasped. My heart ached as my mind conjured the horrific scene. "They were werewolves?"

He nodded. "Shifters that had taken their wolf form during the blue moon."

I swallowed hard. "So, what does this have to do with you meeting Mom?"

"Everything," he replied. "The pack—of the woman and boy— found out what happened to them and planned revenge on your grandfather. One night, when your grandparents and mother were sleeping, they attacked. They kidnapped your grandfather and mother, but your grandmother managed to escape. To this day, no one knows what happened to her. She just . . . disappeared."

"Do you think she's dead?"

"It's likely," he breathed. "If she was alive, I'm sure she would have tried to make contact. But we've heard nothing."

"And you met Mom . . . "

"They took your grandfather and mother deep into the woods where no one could hear their screams. Then, the man whose wife and son your grandfather murdered beat to near death and then bit Aurora —your mother and his only daughter—sealing her fate to become a werewolf. The one thing he hunted and hated most. Then, they beat him and ripped him to shreds.

"Thinking she'd die, they dumped your mother's body in the river. But they didn't know how strong she was. She drew on every bit of strength she had left inside, and clawed herself to the bank." He pressed his thumb and forefinger to the bridge of his nose. "That's where I found her."

A tear trickled down my cheek. "You were her hero."

He sighed, his brow furrowed, his eyes deeply saddened. "She was barely alive. We didn't think she'd survive through the night. My father called a shaman in a nearby town, and he did what he could. And before the shaman left, he pulled me to the side and told me my fate was tied to hers.

"I stayed with her the entire night, made sure she was breathing, and tended to her wounds. My mother didn't want to have anything to do with her at first, because she didn't want trouble with the rival pack. But she came around, after seeing how dedicated I was to keeping her alive."

"Rival pack? Wouldn't that make you . . . "

"Yes, Eris. My family—our family—are shifters."

I swallowed the huge lump in my throat, my heart jackhammering. "Werewolves?"

"Yes."

"The entire family?"

He nodded. "They are all werewolves. Your uncles, aunts, and cousins."

I sat there for long minutes, processing it all. The changes I went through when I turned sixteen, the dream of the woman with the wolf. It started to make sense.

I'd read enough werewolf books to know the heightened senses were part of it, but I'd always thought they were pure fiction. It was no wonder my dad was always asking me if I felt anything unusual. He knew I might experience these things. All that time I'd just thought he was being overprotective.

But in some of the stories I'd read, the wolves shifted at will, while in others, their shifts were controlled by the moon.

"Dad, can the family shift whenever it wants?"

"Our shifts were controlled by the moon and its phases," he started, and I cut in.

"Why haven't I ever seen you change or even be affected by the moon?"

He pulled his necklace from inside his shirt and held it between his fingers. I knew he'd had it for as long as I could remember, and he never took it off.

"This is an amulet. A Tiger's Eye stone. It is supposed to keep you grounded and stabilized, and enhances integrity and willpower. It is also a stone of protection. But *this* one is special." He rubbed it between his fingers. "Before we came to Havenwood Falls, your mother searched and searched, and found a spell that would allow us to change at will, and not be bound by the moon or its phases. Without the amulet, we would have no control."

"But, why haven't I shifted?"

"Most likely because you aren't a pureblood. Your mother was human—with magic in her blood—but she was not born a shifter. She was bitten. Most purebloods make their first shift by the age of thirteen. Those who aren't usually take longer . . . anywhere from the age of sixteen to eighteen. And I've even heard that some half-breeds never shift."

"Has Camden shifted?"

"He has. Garrick said his first shift was a few months after his sixteenth birthday. He was also given an amulet, but here, in Havenwood Falls, they have their own precautions. The tattoos given to the supernatural visitors and residents are magical. Another safeguard to keep the people here protected. For our family, it helps us keep our shifts under control. But with these amulets your mother spelled, we have an even greater advantage to live out normal lives, anywhere. Like we've been doing in New Mexico."

I pulled the pendant from around my neck and held it in my fingers. My dad had given it to me a year ago, when I'd turned sixteen. It was also a tiger's eye stone, in the shape of a heart, on a golden chain. He told me it was a gift from my mother and to never take it off. So I didn't.

"Your necklace was also charmed by your mother. To keep you safe and protected."

I looked up at him, his face solemn.

"What happened to her, Dad?"

"Once your mother regained her health and the new moon hung in the sky, we both transformed, shifting into our wolf forms. It was then I knew without a doubt she was my mate. The pull was strong, undeniable." He paused. "But, enough about that."

"Yeah, thanks. I don't want or need any details." I laughed.

"Your mother became my wife and mate, and we were very happy. But there was a threat we never knew of. A threat we never expected.

"A young woman, a close friend of your mother, saw how happy your mother was, and how happy we were together, and she became furiously jealous. I don't think she was in her right mind, because her obsession made her mad.

"The woman's mother was high priestess of her own coven, but she preferred to frequent your grandmother's coven and ceremonies. There were times she would follow us, hiding in the shadows, but we knew she was there. With the heightened shifter senses, we knew her scent and could hear her footsteps, even if we couldn't see her. At times, she would show up when your mother and I thought we were alone. It became very strange and uncomfortable, until one day, she caught me alone and off guard.

"I know you probably don't want to hear this, but that crazy woman tried to seduce me. I rejected her, of course, pushing away her advances, which infuriated her even more. She left in tears, ranting and raving about how I should have chosen her, and vowed that one day I would pay for my indifference and coldness toward her. I thought she was just a mad woman spouting meaningless threats and paid no heed. And we didn't see or hear from her after that day.

"Years later, we found this place called Havenwood Falls. We saw the kind of protection it offered its citizens, and how we could start a new life and business together as a pack. We settled in this area and made it our home. Being out in the woods, we decided to start the lumberyard business.

"After getting approval from the Court, your mother cast a growth spell over the forest. It makes the trees we cut down regrow to full size in weeks, instead of years. That's how our business can stay stable without leaving Havenwood Falls."

"Mom did a lot of good before she died, didn't she?"

"She did," he replied. "And she stayed true, all the way to the end." I stayed quiet, waiting for him to continue. It was just as hard for him to remember as it was for me to hear it for the first time.

"When your mother became pregnant with your brother, we were overjoyed. But when you were born, our family was complete."

"Dad, why did the picture on our mantel say that mom died giving birth to me?" I questioned.

"I wrote that because I knew I'd forget when we left, and didn't want to remember the truth of how she died."

"What is the truth?"

"I know it seems like I'm bouncing around the answer, but you need to know the entire story to understand."

"I know. I'm not pushing," I said, making a mental note not to keep asking him.

He smiled and continued. "I was walking out in the woods one afternoon when I heard footsteps behind me. I turned to see a woman standing in a long black robe, her face concealed within a large cowl. When she removed the cowl, fear overcame me for the first time since moving here.

"It was the woman. The crazed, jealous woman. And she'd somehow found us here in a place we thought we were safe. Her eyes were dark and evil, holding no emotion, and when I turned to walk away, my body froze in place. I couldn't move, and knew she'd cast a spell on me. I was alpha of my pack and protector of my family, yet this woman had rendered me helpless.

"Then, she offered me a choice. One *last* chance to leave your mother and start a life with her, or suffer the consequence. My temper got the best of me. I told her she was mad, and I would never love her. Then, I watched something inside of her snap. Her eyes went completely black, and I felt an evil power exude from her.

"Her mind was so dark and twisted, and there was nothing but hatred and jealousy in her heart, harbored all those long years. She stormed off, releasing me from the spell. When I chased after her, she was nowhere to be found. Not even a scent.

"I told your mother what happened, but we weren't even sure what she was capable of. What we didn't know was that she'd searched to find a specific spell, so dark and so evil. An unbreakable spell that would change our lives forever. Because I didn't choose her, I would now have to make another choice. To save the life of my wife or my daughter.

"It was on your tenth birthday when you and your mother fell ill. The mages here tried everything they could to stop the curse, to find a loophole, but they couldn't find one in this spell. They told me I had to prepare myself, because one of you would die." A deep sob ripped from my father's chest. His head fell onto his crossed arms on the table. My heart was shattering, splintering for the decision he had to make. Just the thought of having to choose the life of a loved one over another was devastating. It was no wonder he decided to leave this place. He didn't want to be haunted by the memories of that horrifying choice.

I reached over and took his hand, and he squeezed mine.

"I'm so sorry, Dad," I sobbed. "I'm sorry you had to choose between us."

Tears welled again from his bloodshot eyes. "Your mother made me promise to choose you. Made me swear to do everything in my power to protect you, to take you away and keep you safe." He paused and shook his head. "Your brother overheard me making the promise to your mother. He loved you, Eris, but he was just a boy who loved his mother dearly. He wanted me to choose her. Your mother loved you both fiercely, with every part of her heart, and proved she would give her life for either one of you.

"I don't blame him for wanting to choose Mom," I said. "If I'd known . . . If I'd understood what was going on, I would have told you to choose her, too."

"I know you would have." Dad gave my hand another squeeze. "The night before the spell took your mother's life—and half of my heart—Uncle Garrick found Camden in your room. You were sound asleep, and he was standing above you with a knife in his hand."

My chest constricted and ached. "He was going to kill me, wasn't he? Because he wanted Mom to live." Tears streamed down my face. "He must have hated me after she died. Hated that I was alive instead of her." I looked up at my dad. "And hated you for choosing me."

My dad slowly nodded. "I pray that no one else ever has to endure that kind of hell."

I finally realized why my brother had stayed. Why the family knew it was best, and why my father left him behind. And that day, my dad not only lost his wife and mate, he'd lost his son, too.

"I'm so sorry, Dad." I knew those words would never be enough to heal his shattered heart, but they were the only words I could find. "I have something to tell you," I said. Now that he'd told me everything, it was time I told him about me . . . about the changes and the dreams.

So, we sat at that table, and I told him everything, and when I was done, he hugged me.

"What ever happened to the woman who cast the spell?" I asked.

"No one knows. That day I saw her in the woods, she disappeared like a shadow, not leaving any trace of being in Havenwood Falls."

"Do you think she's responsible for what's happening to Camden?"

He shook his head. "I don't know. But I have to consider it a possibility."

"We'll get through this, Dad. Like we always have."

He smiled through his tears. "Yes, we will, sweetheart. Like we always have."

"So, now that all the secrets are out, what's next?" I asked.

"Lyra's daughter, Addie, will be coming to do our tattoos," he said glancing at his watch. "She should be here soon."

"Then what?"

"Then, I have to go meet Sheriff Kasun, and you're going to stay here," he said in his protective, fatherly tone. "We're going to team up, to try and find out what's going on." He swiveled back toward me. "I know your aunts are taking you shopping, but remember stay with them."

"Can't I go with you? I want to help."

"No," he said firmly, then sighed. "I know you want to help, but I don't want you anywhere near the woods. Not until we find out what's going on." His eyes softened. "Go have fun with your aunts. They're excited you're here. Okay?"

"Okay." I threw my arms around his neck, and he hugged me back.

"I love you, Eris."

"I know. I love you too, Daddy."

"I'm going to take a quick shower and change before Addie gets here."

I nodded and watched him leave.

I was trying to be strong. To show him I could handle all of this.

Outwardly, I'd become good at masking what was inside. But inside . . . inside I still had to deal with the overwhelming information about my family, who I was, and how I fit in. All while convincing myself that everything would be all right. My mother died to save me, and my brother tried to kill me. That fact alone made me wonder. Did Camden still harbor those feelings? Did he still hate me?

I'd have to prove to him that I was alive for a reason. I had to find a way to help.

CHAPTER 7

$\mathcal{I}$ was drowning in heaviness. Everything my father had shared with me—the secrets of who I really was, the curse, the promise, the reason my brother stayed—it was pressing me on all sides. The Blaekthorns were werewolves, my mother's side was witches, and her father a werewolf hunter. Talk about dysfunctional. So, what did that make me? And Camden?

My brother had already shifted, so he fit right into the Blaekthorn pack, but I was still in limbo. Maybe I would be one of those who didn't shift. Maybe I would embrace the other side of my heritage. I needed to find out more about my mother's lineage, the Witheridges, and where they came from.

A knock on the door made me jump. I thought it was the girl coming to give us the tattoos, but when I opened the door, Rylan stood there.

At the sight of him, my heart flip-flopped inside my chest, and I forgot to speak.

He laughed and raked his fingers through his hair. "I wanted to ask if, maybe later, you'd like to get a burger. Or whatever it is you like. There's a pizza joint in town, too."

I didn't know what to say. He was asking me to lunch, and we'd just met this morning. "My dad—" I paused, pointing upstairs.

"Yeah, I know. I just thought it'd be cool to get to know my best friend's sister."

God, he was making this hard. "I'm going into town with my aunts. But you're welcome to come by after, if my dad isn't here. The fridge is filled with food. I can whip something up?"

"You're going to cook for me on our first date?"

"Date?" I squeaked. "Definitely not a date. And I won't be cooking. I'll probably be throwing together sandwiches."

"That's fine with me." He shrugged, a crooked grin adorning his handsome face. "I guess I'll see you later."

"Yeah," I said, shutting the door behind him.

I let out a sigh of relief, thankful my dad wasn't here when he came to the door. Rylan was the first boy who'd heard his warning and still dared to come to my house and ask me to lunch. If my dad knew, he would never let me leave. Especially on a motorcycle with a boy I'd just met, who lived next door.

Later, my dad came down, freshly showered and changed. He was wearing blue jeans and a black-and-blue flannel shirt. "You look like you belong in a cabin in the woods," I teased.

"Well, I hope that's a good thing." He chuckled. A smile brightened his face. "I'm meeting the sheriff in town in half an hour, and I'm not sure how long I'll be gone. I told him I'd help, since he's gotten a few tips. I'll be checking out some areas while he talks to those who might have information. Uncle Barney will be coming with me, since he's the second in command. But Uncle Garrick will be next door, in case you need anything."

Not long after, a girl arrived at the house. She was very pretty, around five-six, in her mid-twenties, with light brown hair and brown eyes. She was dressed in black, with a diamond piercing in her nose and a bag slung over her shoulder. She introduced herself as Addie Beaumont, Lyra's daughter. She had come to give me and my dad our protection tattoos. It was strange, considering myself as something other than human. And it also made me wonder . . .

Was Rylan different? Did he have a protection tattoo, too?

Addie was a lot of fun and quick with her work. She did my dad's tattoo first, since he had to leave, and mine was next. Before she left, she told me that if I ever had any questions, I should come see her. It was great being accepted by the people in town, and I felt that maybe in the future, just maybe, Dad and I would return to Havenwood Falls and make it our home.

My dad grabbed his keys and headed for the door. "There is no ward on the property yet, so stay inside and keep the door locked. And when you go out with your aunts—"

"I know," I sighed. "I'll stay with them and be safe. And you be safe out there, too."

"Don't worry, sweetheart. I can take care of myself."

As I watched him walk toward his truck, Uncle Barney jogged from his house to meet him. "Hey princess, if you're bored, head next door. Your Aunt Lydia is starting her yoga session. It'll definitely keep you entertained." He laughed out loud before hopping into the passenger seat and shutting the door.

I giggled, watching them pull away. If Uncle Barney shaved his beard, he would be a mixture of my dad and Uncle Garrick.

And to think they were all werewolves. *Werewolves.* My entire family were shifters. What did they look like shifted? The thought was too overwhelming.

I closed the door and locked it behind me, then went to the fridge to see what kinds of things there were to throw together when Rylan came over. I was relieved to find cold cuts and veggies to make sandwiches. To the right of the fridge was a pantry, and inside I found some bread.

How long did they think we were going to stay here? The shelves were stocked with everything—cereal, crackers, canned goods. Then I remembered Camden was living here, too.

What was it like for him to have gone through his teenage years without a dad?

He truly missed out, because our dad had a lot of love to give. Yes, he was overprotective at times, but it was because he loved me to a fault. And I knew he would have loved Camden the same way. He still did. We were all he had left of our mother.

An hour later, my aunts collected me to go shopping. The drive into town was quick, but it was beautiful. The town was filled with lights and Christmas decorations. The shops were quaint, and it had that small-town feel and charm, and everyone we passed seemed so friendly.

We stopped at a few places, one where Aunt Lydia loaded up on fireworks, and then to a butcher shop where they bought steaks and burgers. For a break, we stopped at a quaint little shop called Coffee Haven. Inside, it smelled like heaven.

"Eris, would you like a coffee?" Aunt Vera asked.

"I'd love a mocha."

"You got it," she said. "After this, we'll walk to the Backwoods Sport and Ski shop, right around the corner. They have some warm jackets and thermals."

"Sounds good." I'd definitely need them.

There was a line, so while my aunts waited, I decided to sit by the window. Outside, I spotted a fountain in the middle of the square, and a gazebo. This area must have looked magical at night with all the twinkle and colored lights.

Out of the corner of my eye, I saw a glimmer of light pass by. I thought I was seeing things at first, until it zipped right past my window again, then returned, making circles directly in front of me.

I gasped, staring at the anomaly. It was my magic glimmer. It had followed me here, to Havenwood Falls.

I looked around the shop to see if anyone else noticed it, but no one did. Even the people it zipped around outside didn't notice.

It suddenly slammed into the window, making me jump, and then zipped away. It wanted me to follow, and the urge to get up and leave was strong. Then, my dad's voice was like a gong in my head. *Stay with your aunts.* Both of them were occupied, talking to other people in line.

Stay or go—that was the question.

To hell with it. This glimmer had been with me as long as I could remember, and always came when I needed it most. It was here for a reason. So, against my dad's wishes, and in spite of the consequences, I stood and walked out the door.

The glimmer zipped around me, like it was happy I'd come, and then it started to move.

We went left down Main Street, passing Shelf Indulgence and The Haven Saloon. We kept going straight, right past the Havenwood Village Apartments. Then it took a right on Sixth and another left on Stuart Street. I had to remember these places in case the glimmer disappeared, so I could find my way back.

The frigid winter air was seeping right through my clothes, making me shiver. Down Stuart Street I began to pick up my pace to a jog. My aunts were going to freak when they found out I was missing, and I prayed they wouldn't call my dad.

This darn glimmer had better be leading me toward something important. As we came to the end of the road, I passed a park with a plaque declaring it Cook's Corner Park and right off it, I slowed and watched the glimmer enter a small graveled path . . . which led directly to the Havenwood Falls Cemetery.

A cemetery. Yep, I was dead. Especially when my dad found out.

Under a thick blanket of white, the cemetery was gorgeous. I could only imagine what it looked like in the summer with flowers and green grass, in its full glory. There were stone pathways, but no headstones, which was odd. But there were plaques with the names of the deceased on the stone walls surrounding me.

The glimmer led me down a maze of pathways, into different sections of the cemetery, farther and farther from the entrance. I started to second-guess myself when we finally reached a more secluded area and the glimmer stopped at the opening of a tunnel.

"Oh, hell no! If you think I'm going into that dark, creepy tunnel, you're crazy!" I huffed at the glimmer. Thank God no one was around, or they would have thought I was mad. It zipped back and forth in front of me. "No way. I'm not going in there." I stepped back. "I'm already in a crapload of trouble, especially when my dad finds out. I might as well pick a burial spot and start digging."

The glimmer zipped around me and then disappeared.

I was pushed forward, gasping as the glimmer touched me. Where it made contact was warm and tingly. It'd never touched me before. It usually just hovered around me.

It was suddenly back in front of me, glowing brighter, lighting the dark tunnel before me.

"You think that's going to help?"

It bobbed up and down as if it were nodding. This glimmer was sassy.

It zipped in front of my face, a foot away, just enough so I could focus on it. Its warmth surrounded me, making my fear and anxiety diminish.

"Fine," I exhaled.

What was the worst that could happen anyway?

The answer: There were too many horrifying things to even attempt to count.

The trip through the tunnel wasn't as daunting as I'd expected, and we reached the other side in no time. It exited into a wooded area, another cemetery.

I followed the glimmer until it stopped in front of a gravestone, and I noticed a large bouquet of fresh-cut red roses lying at its base. My body trembled as I made my way, finally standing in front of it.

A deep sob ripped from my chest, and my legs gave, dropping me to my knees.

"Mom," I cried, my heart shattering into a million pieces. I'd found her. My glimmer had led me directly to her.

My fingers traced the name on the headstone.

Aurora Witheridge-Blaekthorn
Devoted wife, mother, friend

And below that was another inscription.

Those we love don't go away.
They walk beside us every day.

Lying under the earth, right beneath me, was the woman who birthed me. Who loved and raised me, and even died for me. I wished I'd been given the chance to know her. And hoped that every single memory I'd shared with her here, good and bad, returned soon. I wanted them all. I wanted to remember and never, ever forget her again.

I knew the glimmer was near because I could feel its warmth radiating through me, like a warm blanket. But it did nothing to comfort me.

It wasn't fair. "I wish you were here," I wept, resting my forehead against her headstone. I missed her so much, and the ache in my heart was growing, making it hard to breathe.

Footsteps from behind made me jump to my feet and crouch in a defensive stance . . . something my dad had taught me.

I waited, my pulse racing, when Rylan stepped out of the woods.

I quickly wiped my tears and straightened. "What are you doing here?"

His hazel eyes met mine with a hint of concern. "Looking for you. Why? Aren't you glad to see me?"

I huffed, but wasn't going to lie. I was relieved it was him, and not someone—or something—else. "How'd you find me?"

"I have my ways," he said, stepping closer.

I crossed my arms over my chest and narrowed my puffy eyes. "Are you stalking me?"

A playful grin rose on his lips. "I don't need to stalk you, cupcake."

"What the hell does that mean?"

His head cocked slightly to the side as he tapped his left temple. "Intuition." He then took another tentative step closer. "But I think the bigger question here is . . . how did *you* get here? How did you find this place?"

There was no way I was going to tell him I followed a magical glimmer of light. So, I tilted my head slightly, tapped the side of my temple, and replied, "Intuition."

He threw his head back and laughed. "So damn feisty."

As he neared me, he slipped out of his black leather bomber jacket.

"You must be freezing," he said, laying it over my shoulders. The warmth inside his jacket seeped into my skin, instantly warming me. I pushed my arms through the sleeves and hugged it closer. His scent—his unique fragrance of pheromones mixed with hints of pine and wind—made my head tingle.

"Thanks," I breathed, my heart hammering at his closeness.

Glancing around, I noticed the glimmer was gone.

"I'm sorry about your mom," he said, standing next to me, facing her grave. "Your uncle told me what happened. She was brave and selfless."

I nodded, trying not to answer, because I knew if I did, I'd start crying again. As my eyes focused on the headstone, I noticed a subtle etching behind the words. It was of a wolf howling at a full moon, and within the moon was a pentagram. It was who my mom was, and maybe what I was to become. A wolf and witch.

"Why is she buried out here?" I asked. "What is this place?"

"This cemetery is for the supernaturals who live in this town. The other is for the humans." He paused for a moment, then glanced at me. "Just so you know, your aunts are freaking the hell out. Lydia called me, frantic, thinking you were kidnapped. They sent me to look for you, and if I don't get you back soon, she'll blow a major blood vessel."

Crap. "Have they called my dad?"

"Not yet. But the longer you're away, the more likely it is for those two to start gathering a search party." He chuckled.

"Do you have a phone? Can you call them?"

"Yeah," he said, pulling a cell from his back pocket and showing me. "But there's no service here."

Double crap.

"But they said they'll be waiting at Coffee Haven until they hear from me." He extended his hand. "Shall we?"

As soon as I took his hand, a current of vibration traveled from his to mine. I gasped, and his hand flinched, but neither of us let go. His hand was so warm, I didn't want to.

He quickly led me back to the entrance of the Havenwood Falls *human* cemetery, and sitting off to the side was his motorcycle.

Seriously, how did he know I was here?

Rylan hopped on his motorcycle. "Put this on," he said, holding out the helmet to me. I didn't argue. I walked up to him, took the helmet, and pushed it onto my head. It smelled like him.

"I've never been on a bike," I admitted.

"Just hop on the back and hold on."

"To what?"

His head angled to the side, and his smile became serpentine. "To me."

He turned on the ignition and revved his bike. I carefully slipped onto the back and wrapped my arms around his waist. I was so close, my front pressed up against his back. And I liked it. I leaned against him, letting his warmth seep through me.

"When we go around turns, just lean with me," he instructed.

"Okay," I exhaled. "What about your helmet?"

"I only have one. Besides, I have a thick skull." Before I could respond, he pulled out from the cemetery, making my grip tighten around him. He glanced sideways, a broad smile raised on his lips.

A car slowed as we traveled down Stuart Street, and Rylan slowed, too. As both vehicles came to a stop side by side, a guy around our age, with dark hair and eyes, rolled down the back window.

Rylan addressed him. "Hey, Kase."

The boy gave him a nod. "I was going to call you."

"What for?"

"We overheard a couple of human visitors say they saw Camden talking with two guys on black ATVs the night he was found. So keep an eye out."

"Thanks, man. I'll tell the family."

"No problem." Then Kase glanced at me. "Who's that?"

Rylan turned his head sideways. "Cam's sister, Eris."

"Eris?" His eyes widened as I gave him a nod, keeping my helmet on. I didn't want them to see my face, which was probably red, puffy, and splotchy from crying. "Welcome back," he said.

"Thanks." My reply through the helmet was muffled.

"I'm Will Kasun, or just Kase."

Kasun. The sheriff. This must have been his son, because I could see the resemblance.

"Hey, you guys coming to the Festival of Lights on January eighth? It's our first day back to classes," he groaned. "A group of us is meeting after school and heading up to Mt. Mae on the ski slopes. The views up there are killer. Much better than in town."

"We'll think about it," Rylan answered. "Thanks for the info. I'll catch you guys later."

"No problem," Kase answered, then waved as Rylan pulled away.

It wasn't long before we were back in town, pulling up in front of Coffee Haven. I slid off the bike and reluctantly took off the helmet, handing it back to Rylan. "Thanks," I said.

"My pleasure." His head nodded toward the store, where my aunts came rushing out, clearly shaken.

"Oh my God," Aunt Lydia exclaimed, throwing her arms around me, squishing my cheek against her boobs. She then pulled back and held the sides of my face in her hands. "What happened to you? Your face is all red and swollen. Are you okay?"

"I'm fine," I answered.

Aunt Vera hugged me next. "Eris, you were just about to send us to an early grave. What happened? Where did you go?"

There were eyes all around us, making me want to throw on Rylan's helmet and have him whisk me away. "I—I went to the cemetery to see my mom."

They both glanced at each other.

"Sweetie, you should have told us," Aunt Vera replied. "We could have taken you there after shopping."

"I know. And I'm sorry," I sighed. "I just felt like I needed to go there on my own."

"Well, you should have at least told one of us," she said, before her eyes softened. "But we do understand." I felt horrible that I left without telling them, and caused them so much stress. But I couldn't rewind the moment. "We have a few more places to stop before we head home. Did you still want to go to the ski shop?"

"Actually," I turned toward Rylan, "I was wondering if he could take me home. I'm really tired."

Rylan's brow rose. "Yeah, sure. I was headed home anyway."

"Honey, if your daddy found out you were riding on the back of a motorcycle with a boy, he'd not only kill us, he'd kill him."

"I promise, it'll be straight home. And I'll wear a helmet."

Aunt Vera stepped up to Rylan. "First, thank you so much for finding her," she said, laying a hand on his shoulder.

"No problem," he answered.

"Second, promise me that you'll drive super slow and safe, and take her straight home."

"I promise," he said, laying a hand over his heart.

"All right," she sighed. "He found you and brought you here safely. I trust him to take you home just as safely. I know you've had a rough few days. We'll finish up quickly and be home as soon as we're done." She dug a notepad and pen from her bag. After writing on it, she handed it to me. "Here's mine and Lydia's numbers. If you need anything, call us. But Garrick is home too."

"Thank you," I said, hugging them both.

I slid Rylan's helmet back onto my head and wrapped my arms around his waist as he started up the bike.

"Be safe! We'll be home soon," Aunt Lydia yelled as we pulled away.

CHAPTER 8

After a quick tour of the town, Rylan took me home. In no time, he pulled up to my front stairs.

"You want to come inside? It's lunch time, and I can make a pretty mean sandwich."

"Sure. Let me park this bike at home, just in case your dad comes early. And I'm going to tell Garrick what Kase told us."

"Who was that guy?"

"Kase is the sheriff's son. We met during football tryouts. At first, he was an ass, but when he found out what I was, he opened up. He was the one who introduced me to your brother. Even though Camden graduated the year before, they still hung out because they'd played football together. But Cam and I hit it off instantly . . . like two lost brothers finally connecting."

"That's cool," I said, handing him his helmet. I was realizing how much I missed out on Camden's life. He played football, but what were his likes and dislikes? Was he good at sports? I assumed he was, but had no idea. Rylan, a stranger before today, knew things about him I didn't, and it made me a little jealous. "I'll see you in a bit."

"Yeah, be right back." As he drove off, I ran up the stairs and opened the door, quickly ducking out of the cold.

A few minutes later, Rylan knocked.

"Come inside, it's so cold," I greeted him.

He stepped in, raking his fingers through his thick hair. "It's not too bad."

"Are you kidding me? I need to find the temperature control in here. It's freezing."

He stepped toward me, a lazy grin on his lips. "I'm hot blooded. I can keep you warm if you want."

I gulped. His closeness made my blood stir and ignited something inside. A heat. A warm, wonderful heat. I needed distance, so I stepped back.

"You don't have to worry about me, Eris. I'm not a big bad wolf." His eyes traveled to my lips, and I could barely breathe.

I hitched a thumb toward the kitchen. "If you're hungry, we have a bunch of sandwich stuff." I took another step away from his gravitational pull.

He noticed and chuckled. "Maybe in a bit."

"Okay," I exhaled. "Want to watch a movie?"

"Sure." He walked past me, deliberately brushing his arm against mine. *Jerk.*

I followed him into the living room, and he walked straight to a small cabinet under the TV. He knew the place better than I did, and I wondered how much time he spent here with Camden.

"What do you want to watch?" he asked, bending over. I couldn't help but notice his perfect butt. "Besides my ass," he laughed.

Oh hell. Embarrassment heated my face.

"Don't worry, cupcake. I don't mind."

"I wasn't . . . I—I'm going to get us something to drink." I swallowed hard, turning for the kitchen. "Water? Soda?"

"I'll take a Monster."

"A what?"

"Energy drink. They're on the door of the fridge. Second shelf."

"Oh," I exhaled. "Well, at least you know your way around this place."

He gave another wonderful laugh. "Yeah, this was my second

home. It was mine and Cam's place to get away from the adults and the twins."

"Are they bad? The twins?"

"Nah, they're cool. They're fifteen, but your aunt always asks us to keep an eye on them. I think they hate it as much as we do."

"So, you know about the Blaekthorns? About what they are?"

He popped his drink and took a swig. "Well, they don't howl at the moon like the shows suggest."

He did know. So, I pressed him.

"Did you get a tattoo when you came here, the ones for the supernaturals?"

He turned to me, his hazel eyes narrowed. "You can ask me anything, and I'll tell you the truth." He pulled his T-shirt over his head and turned his back toward me.

My breath caught in my throat at the sight. Yes, the almost invisible Havenwood Falls protection tattoo was there, but there was also another, covering his entire back.

Four large slashes were tattooed diagonally from his right shoulder down to the base of his spine. It looked like his skin was being torn apart from the inside out. At the end of the slashes were claws, dripping with blood. But there was something else, peeking from behind those slashes. A wolf, with golden eyes. And its eyes . . . they seemed so real, like they were peering deep into my soul.

My fingers automatically reached out to touch it, and as soon as my fingers grazed his skin, there was a current—a tingling heat, flowing from me to him. The muscles in his back tensed, making me gasp and pull away.

"I'm sorry," I apologized. "I didn't mean to touch it."

His head twisted to the side, the cocky grin back. "You can touch me anytime, and anywhere, you want."

Jerk, I thought. Only because I wanted to.

I was glad when he threw his shirt back on. "And in case you're wondering about the tattoo . . . it's a representation of the beast inside, waiting to be released."

"So, you're—"

"A shifter, just like your family," he answered, as if he were answering any other question. When I paused, his head twisted back to me. "I told you, I'll tell you anything."

"Why? You don't even know me."

He sat down on the couch next to me, the space between us instantly heating. "For one, you're Cam's sister, and your family has taken me in when no one else would."

I couldn't argue with his answer, and I wanted to know, "How did you find Havenwood Falls?"

He smiled, but the smile didn't reach his eyes. Instead, they held a sadness—a look all too familiar. One I'd seen many times in my dad's eyes.

"I came from a protective family and a strong pack. My father was alpha, but being the alpha's son didn't mean anything. Life wasn't any easier for me. From a young age, I had to prove myself . . . to work and fight for everything I got, and didn't get any special treatment.

"Over the past few years, our pack was targeted by rivals because of our strength. We could never settle in one place, so we became wanderers, moving from state to state for the safety of the pack. Even on the move, we still weren't safe. One by one, members were picked off, and our group was whittled down from twenty members to eleven." He turned to me, his face solemn. "About eight months ago, my father went hunting, and he never returned.

"The next morning, a few of the pack members found his body in the woods, shredded to pieces. No one knows who actually murdered him, but we suspected one person. A rogue shifter named Lars." The muscles in his jaw tensed, his eyes staring blankly at the wall. "Lars has been stalking our pack for years, waiting to find a weakness. Wanting to take over. He also had a thing for my mom. The bastard."

My heart ached for him. His story sounded eerily familiar, like my parents', only it was turned around.

"After my father's death," he continued, "his beta and best friend, Axel, took over the pack. Axel is a good guy and has been with my dad from the beginning. The entire pack trusts him."

"Shouldn't you have been the next alpha if you were his son?" I asked.

"I could have, but I didn't want the responsibility. After my dad passed, my mom wanted to leave the pack. She knew things would get worse, especially without my father's protection, knowing Lars was still out there. She felt that if she left, maybe he would finally leave them alone and the pack could survive.

"She asked me to leave with her. And I did. She was my mom, and I had become her protector." His eyes saddened. He leaned back, his head resting on the couch. I could tell that he was struggling with whatever he was going to say next. I could almost feel his pain.

"You don't have to tell me," I said. "Some things are personal, and I respect that."

He glanced at me, his hazel eyes narrowing. "No, I want to tell you. I want you to know my story." He paused, then looked away. "You know, so in case you think I'm a prick, you'll feel pity and cut me slack. Maybe even offer me some solace."

"Well," I said, placing my hand on his shoulder. "The only thing I'm offering you today is a sandwich."

He shrugged, a smile gracing his lips. "Then a sandwich will do."

Crossing one ankle over the other, he exhaled deeply, and I stayed quiet while he continued. "It was my mom who wanted to come to Colorado. She said she had this wonderful dream about a place where people like us could be safe." His eyes found mine again. "My mom had a gift. Her dreams were visions, and most times, when she had them, they came true.

"We were so close, not fifty miles away from this place, but we were starving. We found an old, abandoned barn to stay in for the night, and because she was so weak and tired, I insisted she stay and rest while I went and hunted for food." His eyes closed, and his jaw tensed again. "When I returned, I thought she was sleeping. I went to wake her, but found her throat had been slit." His brow furrowed, and tears welled in his eyes. He quickly turned away and wiped his face on his sleeve.

"Rylan, I'm so sorry." There were no other words. What do you say to someone who lost both of their parents in such a short period of time?

He shook his head, shaking the memory away. "Don't feel sorry for me, cupcake. I've learned hard and fast how to deal with life's twisted games. I'm a shifter. We adapt. We have to or else we die."

For some reason, I wanted to hug him. To wrap my arms around him and tell him I hoped his future was better. It could be, now that he was here. Now that *we* were here.

In the short time we'd spoken, I learned a lot about Rylan. That somehow, fate had brought him to Havenwood Falls. Fate had brought us all here, and we just had to figure out why we were chosen. Even if it was to live out our lives, knowing that there were others like us—different, but still searching for their place on this earth. A place where we all fit. And maybe, Havenwood Falls was that place.

I made us sandwiches, and we sat and watched a few episodes of Supernatural—something we both agreed upon—and after the episode was done, he stood and checked his watch. "I have to run to the warehouse and help them shut down early for the New Year's Eve barbecue tonight."

"The barbecue. Right." It would be the first time, as far as I could remember, that my dad and I would be celebrating the holiday with family. "Thanks for coming over," I said. "I really enjoyed the company."

A wide smile adorned his handsome face. "Thanks for listening. And, sorry about whatever happened in there earlier. I never spill my guts like that, or get emotional . . . with anyone. I guess you're easy to talk to."

"Well, I'm honored," I said and meant it. "Sometimes it's good to spill, you know, so you can fill yourself back up with good things . . . better things."

He nodded, considering my words. "A wise theory."

I shrugged, hoping he wouldn't regret spilling to me. "Will you be at the barbecue?"

"Good food and great company? I wouldn't miss it," he said, heading for the door.

I followed him, and without warning he turned and pressed his warm lips to my cheek. "Catch you later, cupcake," he whispered, his warm breath grazing my face, his lips lingering so close to mine. He'd rendered me frozen and speechless, then winked and walked away. *Jerk.*

I closed the door and pressed my back against it, my heart beating a mile a minute, while butterflies slam-danced in my stomach. The spot he kissed was still tingling and warm and . . . God, it was wonderful.

Rylan's good looks were one thing, but I was finding out there was a lot more to him than the prideful, snarky, testy jerk he first seemed to be. It would be hard to be normal around him, because whenever he was around, he made me feel things I'd never felt before. And there was no avoiding him. For God's sake, he was part of the family and lived next door.

Yawning, I realized how tired I was. The long trip last night and all the crazy events that happened today had taken their toll. I decided to take a nap before my dad got home. Besides, we'd be pulling an all-nighter to welcome in the new year.

Curling up on the couch, I clicked through the channels. The house was too quiet, so I needed the background noise. Especially being alone in an unfamiliar place.

The new version of Beauty and the Beast was on, so I left it and pulled a throw blanket over me. My eyes were heavy, and in no time, sleep had found me.

CHAPTER 9

"*E*ris. E—ris," *a female voice called, but the voice sounded hollow. My eyes opened, and I was on a couch. The TV was off, and the house was dark.*

"Eris," the voice called again.

I sat up, getting my bearings, and realized I was at the house in Havenwood Falls. Feeling a bit frightened, I slowly peeked over the cushions. A bright light illuminated the top of the stairs, and I watched as it slowly hovered downward.

As the light reached the bottom of the steps, it grew bigger and brighter. So big and so bright, it was almost blinding. Then, it suddenly dimmed, and a woman stood in front of me, her body ethereal, illuminating the darkness around her. She was wearing a long white gown, and I realized I knew her.

"Mom?" My voice trembled. Tears blurred my vision as I gazed into honey-colored eyes. Eyes that looked a lot like mine.

"Yes." She smiled, her flawless porcelain face glowing. She was so beautiful, like I remembered, and was wearing a long white gown. "Don't be afraid, my darling," she replied. "Come."

But I couldn't. I was frozen, my body trembling, my heart beating so hard and so fast I thought it might escape my chest.

It was the first time I'd seen my mom since we'd left. But I knew her face. I'd memorized it from the picture we'd had, and I recognized her smile. She had the brightest, most beautiful smile I'd ever seen.

"Come, Eris," she beckoned. "There is something I want to show you."

I gathered my nerves and stood from the couch. Yes, she was my mom, but my mom had also been dead for the past seven years, and now she was hovering inches off the ground.

I stepped toward her, and she waved for me to follow. Gently, slowly, she floated back up the stairs. When she reached the top, she turned right, and headed toward the only room I hadn't been in. My dad's room, and hers . . . once upon a time.

When she reached the closed door, she floated directly through it. As she passed through, it unlocked and creaked ajar. I slowly pushed the door open, noticing her glowing figure near the closet. The rest of the room was dark, in black and white.

"Come," she said, then pointed toward the closet door.

I walked toward the closet, and opened it. It was empty, aside from a few of my dad's dress shirts on hangers. She pointed to the left, and gave me a single nod. I leaned inside but saw a wall. A solid wall and nothing else. What did she want me to see?

"There's nothing here," I said, turning back.

Her hand was still pointing. "The floor, Eris. Look under the floor."

The floor was covered with carpet, but I dropped down anyway, on all fours, and tugged at the edge. To my surprise, it wasn't attached. It was merely a remnant laid on top. Tugging it harder, I folded the carpet back and crawled into the closet.

Then, like I'd seen in the movies, I rapped on the exposed hardwood floor with my knuckles. Sure enough, there was a spot that sounded hollow. Two of the boards had a slightly bigger gap between them, so with my fingertips, I pulled on the lip of a board closest me, and it came right up, leaving a dark hole in the floor.

Turning back to my mom, I watched her smile widen. "Take what is inside, Eris. It's yours now," she said, her voice angelic.

I sucked in a deep breath and reached inside. There was something hard and quite large, so I wrapped my fingers around it and pulled it out. Carrying it out of the closet, I took it to the bed and sat down where my mom was standing—hovering—and placed the rectangular shaped object on the bed. It was wrapped in a red cloth, so I began to unravel it.

It was a book. A leather-bound book with a pentacle—a circle with a pentagram inside—on its front. It was very old and smelled musty, and when I ran my fingers over the cover, the leather was soft, like velvet. I also felt something tingling inside my fingers when I touched it—a power pulsing within.

"What is this?" I breathed.

"A Book of Shadows," she replied. "It belonged to your great-grandmother, Margret Witheridge. It was her diary, so to speak, of all things she practiced. Her spells, herbs, potions, among other things. It was passed to her daughter—your grandmother, Gertrude—when she died. And then, it passed to me. It possesses spells—powerful spells, but mostly spells to protect and spells to heal."

I opened the cover, and on the bottom, written in old script, was:

Margret Witheridge – Salem Village, 1682

Goosebumps riddled my skin. "She was one of the Salem witches?"

"Yes." For the first time, her smile dimmed and her eyes saddened. "She was captured, tried, and found guilty. They hanged her while her husband and daughter watched."

A pain pierced my heart at the thought, and a stray tear trickled down my cheek and dripped onto the open page of the book. I watched the wet spot disappear, as if it were being sucked up. I touched the paper, and it was dry.

"The book has dried your tears," my mom murmured, and I felt oddly comforted.

"What happened after Margret died?" Since she was here, I wanted to learn as much as I could.

"After her death, your great-grandfather took Gertrude, and they left Salem, taking the book with them. Your grandmother treasured it, and entered her own spells she'd learned through the years. She later met and married your grandfather, and had me. When I came of age, the book was passed down."

"Dad told me what happened to you and Grandpa. I know he was a

hunter and that you were kidnapped by werewolves and bitten in front of him. I also know they killed him and left you to die."

"That's true. But there was also a silver lining."

"Silver lining?" I huffed. "Your father was killed, you were beaten and left to die, and your mom ran away, never to be heard of again. Where's the silver lining?"

"If none of that had happened, I would have never met your father, and we would have never had you or Camden or the wonderful time we shared together. It was all a gift . . . the good that came out of the bad." She floated closer, and I could feel her warmth seeping through me. "I love you so much, Eris. I loved you the moment I knew you were in my womb, and even more the first time I held you in my arms and felt that magic pass between us. The very first time I looked into your eyes, I knew you were going to be special. Just like the rest of us Witheridge women. Yes, I loved you then, and I've loved you ever since."

"I've missed you, Mom," I said, my voice exiting in a sob.

"I know, my darling. But I've been with you, watching over you all these years."

Realization slammed me, like a brick to the face.

"You," I gasped, my eyes meeting hers. "You are my glimmer."

When she nodded, I lost it. My tears and sobs became uncontrollable, and my body wouldn't stop trembling.

"I've never left you, Eris. I've been with you all along."

Her words filled me, and wrapped around my shattered heart, attempting to mend it. How could I not know the glimmer was her? It was always there whenever I needed it most.

"Thank you," I finally said, after pulling myself together. "Do you know what happened to your mother? Did she die, too?"

"No," she answered. "When she heard I'd been bitten, and my father had been murdered, she panicked and ran. She was afraid, and I don't blame her."

"If she ran, how did you get the book?"

"When I was strong enough, I returned to the house and was surprised to find the Book of Shadows still hidden in a secret place only she and I knew of. It wasn't long after that when we made our way to Havenwood

Falls." She pointed to the book. "I've added my own spells onto the pages. But remember, these spells should only be used for good. Never for evil or for gain."

I nodded. I would never use a spell to harm anyone. "Dad told me about the dark magic that killed you. The spell that evil woman cast that made him choose between us."

"Yes, it was a very dark and very ancient spell. One that could not be stopped once it was sent," she said sadly. "But the woman had to give part of herself to the spell, and has paid for it."

"I'm so sorry," I sobbed. "I'm sorry he chose me."

"Don't be sorry, sweetheart. Don't ever be sorry. I would have always chosen you." Her hand reached for mine, but passed right through. "You are my life, Eris. You, your brother, and your father." As she came closer, I noticed her body was beginning to fade. "I don't have much time left, so you must listen carefully. The spell on your brother can be reversed. It was cast by a witch, who is attached to the woman who placed the spell against us long ago. It is being conjured out of revenge."

"Revenge? For what?"

"The woman who put the death curse on us is her sister. Because she had to give something to the dark spell, she offered her remaining power. But the spell took more than that. It took her beauty, leaving her face blistered and scarred.

"She twisted her story and told her sister—another powerful witch— that your father tried to seduce her, and that I had become so jealous I placed a curse on her. She lied and never told the truth. That she was the one insanely obsessed with your father, or that the dark spell she had cast was going to take a life.

"Her sister has come to avenge her. To make your father pay for something he didn't do. She spelled your brother, and her goal is to spell your father as well. A spell that will keep them in a deep sleep until they die."

Oh, God. I wasn't sure I could do this alone.

"There is no time, Eris. You must go, but remember, you won't be alone. She is right outside the boundary of Havenwood Falls, getting ready to cast her final spell against your father. She has two men helping her.

They came into Havenwood Falls and took something from your brother, which is how she cast the spell."

Oh, no. The two men. They must have been the ones the sheriff's son was talking about.

"I need to get in touch with Dad," I said, breathless.

"It's too late. She already has him."

My heart dropped. "What do you mean she has him? How?"

"The men. While he was out tracking down a lead in the woods, they knocked him out and have taken him outside of Havenwood Falls, just beyond the wards. She is heavily glamoured, but you can stop her, Eris."

"Me?" I gasped. "I can't stop her. I don't have powers, and I've never cast a single spell in my life. I wouldn't even know where to start."

"Eris," my mother whispered. "Everything you need is inside of you. Magic runs in your blood, and it will guide you. All you have to do is believe in it."

I was terrified. I'd just learned today, a few short hours ago, that I was part witch, and now I was supposed to stop a powerful, practiced witch on my own?

I looked into my mother's eyes and saw something that made me pause my thoughts. It was a look that only a mother could give. Unconditional love, trust, hope, and faith in her daughter. She believed in me, and I not only saw it . . . I felt it.

She leaned forward and rested her hand against the middle of my chest. A surge of power slammed into me, making me fall back.

Gasping, I sat back up. "What happened?"

"The power inside you has been awakened. Find the witch. Stop her. She has the spell that can reverse your brother's curse. As soon as it is broken, cast a spell of protection around the family. There is a powerful spell in the Book of Shadows. It was written by your grandmother. Find it, and speak the words, Eris. Speak them from your heart and feel them with your soul."

I nodded. I could do this. I would do it for my dad and for my brother. The evil witches had already taken my mother, but they weren't going to take anyone else in my family.

I could feel the power inside my blood start to churn. I could feel it growing, writhing, and coiling under my skin.

"How will I find her if she's glamoured?"

My mother placed her pointer fingers on my eyes and spoke, "See that which has been hidden. See the evil lurking in the shadows and bring it to light."

When I opened my eyes, I felt a buzz all around me.

"Find her, Eris. Find her before she spells your father. Once she curses him, she will disappear, and I fear you will never find her again."

I couldn't fail. My mother had given her life for me, and now I would prove that she saved me for a reason. It was my duty now to save my brother and my father.

"I'll find her, mom," I promised. "And I'll reverse the spell."

"I know you will, sweetheart," she said, reaching for me, but her hand passed right through. "I love you, Eris. I always have, and I always will. Remember, I will always be with you."

"I love you too, Mom." With tears streaming down my face, I watched her fade, until I was left in the darkness, alone.

CHAPTER 10

I shot up on the couch in the living room with a cooking show on the TV. I glanced at the time, and a few hours had passed. The sun outside was already starting to set.

"Dad?" I called, but the house was quiet. "Dad!" There was still no answer.

I peered over the back of the couch, to the stairs and wondered about the dream. It felt so real.

Real or not, I had to find out.

Jumping off the couch, I dashed up the stairs and headed straight for my father's room. Inside, the layout was exactly as it was in my dream. I walked up to the closet and pulled open the door, and another surge of déjà vu smacked me.

Dropping to my knees, I pulled the rug back—a remnant that wasn't tacked down. I found the two boards with the larger gap between them and pried the board closest to me open. Without thinking, I reached into the hole. My heart hammered as I felt the hard, rectangular object.

Pulling it from the hole, I sat back, holding the book wrapped in a red cloth. The exact red cloth I'd dreamed of. Overwhelmed with trepidation and excitement, I quickly replaced the board, threw back the carpet, closed the closet door, and ran to my room.

I plopped down on my cupcake bedspread and carefully unraveled the book from the cloth, and there, staring at me, was my great-grandmother's Book of Shadows . . . old and leather-bound, with a pentacle adorning the front.

I could feel the book, feel its power urging me to open its pages filled with magic. But I had one task. To find the spell—the protection spell—that would cover our family, written somewhere inside.

I flipped through the pages, the symbols and drawings calling to me to look and decipher them. To draw from the power of the words written within.

But not now. Right now, I had to stay focused.

As I kept turning, I noticed a section where the handwriting had changed. Where the ink looked a little fresher than the last entry. It must have been the start of my grandma Gertrude's entries.

I turned and turned the pages until I saw it. The protection spell. I could feel the page, feel the words as if they were jumping out at me. The spell was simple. The words powerful.

I quickly dug for my pen and notebook in my bag. I quickly copied the words of the spell, and tore the page out. Shutting the book, I could still feel its power. Feel every spell in the book, luring the power inside me, begging to be set free.

This book—this old, powerful book—was now my responsibility, and I would have to keep it safe and hidden.

A loud knock at the door downstairs sent my heart racing. Wrapping the book back in the red cloth, I tucked it away between my mattresses, until I could find a proper, safe place for it.

Racing down the stairs, I peeked from behind the living room curtain.

It was Rylan. He'd come back.

He was wearing blue jeans and a tight shirt. The sky was icy gray, and the wind was whipping. I ran to the door and unlocked it, letting him in. As it opened, a cold rush of air whooshed in. Rylan stepped inside and quickly shut the door behind him.

We were toe to toe, so close I could feel his warmth wrap around me. I took in a deep breath, because his scent was wonderful, that mixture of pine and fresh wind.

Snapping myself from the fog that had just entered the room, I took a step back, but my heel caught on the mat. I fell backward, but before I hit the ground, Rylan caught me.

I inhaled, folded over his arm, his body above me like he'd dipped me in a dance. There was a buzz in the air between and all around us. His eyes, the gold in them was so—

He broke his stare and then stood straight, pulling me upright.

"Thank you," I exhaled.

"You'd better watch your step, cupcake," he murmured, a cocky grin on his face.

My mind was still buzzing from being in his arms. "I have to go somewhere," I said, moving toward my jacket.

"Eris," he called after me. I started to jog upstairs and get my warmer jacket, but as my foot hit the second stair, he called my name with greater urgency. "Eris!"

"What?" I said, taking the third and fourth step.

"Your father is missing."

I froze, not reaching the fifth, but pivoted back to him. My worst fear was being confirmed. "What did you say?"

"I was next door when Barney came busting in. He told Garrick he hasn't been able to get in touch with your dad. Apparently, they were checking on a lead in the forest, but when Barney called for him, he wasn't there. He wasn't anywhere."

"What about his phone?"

"They tried, but he hasn't answered." His brow furrowed. "The service in this area is spotty. Sometimes it catches, but a lot of times, it doesn't," he added. "Both of your uncles just took off to look for him. They didn't want to tell you because they didn't want to frighten you. But I thought you should know."

"Oh, God." Tears slid down my face. My body trembled, my legs buckled, and I fell onto the stair. "It's true, then. She has him."

"Who?" Rylan asked, taking a few strides across the room to reach me.

"A witch. The one that spelled my brother. She has my dad and is going to spell him too. I need to find her. I need to stop her." I looked up at him. "And I need your help."

"What do you want me to do?" Rylan asked, his gaze softening. "I'm here for you." He held out his hand. "Just tell me how I can help."

I had to gather myself. This wasn't a time to break down. This was a time to prove my worth. To justify my existence.

I took Rylan's hand, and he pulled me to my feet. "I need you to take me to find her."

"You know where she is?"

"No," I sighed, hoping he didn't think I was mad. "But I think she's outside of the town's wards. Once we get on the road, I might be able to find the way." I really wasn't sure, but I hoped. With everything inside me, I hoped I could find them.

"All right," he said, nodding. "Go get your jacket, and meet me outside."

"Thank you," I said, then headed upstairs. I grabbed my warmest jacket, wishing I'd gone to the ski shop, and grabbed the paper I'd written the spell on, tucking it into my pocket.

Outside, Rylan was sitting on his motorcycle. As soon as I stepped out, he handed me the helmet, and I slipped it on and hopped on the back. I wrapped my arms around his waist as he started the bike.

The air was cold, and the sky was growing darker. I hugged him even tighter as the wind whipped around us.

"Relax," I heard him yell. But I couldn't. My body was tense, watching the trees whip by.

When we came to the main road, Country Road 13—aka Burdorf pass—he stopped.

"Which way?" he asked, the bike idling.

I closed my eyes. *Please show me. Lead me to Dad.* When I opened my eyes, I saw my glimmer shoot out from behind a tree. It zipped up to me and touched my cheek, giving me a warm kiss before it took off toward the left.

"Left," I said, and he pulled out.

Rylan maneuvered the bike with ease, and as we left the town of Havenwood Falls, I kept my eye on my glimmer.

It led us farther and farther away from the town, and just when I wondered if we were outside of the wards, the glimmer stopped.

"Stop," I hollered, and Rylan pressed his brake. I squeezed him tight as we skidded off to the side and he cut the engine. Sliding off the bike, I pulled the helmet from my head.

High up on the road were the headlights of someone coming into Havenwood Falls, so he pulled the bike off the side of the road, concealing it behind some trees.

"There is nothing here," he said, looking around. Nothing except the looming dark forest. But my glimmer was still here, zipping in and out of the tree line.

"She's here. The witch is glamoured, but I think I can find her."

"How? How are you getting this information?" he asked. "Not that I don't trust you."

I gazed into his eyes. "My mom," I answered. "She came to me in a dream, and told me what I needed to do."

He nodded and gestured to the forest. "Okay, then. Lead the way."

CHAPTER 11

I took a step into the trees, and the glimmer shot deeper.

"This way," I said, quickly following after it.

Rylan was on my heels, and I was glad he was here with me. I never would have made it this far without his help, and wouldn't have been as brave. Knowing he was a step away, I felt safe.

My feet stumbled a few times on matted roots, but I caught myself and kept going. Pressing on, I hoped I wasn't too late.

Find the witch. Stop her, make her reverse the spell, and then cast the protection spell around my family. That was my task, and I repeated it like a mantra, over and over.

Continuing to follow the glimmer, we went deeper and deeper into the woods, where the trees were tightly knit together. The branches scratched at my exposed skin as I pushed through.

Then, the glimmer stopped. I froze and held my hand up to Rylan; he paused and nodded his head.

I could feel it. A dark power nearby, its evil tendrils seeping out from its master.

The witch was close.

I closed my eyes and called to the power within me. To a power, new and raw, passed down through generations . . . through the Witheridge bloodline.

I felt that power. Felt it stirring in my bones and in my blood. Felt it flowing through my veins, and I welcomed it.

Show me the witch behind her glamour, and give me what I need to overcome her, I begged that power.

This time, when I opened my eyes, the world around me was different. It was glowing and alive. But ahead of me was a wall of darkness shaped like a dome. I saw the magic, the glamour, like a dark wave, and knew behind it was the witch. I could feel her.

Fear tried to strangle me, so I turned to Rylan. As if he could feel my fear, he stepped to my side and grasped my hand. That simple act gave me what I needed . . . told me I wasn't alone.

"Stay here," I whispered.

"Where are you going?" He held my hand firmly, keeping me in place.

"There is a ward, a dark dome of magic concealing the witch, right beyond these trees."

His eyes narrowed as if he were trying to see. "Where?"

"It's a glamour. You won't be able to see it."

"And you can?"

I nodded. "Just stay here. I'll be fine," I lied.

"No way. You're not going in there alone." A fire blazed in his eyes, which had now turned completely golden. The look was one I wouldn't argue with.

"Okay, but please be careful."

His head tilted to the side. "*You* be careful."

With his hand in mine, we stepped forward toward the dark wall.

Inside, I called to my power and felt it growing, tingling inside of me. I let go of Rylan's hand, taking a tentative step forward. Lifting my arms, a wave of light exploded from my palms, slamming into the glamour. The glamour shattered, sparks of magic fell around us like glittering rain, revealing four figures behind it. One was a woman standing in a black cloak, her face concealed behind a large cowl, a black wand in her hand.

As she removed the hood, her evil gaze was frozen on me, her eyes black as night. The sight of it made my skin crawl.

Standing behind her were two men, and between them, bound to a tree, was—

"Dad!" I screamed, running forward.

The witch snapped her wand at me, and its power soared toward me like lightning, slamming into my chest. It threw me backwards, my body crashing against a tree. As I fell to the ground, pain radiated through my chest. I gasped, trying to catch my breath, but it wasn't coming easily.

Behind me, a deep, terrifying growl cut through the night air. Then, a huge, brown wolf came bounding out of the woods, stopping at my side. He was beautiful. His golden eyes fixed on the witch with a predatory focus. Its lip curled back, revealing long, sharp teeth. But he was larger than any wolf I'd ever seen. On his four legs he was just as tall as I was.

"Rylan?" I breathed.

His head twisted back to me, and his golden eyes met mine. He whimpered, and I shook my head. "I'm fine," I exhaled, pulling myself to my feet.

He stepped closer, angling his body in front of me, protecting me. I ran my hand across his side. His fur was soft, and my palm tingled as I stroked him. "Thank you," I whispered. His head bowed before snapping back to the woman.

His body went rigid as the two men stepped forward with knives in their hands. Their heads were covered with black ski masks, only revealing their eyes.

The witch laughed. "What do we have here? A young witch and a wolf? Now that's something you don't see every day."

"Release my dad," I said as bravely as I could.

I tried to take a step closer to her, but the wolf wouldn't let me move. He pushed me back with the side of his head.

"Who are you to give me orders . . . girl?"

"I am not a girl," I roared.

The witch threw her head back in laughter. "Not a girl? Then what are you?"

I glared at her. "I am my mother's daughter. A Witheridge witch," I responded. I could feel the power writhing inside, growing, as if it agreed and responded to my words. "Release my dad," I demanded.

I placed my hand on the wolf and gently stroked his fur. He must have felt my power, because he stepped to the side and let me pass. His eyes still fixed on the threat, his growl deep and guttural.

A sly grin rose on the witch's lips. In a split second, she raised her wand again, but this time I was ready. I raised both hands, and as her power hurled toward me, it struck an invisible wall, instantly dissolving.

Her power didn't touch me, and I barely felt it.

The aghast look on her face mimicked what I was feeling. *I'd stopped her.*

Courage and hope surged inside of me, unfurling through my limbs, while confusion and rage swirled in her eyes.

Raising her wand again, she struck. Her power flew toward us like a ball of flame. I lifted my hands in front of me, and an invisible shield devoured that flame.

She tried again and again, hurling her power at us, trying to hurt us, but my power absorbed every blow.

"How?" she screamed in frustration. Then, her eyes narrowed on us. "Get them," she ordered, her long finger aimed at us.

The two men came charging forward, blades raised over their heads.

Rylan leapt in front of me, sinking his jaws into the first man's waist. With a snap of his head, the man went flying, slamming hard against a tree. When he fell, his body was still. I couldn't tell if he was unconscious . . . or dead.

The wolf then turned his attention to me, dipping his head, and without words, I knew what he meant. He was going after the second man, and he wanted me to go after my dad.

My dad was unconscious, blood dripping from a wound above his left eye. "Hold on, Dad. I'm coming."

The witch turned her attention to him and raised her hands, conjuring a solid wall of wind to surrounded both her and my dad. She was going to cast her spell.

I called on my power, whatever I had left, and pushed it toward her shield. But it had weakened, and I couldn't break through. *No!* There had to be a way to stop her.

A loud yelp made me turn to see the wolf on the ground, the hilt of a blade sticking out from his thigh. The man had escaped Rylan's hold, and his attention was now turned to me.

He sprinted toward me with a look of malicious intent in his eyes. I dropped to my knees and held up my arms in front of me, anticipating the blow. But it never came.

Instead, I heard a growl and a snapping of teeth, followed by an injured scream. Opening my eyes, I witnessed the man's left arm, trapped in the wolf's jaws. He fought back, slamming his fist into the wolf's eye. Then he jumped up, wrapping his legs around the wolf's neck, and squeezed.

"Rylan!" I screamed in horror.

But the wolf was strong. He thrashed his head side to side, slamming the man's head against a nearby tree. As soon as the man's grip loosened, Rylan tossed him into the air, and before he hit the ground, the wolf caught his leg in his jaws, and dragged him into the darkness.

I tried again, to summon the power within, but felt nothing.

"You think you can match my power, young witch?"

I was spent. The power I had called earlier had completely drained.

"She might not be able to, but *you* cannot match *my* power," a voice called from behind us.

From the darkness stepped a small figure, hunched over, with wiry white hair wound in a tight bun.

"Ms. Gingrich?" I blinked a few times, making sure my eyes weren't deceiving me. "How? Why are you here?"

Her eyes met mine. "Because, my darling, I have watched over you all these years, making sure you were safe, and I don't intend to stop now." She smiled, holding a white wand in her hand.

Was Ms. Gingrich a witch?

I watched the old woman step toward the evil witch with no fear.

The witch let out a deep cackling laugh and snapped her wand at the Grinch.

"No!" I screamed, but Ms. Gingrich didn't flinch. She raised her wand, easily deflecting the witch's strike as if it were a wisp of wind.

I watched in complete awe as the hunched old woman walked up to that wall of wind and held up her wand. In the blink of an eye, the wall disintegrated. With another flick of her wrist, the evil witch dropped to her knees, holding her neck as if she were being choked.

"You will release the spell from the boy and his father, or I will release the breath from your lungs . . . forever," Ms. Gingrich commanded.

The witch gurgled, trying to gasp for air. When she finally nodded, Ms. Gingrich released her. She fell to the ground, coughing.

"Do it now!" Ms. Gingrich warned, her wand hovering above the witch in warning.

Ms. Gingrich was even more powerful than I imagined. But a witch? How could I not know this?

I ran over to my dad and released his bonds. His limp body fell to the ground, still unconscious. I rolled him to his back and pressed my ear to his chest. His heartbeat was loud and strong. He was alive.

Rylan stumbled out of the woods, shirtless, wearing jeans that were a bit too baggy. I jumped up and ran over to him, blood seeping through the blue denim where he'd been stabbed. His left eye was red and swollen where the man had slammed him over and over.

"Are you okay?" I asked. It was nearly impossible to avoid admiring his perfectly sculpted chest and abs.

"Fine," he replied, jerking a thumb in the direction he'd come. "But you should see the other guy."

I wanted to laugh, but a thought shot through my head. "Is he dead?"

"No," he replied, with a crooked grin. "But he doesn't have any pants."

Shaking my head, I giggled. He took a step, but his injured leg gave. I caught him, wrapping my arm around his waist to hold him up.

His eyes narrowed. "You caught me," he said, throwing his arm around my shoulders. "I guess this means we're even."

"Yeah, I guess."

"Who's that?" he asked, his head tilting toward Ms. Gingrich.

"She's our neighbor from New Mexico." His eyes widened, and I shrugged. "Don't ask, because I have no idea."

I helped him over to Ms. Gingrich, who still had her wand hovering above the witch as she reversed her spell.

When the spell was finally undone, Ms. Gingrich looked at me and held out her hand.

"Come, Eris. The spell is broken. We have one more thing to do, together."

"How did you know?" I asked, still completely confused at her appearance.

Ms. Gingrich smiled broadly, then began to twirl her wand above her head. Magical dust fell over her, peeling away what appeared to be a glamour. Then, right before our eyes, Ms. Gingrich was no longer there, and in her place stood a tall, slender woman, with long golden hair, braided behind her back. She was wearing a white cloak, but had the same white wand in her hand.

"Who are you?" I asked, although she looked familiar.

Her brow raised. "Don't you know me?"

"You're the woman in my dreams," I murmured. I gazed into her honey-colored eyes and gasped as realization hit me. "Gertrude?"

She smiled widely. "I prefer Gertie. Gertrude makes me sound like an old woman."

My body went weak, and I grabbed on to Rylan's arm for balance. Was this really happening, or was I still stuck in a dream?

Gertie opened her arms wide to me, and as I met her, her arms enveloped me in a warm embrace. My body trembled, and tears flowed from my eyes.

All this time, my grandmother *had* been there, watching over me, glamoured as the Grinch.

"Why didn't you tell me?" I asked. "Why use a glamour?"

Her eyes filled with sadness. "I was afraid. I'd never met your father, and because I ran, after the wolves took your grandfather and mother, I was sure he hated me. I couldn't take the chance to be rejected." She shook her head. "I was a coward back then, but after I heard of Aurora's death, I vowed to watch over her daughter, the next Witheridge witch. I followed you and your father to New Mexico, glamoured myself as an old, nosey woman, and moved next door."

I was overwhelmed. Too much information was hitting me all at once.

"How did you find me here?"

"The brochure that nice lady handed me got me here, but a locator spell led me directly to you." I shook my head, still trying to process it all, when she held out her hand to me. "How about we finish this together, once and for all?"

"Do you really need my help?" I asked, after seeing how powerful she was.

She smiled. "Not really, but I figure it would be nice to do this together, since you made the promise to your mother."

"What?" How on earth could she know that? It was a dream.

She tapped the side of her head with her wand. "The Grinch knows much more than you think."

Oh crap. She knew her nickname.

In the middle of a dark forest, my grandmother and I—Witheridge witches—stood, side by side, hand in hand. The witch on the ground stayed there, unmoving. She'd felt the power of Gertie Witheridge, and she knew she was no match.

Together, we recited the spell of protection over our family, and together we ended the curse. My grandmother told the witch the truth about how her sister had killed my mother, and why. Then she offered a warning—that if she ever saw her again, hell would be unleashed on her and her entire family.

The witch walked up to my grandmother, her head dipped and eyes solemn. "I'm sorry about your daughter and furious my sister lied to me. After what she did and the lies she told, she deserves everything that has returned to her."

"We forgive you," Gertie said, taking hold of her hand. "Now go, and do good."

"I will," she said.

After gathering the two injured men, she left.

While my grandmother went to check on my dad, I went back to Rylan, my eyes darting to the wet crimson seeping through his jeans.

"We need to get you to a doctor."

"Nah," he replied. "It's already healing. By dinner, there will be nothing but a scar."

"Are you serious?"

He laughed, the muscles on his abdomen tightening. "Wanna see?"

His signature cocky grin was back, making my face flush with heat. I wanted to say yes, but shook my head instead.

There was rustling out in the woods. "Piers!" Voices called in the distance. "Piers?"

It was my uncles. "Over here," I yelled back.

In less than a minute, both of them pushed their way through the trees into our area, drenched in sweat.

"What the hell happened here?" Uncle Garrick asked, looking at all of us standing around.

"You missed all the action." Rylan chuckled, leaning back against a tree.

"What happened to you?" He pointed to the blood on Rylan's jeans.

"He got stabbed in the leg, defending me," I answered.

Rylan shrugged. "Battle wounds."

"By who?" Uncle Garrick's eyes turned golden, scanning the area.

"They're gone," I said. "And they won't be coming back."

"How?" he asked.

"It's a long story," I sighed.

Uncle Barney walked toward us. "You saved our niece, Rylan. You deserve an extra-large beef rib at the barbecue tonight."

Rylan pointed a finger at him. "Hey, I'll be looking forward to it."

"How did you find us?" I asked.

"We're family, and with Piers back as our alpha, we followed his scent," Uncle Garrick replied.

"Yeah," Barney cut in. "But if we'd have taken the truck, we would have gotten here faster."

"How would we have caught his scent while sitting in a truck?" Garrick grumbled.

Uncle Barney shrugged. "I could have hung my head out the window." Uncle Garrick groaned and shook his head.

"Eris?" my dad moaned. He was sitting up, a hand pressed to his forehead.

I let go of Rylan and ran to him, dropping to my knees. "Dad, are you okay?"

He nodded slightly. "Aside from the throbbing pain in my head." He leaned forward and grabbed me, pulling me into one of his tight dad hugs and kissed the top of my head. "I'm so glad you're safe."

"What happened?" I asked.

He paused, shaking his head. "Barney and I were following a lead in the woods, somewhere alongside Cooley Creek. I heard something behind me, and when I turned . . . I guess I was knocked out. I don't remember anything else after that." He glanced around. "Where are we?"

"In the woods," Barney answered. My dad moaned, clenching his eyes shut.

"We're outside of Havenwood Falls," I added. "A witch captured you and was going to put a spell on you, but we stopped her." I turned my gaze to Gertie. "*She* stopped her and made her reverse Camden's spell, too."

"Who is she?" My dad tried to stand, so I helped him to his feet.

"Someone I want you to meet," I said softly. Gertie had backed up and stood near Rylan. As we made our way toward her, their eyes met. "Dad, this is Gertrude Witheridge. But she prefers to be called Gertie."

"Gertie?" he exhaled, his eyes narrowing, a deep crease furrowed on his brow.

She stepped forward. "It's nice to finally meet you, son-in-law. In my real form."

Complete confusion riddled my dad's expression.

"Dad, she's Ms. Gingrich. She'd glamoured herself to look like an old woman because she wasn't sure if you'd accept her. Then, she moved next door to watch over us."

My dad's attention fell back to Gertie, his eyes studying her face as if he'd seen a ghost.

"It's true," she said. "I never had the chance to apologize to Aurora, to tell her how sorry I was for running away. But I was afraid. The wolves murdered my husband, and when I couldn't find her, I thought she was dead, too. So I ran. Ran as fast and as far away from that place as I could." Tears rimmed her eyes and spilled down her cheeks. "I'm sorry, Piers."

My dad shook his head. "Gertie, Aurora had already forgiven you. She never stopped loving you, and she understood why you ran." He took hold of her hand. "Thank you for watching over us and keeping Eris safe."

"It was my pleasure," she said with a smile. "I'm sorry for being so hard on you all those years as Ms. Gingrich. I was just being protective."

"I know," he said. "You don't need to apologize." My dad faced the rest of us. "How about we go home?"

"Sounds like a plan," Uncle Barney puffed. "If I don't get my big ol' rear in front of that grill soon, Lydia will kill me."

My uncles helped my dad back to Gertie's car along the roadside, while I walked with Rylan to his bike and helped pull it out from the trees.

"Can you ride this while you're injured?" I asked him.

A smile tugged at the corners of his lips. God, even in the state he was in—sweaty, dirty, his hair in disarray—he was still unbelievably handsome. How was that even possible? "Don't worry about me, cupcake. I'll be just fine."

I smiled, glad he was back to his cocky self.

My dad walked up to Rylan and offered him his jacket.

"Thanks," Rylan said, pushing his arms through it, covering his bare chest.

"Thank you, for protecting my daughter," my dad said, extending his hand. Rylan took it and they shook. "I will never forget it."

Rylan's eyes glanced my way. "It was my pleasure, sir. And I'd do it again in a heartbeat. But you should have seen her. She was pretty badass herself."

My dad's eyes narrowed at me, and I shrugged. "How about I tell you all about it on the way home," I offered.

He smiled, and nodded. "I'd like that."

All of us, except Rylan, piled into Gertie's small hatchback. On the way back to the cabins, I told them everything that had happened —about the glimmer, the cemetery, the dream of my mom, and finding the Book of Shadows. I also told them about Rylan coming over and offering me help, and when I was being attacked, how he shifted into his wolf and took out the two men. I told them about the power I had, and how Gertie came in the nick of time to save us all.

They were quiet, all the way back, listening carefully to every word I said.

"Your mother would have been so proud of you." My dad finally spoke, breaking the silence. Pride lined his voice. "And whether you shift or not, it doesn't matter to me."

"She will shift," Gertie cut in. "Her inner wolf is waiting to be released, but I've kept it calm and quiet over the past year. It's only a matter of time before she shifts."

My head whipped to her. "My dreams. They were true. You were lulling my inner wolf to sleep."

"Yes." She nodded. "I didn't think your first shift should have been in our quiet neighborhood, closely watched by its residents."

"No," I said. "Thank you for that."

We finally pulled into the driveway when my dad leaned forward. "Gertie, we would love it if you joined us for dinner, and help us usher in the new year."

"Yes," Uncle Barney chimed in. "We have more than enough food. And you're family, Gertie. You'll always be welcome."

"Thank you," she said kindly. "But there are a few things I need to take care of back in New Mexico. But you can be sure I'll be around. I won't miss out on my grandchildren's lives."

I leaned over and gave her a hug. "Are you sure you can't stay?"

"Yes. This time is for you and the Blaekthorns to bond. I've had a lot of years with you, as the Grinch." A smile widened on her lips; her hand patted my cheek. "Don't worry. I'll see you again soon."

My chest ached at the thought of her leaving. "Thank you. I couldn't have done it without your help."

"Yes, you could have. You're a Witheridge. We're strong and never give in. You would have found a way."

"I'll miss you."

"I promise I'll see you soon," she said, her eyes glimmering. She leaned forward and pressed a kiss to my forehead.

"Okay," I sighed. "I'll see you soon."

I gave her one last hug and watched her pull away. Then we headed to Uncle Barney's house for the barbecue.

"I need to call the medical center and the sheriff," my dad said. "But I don't have service here."

"Use our house phone," Uncle Barney replied.

I still couldn't believe everything that had happened in one day. It felt like I was still stuck in a dream. But this wasn't a dream. It was real. I had a family. A large family. And a brother and a grandmother.

Tonight, there would be so much more to celebrate than the new year.

CHAPTER 12

*A*s soon as we entered the house, the smell of meat, spices, and baked goods hit us, making my mouth water. Aunt Lydia and Aunt Vera had been busy in the kitchen all afternoon, oblivious to what had happened over the past few hours.

"Damn, Lyd," Uncle Barney said, wrapping his wife in his arms. "This house smells like heaven."

"It'd better. It had to lure you home, didn't it?" He threw his head back and laughed, then gave her a loud kiss. When he pulled back, he smacked her behind, and she yelped.

"Gross, dad," a boy walked in, rolling his eyes.

"Yeah, gross," another repeated, following behind him.

"Boys, come here," Uncle Barney said, wrapping his arms around each of their shoulders. "Weston and Drake, I'd like you to meet your cousin Eris and your uncle Piers."

They each smiled and shuffled toward us, hugging us awkwardly.

They were identical twins and handsome like the rest of the Blaekthorn men—dark-haired with dark features, their eyes flecked in gold. The only difference was one of them had slightly lighter eyes. They were still young, without muscles, but they were already taller than me.

"Don't worry, I still can't tell my sons apart," Uncle Barney laughed.

"Goodness gracious, what happened to you?" Aunt Vera gasped, looking at my dad's bloodied head.

"He got knocked out," Uncle Garrick explained. He headed to the fridge and grabbed a few beers, handing one to my dad.

"Yeah, what he said," my dad muttered, placing the cold bottle to his temple. "I'll be fine. I just need a painkiller, or four."

I heard Rylan's bike outside and went to the window. He'd pulled into Uncle Garrick's driveway.

"Hey, Barney, where's your phone?" my dad asked.

Headlights from a vehicle were headed down the drive. At first, I thought it was Gertie, but I was wrong. A large black truck pulled up right in front of the house.

Rylan noticed and headed our way. He was able to walk on his own now, with a slight limp.

"Dad," I called. "I think the sheriff just pulled up."

Everyone exited the house and stood on the porch as Sheriff Kasun slid out of his vehicle. Then they all went quiet as another figure exited from the passenger side.

My pulse started to race, and even with the chill in the air, I started to sweat.

"Oh my, it's Camden!" Aunt Vera exclaimed.

Seeing my brother, conscious, for the first time in seven years sent a wave of emotions coursing through me. I was happy to see him, but I was also nervous as hell. He'd hated me and wanted to kill me. He wanted my dad to choose my mom, instead of me. And I didn't blame him.

I stayed on the porch as everyone else ran down to greet him. He'd been here all these years, and had become like a son to them all.

I heard my dad ask Sheriff Kasun if he could come by and explain everything in the morning.

"Have fun with your family tonight," the sheriff said before jumping back in his vehicle. "I'll see you tomorrow."

As the family greeted Camden, Rylan came and stood by my side.

He knew what happened between me and my brother, and I had a feeling he was standing beside me because he wanted to make sure I was safe, and that Camden wouldn't try anything stupid.

The family made their way back to the stairs, and as they reached the top, Camden stopped in front of me. He was tall, about the same height as Rylan, and handsome—a mixture of my dad and mom. His face held no expression, and it made my heart ache.

Rylan moved slightly, and Camden's eyes snapped to him, narrowing. "I see you've met my sister."

Rylan gave his signature grin and glanced at me. "I have, and she's pretty special."

I heard a growl rumble from my brother's chest before his eyes turned back to me with a harsh glare.

"Camden," I breathed, my voice shaky.

He shook his head, his brow furrowed, and my heart shattered. *He still hates me.*

Then, his gaze suddenly softened, and his fingers touched the side of my face.

"Eris. You've grown up," he said. Then, without another word, he grabbed my arms and pulled me into a hug. I hugged him tight and felt his chest heave.

Both of us stood there, in the cold, surrounded by family, and wept. Our hearts healing, mending, after all these years. When he finally let go, his bloodshot eyes stared into mine. "I'm sorry, sister. I was young and confused, and Mom was my world."

"I know," I breathed. "She was mine too."

"Can you forgive me?" he asked.

I nodded, tears refilling my eyes. "I already have."

He wrapped me in a tight embrace one more time. "Thank you." He pressed his forehead against mine. "I'll see you inside."

The family headed into the house, leaving me and Rylan alone.

"Hey," he said, his hand brushing against mine. "I'm gonna head over to shower and change."

I grabbed hold of his hand, halting him. "Thank you," I said.

"For what?"

"For being here."

He shrugged. "I was just making sure things were copacetic."

"Yeah, I know you were. But not only for that . . . for everything you did today. You were there for me, and I appreciate it." I rose up on my tiptoes and kissed his cheek.

A crooked grin lifted on his handsome face. "You don't think getting stabbed in the leg was worth a real kiss?"

"How about you take a rain check, for a time when my entire protective family isn't standing right on the opposite side of the door."

"I'll take it," he said, then winked and walked away.

THE BARBECUE WAS AMAZING, and everyone was stuffed and happy to be together again, as it should have been all along. We ushered in the new year, knowing change was imminent. But I was ready for it and welcomed it. We all did.

Over the next week, our family began to mend. My memories were still returning, but now it was time to create new ones. It was great having an older brother, who I found was just as protective as my dad.

On top of that, my dad decided to move us back to Havenwood Falls, where he would take his place as alpha of the Blaekthorn Shadow Pack and help with the family business. I also decided that I'd be enrolling the next year at Havenwood Falls High as a senior.

I really hoped my grandma Gertie would follow us here. But that was still uncertain. I was just glad to have her back in my life, knowing I could connect with her anytime I wanted.

Rylan and I spent a lot more time together, especially since winter break was still on. He was a senior at Havenwood Falls High and would be graduating soon, but he already had a steady job at Blaekthorn Lumber and Supply.

My dad let him get closer than any other guy had, and even let him take me out a few times, only not on his motorcycle. And Camden sort of tagged along.

For the first time in my life, I felt a sense of stability. That hole I'd had in my heart for all those years was steadily being filled. And I noticed it in my dad, too. Things were finally taking a turn in the right direction, and we were finally becoming whole.

~

IT WAS the eighth of January, the first day of school after the winter break, and the night before we had decided to head back to New Mexico to pack our things for the big move. It was also the night of the Festival of Lights—a time when the residents of Havenwood Falls gathered in the town and on the mountainsides, offering tribute to all those who had fallen and lost their lives while protecting the people of the town and its secrets during the massacre of 1876.

Rylan asked my dad if I could go, and because Camden and the twins were going, too, he agreed. After school, Camden and I met Rylan and the twins at the school, and drove up Mt. Mae. We were all given paper lanterns and lighters before we rode the ski lifts up the slopes. There, we met other students from Havenwood Falls High.

I recognized the sheriff's son Kase in a group of guys, and was introduced to Rowan, River, Zaltana, Julianna, Viv, Breckin, and Zara, who also rode the lifts up. It felt great to be a part of something, with kids my age, especially after being homeschooled for the past three years.

We made a bonfire between a few trees and waited for nightfall.

One of the kids explained to our group about the event. That it was meant to honor those who had given their lives for the town and its residents throughout the centuries. Also, every year on this same night, all residents of Havenwood Falls turned off their Christmas lights for the last time until the next season.

Not long after, we watched as the entire town below went dark, and then stood in a moment of silence.

I couldn't help but think of my mother. She'd sacrificed her life for me. Gave everything so I could live, and I was standing here because of her.

A bright red flare shot high into the sky from city hall, a sign for everyone to begin lighting their lanterns. Rylan held ours between his hands while I lit it.

I placed my hands over his as a cold wind whipped around us. Our eyes met; the panes of his handsome face illuminated from the lantern's warm glow.

"You ready?" he asked.

"Ready."

We let go and watched our lantern slowly ascend. Then, my glimmer appeared out of nowhere and circled around it. Seeing it, knowing it was my mother, knowing she was here to witness it, made me emotional.

Tears pooled in my eyes, blurring my vision as I watched the lantern lift higher and higher, along with the thousands of other golden-lit lanterns filling the onyx sky. It was unbelievably beautiful and so peaceful, and with the darkened town below, it was a wonder to be seen.

Then, as if the moment weren't already magical, wisps of snow curled and danced around us, and gasps and laughter filled the air.

I turned, looking into Rylan's eyes, and his gaze softened, making my heart burst. I placed my hand against his cheek, his fingers gently grazed against mine.

God, I loved the way he looked at me, when his eyes looked like molten gold.

I gnawed on my lower lip, which caused a low laughter to rumble from his chest.

He held the sides of my face, then slowly leaned in. The warmth of his breath against my cold cheek sent tingles down my spine and through my belly.

"I'm cashing in my rain check right now," he whispered, and I nodded.

Heat rushed to my core as his warm lips found mine, sweeping gently across them. I opened to him, and his kiss deepened, becoming intimate. At that moment, I was lost, a paper lantern floating high in the sky above.

"Hey, Rylan." Camden's voice yanked me from bliss and pulled me back down to earth. "Rylan!"

Rylan's lips lingered a bit longer before he pulled away. When we turned, there was a girl standing next to Camden.

"She's been looking for you," he said, hitching his thumb toward her.

The girl was around our age, very thin and tall, with long brown hair and dark brown eyes. She looked sickly and tired, with pronounced, dark bags under her eyes.

Still in Rylan's arms, I felt his muscles stiffen as the two of them stared at each other.

"Keira, what are you doing here?" he asked in a not-so-friendly tone.

"Rylan," she breathed, taking a tentative step forward, her head dropping. "The pack needs you."

"What are you talking about?" Rylan bit, "Axel is in charge. He's more than capable to run the pack."

"No, he's not," she said, her voice trembling. "Lars killed him, or at least we think it was him, leaving us leaderless. We've been on the run, trying to survive." Her hands twisted around themselves. "You're the rightful alpha of our pack, Rylan. If we don't get protection, we're all going to die."

He shook his head. "I left. I'm no longer a part of the pack," he snapped, releasing me. As he did, a coldness swept over me.

"Lars has threatened to take over, and the pack is frightened. They need you. *We* need you," she said, her eyes pleading. "And although you don't think you are, you'll always be a part of the pack."

"How did you find me?" he asked, his tone guarded.

"You're an alpha, Rylan. We're all connected."

He exhaled loudly. "Where is Lars?"

"Last we heard, he was in Gunnison, probably heading this way."

Rylan cursed under his breath, his hands raking through his hair. "And where's the pack?"

"They're in Montrose, a little over an hour away." Rylan was clearly disturbed. "I'm sorry," she said, looking between us. "I had to come.

The pack needs a leader, and if Lars finds them, you know what he's capable of doing. There are only six of us left."

Rylan cursed again. "I'll think about it," he finally exhaled, looking up at her.

"How is your mother?" Keira asked.

He gave her a pained look that made my heart ache. "She's dead."

"What?" Keira's eyes shut tight, and a tiny tear trickled down her frail cheek. "I'm so sorry," she whispered. She stepped closer and handed him a piece of paper. "We'll be here until tomorrow night." Rylan took the paper and shoved it in his pocket.

The entire atmosphere had changed as we watched the girl, Keira, walk away. My heart was breaking for her, understanding what she was going through, but it wasn't my place to say anything.

"What was that all about?" Camden asked, stepping toward Rylan.

"Pack issues," Rylan exhaled. "I'll deal with it later."

"We'll talk later," Cam said and walked away. He also knew it was better not to interfere right now.

Rylan walked back to me and laced his fingers through mine.

"Are you okay?" I asked, gazing deep into his hazel eyes.

But I knew he wasn't okay. I could read his body language and see stress clearly etched on his face. Keira's news had greatly affected him.

But Rylan was strong, a survivor. I had learned he didn't like to wear his emotions on his sleeve, and didn't like to involve anyone else in his problems. He was the type who handled issues his own way. And after hearing what kind of person Lars was, I had a feeling Rylan would avoid bringing his pack into Havenwood Falls. He wouldn't want to risk the safety of my family, or me, and what he was still building here. If anything, he would keep the issue outside of town until it was resolved. And that's what scared me most.

"Hey, you," he said, kissing the tip of my nose. His signature grin was instantly back, putting a smile on my face. "Don't worry about me, cupcake. It's nothing I can't handle."

"I know," I sighed, taking his other hand. I wanted him to know that we were here for him, like he was for us . . . for me. And we would fight for him, no matter what. "We're all here for you. You know that, right?"

His eyes went distant for a moment. I wrapped my arms around his waist and he hugged me closer to his chest. His wonderful scent wrapped around me, instantly calming my nerves.

"I know," he breathed, pressing his lips to my forehead. "I know."

We stood in silence, holding each other tight, watching the last of the glimmering lanterns sail into the endless sky above, until they faded from view.

There were so many new and unanswered questions floating around us. But I still believed in fate and held tightly to it, believing it brought us to this town for a reason.

What did the future hold for us? I didn't know. But like my dad always said:

We'll get through it together . . . like we always have.

WE HOPE you enjoyed this story in the Havenwood Falls High series of novellas featuring a variety of supernatural creatures. The series is a collaborative effort by multiple authors.

Look for the continuation of the stories in this volume:

Blood & Iron by Amy Hale
Avenge the Heart by Michele G. Miller
Shadows & Spells by Cameo Renae

Stay up to date at www.HavenwoodFalls.com

ABOUT THE AUTHOR

USA Today bestselling author Cameo Renae was born in San Francisco, raised in Maui, Hawaii, and now resides with her husband and children in Alaska.

She's a daydreamer and a caffeine and peppermint addict, who loves to laugh and loves to read to escape reality.

One of her greatest joys is creating fantasy worlds filled with adventure and romance and sharing it with others.

One day she hopes to find her own magic wardrobe and ride away on a magical unicorn. Until then . . . she'll keep writing.

ACKNOWLEDGMENTS

First, I'd like to thank Kristie Cook who invited me to be a part of this amazing world. It's been such an honor and privilege to write alongside all the other outstanding Havenwood Falls authors.

I'd also like to thank the readers. It's because of you that our stories come to life. We appreciate you.